IT'S ONLY ROCK AND ROLL

It's Only

Rock and Roll

an anthology of rock and roll short stories

edited by Janice Eidus & John Kastan

d r g
david r. godine, publisher
boston

A Godine Paperback Original
first published in 1998 by
DAVID R. GODINE, PUBLISHER, INC.
Box 450
Jaffrey, New Hampshire 03452

*Due to limitations of space, permissions acknowledgments appear on page 287.
Frontispiece photograph used by permission of Michael Ochs Archives.*

LIBRARY OF CONGRESS CATALOGING IN PUBLICATION DATA

It's only rock and roll : an anthology of rock and roll short stories
/ edited by Janice Eidus & John Kastan.
p.   cm.
1. Rock music—Fiction. 2. United States—Social life and customs—20th century—
Fiction. 3. Rock musicians—United States—Fiction. 4. American fiction—
20th century. 5. Short stories, American. I. Eidus, Janice. II. Kastan, John, 1953-   .
PS648.R63187   1998
813'.0108357—DC21   98-35749
CIP

ISBN 1-56792-089-6 (PBK.)

Text design by Mark Polizzotti

First edition, 1998
This book was printed on acid-free paper
Printed in Canada

contents

ROCK AND ROLL IS HERE TO STAY

"There's a communal religious feel to rock music; that and sports are the closest a lot of us will ever come to religious fervor. At the end of the concert, you raise your hands and hold a lighted match or lighter. We put an awful lot of faith in rock and roll."

—Susan Neville, *Indiana Winters*

introduction

As one of thousands of crazed, screaming teenyboppers, I stood, in 1964, for hours and hours in front of various New York City hotels, trying desperately to get past the police and hotel security to catch a glimpse—or perhaps even to touch—my flesh-and-blood idols, the so-called British Invasion groups: the Beatles, the Rolling Stones, the Dave Clark Five, Herman's Hermits, Gerry and the Pacemakers, and others. I wept and screamed for all of them, but none so much as my personal favorites, George Harrison and Mick Jagger. (Mick once dropped his sunglasses at my feet on the steps of Carnegie Hall before a concert, and—good girl that I was—I picked them up and handed them back to him, eliciting the most genuinely shocked "Thank you" I've ever heard.)

I didn't dream back then that I would grow up to be a writer of novels and short stories, many of them focused on my continuing love of the rock music world and its charismatic heroes and heroines. At one point in my literary career, I began to notice that many of my favorite writers were also using this music as a central metaphor in their work. Over breakfast one morning, the Velvet Underground playing in the background, my husband, John, and I began discussing the connection between rock and contemporary literature, and ultimately decided to co-edit a collection of the best of these stories.

We were both inspired and driven as we assembled the collection we now present to you, the first of its kind, featuring fiction that explores the wide range of rock and roll: from the doo-wop of the fifties, to Elvis and the Beatles, to punk and heavy metal, and on to the wild women and alternative rock of the 1990s.

It seems to us that each story in this book is like a good song: entertaining and powerful in its own right. Our aim was to offer a dramatic and revealing (and often very funny) look at the rock and roll way of life, in which the individual pieces—like the music itself—range from the outrageous to the mellow. Illustrating the music's extremely widespread appeal, the authors represent diverse cultures as well—from "Downtown" to "Down South," and from those who remember Elvis Presley provocatively swiveling his hips on *The Ed Sullivan Show,* to those who were born after the King died.

*   *   *

Rock has now been around for forty years, with roots reaching back to the blues and jazz (whose own roots are in Africa), to European classical music, to American folk and country and western. In other words, this is a music that reflects the cultural diversity and synthesis which *is* the American experience, and which has become a kind of soundtrack for our contemporary lives, used by innumerable filmmakers to situate us in time and place, as well as to stir up our deepest memories and feelings.

Like these filmmakers, and like so many of us, the writers in this book have been profoundly affected by rock and roll. We've divided the book into five sections, representing the main themes that emerged from this group of stories, even as these themes accommodated a wide range of mood, imagery, and style. Broadly speaking, they veer from the raw, street-savvy quality of the early days of fifties rock, to the urgent desire for release, escape, and social change in the sixties, to the angst and edgy unease associated with the end of the millenium.

The first section, "Glory Days," evokes the past. In "The Day I Met Buddy Holly" by Kim Herzinger, a twelve-year-old boy hangs around the local train station, convinced that the bespectacled young man waiting on the platform is the world-famous rocker. Jill McCorkle's "Final Vinyl Days," meanwhile, eulogizes the passing of the LP through its impact on the life of the emotionally adrift narrator.

"Keepin' the Faith," (the title of the next section) has always been a significant part of the lives of both musicians and fans. Jodi Bloom's "Shrine" is about a teenage girl who, while living with her family in a trailer, must contend with her younger sister's "stupid" love for Kurt Cobain—complete with a bona-fide shrine. In Kim Addonizio's "'Til There Was You,'" the girlfriend of the keyboard player in a "loser" San Francisco band surprises everyone by turning out to be the one true winner of the whole bunch.

In the third section, "You've Really Got a Hold on Me," the writers explore the nature of rock and roll obsession. François Camoin's "A Hunk of Burning Love," introduces us to Gene, an aging Texas "good old boy," who's equally obsessed with Elvis Presley and Rita, the waitress at the New Deal Cafe & Bar. T. Coraghassen Boyle's "Rock & Roll Heaven" follows the recently deceased lead guitarist of a band called "the Toads" as he desperately tries to find his way to rock and roll heaven, but keeps landing in all the wrong places.

The writing in "Welcome to the Jungle" is wild. Roberta Smoodin's fanciful "Ursus Major" concerns a talking bear whose only passion in life is "to dance to the music"—leading him to join the Ungrateful Wretches, a second-rate, drug-taking, sixties band in Denver. The tightly-wound lead singer in Lee K. Abbott's "The Unfinished Business of Childhood" becomes increasingly delusional and megalomaniacal, taking the lyrical prose of the story with him. And Harold Jaffe's "Madonna" is an offbeat, stylish discourse on the myriad facets of our contemporary diva.

The final section, "Rock and Roll is Here to Stay," showcases and applauds the remarkable durability of the music. The son in Bruce Jay Friedman's "Brazzaville Teenager" embarks on a mad quest to save his father's life by recording a most unusual song in his honor. In Lucinda Ebersole's Kafkaesque "Bigger Than Jesus," a nineties guy named Sammy suddenly metamorphoses into a sixties moptop Beatle. The road trip taken by a guitar-playing father and his teenaged son in Geoffrey Becker's "Bluestown" leads to their understanding of the real meaning of the blues.

*   *   *

All the fiction in this collection—with its extraordinary variety of styles, voices, and visions—explores and celebrates the significance of rock and roll in our lives by evoking the singers, the songs, the fans, and the passion that are a part of this powerful music. We trust that these stories, like the music itself, will trigger memories and associations for you, whether they are joyous, mournful, romantic, sexual, angry, or humorous. And we're optimistic that this book will be the first of others to come, since rock and roll will undoubtedly continue to inspire and play muse to the literary imaginations of future generations of writers and readers.

Perhaps we can conclude best by quoting the singer in Ava Chin's "Belgrade, New York" as she describes the pure intensity and ardor of the world of rock and roll: "When the band enters, there is a tension I have felt before and a rise in the audience... On stage, where a minute is a century and at the same time less than a second, the extraneous is stripped away like bones in the floor of the Atlantic and you treat every moment like it's both forever and lost in a child's song. You do not think of last month's rent or yesterday's weather, only of what you do."

—*Janice Eidus*
December 1997

GLORY DAYS

The Day I Met Buddy Holly

kim herzinger

I MUST HAVE BEEN ABOUT TWELVE, living in Eugene, Oregon, and somehow I was by myself down at the train station. I don't know how that could have been, but I was down there anyway, and I saw this guy. He looked familiar to me, not familiar like someone I had seen around town, but familiar in another way, a famous way. He had famous written all over him. He was just standing there, next to the tracks, smoking a cigarette and looking for the train. Once in a while he'd put his foot on his bag—he only had the one bag—and then take a deep drag on his cigarette and look down the tracks real seriously. I sat on a mail cart to consider him. He had the famous glasses on, black and thick—too black for an ordinary guy even in 1958—and he was wearing a kind of bluish checkered shirt that was open at the collar. His pants, I remember, were rumpled, as if he'd spent an awful long time sitting in the station, or if he'd slept in them even. Then he glanced over at me and gave himself away. It was the glance that tipped me off, just a flash of the eyes and something he did with his lips—he was through with his cigarette at that particular moment—and I could tell from that he was Buddy Holly, the real Buddy Holly right there on the station platform waiting to catch a train. I don't know if you remember what Buddy Holly looked like, when he was singing songs with the Crickets, but if you'd seen the way he glanced and what he did with his lips you would have recognized him. And now everything made sense. His shirt was expensive, I could see now,

3

but made to *look* inexpensive, like an ordinary guy's shirt except that it wasn't really. And his pants were the kind that gave him a lot of room to move around inside them, the kind that got rumpled because he was on the road and there wasn't anybody to iron them who wouldn't have paid too much attention to him and called up the newspaper and everything. It was pretty clear that Buddy wanted to be alone there—I looked around to see if I could see any Crickets but there wasn't anybody who looked like he could have been one—and the reason he was standing and looking so hard down the tracks was because he was composing something. Right there, on the station platform, composing a song that would have this twelve-year-old kid in it, sitting on an empty mail cart, staring out toward the tracks. It's the kind of thing Buddy Holly would write about if he saw the right kid.

I sat for a long time trying to decide whether I should go up to him and tell him that I knew who he was and that I liked his music and that I hoped he'd keep singing with the Crickets. I sat there trying to decide whether I should do that, and wishing that my friend Charles Krietz was there, because he would do it if I didn't and just wishing that somebody I knew was there so I could tell them about what I was seeing so I could feel famous for a minute. And then I thought maybe Buddy was unhappy because nobody recognized him, that he had gone out among the people like a king to hear what they had to say about him, and nobody had said anything at all.

When I was ten a friend of the family had been involved in getting famous people to star at the rodeo; he was in charge of the Kiwanis Buckaroo Breakfast and Chuckwagon Dinner, where the star would sit up at the head of the table and sign autographs after the meal and, if he sang, sing. Lee Aaker, who played Rusty on *Rin Tin Tin,* came to town when I was ten. He wasn't much older than I was and I couldn't understand why he got to be on that show and I didn't. Then I heard that he played shortstop for a Little League team in Hollywood.

Now I was a pretty fair little ballplayer then, better than almost any of the kids my age—though I didn't have any power to speak of—and there wasn't any question in my mind that I was a better ballplayer than Lee Aaker, who just looked like a haughty little fat kid in a Fort Apache cavalry suit eating pancakes up on the stage at the Buckaroo Breakfast. So after he was through I went up there to talk to him. I was mad at him. I said, "So, you play baseball. Well, we got a pitcher could strike you out. Three pitches." And I held up my fingers to show him just exactly how many pitches it would take.

He just looked at me like I was nothing.

That was the last time I talked to anyone famous, and I'd blown my chance. So you can see how I would be pretty nervous going up to Buddy Holly.

Now Buddy was beginning to look a little nervous, too. He was beginning to pace up and down the platform. I was worried because I imagined my chance to talk to him was going. When they get agitated, famous people don't want much to do with anybody who is not famous. I'd learned that from Lee Aaker, and you could see it on television any day of the week. But while he was pacing up and down I got a good look at Buddy Holly's shoes. They were wing-tips, but not like my father's wing-tips, which looked blocky and oversized, like orthopedic shoes. Everybody he knew wore those same shoes, walking around as if they lived in a town where everybody had foot problems, clumping around in shoes I said I'd never wear, ever. Buddy Holly's shoes weren't like that though. They were sleeker, and the tip seemed to shark out of the front of them like it had real wings on it, and the design was low on the sides and tense, sort of stretched out, like the orange flames on Charles Krietz's brother's '55 Chevy. They were custom-made shoes, that was pretty clear. You couldn't go down to Kinney's and buy a pair of those. Even the soles were different—thinner, barely even there. Buddy Holly didn't look like he was walking on iron bars the way my father and all of his friends and business associates looked like.

Anyway, I thought I'd better do something and quick. What I thought I'd do was to sort of saunter up near to where Buddy was pacing and wait for him to drop something, or hesitate, or maybe say something to me. If I said something first, it would have to be *knowing*, like I knew who he was and that I liked him and the Crickets, that I wasn't one of those Christians who hated him and his music and thought he was a bad influence on youth, that I wasn't going to give him away, and I could take talking to him even if he was famous. All of this had to be done in a stroke. I didn't know how I would do all that, but I made my way over toward where he was anyway. Buddy Holly saw me coming, he looked right at me, took a deep drag on another cigarette—sort of sized me up in a glance—then looked down the tracks again. I looked at the tracks for awhile myself. I don't know what Buddy must have been thinking, seeing a little kid standing on the platform like that, looking down the tracks for the train as if he was going to be getting on any minute, but he didn't show any surprise or anything. Then I could see that Buddy was looking at a big old house on the Skinner's Butte, a sort of hill that stuck up right at the end of town and overlooked the train station, a place where teenagers would drive their cars up to the top of and make out, listening to his music.

The house was the pride of that butte. It was huge, bigger than it should have been, it had gables and towers, and no one seemed to know who lived in it. It was a great place for Halloween. Charles Kreitz told me once that he'd tried to rouse somebody in there on Halloween night, but no one ever even answered the door. He thought that the people who lived there had probably made sure that the police were watching it so kids couldn't come around and cause mischief. Buddy was looking at this house when what to say came to me.

"That's the Kreitz house," I said. "I know them."

Buddy smiled, but kept his eyes steady on the house.

"It's pretty old," I said.

Then Buddy Holly said, "How old is it?"

Now this is what bothers me. I'd just made up the people who lived in the house, but I couldn't think of a thing when he asked me how old it was. I suppose I could have said anything, thirty or fifty or a hundred years old, anything—I doubt if Buddy Holly knew enough about houses to think I might be lying to him—but his question about how old it was stymied me.

After a long time, with Buddy and me both looking at the house as if it would get up off its foundation any minute and tell us how old it was, I said, " I don't know. It's old enough. I know that."

He said, "I've been through Eugene quite a few times, you know, but I've never noticed that house before."

Now I hadn't known that Buddy Holly had been in Eugene before, and I thought maybe he had performed over at the college and I just hadn't heard about it because I was too young or something, or maybe he had been through town a lot before he had gotten famous. Being in Eugene didn't seem strange to me. I had lived there all my life. It seemed strange to think, though, that Buddy had been there a lot and I was evidently the only one who knew about it.

The sun was shining down onto the top of Buddy's head; like most rock and roll stars Buddy had sort of short hair, with just a tiny curl coming down in the front. I had to squint to see him.

"Well, usually the trains are here on time," I said.

He lit a cigarette. "Not today."

"No. Not today. There might be something wrong. Maybe a log problem or something. Sometimes we get a log problem in town because of all the lumber companies here. You've probably smelled some of them. Maybe some logs have fallen off and hurt the tracks. That's lumber for you."

Buddy Holly shook his head. "Do they like living there? I'll bet it's kind of noisy."

Buddy was asking about the Kreitzes. It flustered me.

"I don't think its too bad up there really," I said, and then I said, "You're Buddy Holly, aren't you?" I was surprised at myself, and I thought for a minute that Buddy was going to turn and walk away from me. But he didn't, he took it in stride.

"I wish," he said finally. "My name is Tom Truehaft. I'm from Lake Oswego. I'm a barber."

I looked at his shoes. They were not the shoes of a barber. No barber would have ever known that they had shoes like that. I gave Buddy Holly a knowing smile.

"I think those shoes are pretty keen," I said. "Not like my dad's."

When I was seventeen I took a girl to a school dance who had the reputation of being impure. Her name was Tanya Vincent and she came from this crummy little town outside of Eugene called Coburg. We thought all the girls from there lived on farms; anyway, they all looked a little smudgy, like they didn't have much to do and spent a lot of time out in the furrows reading magazines or something. My friend Scott Webber, whose father was a doctor and was rich, had had a date with Tanya earlier in the school year. It ended with Tanya running through their big ranch-style house in her panties, which were kind of rubbed-looking and gray, but still satiny, he told me. The picture of Tanya running around Scott Webber's living room in her panties was banging around in my mind when I told her about the time I met Buddy Holly at the train station. When I told her about it I changed the station from Eugene to Portland, after deciding against San Francisco at the last minute. I didn't think she'd ask me why I was waiting around alone at the Portland train station, and she didn't. Buddy was dead by then, of course. He'd died with the other two in that plane crash in Iowa. She said she liked Buddy Holly and that he reminded her a little of Roy Orbison. She didn't remember too much about him, she said, but her older brother—who was a mechanic in Coburg and a guy I thought might be a major obstacle when I took

Tanya back home after the dance—used to play his music a lot. I was trying to raise the stakes with Tanya. I was pretty popular in high school and played varsity basketball and she should have been happier to be out with me than she seemed to be. I thought maybe she had gotten a little jaded after her date with Scott Webber. So it made me mad to think that what she remembered of Buddy Holly was being strained through her hayseed brother, probably out in the family barn working on getting a tractor going. Somehow, her memory of Buddy Holly seemed to reflect on *me*.

So I told her that he'd given me his shoes. I didn't think that she'd ask me if Buddy Holly ended up getting on the train in his socks, and she didn't. I told her that I had had the shoes until last year, and that I only showed them to my very best friends, and that I would have liked to let her see them, but that my mother had thrown them out when she had invaded my closet one day and thrown out a lot of stuff from my childhood days. I talked as if it didn't bother me so much except that now I couldn't show her that pair of Buddy Holly's wingtips.

The dance ended with Bobby Vinton singing "Mr. Lonely" twice in a row. By then I thought Tanya Vincent was pretty much going my way, except that she said it was too late for her to go up to Skinner's Butte with me, and when I took her back to her house in the country it turned out to be low-slung, with that white gravel on the roof, and more modern than mine. Her older brother wasn't there, but everybody else in her family was. After she introduced me she told her mother that I had met Buddy Holly when I was twelve and that he had given me his shoes. Her mother thought that was nice of him and wondered what he worn on the train.

That next summer, after I had started seeing Tanya regularly, she climbed up onto my roof in the middle of night and knocked on my upstairs bedroom window and woke me up. She wanted to come in. She was squatting down on the slope of our roof and twisting around on her haunches. She looked excited, as if she was going to start giggling real loud any minute. The whole thing scared the hell out of me, because there wasn't carpeting on my bedroom floor and you could hear everything downstairs even if you walked on tiptoe. Mostly it was embarrassing; I had on my green pajamas with the beige piping and I was too scared to act like this kind of thing happened to me all the time. She spent about a half an hour in my bedroom, whispering the story of how she had been riding around with her Coburg girlfriends, how she told them what she was going to do, how she had them drop her off at my corner, and that they were going to drive around the neighborhood until she came back down. Thinking of my mother, who was a light sleeper and who got up a lot in the middle of the night to wash or something, I told Tanya that the police patrolled the neighborhood all the time, and her friend's car would be suspicious. She said she didn't want her friends to get in any trouble and we went into a long kiss.

As she was climbing out the window, she said, "Could I see those shoes you got from Buddy Holly?" It made me mad. My parents were just downstairs, probably waking up now and rubbing their eyes and wondering why I was up so late, probably wondering if I was sick and Tanya Vincent was stuck halfway out my window asking if she could see some shoes that I had told her my mother threw away a long time ago. It really did make me mad.

Now what I told Tanya Vincent about the shoes was, naturally, not really what happened when I met Buddy Holly. I took in his information about being a barber from Lake Oswego and considered it for about a minute. Even though I had been flustered, I thought that I had asked him if he was Buddy Holly in a pretty casual way, casual enough not to make him think that I was going straight to a phone and call up the paper. But there wasn't any other reason why he would have told me his name was Tom Truecraft.

So I said, "Well, you really look like Buddy Holly. A *lot* like him."

"I wish I had his money," said Buddy. Then he sort of twisted around in his pants a little bit and looked down the tracks, flipping his cigarette onto the rails.

"Do you want me to check it out and see when the train will be coming in? I can find out inside." Buddy said thanks and I went in to find out. The train station in Eugene was one of the old kind, all wood and with the name of the town hung out in the middle of it. It wasn't orderly, but it made sense. When you were in there you knew exactly what you were supposed to do. A big chalkboard said that the train was supposed to be at 12:17 and nothing said it was going to be late. Although now it was 12:45. Nobody seemed surprised about it and nobody in the waiting room looked like he might have been a Cricket. The man behind the ticket counter wore suspenders and had a red face.

"What time is the train coming in?" I asked him. "Buddy Holly's out there and I'm checking for him."

The man smiled and told me it would be there in an hour or so.

That's what I told Buddy Holly when I came out. He told me thanks and said he was going to go over to the restaurant right next to the station and get some coffee and a paper.

It's true that when I told Tanya about the time I met Buddy Holly I lied about getting those wing-tips. I suppose I thought that Tanya was a mouth-breather, and that I could put the shoes in the story and she'd believe me. And, of course, that's what she did. Later on, though, Charles Krietz started taking her out—this was after I'd told him about how Tanya had climbed onto my roof—and he wondered why I'd never shown him those shoes.

"I'm a good enough friend of yours, aren't I? I'm a good enough friend to have had a chance to see your own personal pair of Buddy Holly shoes." Charles thought Tanya was a little dim, too, but he said it didn't matter much to him. "Maybe your mother remembers about them." He said. "Maybe she never even threw them away, since they must have meant so much to you. Maybe they're still in the house somewhere. Maybe your mother is saving them for a special occasion."

I told Charles that I didn't think my mother even knew what they were.

"Seems like she would have," said Charles. "Seems like I would have. At least that's how it seems to me. You know what I mean?" I knew what Charles meant, all right, but it was too late to come clean about the shoes.

Charles always said that he really didn't care anything at all about Tanya Vincent, but when she dropped him for a guy named Mike, who lived out on some farm near where she lived, he came out against girls altogether for a while. Charles had turned philosophical for a time about this, and he'd corner you and want to have long talks about women. He had never been dumped by a girl before and the experience had brought out a new side of Charles.

"What women want," I remember he told me, "is for guys to want to make out with them. They don't really want to make out, you understand—except sometimes, you know, when they do it just to keep up the image. No. They just want to make sure that you *want* to. We're talking barely human here. It's like when we drive down the gut on the weekend and see all these damn girls in their cars. *We* think they're down there for the same reason we're down there. *We* think they're down there *looking* for something. They get in their damn cars, and then stare straight ahead like they've got pretty important things to do just ahead of them—you know, as if they've got *big doings* waiting for them just down the street. And if they're not doing that they'll be putting on some of those damn toiletries they've got. They flash out these compacts, and they've got cotton balls all over the interior, and then they sort of apply this stuff with the most intense kind of concentration, as if this one last *dab* is the thing that's going to do it, you know, like this is last little *touch* that's the only thing they need to make the sugar plums dance."

Charles was bitter because I'd been telling him that I thought that one of Buddy Holly's songs had it pretty close about women. I was thinking of when Buddy sang about "the dreams and wishes you wish in the night when lights are low." Charles was in no mood for this sort of thing, and said that he thought all the songs were stupid, although probably "Do You Love Me?" by the Contours had some truth to it.

"So we always roll our windows down, like fools, and make some kind of noise about how would they like to go somewhere with us or what high school do you go to or say something from a song. Then what do they do? They stare straight ahead of themselves and intensify their dabbing. And then they act like we've got hair growing out of our palms. A visible *pall* falls over their car. A goddamn *visible pall*. Then the light changes and they gun their car down to the next light, giggling like hell. Animals."

I told Charles that for women to stick with you that even money wasn't enough, that you probably had to be famous. I told him that I knew this from the day I'd met Buddy Holly.

"Or maybe being really good-looking," he said.

"Yes. Good-looking too," I said.

"Only my mother loves me now," he said.

I had sat down on the mail cart for a while and then went over to the restaurant where Buddy had gone to wait for the train. It was just a little place called Thurber's with a counter and a few booths. The outside of it had some kind of covering that was supposed to look like red and black bricks. It had greasy menus and a little jukebox thing installed in every booth so people could play music without having to get up. When I visited Eugene again in the seventies I noticed that it had been taken over by some hippies. The sign was hand-lettered and so were the menus and the town sanitation board had given it a B rating—not very good. They renamed it the Eugene Creamery. Later the hippies left and the place became part of a restoration project that swept the train station end of town. This was at the same time that the Smeed Hotel, which was just across the street, got turned into a toy store, a kite shop, and a place that sold Birkenstock shoes. During this time the restaurant was called the Buttery, and it always looked like it was just about to be open for business, but it never was. The last time I was there I saw it again, and it looked almost like it had when Buddy Holly sat there at the counter and had his coffee and read the paper. The individual jukeboxes were gone, though.

I was keeping an eye on Buddy from outside the restaurant when another kid I didn't know came up on his bike. Ordinarily I wouldn't have said anything, but this was too big a thing to keep to myself.

"Guess who's in the restaurant, at the counter," I said.

"Who?"

"Buddy Holly."

"*The* Buddy Holly?"

I nodded.

"Which one?" he asked

"Right there, next to the pies, reading the paper. He's got a blue shirt on. I was talking to him earlier. He's waiting for the train."

The kid looked in through the window.

"Are you sure that's Buddy Holly?" he said. "It doesn't look like him."

"I asked him," I said.

The kid cupped his hands right up against the glass of the door and looked at Buddy. After a while he went for his bike. "I'm going to tell my friend Darrel. He'd know. His sister's got all of Buddy Holly's records. She thinks he's cherry."

"I *asked* him," I said.

"I'm going to go get Darrell," he said.

While the kid went to go get Darrel, Buddy Holly ordered a piece of the Dutch Apple pie they had and I told some people going into Thurber's that they had Buddy Holly in there, eating a piece of pie and drinking some of their coffee. The word started getting around outside, and then inside too. A few other kids joined me, and we took tuns putting our faces up against the door window, and watching him eat and drink. Somebody put on one of Buddy's songs from a booth, and everybody started tapping their feet and looked longingly over toward his direction. The people at the counter tried not to look at him at all, but most of them did it anyway, peeping over their newspapers or pretending to stare at the wall behind him where all the whole pies were stacked up in a refrigerator. Between the times she was refilling Buddy's coffee, the waitress would stand next to another waitress, and they would giggle and talk with their hands covering their mouths and then laugh hard and bump their hips together. Once, the waitress spoke in what looked like low tones to Buddy and pointed out somebody in a booth. Buddy turned around slightly and nodded and smiled when the man in the booth gave him a salute.

About the time the friend of Darrell's got back with some other kids on bikes, Buddy got up from his spot at the counter, paid the waitress, and came out. By now there was a lot of us outside of Thurber's and at first we all just stood back, gave him plenty of room, and watched him while he started to walk toward the station. He was tapping his newspaper against his leg and smiling. Since I had a special connection with Buddy Holly, I moved up next to him as he went towards the tracks.

"Thanks, buddy," he said just before we got there. "This is great."

When Buddy got back to the platform, he lit another cigarette. I sat down on the mail cart again. By now all the kids had walked their bikes up the edge of the platform, and people from the restaurant had trailed up behind them just to get one last look at Buddy before he got on his train. Some of them had bought coffee to go in cardboard cups, and drank it and talked and pointed with their elbows. A little wisp of a dust devil blew some bits of paper and cellophane and cut grass up and around, and it circulated through the crowd and the people stepped out of the way. It was as if they were dancing. But they still kept their eyes glued on Buddy while he smoked his cigarette. Both of the waitresses stuck their heads out of the restaurant door, kind of stacked up like the pies, and Mr. Thurber stood out in his sidewalk and watched Buddy with his arms crossed and with a spatula in one hand.

This was all pretty amazing, of course, and not the kind of thing that you get to see very often. Fame up close rubs off on you, makes you feel that you're different and special just because you're there. I saw it again once when I was in Florence, Italy, on leave with some friends. One of my friends knew this girl from his hometown, and she was one of these girls who was so gorgeous it was like she was from another planet. She was a model for *Vogue* magazine and some other magazines too, but she was in Florence cleaning art for the summer. She'd been on the covers of these magazines, but she was just as amazing in person. I felt that a girl like that must have feelings that were especially acute in order to go along with her looks, so everything I said to her sounded dumb.

Now this girl wasn't really famous. I mean probably nobody in Italy actually knew her name. But she was spectacular, so she didn't need to be famous, too. She must have felt famous just for being around herself. She had a favorite restaurant on a back street across the river and so the four of us—she was in the lead because she knew where she was going and she knew the Italian language—went on a long walk down there. So here I am, walking along beside this woman who's pretty obviously not from the world as we know it, looking as if the space has been cut out from around her, and I start seeing these Italian men begin to gather around doorways and windows, watching us as we come down the street. They start holding their heads and pretending to weep, they slap their foreheads and run inside and call for their friends to come out on the street. Some whistle and lay their heads back and howl. Men stick their heads out of bars and restaurants, still wiping away some sauce from their mouths. One guy reaches out from a window as if to shake my hand when I pass by him and says, "Bravo, signor, bravo." He says this with his eyes big and a huge grin, like he's in awe. By now a pretty decent crowd is trailing along beside us, laughing and smacking each other and singing, holding wine bottles up to the great appreciation of all the people hanging out of windows and lounging outside of doors up and down the street. They take turns running up alongside of us, grabbing our elbows and jacking themselves down on their knees, giving out pleading sounds in Italian and clasping their hands and shaking them like they're praying. A few throw themselves in front of her and scuff along the street backwards on their knees. Some of them still have their dinner napkins tucked in their collars. They offer her flowers or wine or whatever they can find. One talks like mad and keeps pointing at an entire fruit and flower stand, wiping fake tears away from his eyes the whole time. And this lovely girl we're with walks on straight ahead, doesn't miss a beat; she just nods slightly and smiles at everybody as they howl and sing and wail like sirens.

It was pretty amazing. We ate and drank everything after we got to the restaurant. I told them about the time I was twelve and Buddy Holly gave me a pair of his shoes. We made so much noise at our table that even our Italian waiters got a little nervous.

Just before the train came into view a sort of hush came over the station. Now I've been to a few train stations since and this is something that always happens. Nobody can see anything yet, and the train isn't blowing its whistle, but the ticket takers swivel around in their chair, the porters start putting bags on carts, and people standing around begin to kiss each other or stand up straight and adjust their clothing. People begin to get out of their cars and walk fast toward the platform. Maybe there's a deep hum in the rails or something. It's a special time. Buddy Holly flicked his cigarette onto the tracks, took a comb out of his back pocket and ran it through his hair.

When the train finally stopped at the station there were a lot of people around, more people than could possibly have been waiting for a train. I could tell from the way the porter said to get on board that he knew that he would helping Buddy Holly, *the* Buddy Holly, onto his train. I moved up close to him again while he fixed his pants one last time. When he leaned down to pick up his bag, he put his hand on my shoulder. He shook his head slowly in a resigned kind of way, but he was still smiling. It was better than shoes.

"Son," he said, "son."

Then Buddy went inside and sat down.

I could see him from where I was on the mail cart. He looked outside at the platform but didn't seem to be focusing on anything in particular. Then he sort of nodded at all of us out on the platform, opened up the paper that he'd bought at the restaurant and started reading it. The train got going again after a little while and I watched it as it went up the tracks, toward Portland.

When the train was gone, everything seemed to relax, everybody went inside again. The house on the side of Skinner's Butte got a little smaller. The whole town let its breath go and settled back. Nothing had changed. Buddy Holly had been there, and now he was gone, and we were back to being what we'd always been.

Final Vinyl Days

jill mccorkle

I'LL NEVER FORGET THE DAY Betts moved in. How could I? Open the apartment door and there she was with two suitcases, a purple futon, and two milk crates full of albums. It was 1984, the day after Marvin Gaye died. That's how I remember so well. I had just gotten home from my job at Any Old Way You Choose It Music, where the Marvin Gaye bin had been emptied within a couple of hours. I'd spent the afternoon marveling at what happens when somebody kicks. For years, other than the Motown faithfuls and a brief flurry after *The Big Chill,* that bin was neglected; I had even dusted it back when everybody was BeeGee Disco Crap Berserk. Now Marvin is dead and there's a run on his music. Same thing happened with Elvis and John Lennon, always good sellers, but incredibly so when they died.

"You want me here, don't you?" Betts asked, her thick, dark hair hitting her shoulders. Her eyes were always wide open as if she were seeing the world for the first time, every object catching her attention for the moment. She was staring at me; I was the object of her attention for the moment. "I mean I've been staying every night so I might as well have my things, right? And by the way," she was saying, "I could use some help." The purple futon was unrolled and halfway in the apartment. "We don't need this, but Helen said she didn't want it." Helen was the roommate, a physics major who liked to test all the physical properties during sex. Betts had said (before she started coming to my place) that it was driving her crazy (the shaking plaster and peculiar sounds). I didn't tell her but it was driving *me* crazy, for different reasons, the main one being was that I was a wee bit curious about what took place on the other side of that wall. Betts's side was pretty tame: a bulletin board covered in little notes and photos and ticket stubs, a huge poster of a skeleton. She was majoring in physical therapy and was taking it all real seriously (too seriously if you ask me) or, depending, not seriously enough. "I am not a masseuse," she said often enough, with no smile whatsoever. Short on sense of humor but long on legs. Sometimes you have to pick and choose. Sometimes you buy an album for just one song, thinking that the others will start to grow on you. When she finally got that futon in, she pulled out her Duran Duran album and that's when I put my foot down. We were from different time zones. She had a whole list of favorite *good old songs:* "Afternoon Delight" and "Muskrat Love" to name two.

I played Marvin: "Stubborn Kind of Fella," "It Takes Two," "Mercy Mercy Me." She just shrugged and went back in my room to arrange her little junk all over the top of my dresser and all over the back of the commode. I just sat there with Marvin, tried to imagine what it must feel like to know that your old man is about to kill you like Marvin did.

"Why did he wear that hat all the time?" Betts asked, looking the same way she did when she asked me why I still wore my hair long enough to pull back in a ponytail. "Is he the guy who sings that 'Sexual Healing' song?" She was standing in the kitchen with a two liter Diet Coke in one hand and a handful of Cheetos in the other. She's the healthy one. She's the one bitching about an occasional joint. It's okay for her to go downtown and pound down beer with her girlfriends but for goddsakes don't do anything illegal. "We've got to fix this place," she was saying. "And did you say you were going back to graduate school in the fall?"

"No." I shook my head and watched her peek under a dishcloth like she expected a six foot snake to pop out. She sounded just like my mother, asking me if I just said what she knows I never in the hell did. Those were her words: *graduate school*. When my mom does it, the secret words are electrical appliance store. My old man owns one in a town so big it actually has two gas stations, and he'd rather pull his nose off of his face with a wrench or beat up my new Maytag washer than to have me in his employment. Mom says things like, "Didn't you say you were looking for a job where you can advance in business?" That's when I always click the phone up and down or flip on the blender and plead bad connection. It's a real bad connection, Mom. And there stood Betts, swinging her NutraSweet, eating her fluorescent cheese, waiting for an answer.

"You know that night we first met, you said you had been in law school and were thinking about going back."

"I said that?" I asked and she nodded. "Did I tell you I quit law school and joined VISTA? Spent a year in the Appalachian Mountains with diarrhea?" She nodded a bored affirmative. "Did I tell you I loved it?"

"No."

"Well, that's because I didn't. But what I learned in that year is that I could do anything I wanted to do, you know?"

"So?" She took a big swallow of NutraSyrup, then wiped her mouth and hands with enough paper towels to equal a small redwood. "What are you going to do?"

"I'm doing it." I lifted the stylus off of Marvin and cleaned the album, my hand steady as I watched the Motown label spin. She was staring in disbelief. It was a real bad connection. As good-looking as she was, it was a real bad connection. I left for five seconds, long enough to go and pee and see her little ceramic eggs filled with perfumed cedar shavings on the back of the john, and in that brief five minutes, she put on Boy George. What we prided ourselves on most at Any Old Way You Choose It Music then was that we did just that, chose it without regard to sales and top tens and who's who. Like if I was in one mood, I might play the Beatles all day long, maybe play "Rubber Soul" two times in a row: I had whole weekends where all I played were the Stones, Dylan, or the Doors, and then followed it with a Motown Monday, a Woodstock Wednesday. Some days I just went for somebody like Buffy St. Marie or Joan Baez, which always surprised the young clientele, people like Betts, people who might say, Who's that? Screw them.

"You mean you're going to work there forever?" Betts asked, Boy George staring up at me from the floor. Her fingers were tapping along to "Do You Really Want to Hurt Me?"

"I'm buying in," I told her, which was not entirely a lie. The owner, a guy my age who had already made it big in the local business scene, was considering it. He had graduated with a D average from a small second rate junior college, and found a small empire already carved out by his old man. I graduated from the University with a 3.7 in English and philosophy, highest honors for some old paper I wrote about Samuel Coleridge, and what I got was one of those little leather kits for your toiletries. What toiletries? I had wanted to ask my mom, who said she remembered me saying I needed one of those. Yeah right. I need a toiletries kit.

"I'm doing okay," I said and lifted the stylus from Boy George, searched in earnest for the Kinks so Betts could ask some more dumb questions. She came over and knelt beside me, put her head close to mine, little orange Cheeto sparkles all above her lip.

"I know you're doing okay," she whispered and pressed her mouth against my neck. "You're better than okay," she said. "My friends all think you're interesting in a kind of weird way, you know, mysterious." Though her knowledge of gross anatomy was limited at that stage of the game, her own anatomy was doing quite nicely. Too nicely really because it made me a dishonest person. I was thinking *bad connection, bad connection,* and yet I let her play her albums and pull me to the floor. "Isn't it great that I've moved in?" she asked ten minutes later, the needle hugging the wide smooth grooves of the last song, a long silent begging for the needle to be lifted. "Isn't it going to be wonderful?" she asked, but all I could think about when I closed my eyes was Marvin standing there in his hat, his old man with pistol aimed. Betts moved in the day after he died and he hadn't been dead three months when she moved out; she pled guilty to not *truly* loving me, and I turned on the somber broken-hearted look long enough to pack up her books and hand them out to the squat-bodied pathology resident who she had taken up with and who was waiting for her. "Here's a live one for you," I told him and patted her on the back.

I didn't really miss *her* so much as I just *missed*. The young jerky store owner was still dangling his carrots about *maybe* letting me buy in. I told him that he was getting too far away from the old stuff, the good stuff, but he insisted that we *go with the flow*. He didn't want me monopolizing the sound system with too much of the old stuff; he said Neil Young made his skin crawl. He was just sick all over that he hadn't kept his Rick Nelson stock up to date. I figured what the hell, did I really want to be in business with such a sleaze? I took a little vacation to get myself feeling up, to get Betts out of my bones, and then I was back full force, nothing on the back of my john, no album that never should have been on my shelves. But before too long, there I was hanging up T-shirts of the Butthole Surfers. Things were getting bad.

I thought things couldn't get worse, but let a couple of years spin by and they did. There were prepubescent girls with jewelry-store names running around the shopping malls singing songs they didn't deserve to sing. It was plagiarism; it was distasteful. Where were the *real* women? Where was Grace Slick? Then there was a run on Roy Orbison's music, and once again, my jerk of a boss was in a state of panic that he'd missed yet another good-time post-mortem sale. He was eating cocaine for breakfast by then and had a bad case of DBC's (Dead Brain Cells). I might sleep around now and then; I might even end up with someone born after 1968, but at least I'm moral about it. He gets them tanked and snorted and then goes for the prize. One step above being a necro if you ask me. And what really pisses me off is that society sees me as the loser, the social misfit who's living in the past. The guy drives a BMW and owns a condo and a business, stuffs all his money up his nose, pokes teenage coeds who don't remember he did it, and he's successful.

I was just about to the point where I couldn't tune it all out when I landed up with a bad hangover that turned into the flu and landed me in one of those fast-food medicine places. You know; Doc in the Box, planted right beside Revco so you can rush right over and fill your prescription. I felt like hell and I was about to stretch out on their green vinyl couch when I saw someone familiar. It was Marlene Adams, a girl from home, a woman of my time, no ring on her hand, good-looking as ever. I sat straight up and was about to say something when she turned calmly and called my name. "I was wondering when you'd recognize me," she said and laughed, her eyes as blue as the crisp autumn sky. "I had heard you were still living around here. Who told me that? Somebody I saw at a wedding not too long ago." For a split second I was feeling better, felt like grabbing a bucket of chicken and sitting in the park, throwing a Frisbee, going to some open-air concert. "You haven't changed a bit," she said, and I felt her gaze from head to toe. It was the first time in years that I was *worried* about how I looked.

"Neither have you." I sat up straight, smoothed back my hair. God, why hadn't I taken a shower? "Why're you here?" I asked and glanced to the side where there was a cloudy aquarium with one gold-fish swimming around. "I thought you were some place like California or Colorado or North Dakota. I thought you were married." I thought the fish must feel like the only son of a bitch on the planet, thirty gallons of water and nobody to swim over and talk to.

"Divorced. I'm back in graduate school, psychology," she said and laughed. "And I'm in this office because I tripped down some steps." I turned back from the dismal fish to see her holding out her right foot, her ankle blue and swollen. She had on a little white sock, the kind my mother always wore with her tennis shoes, little colored pompom balls hanging off the back.

"Can you believe it?" She shook her head back and forth. "It was really embarrassing. There were loads of people in the library when it happened." She leaned back, her thick hair fanning behind her as she stared up at the ceiling. I kept expecting her to say something really stupid and mundane and patronizing like, *So, you say that you're living here but not in graduate school, you sell albums and tapes to coeds who you occasionally sleep with, you say you have a hangover, what I'm hearing from you is that you are in search of a sex partner who has possibly heard of some of the songs of your youth.*

"I'm just as clumsy as I was the time we went camping," she said, her voice light and far removed from that psychological monotone Id just imagined. "Remember? You swore you'd never take me again?"

"And I didn't," I said. "I never got the chance." I turned back to the fish. It was an awkward moment. You don't often get to discuss breaking up years after the fact, but we were doing it. She dumped me, and now that I had reminded her of that fact, she was talking in high gear to cover the tracks. *Why does it take so long to get seen in this place?* And *When have you ever been home? Does your dad still have the refrigerator store,* and *Is your mom well?*

I was relieved when the door opened and the nurse called me in. "See you around," I said politely, half hoping that she'd disappear while I was gone. Marlene and I were the same age from the same small town, the same neighborhood even. I had known her since my family moved to that town when I was in the fifth grade and we had all run around screaming the words to "I Want to Hold Your Hand" and crossing our eyes like Ringo. That was the common ground that had brought us together that month in college to begin with.

I thought about it all the while they stuck a thermometer in my mouth and instructed me to undress. Marlene had been pretty goofy as a kid, and though I considered her a friend, I never would have ridden my bike over to her house to visit. She had this dog named Alfie, who smelled like crap, thus leaving Marlene and her wet-dog-smelling jeans rather undesirable. In junior high, Matt Walker and I suggested we put Alfie in front of a firing squad, and Marlene didn't speak to me for weeks after. No big deal, but then high school we got to be pals just sort of hanging outside the breezeway where you were allowed to smoke in between classes. Can you believe that they let us smoke in school? That *they,* the administrators, those lopsided adults had *designated* an area? I spent a lot of time there and so did Marlene. She was on the Student Council, which most of us thought was a bunch of crap, but still she was forever circulating a petition. She was really into womanhood, which I found kind of titillating in a strange way, don't ask me why, though I never did anything at all. She was a hard worker, a smart girl. That's the kind of shit people wrote in her yearbook if they wrote anything at all. Nineteen-seventy was not a big year for yearbook signing. But then, get the girl off to college and there was a major metamorphosis; it was like I could watch it happen there in poli-sci lecture, blonde streaks in her hair that hung to her waist, little cropped T-shirts and cutoff jeans, her tinted wire-rim glasses (aviator style like Gloria Steinem's) always pushed up on her head. Guys waited to see where she was going to sit and then clustered around her. God, she was beautiful, and then I had to take a turn just sitting and *listening* to all that was going on in her life just as she had *listened* to me there in the smoking area. I had a girlfriend here and there along the way, but I guess I was really waiting for Marlene to come around. Her boyfriend had been drafted, and though she told me how lucky I was not to have been taken (lucky break, legal blindness; my brother winged me in the left eye with a sharp rock when I was seven), I could tell that I was somehow weakened in her eyes. There would have been much more admiration had I had 20-20 vision and fled to Canada. It was a brief affair, the consummation of any likes we'd had for each other since adolescence, and then it was over, one fiasco of a camping trip, pouring down rain, Marlene sprained her thumb when she tripped over a tree limb and landed face down in the mud. It amazed me the things that that dumb thumb *hindered* her from doing. It was a loss of a weekend.

"You have the flu," the nurse told me after I'd waited forever in my underwear, and I made my way back out to the lone-fish lobby to find her still there, though now her ankle was all neatly bound up in an ace bandage.

"You don't look so great," she said. "Why don't I go home with you and fix you something for lunch?" I just shrugged, thinking about what was in my kitchen cabinet, a molded loaf of bread, a couple of cans of tomato soup, one can of tuna. If she could turn it into something, I'd beg her never to leave me.

"What about your car?" I asked, and again she pointed to her ankle.

"I can't drive. My ankle." For a minute she sounded just like she had years before, *I can't do that, my thumb,* and I should have listened to the warning but I was too taken back by her features, a face that needed no makeup of any kind, a girl who *looked* like she *ought* to be a perfect camper. "I rode the bus here," she said and extended her hand for me to help her out. "It'll be fun to catch up on things."

Marlene and I picked up with each other like we'd never been apart. It was like we could read each other's mind, and so we carefully avoided talking about the time we broke up. Instead we focused on all the good stuff, things we had in common, just by being the same age and from the same town. Like I might say "Remember when Tim Oates cut off the top of his finger in shop?" and she'd say, "Yeah, he was making a TV table for his mama." Things like that. We had things in common that might seem absolutely stupid to an outsider. After three glorious months, tripling our first time together, Marlene and I finally came around to talking out all the things that ruined us before. She was starting to kind of hint about how she was going to be a professional and how maybe I would want to be a *professional* too. I started singing that song, "I see by your outfit that you are a cowboy, you see by my outfit that I'm a cowboy, too."

"C'mon," she said and wrapped her arms around my neck. "I don't mean to give you a hard time, it's just that I've heard you say how you really want..." Bad connection, bad connection.

"So you get an outfit and let's all be cowboys," I finished the song, and she went to take her exam in a real pissed-off state. I did what I always do when I'm feeling lousy, which is to sort through my albums and play all of my favorite cuts. I should have been a deejay, the lone jockey on the late-night waves, rather than employee to a squat coked-to-the-gills little rich shit. I thought of Marlene writing some little spiel about *composure, heal thyself*. I was playing Ten Years After full blast. Sly and the Family Stone on deck. And then all in one second I felt mad as hell, as mad as I'd been on that pouring-rain camping trip when Marlene told me that it was hard for her to think of me as anything except a *friend*. She actually said that. It all came back to me when I saw that old Black Sabbath album, which is what she had left behind the other time she moved out. That's a whole helluva lot. Warms my heart to see a green faced chick draped in scarves wandering around what looks like a mausoleum. She had all the routine things you can think of to say. "I know you don't really care about *me*," she had said. "I could be *anybody*."

"Yeah right," I told her. "I could cuddle up with Pat Paulson and not care. I'm just that kind if insensitive jerk."

"But you don't care about *me*," she had said and pounded her chest with her hand, which was wrapped in a bath towel to protect the sprained thumb which had left her an absolute invalid. "I need to be my own person, have my own life." I found out a day later that she already had all the info on all these schools in the West; she had been looking for a good time to bale out and it seemed camping in the monsoon was as good as any. It was hard to remember but it seemed I said something like, "And I don't need to have my own life?" and then the insults got a little thicker until before long I was told that I was apathetic and chauvinistic and my brain was stuck between my legs.

"So, that's why you're always asking what I'm thinking," I said in response. By that time we were soaking wet and driving back *down* the rest of the mountain in a piece-of-crap car I had at the time, an orange Pinto, with a Jimi Hendrix tape playing full blast (eight track, of course). "And what kind of stupid question is that anyway, and yet you always ask it. *What are you thinking?*" Yeah, that was how the whole ride home went, and of course any time I had a good line, any time I scored, then she got to cry and say what an ass I was.

By the time she got home from her lousy test, I was as mad as if I was there in the pouring rain, jacking that screwed-up Pinto to change a flat while she sat on the passenger side and stared straight ahead at that long stretch of road we had to travel before I could put her out. Apparently she had been thinking through it all as well because she walked into my apartment looking just as she had when I dumped her out in front of her dorm years before. We had both played over the old stuff enough that we had independently been furious and now were simply exhausted and ready to have it all end, admit the truth. Nothing in common other than walking the planet at the same time. She was barely over her divorce, she rationalized (he had dumped her, I was delighted to find). I handed her that Black Sabbath album on her way out, and we made polite promises about keeping in touch.

And now I've come to this: Final Vinyl Days, the end of an era. Perfectly round black vinyl discs, their jackets faded, sit on the small table before my checkout and await extinction. I stare across the street, the black asphalt made shiny by the drizzling rain, the traffic light blinking red and green puddles in the gray light where a mammoth parking deck is under construction. There I see the lights in the store we compete with, Record City, and I can't help but wonder when they'll change their name: CD Metropolis. But what can I say about names? Any Old Way You Choose It ain't exactly true either.

"Record City doesn't have *these*," my boss said just last week and began putting this crap all over the place, you know, life-size cutouts of Marilyn Monroe and Elvis, little replicas of the old tabletop jukeboxes that are *really* CD houses, piñatas and big plastic blowup dinosaurs. I work nights now, not as much business and I don't have to argue with the owner about what I play overhead. As far as I'm concerned, the new kids on the block are still Bruce Springsteen and Jackson Browne. My boss said it was a promotion, but I know better. Janis Joplin's singing now, "Me and Bobby McGee," and the Stones are on deck with "Jumping Jack Flash." The Stones are the cockroaches of rock. They'll be around when civilization starts over, and I cling to this bit of optimism.

I had no choice but to give in to CDs. And yeah, they sound great, that's true. It's just the principle of the thing, your hand forced to change. Not even to mention the dreaded task of *replacing*. It's impossible. Think of what's *not* available. I'm just taking my time is all. I figure if I just go from the year of my birth to the year I graduated from college, it'll take the rest of my life. I'm going alphabetically so that I don't miss anything, and it's a real boring calculated way to approach life. I mean, what if that's how I dealt with women? Imagine it: Betts, Erica, Gail, Marlene, Nancy, that one who always wore black, either Pat or Pam, Susie, Xanadu. Yeah right, Xanadu. I thought it was kinda cute that she had gone and renamed herself. Then I learned that she had never even heard of Coleridge, but rather had some vivid childhood memory of Olivia Newton John. Scary. We were in a bar and it was very very late so what could I expect? "Let's get physical," I suggested, and she raised her pencil-thin eyebrows as if trying to remember where she'd heard *that* line before. "Can I call you Xan?"

"Oh, sure," she said, "everybody does." And when she walked ahead of me to the door, I noticed her spiderweb stockings complete with rhinestone spider. She wore a black spandex miniskirt, and I realized that my knowledge of women's fashion had come full circle. I looked at myself in the beer-can-lined mirror to affirm that yes, I had hit bottom. Xan and I had *nothing* in common except cotton mouth and body hair.

Now Del Shannon had gone and shot himself, and no one has even asked about his music. I hear the song "Runaway," and I see myself, a typical nine-year-old slouch, stretched out on my bed with a stack of comic books and the plug of my transistor radio wedged in my ear. My mom made me a bedspread that looked like a race car the headlights down at the end facing into the hallway where my dad was standing in his undershirt, his face coated in lather. "C'mon, honey," my mom said. "We've got to go down to the store," and then there we all were in front of this little cinder-block store at the edge of town, our last name painted in big red letters on the window. There must have been at least ten people gathered for the event, which my dad later said (while we waited for foot long hot-dogs to be delivered to the window of the car) was just about the proudest moment of his life. He said it was second only to marrying my mother (she had a ring of vanilla shake around her mouth as she smiled back at him) and having my younger brother and me. My brother was in a French-fry frenzy, bathing in a pool of catsup he'd poured on the little checkered cardboard container, but he stopped to take in the seriousness of my dad's announcement. I was wondering even then how you *know* when its the happiest moment. I was dumbfounded that anyone could build a life on refrigerators and stoves and be happy about it. It amazes me now to think that I sat in the backrest of that old

Chevrolet and looked at my parents (younger then than I am now) and thought how ridiculously *outdated* they were.

Now this coed comes in. Tie-dye is *back,* torn jeans, leather sandals. If her hair wasn't purple and aimed at the ceiling, I could just about console my grief. "Can I help?" I ask, totally unprepared for the high squeak of a voice that comes out. She sounds like she just inhaled a balloon full of helium.

"I want *The Little Mermaid,*" she said, a high-school ring still on her finger. "You know, the video? It's for my little brother."

"Yeah, right. Over there." I point to the far wall, the latest addition to my record/CD/video store, a menagerie of colorful piñatas swinging overhead. "We got 'em all."

Oh yeah. We've got a two-foot table boasting the end of my youth, leftover albums, the bottom of the barrel. It's all that's left, and nobody even stops to look, to mourn, to pay respect. I arranged them such that Joni Mitchell is the one looking out on the dreary day. I imagine someone coming from the street and saying, "Oh, I get it, *paved paradise and put up a parking lot,*" but no such luck; there is no joy in Mudville.

I try to make myself feel better. I think of the positive factors in my life. I recycle my cans and glass and paper. I ride a bike instead of driving a car. Though my old man and I don't always see eye to eye, I know that I'll never turn to find him with a gun pointed my way like Mr. Gaye did to Marvin. I sleep peacefully, all bills paid, no TV blasting MTV like the one across the street in the cinder-block house where a couple of girls come and go. One of them is real nice-looking in a kind of Marlene way, wears gym clothes all the time, no makeup, hair long and loose. Though I know sure as hell if I slept with her she'd get up and put on lipstick and control-top panty hose and ask me why I don't cut my hair and get a real job. It's the luck of the draw, and my luck is lousy. "Give up the Diet Coke," I had told Betts. "Give up the fluorescent foods." I told Marlene to give up the self-pity; if she wanted to be somebody, then to stop talking about it and be it. I had suggested to Xan that she give up the body hair. I told the boss to be *different*, not to cave in to all this crap. The bottom line? Nobody likes suggestions. So why I am supposed to be different?

"What can you tell me about the Byrds?" My heart leaps up and I turn to face the purple-haired, squeeky-voiced girl, who has placed *The Little Mermaid* on the counter and has a twenty clutched in her fist.

"Yeah? The Byrds? Like turn, turn, turn?"

She looks around, first one way than the other. Then she looks back at me, face young and smooth and absolutely blank. "The pink ones," she squeaks and points upward where flamingo piñatas swing on an invisible cord. "How much?"

I watch her walk off now, her pilgrim-looking shoes mud-spattered as she heads through the construction area, her pink bird clutched to her chest along with *The Little Mermaid*. It's times like this when I start thinking I might give my dad a call and say, "I know you've been saying how you want me to take over your business some day…" It's times like this when I start thinking about Marlene, when I start forgetting how bad it all got. I do crazy things like imagine us meeting again, one more try at this perfect 1970s romance. Like maybe I *will* go to work for my dad, and in my off-hours maybe I'll get out the old power saw and make my mom a TV table (just like you've been saying you wanted, Mom), and maybe I'll circumcise the old index finger and end up in the emergency room and I'll look down that row of vinyl chairs and there she'll be. It's not the *perfect* fantasy but it's one I have. It's one that more and more starts looking good after I watch Marvin's music revived by a bunch of fat raisins dancing around on the tube, or after I see a series of women getting younger and younger, arriving at my door in their spider hose and stiff neon hair, their arms filled with little plastic squares, a mountain of CD covers dumped on my floor.

Bobby's Girl

rochelle ratner

ANNETTE FUNICELLO, WHO USED TO BE ON *The Mickey Mouse Club* and then went out on her own as a singer, was her best friend. Shelley Fabares, who played Mary, the daughter on *The Donna Reed Show,* was her second-best friend. The three of them were all but inseparable when they were in California at the same time, though that happened rarely.

Frankie Avalon and Fabian were the men she was closest to, because Bob Marcucci and Pete DeAngelis managed all three of them. She and Frankie had more or less dated at times. Fabe was really too young for her. But Bobby Rydell was the man she dated mostly— though only when their schedules permitted it. Then there was Paul Anka, who mostly dated Annette.

Her parents' living room–dining room combination was maybe thirty feet wide by twenty feet long, not a bad shape for pacing. She had to pace to keep her show-biz friends with her. Otherwise they left the way real kids did, and she was alone again. She paced counterclockwise, a big circle in front of the sofa and behind the coffee table, around the diningroom table, past the kitchen door, and back again. Every so often she briefly reversed the circle, so as not to get dizzy. The dachshund entered after the first ten minutes or so and crouched safely underneath the dining room table where he wouldn't get stepped on, his body stretched out long, neck and chin on the floor, eyes wide open, watching, his left ear tossed back over his

34

head and inside out in a gesture of I don't care. *She* was the one who didn't care. Sometimes her father pointed to the dog and told her the dog was confused, that she was making her dog crazy and he was going to turn vicious on account of her. This could go on for hours. She could wear out a track in the carpet, as her father accused her of doing. Her body rocked slightly. Pacing helped her focus.

Annette Funicello and Shelley Fabares both lived with their parents. She envied them because their parents went along with their careers and encouraged them. She thought it was funny, when she stopped to think about it, that Bobby, Paul, Frankie, even Fabe—all the boys—had moved out on their own, just as she had. Her managers, Bob Marcucci and Pete DeAngelis, especially Bob, were like substitute parents. She sometimes dared them by purposely acting up, and Bob sometimes had to take a firm hand with her. She pretended to be how old? Seventeen. Sometimes eighteen or nineteen, depending. Just so long as she was over ten, past this awful time she was going through now. It was good having Fabe and Frankie going through the same scenes with Bob and Pete. They were like her brothers and consoled her.

Take last night, for instance. She had a TV show to do next weekend, and Bob told her to go home and get to bed early. Then Bobby called, and she went out with him. Usually no one found out, but people were starting to know her around town. Dick Clark, who was supposed to be her friend, ran into them and might well have told on her. She woke up scared this morning.

She called Frankie and asked him if he'd drive into the office with her, just in case. It wasn't all that unusual. It was expensive to park downtown, and they frequently drove in together.

"Bobby's in town, by the way." She strained to make her voice sound casual. At times like that, all the acting lessons in the world didn't seem to help much. "He came over last night, and we went out for a while, did the gallery tour."

"I thought Bob wanted you to get to bed early."

"Yeah, well..." Oh Christ, Frankie was slipping into his big brother know-it-all role again. All of twenty-one, the hot shot.

"Look," he said. "You know you have to look good for the show. It's stupid to overdo things."

"We ran into Dick in Molly Barnes' Gallery." She said it softly, her voice rising at the end, almost to a question.

"That was smart. Why the hell did you go where people might see you? Haven't you at least learned that much by now? And I'll bet you stayed up half the night worrying, too. Jesus."

Silence. Frankie looked straight ahead at the traffic. Two full stoplights before he turned to her. "Dick won't tell," he said with that smile she loved so much. Now he knew why she called him this morning. His whole scolding game was just something to pass the time in traffic.

And, anyway, it turned out Bob didn't know this time.

Her father tiptoed into the kitchen for a glass of milk. She could feel him staring at her. He was as sad and confused as he claimed the dachshund was, but with his bushy black mustache, too large for his small face, he looked more like a chipmunk. He was nearing sixty, exhausted from a twelve-hour day at work, too old for children. His thick, black-framed reading glasses were pushed up on his forehead, as if he didn't have the energy to take them off completely. His feet were popping out of his backless slippers.

Not now, please not now—they were all in Bob's office, joking, really being friends, carefree. She was almost tempted to confess she went out last night, Bob knew in the end that kids needed their fun, needed to be somewhat reckless. That was why she loved him.

Then the blow came. "The news is almost on," her father said. Silence. "They're broadcasting parts of Castro's speech today. You ought to hear it. You ought to find out what's happening in the world. You might realize there are people with larger problems than you have. Real problems, not imaginary ones."

She reversed the circle to avoid walking past him. He stood there, fidgeting, his eyes blinking from the strain of watching her. A louder silence.

He walked quickly back to the den, turned the television up a little louder, so he wouldn't have to think about her. Either that or he was getting hard of hearing, but he would never admit that. She slowed down her pace. Her thoughts were starting to wander. What would it have been like if she had brothers and sisters, a real family? Maybe she wouldn't have needed to pace, if she'd had real friends, at least. This sort of thought led nowhere and broke into the fantasy. It was her father's fault. Damn him. She stooped to fix the dog's ear and felt his body tighten up, his long backbone coiling away from her ever so slightly. He couldn't make up his mind. She petted him, spoke softly, took some sleeping pills—two Tuinol and a couple of Valium—and went into her room and closed the door. Peace and quiet.

Actually the circle used to be a straight line. The pacing used to have a purpose. It used to lead somewhere, to school, Union Avenue School, ten blocks from home, blocks in alphabetical order: Kenyon, Lancaster, Manchester, Nassau, Osborne, Pembroke, Quincy, Rumson, Swarthmore, Thurlow, Union. Her whole life ordered. Annette, Shelley, Frankie, Fabe—they were her friends for the walk at least, out in the open air where they could breathe. They didn't forget her the way Arlene had back in first grade. Arlene was the daughter of her mother's best friend and was supposed to walk her home at lunchtime. One day Arlene got talking with her friends and just left her standing there.

Ever since that day, she'd had her own friends on the walk home. She had her friends to console her two years ago, when she was eight years old and Rebel, her beagle puppy, was run over by a dump truck on Jerome Avenue. Even Harriet, her grown-up next-door neighbor, who would have understood how she felt, wasn't at home. Rebel had dug his way out of the pen her father had built for him.

Of course, as she aged, her circle of friends had grown. There were fights, and there were people who didn't like each other, just as in life, but in the end they were all her friends, and they always forgave her. That was what real friendship was.

Shelley Fabares and Annette Funicello were both tutored on the sets when they were working. Fabe went to public schools in Philadelphia a good part of the year. His parents insisted that he not be singled out. Paul, Frankie, and Bobby had all graduated, though they talked of going to college someday. But, for her, there never seemed to be a question of studying. She simply avoided that.

She turned the music louder, the way her father turned up the TV or her mother raised her voice talking on the phone when she could hear her daughter's footsteps pacing the next room. All that thought of school was starting to upset her. She tried hard to focus on the words of one song after another:

Venus, if you will...

all the way down to the part where Frankie's pleading for some "little girl" just like her.

Probably the other kids had stereos. She was seldom in their houses long enough to find out, and when she was, she found herself too nervous to look around. Arlene had a Victrola, with a black plastic case and a long thick thimble that you piled the forty-fives on and let them drop one after another. She knew she didn't want that, didn't want anything Arlene had.

She remembered the small record player she had as a little girl, with decals on its lid of Mary and her little lamb. She loved to put the records on one by one, playing games like "I choose you because you're yellow" or "I choose you because you've been sitting there so patiently." Half the fun was playing them one by one. So she convinced her parents to buy her the best manual record player they could find, but it was still, they told her, a glorified child's toy, since, they told her, everyone with any sense bought the other kind, like Arlene.

Records were also a problem. Her parents had one or two cha-cha records that they played when they practiced steps from their dance class. They took lessons from the same teacher they later sent her to. Watching them dance so awkwardly on her pacing carpet, with her father stepping on her mother's feet, anyone would have thought they'd learn that dancing couldn't be taught. But they didn't seem to notice.

My Son the Folk Singer, by Allan Sherman, was another record her parents owned, but you didn't have to dance to it. She enjoyed that. And about once a month, when her parents went shopping at Garwood Mills, the first discount store in Atlantic City, she prevailed upon them to let her buy a forty-five, and she got "It's Only Make Believe" by Conway Twitty, "Diana" by Paul Anka, "All I Have to Do Is Dream" by the Everly Brothers, and Frankie's recording of "Venus." She also had a record by Marty DeNico, the South Philly teenager Uncle Steve managed. He'd actually grown up with Fabe, Frankie, and Bobby, and the record was a demo that said NOT FOR SALE on its label: her most treasured possession.

For her tenth-birthday present, her parents said she could choose any album she wanted. She went up to Garwood Mills alone and stared and stared, with nobody rushing her this time. She looked at the album covers, picked up a few to read the backs, but most of the companies were smart enough to put the important notes inside so you had to buy the record if you wanted to read them. At last she chose an album by Fabian, his first. It had a bright orange cover with the face of the handsome thirteen-year-old staring almost shyly at her. It was a false-double album, only one record. Inside, the cover promised more color photos, a pull-out portrait suitable for framing, plus the liner notes. She read, for the first time, how Fabe was discovered sitting on a stoop in South Philly after his father had just been taken to the hospital with a heart attack. Fabe agreed to sing only because he knew it was up to him to look after the family now. It said his father was a policeman: Dominic Forte. She already knew that Bob Marcucci and Pete DeAngelis owned Chancellor Records, which produced the album. She did what little she could to help support them.

She held the pull-out portrait in her hands. For a moment she thought of just tacking it up on the wall over her bed, where maybe she would dream of him. But she never remembered her dreams anyway, only the nightmares. Besides, she had something better than dreams and much more private. To tack it up on the wall would cheapen it. That was what the other kids did. She imagined pinups all over their rooms, the girls talking about new records in voices as shrill as her mother's. Gossip, that's what it was. She wanted no part of it. She put the portrait back in the album and tucked the album away in a drawer where even the maid wouldn't find it. No one must know of this.

Elvis in Wonderland

kathleen warnock

I AM NOT A READER OF the supermarket tabloids (except when the checkout line is very long). I do not see the face of Jesus in the mold in my refrigerator (though I probably shouldn't hang onto things until they turn bad). I am not prone to gullibility or given to leaping over facts to miraculous conclusions. I'm an elementary school teacher: history, arithmetic, science. History repeats itself. Two and two always make four. Matter cannot be created or destroyed, it can only change form.

I'm not comfortable telling a story. I feel much more at home with a red pencil and a box of gold stars, a pile of students' work on one side—uninformed to informed. I believe my kids think me tough. Tough but fair. The pictures they draw, their heartfelt letters, those are the proof they give me I was there for them. That they can read, write, and add is their evidence of me.

These days, summers are unbearable in Wonderland, Maryland. Someone has written on the town limits sign: "Not much of a..."

Back when old Route 2 was the only way to the shore (up and over through Delaware), then it was something. People would stop off for a few hours or days on their way to the ocean and stay in the grand old hotel (at least until 1914) and visit the amusement park that gave the town its name.

The park was still a popular destination until the late sixties, when the Key Bridge and the Harbor Tunnel made Route 2 a road to nowhere. Who would take a cracked old two-lane blacktop for five hours when you could blow down a modern throughway in under three? Not you, not anybody else either, and that was it for Wonderland.

I was pushing my bike back to my house because the damn thing had a flat. Late June felt like August and thirty years old felt like a hundred. The sweat ran in my eyes as I squinted—walking right into the sun. My ankles and calves were covered with bug bites. And it was another mile home. No one comes down Wonderland Lane anymore *except* me, so I was walking down the middle of the road. The glare created mirages on the road, pools of water that seemed quite real, but evaporated into nothing as I got closer. I had my headphones on—the oldies station faded in and out, as if Baltimore were on another planet. I was singing along with *Heartbreak Hotel*, so I didn't hear the screech of brakes, but I felt the wind as the car swerved to avoid me. I froze and felt my heartbeat in my ears.

The car, a big white pimpmobile, ended up in the drainage ditch. I felt terrible for not paying more attention. I threw my bike down and ran over, and as I got there, the passenger door opened—the driver's side was jammed against the grass at the bottom of the ditch.

"Are you all right, little lady?" he asked. And for a moment I thought I was going to faint. The heat hit me like a wave, and the whine of the seventeen-year locusts grew into a roar.

"I'm fine... Am I?" I replied. I wasn't too sure.

"You look a mite peaked," he told me in that unmistakable drawl. "I expect it's the heat. And the close call."

"Yeah," I chose to agree. I took another look at him. The hair was now gray, but combed into an old-fashioned pompadour. He'd lost weight and his form had the lean lines of the early days. And those were his hooded eyes, if they did have crows feet. The curled lip.

"What about you?" I asked, "Are you OK?"

"All in one piece," he affirmed. "Ah'm kinda surprised."

"So am I!" I sat down right there at the side of the road. I closed my eyes and fully expected to open them on an empty road.

"Honey, are you sure you're all right?" I felt his hand on my shoulder. A shock, like jumping into cold water and losing your breath, ran through me. And when I looked up, I was staring into the eyes of the King.

"Is anything wrong?" he persisted.

"I just thought—" I began. Then considered. A man doesn't go to all that trouble for no reason. And if I called his name, he might disappear. "Nothing. For a minute, I thought you were someone I used to know. Someone I haven't seen in a long time."

He nodded slightly.

"Kinda funny when that happens, isn't it?" And he helped me up.

His car wasn't damaged, so I found a couple of boards and we stuck them under the front tires. It took a while, but we got the Caddy out of the ditch. Then he threw my bike in the trunk, and insisted on giving me a ride home. As I sank into the velour bucket seat and he cranked up the air conditioner, I thought that if this was a hallucination, it was awfully specific.

My house is on the other side of Wonderland Park, and as we drove down the winding, tree-lined lane I saw him looking through the cyclone fencing at what was left of the place.

"You live here?" he asked.

"The old caretaker's place, back of the park. It was either that or a mobile home."

"Must be kinda lonely."

"It is. But I like it. It's like living in a different part of the world," I tried to explain. "I mean—what's that quote? 'The past is another country. They do things differently there.' I like to explore that other country." He didn't say anything, but nodded again.

We pulled up in front of my place, a Victorian-style cottage (ca. 1908) with gingerbread trim. He helped me with my bike, then started to get back in his car.

"Don't go!" I said, surprised at the vehemence in my voice. "I mean, come in for a minute. Let me give you something to drink. Least I can do after running you off the road..."

I could see him weighing the decision. He slammed his car door, and grinned. "I'd say that's the least you can do, darlin'!"

I'd made a batch of iced tea that morning, and I poured it into tall glasses with a shaking hand. He shut his eyes and drained half the glass in one gulp, leaning against the refrigerator, then he rubbed it against his forehead.

"You're lookin' at me funny," he said, through half-open eyes.

"I got a sudden image of Jimmy Dean in *Rebel Without a Cause*," I told him. "Y'know, the scene when he goes home after the chicken race, and drinks milk from the bottle, then holds it to his head."

"You're not old enough to remember James Dean," he scoffed. "Me, I saw his movies when they first came out. I wanted to be him. I copied the look, the moves." He put the glass on the counter. "I guess I still do. I remember how I felt the day he died. I wanted to meet him. And I knew I never would. It tore me up."

He moved out of the kitchen quickly, through the bead curtain that hangs in the arch to the living room. If the beads hadn't still been swaying, I would have sworn he'd disappeared. I gave him a minute, then followed.

He was staring at my memorabilia, the clutter and detritus abandoned and forgotten over the course of a century in a place where people used to play. I've hung up old faded pennants with "Wonder-Land" written on them, lined the molding around the room with souvenir plates showing ladies in long dresses and men in boaters carrying bamboo canes. There's a large poster, hand-tinted, with scenes of the park, showing the "Wonder-Wheel", the swan boats, the carousel. I even found some pipes from the old steam organ, and brought them in.

"What's this stuff?" he asked, picking up a room key, a worn brass tag dangling from it.

"Stuff from the old hotel," I told him. "They never rebuilt after it burned down. They just paved it over. But even parking lots aren't indestructible, and there's lots of holes I can go poking through."

"I don't remember a hotel," he murmured.

"You wouldn't, unless you're a lot older than you look. Burned down before World War I. When were you here?"

"During my James Dean days. I came through here a few summers."

I went to the bookcase and hauled out some of my scrapbooks,

"This is stuff I found from the Fifties," I told him. He gently opened the first bulky book, and flipped through the pages, slowing here and there to gaze at a photo for a moment, running his finger down a handbill, smiling a private smile. I looked over his shoulder at the old black-and-whites of teenagers who were probably grandparents by now, girls and boys with funny hairstyles dancing in the outdoor ballroom to the glow of Japanese lanterns.

The shots of the singers were taken from floor level, looking up at the stage, and caught the performers at moments of abandon— with their eyes closed, or hunched over the microphone, or with their heads thrown back, drops of sweat flying. Summers then were just as hot as they are now. There were unknowns, and has-beens, and never-made-its, and skinny young guys barely recognizable as the stars they became.

Bobby Darin smiled from one glossy. I'd also found shots of the Crickets, Bobby Rydell, Chuck Berry, Frankie Avalon, Ricky Nelson, Carl Perkins, Jerry Lee Lewis, Bobby Vinton, Vito and the Salutations, Frankie Ford, Freddy "Boom Boom" Cannon, Ray Charles, the

Moonglows, the Orioles, the Ink Spots (the black acts played on "colored days" in the Jim Crow era).

He turned the page and found himself looking at himself. In the picture, he was wearing a pair of baggy pegged pants with a pleat, and two-toned shoes. He had on a big boxy jacket with a shiny lining, and a skinny dark tie that was flapping up. One hand was out in a windmill gesture, the other grabbed the mike. His feet were off the ground, and he looked like he was flying.

"I bet that was a pink jacket," I said.

"I bet it was, too," he replied, turning the page, then closing the book. He got up again, and paced back to the kitchen. I put the book away and followed.

"Where'd you get that stuff?" he asked. "Why do you save it?"

"It's here. Everywhere you look, there's another pile from another summer. The people are gone, but they were here. Who were they? What were they like?"

"I knew them. I knew me. But now I don't. Everything's changed. Everyone's different. They're strangers to me, even if they think they know me. And I go looking for a familiar face, something I can grab onto, and I see glimpses, sometimes I think I see myself. But that's not it. Something's missing. And no one seems to notice."

"Most people don't," I agreed. "But some do. They try to remember who we were. Maybe that's why I trashpick through history. Bits of paper and curled up old black-and-whites. Looking for America or something." Suddenly, I was embarrassed to the point of misery. "I'm just a nutty schoolteacher out in the boonies, gone a little stir crazy, I guess." More than a little, I told myself, staring at my feet.

"I'm not sure what you're lookin' for, darlin', but I hope you find it," he said. "Sometimes we can't put a name on what we want. Goin' on twenty years I've been on the road, and I still don't know what I'm hopin' to find." He looked around. "I came here because I wanted to see where I'd been. So maybe you're right, sugar."

"It's too dark in here. Let's go outside."

I took him back to where they keep the cars from the various rides. There are still a few left, wrapped up like mummies in their old canvas coverings. On sunny days, light falls in puddles through all the broken panes in the belfry of the roundhouse. The sunbeams caught the motes of dust in the musty air. Pigeons flutter in and out of the roof, and at sunset, the bats wing out of their nests. A set of railroad tracks leads from the barns past my house to the park proper, an area sealed off by the barbed-wire topped metal fence. I could unlink the chain, and we squeezed through and followed the tracks into the old amusement ground.

A feeling of melancholy descends on me whenever I walk in the park. It's a place built for people that no one comes to anymore. The swan boats list, half-sunk in the algae-covered lake, which is filling in. The food stalls and games booths are shuttered. The cement bases are all that remain of the picnic tables.

It's been vandalized plenty, and the names of teen couples are spray-painted on the band shell. Anything that could be carried away is gone. There are fires every now and then, one of which destroyed most of the wooden roller coaster a few years back.

He took my hand, and I was glad to be walking through the park with someone for once. We didn't say much as we made our way to the entrance, where Alfunzo the Clown still perches over the gates, his painted smile faded but still grinning through the graffiti, his hands stretched out on either side to juggle the word W-ND-RLA-D in an arch over his head.

"The ol' boy's still standin'," he commented.

"Somewhat the worse for wear, as are we all." I smiled a little.

"Didn' anyone ever try to open it up again?" he asked me. "You'd think they'd try to bring back somethin' that was so alive once."

I told him about the attempt in the late seventies when they actually had one showcase weekend before it failed; and the time in the mid-eighties when a group of investors tried to turn the place into a theme park. They built some waterslides before declaring bankruptcy, and drove the local S&L into collapse. A holding company, rumored to be Arab-owned, holds title to the place these days. It is not worth their while to fix it up, or tear it down. It is always for sale.

There has always been talk—about getting the state to declare gambling legal and opening a casino, about inviting the Japanese to turn it into a golf course, about building Wonderland Condos. But real estate is only valuable when it's someplace people want to be and Wonderland is too far to be a bedroom community for Baltimore or Wilmington; not close enough to the Bay to draw sailors. The Choptank's not a particularly inspiring river.

"What do the people around here do?" he asked.

"Mostly, they move away," I told him. "There's some truck farms, a couple of strip malls, people retired on pensions. Lot of 'em on welfare. There hasn't been any industry here since Perdue bought out the poultry plant and moved operations down the Eastern shore."

"It shouldn't be like this. Things shouldn't be like this!" He strode back through the arch, hunched over like an old man. I caught up with him at the roller coaster, and timidly tugged on his sleeve.

"Hey, wanna go for a ride?" I asked, spinning the turnstile.

"It don't work!" he angrily replied. "Nothin' works!"

"Come on," I insisted, and jumped on the stairs. At the top, I turned back to him and held out my hand. He hesitated a minute, then straightened up and followed. I released the brake and the first car slid into view. I climbed in, and he hopped in after me. We pulled the bar across our laps.

"Now what?"

"Now we shut our eyes and go for a ride," I told him. A light breeze kicked up as we leaned back and I narrated the voyage.

"Click-click-click—that's the chain pulling us up the first hill," I started. "Hold on, the first drop is spectacular!"

"I'm not scared!" he boasted.

We let out long, high yells.

"Watch the turn!" I shrieked, and he thudded into me as though we'd just taken a hairpin at top speed. Then we both bounced up and down as though the car were cresting a series of hills. The wind whipped my hair back, and we both caromed around the car on the biggest, scariest, roller coaster ride ever. Then the final drop, and I swear I could feel my insides falling away and I threw my hands up, screaming at the top of my lungs.

I opened my eyes and we were both breathing hard—he'd taken the last hill with his arms in the air, too, and we started laughing like a couple of crazy people. He helped me out of the car and my legs were actually shaky.

We walked back around the other side of the lake, past the outdoor ballroom and bandshell.

"I wonder who's playing tonight?" I asked, wandering over to the stage. I applauded and whistled. He stood motionless, looking up at the stage. I could see the tension running up his back. Then, in one swift movement, he was on the stage, still turned away from me, looking up, down and around. Suddenly, he whirled around, an imaginary mike in one hand, pointing at me.

"Well, that's all right Mama…"

I slowly approached the edge of the stage, my eyes riveted on him. He sang right to me, kneeling down over the invisible mike, jumping up, stalking the stage, working his audience of one.

He was so beautiful, and that voice—it was older, deeper, but it still filled up my heart. No one could ever sing like him, or take his place. He sang and sang—his own songs, other old ones, new songs, rock, blues, gospel, He must have sung for hours. As it turned twilight, and the first lightning bugs shone green and orange, I could still see him, glowing like the sunset, through the gathering dark.

"In Graceland, in Graceland, I'm going to Graceland," he sang, and I joined him for the final verse.

> *For reasons I cannot explain,*
> *there's some part of me wants to see Graceland...*

And he stopped, soaked with sweat, and slowly sank to the stage. I went up beside him and helped him sit up. We swung our legs over the edge of the stage. He leaned his head on my shoulder and looked up at me, blissful. He was slick with sweat and his shirt was damp, but I didn't mind. I like the heat of a man who's been working hard, the smell, the stubble of beard, the tension waiting to be discharged.

"Wanna dance, sweet thang?" he asked. He jumped down and held out both hands. I moved right into his arms and he swung me around. He spun me and twirled me, and even dipped me to his own accompaniment.

"Shall I stay? Would it be a sin?..." Just then the wind really kicked up, and the outdoor ballroom was lit up like day by a flash of lightning, and at the crunch of thunder we both skedaddled.

We ran back through the park, hoping to beat the rain, but by the time we ducked back through the fence the hard, heavy drops were pelting us in a downpour we could barely see through.

We crashed through my back door and stood in my kitchen, breathing hard and dripping. I shivered.

I went up to my room to get towels and a change of clothes. I turned as I heard his footsteps and saw him silhouetted in the door. I clutched the clothes to my chest and dropped some of them on the floor.

"Can I use your shower?" he asked, peeling off his sodden shirt.

"N-no problem," I told him, offering him a towel, along with a T-shirt and a pair of sweats. "You should get out of those wet things." He started to unbutton his Levis, and I looked away. He laughed and went into the bathroom.

I sat on the edge of my bed and heard the shower spurt on. I was shivering so hard my teeth chattered. I stripped off my clothes and rummaged in my bureau for clean, dry things. I turned as he came out of the bathroom, a towel around his waist.

"You got any more shampoo?" he asked, looking me in the eye.

"Try under the sink," I managed to get out.

"Honey, you got nothin' to be ashamed of," he said. As he went back into the bathroom, he dropped his towel. He left the door open, and I caught an eyeful of his bare ass as he rooted for the shampoo under the sink, then climbed back into the shower. I pulled on a T-shirt and shorts, and fled barefoot down the stairs.

In a few minutes he was in the kitchen, still glistening, his hair slicked back, his chest stretching one of my old Wonderland shirts, watching as I readied some chicken for the broiler.

"This do for you?" I asked. "Or would you rather have a fried peanut butter and banana sandwich?" He cocked one eyebrow.

"Can't eat 'em anymore," he replied. "Gotta watch my cholesterol. The chicken'll do fine if you don't mind takin' off the skin."

"Mr. Heart Healthy," I teased him. "You eat salad, too?"

"Yes, ma'am," he shot back. "I have cleaned up my act."

"Not too clean, I hope."

"Just clean enough to keep havin' dirty thoughts," he grinned, and damned if I didn't drop the salad bowl. Fortunately, it was plastic and didn't break.

"Aw, I don' mean to embarrass ya, darlin'," he smiled. "I'm just funnin'." I gathered the lettuce and rinsed it off again.

He came up behind me, reached around and grabbed my hands. The water from the faucet splashed over his big brown hands, and my smaller, paler ones. For a moment, that was all I could see, the hands, the water, and feel his body pressed full length against mine, his arms down my arms. I felt his breath in my ear, a husky whisper: "What do you say, darlin'?"

"I say to hell with the chicken."

*　　*　　*

Just before dawn, I wandered between sleep and waking and reached out for the other person in my bed. And when he wasn't there, I woke.

Where he had been was still warm, the imprint of his head on the pillow. I heard a distant, scraping noise—my back door.

I ran down the stairs and outside as he closed his car trunk.

"Elvis!" I called. He started to smile, then looked away, then back at me, a pained look on his face. "Take me with you!" He walked back to the porch. "Maybe I can help you find what you're looking for," I told him.

"You helped me already," he replied, covering my mouth with one final kiss.

"Come back any time," I said. I pushed back a lock of hair that had fallen into his eyes. He swam in and out of focus as my own eyes betrayed me by brimming over. "You call me if you ever need anything."

"I will," he said. "You take care of yourself, hear?" He started up the Caddy and drove away. I watched until the taillights merged with the morning. The sun boiled big and orange as it crept above the trees. A flock of crows flapped and cawed, black as ink. I saw the red tail of a fox disappear into the bushes.

Probably would be another scorcher.

Vito Loves Geraldine

janice eidus

VITO VENECIO WAS AFTER ME. He'd wanted to get into my pants ever since tenth grade. But even though we hung around with the same crowd back at Evander Childs High School, I never gave him the time of day. I, Geraldine Rizzoli, was the most popular girl in the crowd, I had my pick of the guys, you can ask anyone, Carmela or Pamela or Victoria, and they'll agree. And Vito was just a skinny little kid with a big greasy pompadour and a cowlick and acne and a big space between his front teeth. True, he could sing, and he and Vinny Feruge and Bobby Colucci and Richie DeSoto formed a doo-wop group and called themselves Vito and the Olinvilles, but lots of the boys formed doo-wop groups and stood around on street corners doo-wopping their hearts out. Besides, I wasn't letting any of them into my pants either.

Carmela and Pamela and Victoria and all the other girls in the crowd would say, "Geraldine Rizzoli, teach me how to tease my hair as high as yours and how to put my eyeliner on so straight and thick," but I never gave away my secrets. I just set my black hair on beer cans every night and in the morning I teased it and teased it with my comb until sometimes I imagined that if I kept going I could get it high enough to reach the stars, and then I would spray it with hairspray that smelled like red roses and then I'd stroke on my black eyeliner until it went way past my eyes.

The kids in my crowd were the type who cut classes, smoked in the bathroom, and cursed. Yeah, even the girls cursed, and we weren't the type who went to church on Sundays, which drove our mothers crazy. Vito was one of the worst of us all. He just about never read a book or went to class, and I think his mother got him to set foot in the church maybe once the whole time he was growing up. I swear, it was some sort of a holy miracle that he actually got his diploma.

Anyway, like I said, lots of the boys wanted me and I liked to make out with them and sometimes I agreed to go steady for a week or two with one of the really handsome ones, like Sally-Boy Reticliano, but I never let any get into my pants. Because in my own way I was a good Catholic girl. And all this time Vito was wild about me and I wouldn't even make out with him. But when Vito and the Olinvilles got themselves an agent and cut a record, "Teenage Heartbreak," which Vito wrote, I started to see that Vito was different than I'd thought, different than the other boys. Because Vito had an artistic soul. Then, on graduation night, just a week after Vito and the Olinvilles recorded "Teenage Heartbreak," I realized that, all these years, I'd been in love with him, too, and was just too proud to admit it because he was a couple of inches shorter than me, and he had that acne and the space between his teeth. There I was, ready for the prom, all dressed up in my bright red prom dress and my hair teased higher than ever, waiting for my date, but my date wasn't Vito, it was Sally-Boy Reticliano, and I wanted to jump out of my skin. About halfway through the prom, I couldn't take it any more and I said, "Sally-Boy, I'm sorry, but I've just got to go over and talk to Vito." Sally-Boy, who was even worse at school than Vito, grunted, and I could tell that it was a sad grunt. But there was nothing I could do. I loved Vito and that was that. I spotted him standing alone in a corner. He was wearing a tux and his hair was greased up into a pompadour that was almost as high as my hair. He watched me as I walked across the auditorium to him, and even in my spiked heels, I felt as though I was floating on air. He said, "Aay, Geraldine, how goes it?" and then he took me by the arm and we left the auditorium. It was like he knew all along that one day I would come to him. It was a gorgeous spring night, I could even see a few stars, and Vito put his arm around me, and he had to tiptoe a little bit to reach. We walked over to the Gun Hill Projects, and we found a deserted bench in the project's laundry room, and Vito said, "Aay, Geraldine Rizzoli, I've been crazy about you since tenth grade. I even wrote 'Teenage Heartbreak' for you."

And I said, "Vito, I know, I guessed it, and I'm sorry I've been so dumb since tenth grade but your heart doesn't have to break any more. Tonight I'm yours."

And Vito and I made out on the bench for awhile but it didn't feel like just making out. I realized that Vito and I weren't kids anymore. It was like we had grown up all at once. So I said, "Vito, take me," and he said, "Aay, Geraldine Rizzoli, all right!" He had the keys to his older brother Danny's best friend Freddy's car, which was a beat up old wreck, but that night it looked like a Cadillac to me. It was parked back near the school, and we raced back along Gun Hill Road hoping that Sally-Boy and the others wouldn't see us. Even though Vito didn't have a license, he drove the car a few blocks away into the parking lot of the Immaculate Conception School. We climbed into the back seat and I lifted the skirt of my red prom dress and we made love for hours. We made sure I wouldn't get pregnant, because we wanted to do things just right. Like I said, I was a good Catholic girl, in my own way. Afterwards he walked me back to Olinville Ave. And he took out the car keys and carved "Vito Loves Geraldine" in a heart over the door of the elevator in my building, but he was careful to do it on another floor, not the floor I lived on, because we didn't want my parents to see. And then he said, "Aay, Geraldine Rizzoli, will you marry me?" and I said, "Yeah, Vito, I will." So then we went into the staircase of the building and he brushed off one of the steps for me and we sat down together and started talking seriously about our future and he said, "Aay, you know, Vinny and Bobby and Richie and me, it's a gas being Vito and the Olinvilles and singing those doo-wop numbers, but I'm no fool, I know we'll never be rich or famous. So I'll keep singing for a couple more years, and then I'll get into some other line of work and then we'll have kids, okay?" And I said sure, it was okay with me if he wanted to sing for a few years until we started our family. Then I told him that Mr. Pampino at the Evander Sweet Store had offered me a job behind the counter which meant that I could start saving money right away. "Aay, Geraldine, you're no fool," he said. He gave me the thumbs up sign and we kissed. Then he said, "Aay, Geraldine, let's do it again, right here in the staircase," and he started pulling off his tux, but I said I wasn't that kind of girl, so he just walked me to my door and we said good night. We agreed that we wouldn't announce our engagement until we each had a little savings account of our own. That way our parents couldn't say we were too young and irresponsible and try to stop the wedding, which my father, who was very hot-tempered, was likely to do.

The very next morning, Vito's agent called him and woke him up and said that "Teenage Heartbreak" was actually going to get played on the radio, on WMCA by the Good Guys, at eight o'clock that night. That afternoon, we were all hanging out with the crowd and Vito and Vinny and Bobby and Richie were going crazy and they were shouting, "Aay, everyone, WMCA, all right!" and stamping their feet and threatening to punch each other out and give each other noogies on the tops of their heads. Soon everyone on Olinville Ave. knew, and at eight o'clock it was like another holy miracle, everyone on the block had their windows open and we all blasted our radios so that even the angels in Heaven had to have heard Vito and the Olinvilles singing "Teenage Heartbreak" that night, which, like I said, was written especially for me, Geraldine Rizzoli. Vito invited me to listen with him and his mother and father and his older brother Danny in their apartment. We hadn't told them we were engaged, though. Vito just said, "Aay, ma, Geraldine Rizzoli wants to listen to 'Teenage Heartbreak' on WMCA with us, ok." His mother looked at me and nodded, and I had a feeling that guessed that Vito and I were in love and that in her own way was saying, "Welcome, my future daughter-in-law, welcome." So sat around the kitchen table with the radio set up like a centce and his mother and I cried when it came on and his father Danny kept swearing in Italian and Vito just kept combing his padour with this frozen grin on his face. When it was over, everyon the block came pounding on the door shouting, "Aay, Vito, opp, you're a star!" and we opened the door and we had a big party everyone danced the lindy and the cha-cha all over the Venecio apartment.

Three days later "Teenage Heartbreak" made it to nber one on the charts, which was just unbelievable, like twenty tsand holy miracles combined, especially considering how the gunce counselor at Evander Childs used to predict that Vito would end up in prison. The disk jockeys kept saying things like, "The four boys from the streets of the Bronx are a phenomenon, ladies and gentleman, a genuine phenomenon!" Vito's mother saw my mocer at Mass and told her that she'd been visited by an angel in whi when she was pregnant with Vito and the angel told her, "Mrs. Venecio, you will have a son and this son shall be a great man!"

A week later Vito and the Olinvilles got flown out to L.A. to appear in those beach party movies, and Vito didn't ever call me to say good bye. So I sat in my room and cried a lot, but after a couple of weeks, I decided to chin up and accept my fate, because, like Vito said, I was no fool. Yeah, it was true that I was a ruined woman, labeled forever as a tramp, me, Geraldine Rizzoli, who'd made out with so many of the boys at Evander Childs High School, but who'd always been so careful never to let any of them into my pants, here I'd gone and done it with Vito Venecio who'd turned out to be a two faced liar, only interested in money and fame. Dumb, dumb, dumb,

Geraldine, I ht. And I couldn't tell my parents because my father would taken his life savings, I swear, and flown out to L.A. and kill. And I couldn't even tell Pamela and Carmela and Victoria, bec we'd pricked our fingers with sewing needles and made a pact l in blood that although we would make out with lots of boys, uld stay virgins until we got married. So whenever I got togethe h them and they talked about how unbelievable it was that ski little Vito with the acne and the greasy pompadour had become ch and famous, I would agree and try to act just like them, like I just so proud that Vito and Vinny and Bobby and Richie were millionaires. And after a month or so I started feeling pretty g and I thought, ok, Vito, you bastard, you want to dump Gera e Rizzoli, tough noogies to you, buddy. I was working at the Evan Sweet Store during the day and I'd begun making out with some the guys in the crowd in the evenings again, even though my rt wasn't in it. But I figured that one day someone else's kisses mig ake me feel the way that Vito's kisses had made me feel, and I'd ne know who it would be unless I tried it.

And th one night I was helping my mother with the supper dishes, w h I did every single night since, like I said, in my own way, I was good Catholic girl, when the phone rang and my mother said, "Ger ine, it's for you. It's Vito Venecio calling from Los Angeles," and e looked at me like she was suspicious about why Vito, who'd bee trying to get into my pants all those years when he wasn't famou and I wouldn't give him the time of day, would still be calling m at home now that he was famous and could have his pick of girls. When she'd gone back into the kitchen, I picked up the phone but my hands were so wet and soapy that I could hardly hold onto the receiver. Vito said, "Aay, Geraldine Rizzoli," and his voice sounded like he was around the corner, but I knew he was really three thousand miles away surrounded by those silly looking bimbos from the beach party movies. "Aay, forgive me, Geraldine," he said, "I've been a creep, I know, I got carried away by all this money and fame crap but it's you I want, you and the old gang and my old life on Olinville Ave."

I didn't say anything, I was so angry and confused. And my hands were still so wet and soapy.

"Aay, Geraldine, will you wait for me?" Vito said, and he sounded like a little lost boy. "Please Geraldine, I'll be back, this ain't gonna last long, promise me, you'll wait for me as long as it takes."

"I don't know, Vito," I said, desperately trying to hold onto the phone, and now my hands were even wetter because I was crying and my tears were landing on them, "you could have called sooner."

"Aay, I know," he said, "this fame stuff, it's like a drug. But I'm coming home to you, Geraldine. Promise me you'll wait for me."

And he sounded so sad, and I took a deep breath, and I said, "I promise, Vito. I promise." And then the phone slipped from my grasp and hit the floor, and my mother yelled from the kitchen, "Geraldine, if you don't know how to talk on the phone without making a mess all over the floor, then don't talk on the phone!" I shouted, "I'm sorry, Ma!" but when I picked it up again, Vito was gone.

So the next day behind the counter at the Evander Sweet Store, I started making plans. I needed my independence. I knew I'd have to get an apartment so that when Vito came back, I'd be ready for him. But that night when I told my parents I was going to get my own apartment they raised holy hell. My mother was so furious she didn't even ask whether it had something to do with Vito's call. In fact, she never spoke to me about Vito after that, which makes me think that deep down she knew. The thing was, whether she knew or didn't know, seventeen-year-old Italian girls from the Bronx did not leave home until a wedding ring was around their finger, period. Even girls who cut classes and smoked and cursed. My parents sent me to talk to a priest at the Immaculate Conception Church, which was right next door to the Immaculate Conception School, the parking lot of which was where I gave myself to Vito in the back seat of his older brother Danny's best friend Freddy's car, and the priest said, "Geraldine Rizzoli, my child, your parents tell me that you wish to leave their home before you marry. Child, why do you wish to do such a thing, which reeks of the desire to commit sin?"

I shrugged and looked away, trying hard not to pop my chewing gum. I didn't want to seem too disrespectful, but that priest got nowhere with me. I was going to wait for Vito, and I needed to have my own apartment ready for him so the instant he got back we could start making love again and get married and start a family. And besides, even though the priest kept calling me a child, I'd been a woman ever since I let Vito into my pants. I ran my fingers through my hair trying to make the teased parts stand up even higher while the priest went on and on about Mary Magdalene. But I had my own spiritual mission which had nothing to do with the Church, and finally I couldn't help it, a big gum bubble went pop real loudly in my mouth and the priest called me a hellion and said I was beyond his help. So I got up and left, pulling the pieces of gum off my lips.

The priest told my father that the only solution was to chain me up in my bedroom. But my mother and father, bless their hearts, may have been Catholic and Italian and hot tempered, but they were good people, so instead they got my father's best friend, Pop Giordano, who'd been like an uncle to me ever since I was in diapers, to rent me an apartment in the building he owned. And the building just happened to be on Olinville Ave., right next door to my parents' building. So they were happy enough. I insisted on a two bedroom right from the start so that Vito wouldn't feel cramped when he came back, not that I told them why I needed that much room. "A two bedroom," my mother kept repeating. "Suddenly my daughter is such a grown up she wants a two bedroom!"

So Pop gave me the biggest two bedroom in the building and I moved in, and Pop promised my father to let him know if I kept late hours, and my father said he'd kill me if I did, but I wasn't worried about that. My days of making out with the boys of Olinville Ave. were over. I would wait for Vito, and I would live like a nun until he returned to me.

My mother even ended up helping me decorate the apartment, and to make her happy I hung a velour painting of Jesus above the sofa in the living room. I didn't think Vito would mind too much since his mother had one in her living room too. I didn't intend to call Vito or write him to give him my new address. He'd be back soon enough and he'd figure out where I was.

And I began to wait. But a couple of weeks after I moved into the apartment I couldn't take not telling anyone. I felt like I'd scream or do something crazy if I didn't confide in someone. So I told Pop. Pop wore shiny black suits and black shirts with white ties and a big diamond ring on his pinky finger and he didn't have a steady job like my father who delivered hot dogs by truck to restaurants all over the Bronx, or like Vito's father who was a construction worker. I figured that if anyone knew the way the world worked, it was Pop. He promised he'd never tell, and he twirled his black mustache and said, "Geraldine Rizzoli, you're like my own daughter, like my flesh and blood, and I'm sorry you lost your cherry before you got married but if you want to wait for Vito, wait."

So I settled in to my new life and I waited. That was the period that Vito kept turning out hit songs and making beach party movies and I'd hear him interviewed on the radio and he never sounded like the Vito I knew. It sounded like someone else had written his words for him. He'd get all corny and sentimental about the Bronx, and about how his heart was still there, and he'd say all these sappy things about the fish market on the corner of Olinville Ave., but that was such crap, because Vito never shopped for food. His mother did all the shopping, Vito wouldn't be caught dead in the Olinville fish market, except maybe to mooch a cigarette off of Carmine Casella, who

worked behind the counter. Vito didn't even like fish. And I felt sad
and worried for him. He'd become a kind of doo-wop robot, he and
the Olinvilles, mouthing other people's words. I noticed that he'd
even stopped writing songs after "Teenage Heartbreak." Sometimes I
could hardly stand waiting for him. But on Olinville Ave., a promise
was a promise. People had been found floating face down in the
Bronx River for breaking smaller promises than that. Besides, I still
loved Vito.

Pamela married Johnny Ciccarone, Carmela married Ricky
Giampino, and Victoria married Sidney Goldberg, from the Special
Progress Accelerated class, which was a big surprise, and they all got
apartments in the neighborhood. But after a year or two they all
moved away, either to neighborhoods where the Puerto Ricans and
blacks weren't starting to move in, or to Yonkers or Mount Vernon,
and they started to have babies and I'd visit them once or twice with
gifts but it was like we didn't have much in common any more, and
soon we all lost touch.

And Vito and the Olinvilles kept turning out hits, even though
like I said, Vito never wrote another song after "Teenage Heartbreak." In addition to the doo-wop numbers, Vito had begun letting
loose on some slow, sexy ballads. I bought their forty-fives and I
bought their albums and every night after work I would call up the
radio stations and request their songs, not that I needed to, since
everyone else was requesting their songs, anyway, but it made me
feel closer to Vito, I guess. And sometimes I'd look at Vito's photograph on the album covers or in the fan magazines and I'd see how his
teeth and hair and skin were perfect, there was no gap between his
front teeth like there used to be, no more acne, no more cowlick. And
I kind of missed those things, because that night when I gave myself
to Vito in the back seat of his older brother Danny's best friend
Freddy's car, I'd loved feeling Vito's rough, sandpapery skin against
mine and I'd loved letting my fingers play with his cowlick and let-

ting my tongue rest for a minute in the gap between his front teeth.

So, for the next three, four years, I kind of lost count, Vito and the Olinvilles ruled the airwaves. And every day I worked at the Evander Sweet Store and every night I had dinner with my parents and my mother would ask whether I was ever going to get married and have babies and I'd say, "Come on, Ma, leave me alone, I'm a good Catholic girl, of course I'm gonna have babies one day," and my father would say, "Geraldine, if Pop ever tells me you're keeping late hours with any guys, I'll kill you," and I'd say, "Come on, Pa, I told you, I'm a good Catholic girl," and then I'd help my mother with the dishes and then I'd kiss them goodnight and I'd go visit Pop for a few minutes in his apartment on the ground floor of the building and there would always be those strange men coming and going from his apartment and then I'd go upstairs to my own apartment and I'd sit in front of my mirror and I'd tease my hair up high and I'd put on my makeup and I'd put on my red prom dress and I'd listen to Vito's songs and I'd dance the lindy and the cha-cha. And then before I went to sleep, I'd read through all the fan mags and I'd cut out every article about him and I'd paste them into my scrapbook.

Then one day, I don't remember exactly when, a couple of more years, maybe three, maybe even four, all I remember is that Carmela and Pamela and Victoria had all sent me announcements that they were on their second kids, the fan mags started printing fewer and fewer articles about Vito. I'd sit on my bed, thumbing through, and where before, I'd find at least one in every single mag, now I'd have to go through five, six, seven magazines and then I'd just find some real small mention of him. And the radio stations were playing Vito and the Olinvilles less and less often and I had to call in and request them more often because nobody else was doing it, and their songs weren't going higher than numbers fifteen or twenty on the charts. But Vito's voice was as strong and beautiful as ever, and the Olinvilles could still do those doo-wops in the background, so at first I felt really dumb, dumb, dumb because I couldn't figure out what was going on.

But I, Geraldine Rizzoli, am no fool, and it hit me soon enough. It was really simple. The girls my age were all mothers raising kids, and they didn't have time to buy records and dance the lindy and the cha-cha in front of their mirrors. And the boys, they were out all day working and at night they sat and drank beer and watched football on TV. So a new generation of teenagers was buying records. And they were buying records by those British groups, the Beatles and the rest of them, and for those kids, I guess, an Italian boy from the Bronx with a pompadour wasn't very interesting. And even though I didn't look a day older than I had that night in the back seat of Vito's older brother Danny's best friend Freddy's car, and even though I could still fit perfectly into my red prom dress, I had to face facts, too. I wasn't a teenager any more.

So more time went by, again I lost count, but Pop's hair was beginning to turn grey and my father was beginning to have a hard time lifting those crates of hot dogs and my mother seemed to be getting shorter day by day, and Vito and the Olinvilles never got played on the radio at all, period. And I felt bad for Vito, but mostly I was relieved, since I was sure then that he would come home. I bought new furniture, Pop put in new windows. I found a hairspray that made my hair stay higher even longer.

But I was wrong. Vito didn't come home. Instead, according to the few fan mags that ran the story, his manager tried to make him into a clean cut type, the type who appeals to the older Las Vegas set. And Vito left the Olinvilles, which, the fan mags said, was like Vito had put a knife through their hearts. One mag said that Vinny had even punched Vito out. Anyway, it was a mistake on Vito's part not to have just come home right then. He made two albums and he sang all these silly love songs from the twenties and thirties, and he sounded really off-key and miserable. After that, whenever I called the disk jockeys they just laughed at me and wouldn't even play his records. I'd have to go through ten or fifteen fan mags to find even a small mention of Vito at all. So I felt even worse for him, but I definitely figured he had to come home then. Where else could he go? So I bought a new rug and Pop painted the wall. And I sat in front of my mirror at night and I teased my hair and I applied my make up and I put on my red prom dress and I danced the lindy and the cha-cha and I played Vito's albums and I'd still cut out the small article here and there and place it in my scrapbook. And I hadn't aged a day. No lines, no wrinkles, no flab, no grey hair. Vito was going to be pleased when he came home.

But I was wrong again. Vito didn't come home. He went and got married to someone else, a skinny flatchested blonde model from somewhere like Iowa or Idaho. A couple of the fan mags ran little pieces, and they said she was the best thing that had ever happened to Vito. Because of his love for her he wasn't depressed any more about not having any more number one hits. "Aay," he was quoted, "love is worth more than all of the gold records in the world." At first I cried. I kicked the walls. I tore some of the articles from my scrapbook and ripped them to shreds. I smashed some of his albums to pieces. I was really really angry, because I knew that it was me, Geraldine Rizzoli, who was the best thing that had ever happened to him! That blonde model had probably been a real goody-goody when she was growing up, the type who didn't cut classes or smoke or tease her hair or make out with lots of guys. No passion in her skinny bones, I figured. And then I calmed down. Because Vito would still be back. This model, whose name was Muffin Potts, was no threat at all. Vito would be back, a little ashamed of himself, but he'd be back.

Soon after that, Vito's mother and father died. A couple of fan mags carried the story. They died in a plane crash on their way to visit Vito and Muffin Potts in Iowa or Idaho or wherever she was from. I didn't get invited to the funeral, which was in Palm Beach.

Vito's parents had moved there only six months after "Teenage Heartbreak" became number one. Five big moving vans had parked on Olinville Ave., and Vito's mother stood there in a fur coat telling everybody about the angel who'd visited her when she was pregnant with Vito. And I'd gone up to her and kissed her and said, "Good bye, Mrs. Venecio, I'm going to miss you," and she said, "Good bye, Carmela," like she was trying to pretend that she didn't remember that I was Geraldine Rizzoli, her future daughter in law. The fan mags had a picture of Vito at the funeral in a three piece suit, and the articles said he cried on the shoulder of his older brother Danny, who was now a distributor of automobile parts. There were also a couple of photos of Muffin Potts looking very bored.

Then I started to read little rumors, small items, in a few of the magazines. First, that Vito's marriage was on the rocks. No surprise to me there. I was surprised that it lasted an hour. Second, that Vito was heavy into drugs and that his addiction was breaking Muffin's heart. Really hard drugs, the mags said. The very worst stuff. One of the mags said it was because of his mother's death and they called him a "Mama's Boy." One said he was heartbroken because of his break-up with the Olinvilles and because Vinny had punched him out. And one said he'd been doing drugs ever since Evander Childs High School, and they had the nerve to call the school a "zoo," which I resented. But I knew a few things. One, Vito was no Mama's Boy. Two, Vito and the Olinvilles still all loved each other. And, three, Vito had never touched drugs in school. And if it were true that he was drowning his sorrows in drugs and breaking Muffin Pott's heart, it was because he missed me and regretted like hell not coming home earlier!

Soon after that I read that Muffin had left him for good and had taken their child with her. Child? I stared at the print. Ashley, the article said. Their child's name was Ashley. There was no photo, and since Ashley was a name with zero personality, I wasn't sure whether Ashley was a girl or boy. I decided it was a girl, and I figured she looked just like her mother, with pale skin and a snub nose and milky-colored hair, and I wasn't even slightly jealous of that child or her mother because they were just mistakes. True, Vito kept acting dumb, dumb, dumb, and making some big fat mistakes, but I didn't love him any less. A promise was a promise. And I, Geraldine Rizzoli, knew enough to forgive him. Because the truth was that even I had once made a mistake. The way it happened was this. One day out of the blue, who should come into the Evander Sweet Store to buy some cigarettes but Petey Cioffi, who'd been one of the guys in our crowd in the old days. A couple of years after graduation he married some girl from the Grand Concourse and we all lost touch. But here he was in the old neighborhood, visiting some cousins and he needed some cigarettes. Anyway, when he walked in, he stopped dead in his tracks. I could tell he was a little drunk, and he said, "Aay, Geraldine Rizzoli, I can't believe my eyes, you're still here, and you're gorgeous, I'm growing old and fat, look at this belly, but not you, you're like a princess or something." And it was so good to be spoken to like that, and I let him come home with me. We made out in my elevator, and I felt like a kid again. I couldn't pretend he was Vito, but I could pretend it was the old days, when Vito was still chasing me and trying to get into my pants. In the morning, Petey said goodbye, looked at me one last time, shook his head and said, "Geraldine Rizzoli, what a blast from the past!" and he slipped out of the building before Pop woke up. He probably caught holy hell from his wife and I swear I got my first and only grey hair the next morning. But my night with Petey Cioffi made it easier to forgive Vito, since I'd made my mistake too. And I kept waiting. The neighborhood changed around me. The Italians left, and more and more Puerto Ricans and blacks moved in, but I didn't mind. Because everyone has to live somewhere, I figured, and I had more important things on my mind than being prejudiced.

Then I pretty much stopped hearing about Vito altogether. And that was around when my father, bless his heart, had the heart attack on the hot dog truck and by the time they found him it was too late to save him, and my mother, bless her heart, followed soon after. I missed them so much, and every night I came home from work and I teased my hair at the mirror, I put on my make up, I put on my red prom dress, I played Vito's songs, I danced the lindy and the cha-cha, and I read through the fan mags looking for some mention of him, but there wasn't any. It was like he had vanished from the face of the earth. And then one day I came across a small item in the newspaper. It was about how Vito had just gotten arrested on Sunset Strip for possession of hard drugs, and how he was bailed out by Vinny of the Olinvilles, who was now a real estate salesman in Santa Monica. "I did it for old times' sake," Vinny said, "for the crowd on Olinville Ave."

The next morning, Pop called me to his apartment. He had the beginnings of cataracts by then and he hardly ever looked at the newspaper anymore, but of course he'd spotted the article about Vito. His face was red. He was furious. He shouted, "Geraldine Rizzoli, you're like my own daughter, my own flesh and blood, and I never wanted to have to say this to you, but," he waved the newspaper ferociously, which was impressive, since his hands shook, and he weighed all of ninety pounds at this point, although he still dressed in his shiny black suits and those strange men still came and went from his apartment, "the time has come for you to forget Vito. If he was here I'd beat the living hell out of him." He flung the paper across the room and sat in his chair breathing heavily.

I waited a minute before I spoke just to make sure he was going to be okay. When his color returned to normal, I said, "Never, Pop. I promised Vito I'd wait."

"You should marry Ralphie."

"Ralphie?" I asked. Ralphie Pampino, who was part of the old crowd, too, had inherited the Evander Sweet Store from his father when Ralphie Sr. died the year before. It turns out that Ralphie Jr., who'd never married, was in love with me, and had been for years.

Poor Ralphie. He'd been the kind of guy who never got to make out a whole lot. I'd always thought he looked at me so funny because he was constipated or had sinuses or something. But Pop told me that years ago Ralphie had poured out his heart to him. Although Pop had promised Ralphie that he'd never betray his confidence, the time had come. It seemed that Ralphie had his own spiritual mission: he was waiting for me. I was touched. Ralphie was such a sweet guy. I promised myself to start being nicer to him. I asked Pop to tell him about me and Vito, and I kissed Pop on the nose and I went back upstairs to my apartment and I sat in front of my mirror and I teased my hair and I put on my makeup and I put on my red prom dress and I listened to Vito's songs and I danced the lindy and the cha-cha.

The next day, Ralphie came over to me and said, "Geraldine Rizzoli, I had no idea that you and Vito—" and he got all choked up and couldn't finish. Finally, he swallowed and said, "Aay, Geraldine, I'm on your side. I really am. Vito's coming back!" and he gave me the thumbs up sign and he and I did the lindy together right there in the Evander Sweet Store and we sang "Teenage Heartbreak" at the top of our lungs and we didn't care if any customers came in and saw us.

But after that there wasn't any more news about Vito, period. Most everyone on the block who'd known Vito and the Olinvilles was gone, and I just kept waiting. Just around that time an oldies radio station, WAAY, started up and it was pretty weird at first to think that Vito and the Olinvilles and all the other groups I had spent my life listening to were considered "oldies" and I'd look at myself in the mirror and I'd think, "Geraldine Rizzoli, you're nobody's oldie, you've got the same skin and figure you had the night that you gave yourself to Vito." But after awhile I got used to the idea of the oldies and I listened to WAAY as often as I could. I played it every morning first thing when I woke up and then Ralphie and I listened to it together at the Evander Sweet Store, even though most of the kids who came in were carrying those big radio boxes tuned to salsa or rap songs or punk and didn't seem to have any idea that there was already music on. Sometimes when nobody was in the store, Ralphie and I would just sing Vito's songs together. There was one DJ on the station, Goldie George, who was on from nine in the morning until noon and he was a real fan of Vito and the Olinvilles. The other DJs had their favorites too. Doo-Wop Dick liked the Five Satins, Surfer Sammy liked the Beach Boys, but Goldie George said he'd grown up in the Bronx just two subway stops away from Olinville Ave. and that he and his friends had all felt as close to Vito as if they'd lived on Olinville Ave. themselves, even though they'd never met Vito or Vinny or Bobby or Richie. I liked Goldie George, and I wished he'd been brave enough to have taken the subway the two stops over so that he could have hung around with us. He might have been fun to make out with. One day Goldie George played thirty minutes straight of Vito and the Olinvilles, with no commercial interruptions, and then some listener called in and said "Aay, whatever happened to Vito anyway, Goldie George, he was some sort of junkie, right?"

"Yeah," Goldie George said, "but I'm Vito's biggest fan, like you all know, because I grew up only two subway stops away from Olinville Ave. and I used to feel like I was a close buddy of Vito's even though I never met him, and I happen to know that he's quit doing drugs and that he's found peace and happiness through the Chinese practice of Tai Chi and he helps run a mission in Bakersfield, California."

"Aay," the caller said, "Goldie George, you tell Vito for me that Bobby MacNamara from Woodside says, 'Aay, Vito, keep it up, man!'"

"I will," Goldie George said, "I will. I'll tell him about you, Bobby, because, being so close to Vito in my soul when I was growing up, I happen to know that Vito still cares about his loyal fans. In fact, I know that one of the things that helped Vito to get through the hard times was knowing how much his loyal fans cared. And, aay, Bobby, what's your favorite radio station?"

"AAY!" Bobby shouted.

And then Goldie George played another uninterrupted thirty minutes of Vito and the Olinvilles. But I could hardly hear the music this time. I was sick to my stomach. What the hell was Vito doing in Bakersfield, California running a mission? I was glad he wasn't into drugs any more, but Bakersfield, California? A mission? And what the hell was Tai Chi? I was so pissed off. For the first time I wondered whether he'd forgotten my promise. I was ready to fly down to Bakersfield and tell him a thing or two, but I didn't. I went home, played my albums, danced, teased my hair, frowned at the one grey hair I'd gotten the night I was with Petey Cioffi, and I closed my eyes and leaned my head on my arms. Vito was coming back. He just wasn't ready yet.

About two weeks later I was behind the counter at the Evander Sweet Store and Ralphie was arranging some Chunkies into a pyramid when Goldie George said, "Guess what, everyone, all of us here at the station, but mostly Vito's biggest fan, me, Goldie George, have arranged for Vito to come back to his home town! This is Big Big Big Big News! I called him the other day and I said, `Vito, I grew up two subway stops from you, and like you know, I'm your biggest fan, and you owe it to me and your other loyal fans from the Bronx and all the other boroughs to come back and visit and sing 'Teenage Heartbreak' for us one more time, and I swear Vito got choked up over the phone and he agreed to do it, even though he said that he usually doesn't sing any more because it interferes with his Tai Chi, but I said, `Vito, we love you here at AAY, man, and wait'll you hear this, we're going to book Carnegie Hall for you, Vito, not your grandmother's attic, but Carnegie Hall!' How about that, everyone. And just so you all know, the Olinvilles are all doing their own things now, so it'll just be Vito alone, but hey, that's okay, that's great, Vito will sing the oldies and tickets go on sale next week!"

And I stood there frozen and Ralphie and I stared at each other across the counter, and I could see a look in his eyes that told me that he knew he'd finally lost me for good this time.

Because Vito was coming back. He may have told Goldie George that he was coming home to sing to his fans, but Ralphie and I both knew that it was really me, Geraldine Rizzoli, that he was finally ready to come back to. Vito worked in mysterious ways, and I figured that he finally felt free of the bad things, the drugs and that boring Muffin Potts and his own arrogance and excessive pride, and now he was pure enough to return to me. I wasn't wild about this Tai Chi stuff, whatever it was, but I could get used to it if it had helped Vito to get better so he could come home to me.

Ralphie sort of shook himself like he was coming out of some long sleep or trance. Then he came around the counter and put his arm around me in this brotherly way. "Geraldine Rizzoli," he said really softly, "my treat. A first row seat at Carnegie Hall."

But I wouldn't accept, even though it was such a beautiful thing for Ralphie to offer, considering how he'd felt about me all those years. I got teary-eyed. But I didn't need a ticket, not me, not Geraldine Rizzoli. Vito would find out where I lived and he'd come and pick me up and take me himself to Carnegie Hall. He'd probably come in a limo paid for by the station, I figured. Because the only way I was going to the concert was with Vito. I went home after work and I plucked the one grey hair from my scalp and then I teased my hair and I put on my make up and I put on my red prom dress and I danced and sang.

All week Goldie George kept saying, "It's unbelievable, tickets were sold out within an hour! The calls don't stop coming, you all remember Vito, you all love him!"

On the night of the concert Pop came by. He had to use a walker to get around by then and he was nearly blind and lots of things were wrong. His liver, gall bladder, stomach, you name it. He weighed around seventy-five pounds. But he still wore his shiny black suits and the men kept coming in and out of his apartment. And he sat across from me on my sofa, beneath the velour painting of Jesus, and he said in a raspy voice, "Geraldine Rizzolli, I didn't ever want to have to say this, but you're like my own daughter, my own flesh and blood, and as long as Vito wasn't around, I figured, okay you can dance to his albums and tease your hair and wear the same clothes all the time and you're none the worse for it, but now that he's coming home I've got to tell you he won't be coming for you, Geraldine, if he cared a twit about you he would have flown you out to L.A. way back when and I'm sorry you let him into your pants and lost your cherry to him, but you're a middle-aged lady now and you're gonna get hurt real bad and I'm glad your mother and father, bless their souls, aren't around to see you suffer the way you're gonna suffer tonight, Geraldine, and I don't wanna see it either, what I want is for you to drive down to Maryland tonight real fast, right now, and marry Ralphie, before Vito breaks your heart so bad nothing will ever put it together again!"

I'd never seen Pop so riled up. I kissed him on the nose and I told him he was sweet, but that Vito was coming. And Pop left, shaking his head and walking slowly, moving the walker ahead of him, step by step, and after he left, I played my albums and I teased my hair and I applied my lipstick and I danced the lindy and the cha-cha and I waited. I figured that everyone from the old crowd would be at the concert. They'd come in from the suburbs with their husbands and their wives and their children, and even, I had to face facts, in some cases, their grandchildren. And just then there was a knock on my door and I opened it and there he was. He'd put on some weight, but not much, and although he'd lost some hair he still had a pompadour and he was holding some flowers for me, and I noticed that they were red roses, which I knew he'd chosen to match my prom dress. And he said, "Aay, Geraldine Rizzoli, thanks for waiting." Then he looked at his watch. "All right, let's get a move on! Concert starts at nine." And I looked in the mirror one last time, sprayed on a little more hairspray and that was it. Vito took my arm just the way he took it the night I gave myself to him in the back seat of his older brother Danny's best friend Freddy's car, and we went downtown by limo to Carnegie Hall, which was a real treat because I didn't get to go into Manhattan very often. And Carnegie Hall was packed, standing room only, and the crowd was yelling, "Aay, Vito! Aay, Vito! Aay, Vito!" and Pamela and Carmela and Victoria were there, and all the Olinvilles came and they hugged Vito and said there were no hard feelings, and Vinny and Vito even gave each other noogies on the tops of their heads, and everyone said, "Geraldine Rizzoli, you haven't aged a day." Then Goldie George introduced Vito, and Vito just got right up there on the stage and he belted out those songs, and at the end of the concert, for his finale, he sang "Teenage Heartbreak" and he called me up on stage with him and he held my hand and looked into my eyes while he sang. I even sang along on a few of the verses and I danced the lindy and the cha-cha right there on stage in front of all those people. The crowd went wild, stamping their feet and shouting for more, and Goldie George was crying, and after the concert Vito and I went back by limo to Olinville Ave. and Vito gave the limo driver a big tip and the driver said, "Aay, Vito, welcome home," and then he drove away.

And ever since then Vito has been here with me in the two bedroom apartment. He still does Tai Chi, but it's really no big thing, an hour or two in the morning at most. Pop died last year and Vito and I were with him at the end and his last words were, "you two kids, you're like my own son and daughter." Vito works in the Evander Sweet Store now instead of me because I've got to stay home to take care of Vito Jr. and Little Pop, who have a terrific godfather in Ralphie and a great uncle in Vito's older brother, Danny. And, if I'm allowed to do a little bragging, which seems only fair after all this time, Vito Jr. and Little Pop are very good kids. They go to church on Sundays and they're doing real well in school because they never cut classes or smoke in the bathroom or curse, and Vito and I are as proud as we can be.

KEEPIN' THE FAITH

Shrine

jodi bloom

LISSA IS A FREAK. A snot-nosed, slippery little Kurt Cobain–loving freak of nature. I hate her. I hate living with her in this trailer, in this room, in this life. She sucks.

I'm writing all this down because Miss Carter says anger and hostility will eat away at you a little at a time, eat you up from the inside out. That is so totally gross isn't it? She said, "Just write it all down Joanie." Her voice is kind of nice in that guidance counselor way. Anyways, I'll try it. But I have to hide it from Mama and Dad and the dork. Because it's supposed to be utterly private.

It was all Julissa's fault I ended up in Miss Carter's office to begin with. She's the one with major problems. She's the one who fell in love with Kurt Cobain, the skanky, creepy lead singer of Nirvana, and put magazine pictures of him up on her side of the bureau—this big old dresser that separates our beds. Which I thank God for so I don't have to see either of their stupid faces when I go to sleep.

Should I describe the rest of our room? So you can picture this scene? Miss Carter called this my memoir, which I kind of like because it sounds French or something. *My Memoir,* maybe that's the title. Oh yeah, the room. Well, I don't know what to say. It's a room. It should be all mine, but I have to share it with a freak. That's about all there is to say right there.

Oh, one other thing. Our room is divided exactly in half. One hundred percent halvsies all the way. I wanted to paint a line down the middle, across the floor, but Mama said no way and I guess I could see her point about that. Later on though, when Lissa totally freaked out, I got some of what they call water-base paint and did it anyway—a bright yellow line, nice and thick, all the way down the wall, right across the dresser and floor and up the other wall—as far up as I could go without standing on a chair, which is about three-fourths or so.

It was kind of like a highway. You could really imagine driving along, right out the trailer window, following that yellow line away from this miserable life. But I'm getting ahead of my memoir here.

You can see that Kurt Cobain made me and Lissa do some pretty bad stuff, right? I mean the only reason I ever did that destructive thing of painting my bedroom up like the Interstate was because his picture was all over the place and creeping up on my side of the room which is strictly off limits and Lissa knows it. But she was just stupidly in love with that hideous boy.

After the first picture went up on Lissa's side of the dresser, it wasn't long before she was just completely messed up, and there was nothing less than a shrine to Kurt Cobain right there on Lissa's old desk: pictures, candles and other stupid junk. She even put dead flowers all around and started burning some stinky incense shit that she lifted from the drugstore at the mall.

I know all about her shoplifting because Ornette, her supposedly best friend, told me one day when she was in a fight with Lissa. Which just goes to show what kind of a best friend Ornette is, going and tattling like that. Even I won't tattle, and I *hate* Lissa. Can you figure that out? I can't.

By the way, I'm allowed to curse in this memoir if I want to. Miss Carter said so. I didn't ask or anything. She said, "Joanie, give yourself permission to write anything you want." Ok, permission.

Anyway, I know just where Julissa got the crazy notion of a

shrine; anyone with half a brain can see where she got it. From Mama, who has a real shrine to Jesus with a statue and candles and everything and almost had one to Bruce Springsteen, but Dad nipped that in the bud. He said he wasn't having a bunch of magazine pictures around of some stupid old has-been rock and roller who Mama still had a thing for.

Of course Mama is allowed to have her shrine to the Lord Jesus and no one can argue with that—dead flowers and all. Just remember, Julissa is not original, so don't think she is. Still, I don't know where she got the idea to pray at the shrine of Kurt Cobain, because like even Mama doesn't *pray* at the shrine of Jesus. Probably because Mama doesn't want to be embarrassed in front of me and Dad. But did that stop Julissa? What do you think?

Ok, picture this: our bedroom, which is nothing but a stupid little room in a trailer, with old furniture and barely enough space to begin with but at least it's partly mine, turns into a museum of an ugly and dirty-looking boy who makes the worst faces I ever saw anyone make in front of a camera. It's like he doesn't even know how to be a rock star, that's how plain stupid he is.

Kurt wearing a torn-up sweater, Kurt looking like a total perv in a girl's dress—a beat-up looking one too, not even a nice dress—Kurt on the cover of *Sassy* magazine with his slut of a real girlfriend, who's last name I'm sure is really Love, yeah right. In that one, Kurt's hair is red. I don't mean red like normal red hair. Red like... a *stop sign*. You know, fire engine red.

All this time, while Lissa was building the Kurt Museum in our bedroom, she was starting to act weirder and weirder, and I was hating her more than ever. Like, she stopped taking baths and stuff; I mean she kind of smelled disgusting. It was so totally gross; our room smelled like Lissa and incense. And she never had much to say before all this happened, but after awhile, if you wanted to talk to her you practically had to throw a rock at her head.

Which is exactly what I did after she came home with that Walkman, and the tape of Nirvana.

You know, the one with that filthy picture of the baby—with his peepee hanging right out—floating underwater so you think maybe he's dead. And it's like someone is fishing for the dead baby with a dollar bill. *How totally perverted can you get?* So, on the way to school one day I was trying to ask her something and she was plugged in as usual with her headphones, and I picked up a rock—well it was really a pebble—and threw it at her stupid head.

Which I got grounded for later on account of there was a little bruise there and Lissa lied and said it hurt like hell. Of course she didn't get in trouble for saying the h-word. Only because I was already in trouble and usually only one peron gets in trouble at a time; that's just the way it is around here.

No one knew where Julissa got the Walkman, which she like… attached to herself… *permanently.* Lissa says she saved up her pitiful allowance and bought the Walkman. But I suspect it was just her slippery little thievery, after what Ornette told me. My little sister, the criminal. Anyway, she even slept with it and I swear, Nirvana was working on her subliminal mind, you know, like those quit-smoking tapes which Mama tried once… and they worked. It's very powerful, she told us, when something *manipulates* your subliminal mind.

I got so fed up with my dumb sister I just started hanging out over at Carol Leigh's house until I absolutely *had* to go home… until I would be ashamed to stay any longer. Carol Leigh actually gets on my nerves too but not half as much as Julissa.

Then one day I got home and there was a new picture on the wall of Kurt Cobain, looking like he just rose up from the grave. Maybe I could have ignored it, but in this picture you could tell, once and for all, that Kurt Cobain was a true agent of Satan himself. Plus, this one was on my side of the room—above the dresser, but past the middle. On *my* side.

I guess you could say I kind of freaked out of my rational mind. But I already told about that. Did I tell how I had to scrub the yellow paint with a toothbrush and Ajax for an entire weekend to get it off the natural wood-grain paneling? The bureau got kind of ruined too. I got grounded. Again. Which I blame Kurt Cobain for. You could easily say he was ruining my life. Totally.

But all that was nothing compared to what was happening to Julissa because her mind was being taken over. Thank God I'm not a weakling like my dumb sister. Because when you think about it, I could have been manipulated and possessed too, with Kurt's eyes staring down on me all the time, with Lissa and her nightly prayer services. But see, I think it was the playing of that dead baby tape all the time that pushed Julissa over the edge.

Lissa never got the next tape, the one with the even more disgusting picture of a naked lady on the front. I saw it at K-Mart but I kept it a secret from Julissa. Later I found out she knew about it but she just didn't care because she was an addict of the dead baby one and it was the only thing in life she cared about.

When Lissa went over the edge it was on a Wednesday. I remember because that's Mama and Dad's bowling night. I was over at Carol Leigh's, working on our diorama for social studies, which is my favorite subject. Carol Leigh sucks at social studies, but she's good at art so I decided to let her help me with the diorama of *Abraham Lincoln Meets President Clinton*. It was coming out pretty good.

By the time I got home it was dark, and I might have been in trouble for being out late, except like I said, no one was home. Ok, maybe I should have known something strange was going on because the place was completely dark, pitch black and dead quiet. It made me kind of nervous, like I got a little chill, but I didn't think anything of it.

I went in and flipped on the kitchen light. I called out for the dork, just to see what was up. But no answer. I called her again, louder: *LISSA*. Still no answer, so for a joke I yelled: *Julissa Mary Lucille,* which is her entire Christian name. Which she totally hates because it means she's in some *major* trouble and because it is the dumbest sounding name. Really, you have to admit.

There was no answer from Julissa Mary Lucille, so I did what I always do, which is get a root beer from the fridge and head for my room. I mean *our* room. But the door was shut and then it dawned on me that Lissa was probably in there doing some stupid high mass for Kurt Cobain since she had the place to herself and all.

I decided to spy on her so I opened the door just a crack. And sure enough the candles were lit, the incense was burning away, stinking the place up to high hell. But here's the thing. Lissa, the little creep, had stolen the VCR and the TV from the living room, *can you believe it?* I mean we're not supposed to touch the VCR, let alone move it around. Strictly off limits. I was thinking Lissa was gonna get it bad, because I doubted she'd have the brains to get it moved back and all hooked up again before Mama and Dad got home. I was thinking, man, she is really gonna get it bigtime.

Of course Lissa didn't even know I was standing in the doorway— I was hidden pretty good. And maybe I was wrong to be spying like that. But just think if I didn't. I never would have known how truly messed up Lissa was. See, Lissa was lying on the bed, with her eyes closed, buck naked, which I would have told right off, but I can't help it; it's embarrassing just to tell about, even in my private memoir.

She had her stupid Walkman on, you figured that out right? Her eyes were shut tight and the VCR was stuck on the face of her master, Kurt Cobain. She had the machine on pause or something, so it was like stuck on this glowing picture of him.

Then I got the true shock of my life. It's hard for me to say, but my stupid sister had her finger right up her *thing*. I didn't know what to do. I mean, I knew I had to get out of there but I wasn't quick enough because just when I turned to leave, Lissa opened one eye, and that eye shined right on me like something totally crazy and possessed.

I was busted. I got so freaked out that I just shut the door and ran outside and sat on the stoop, trying to catch my breath. My mind was all a mess. I wanted to cry. I felt sorry for Lissa, but I hated her at the same time. It was bad enough that she was so out of control, but how could she do that thing? I was scared for all of our lives at that point because I knew for sure that we were being invaded by an evil Satanic force.

Then after awhile Lissa came out and had the nerve to sit down next to me on the stoop. I couldn't even look at her; I just looked up at the sky. The moon was beautiful. I thought it would be so nice to go and live there. Maybe it's a little immature, but I closed my eyes, and sort of started wishing. Then Lissa said, "Why do you hate me so much?"

"Because, Lissa," I said, "you're a creep and a sinner. Besides playing with the VCR, you shouldn't do that thing you were doing. It's a sin and you know it." I was whispering, in case the neighbors were around snooping. "You're bringing your sins on all of us," I said.

"It's not a sin," Lissa said.

"Is so," I said. "Is so, SINNER." I was really mad by now. I ran back inside.

"You do it too," Lissa yelled after me. "And besides, Miss Carter says it's *natural.*"

That was the thing that made me the maddest of all—Lissa's big lie about Miss Carter. I knew Miss Carter would never, ever say a thing like that. That was what made me spitting mad.

And by the way, I only did it like once you know, and I don't think that counts. I don't think God would even count that.

That night I dreamed of painting another yellow line. It was just like in *The Wizard of Oz,* leading you straight into the night sky, around and around the twinkling stars and right up to the moon. Which in my dream was a beautiful place you could live, like the Emerald City. And there was no Julissa and no Kurt Cobain either, but you probably figured that much. Anyway, at least Kurt was out of my life soon enough.

I heard about it at school, about Kurt Cobain offing himself with a shotgun, from this girl Georgia, who thinks she's cool and wants to be a TV reporter like on *A Current Affair*—so she's always in everyone's business. You would think she already has the job or something.

"Hey," she said, right out in the hallway so everyone could hear. "Go tell your freaky sister that her boyfriend just killed himself."

"What?" I said. Because really, I didn't get what she was saying.

"Lissa's boyfriend," Georgia said. "You know, Kurt No-brain." She was laughing hysterically.

That's when Carol Leigh came up to me and told me about how they found Kurt Cobain dead in his own house. "By his own hand," she said, "shotgun, *right to the brain.*"

Even I felt sort of bad when I heard this and don't ask me why. It was like I knew it was some kind of sign of something else really bad coming, like the opposite of *déjà vu.* I just started walking. I walked right down the hall to Mrs. Wilkes's eighth-period geometry class, where I knew I would find my sister. I stood outside the door and waited. I saw Lissa coming but she didn't see me on account of I was sort of hiding behind the door, watching through the little window. She went in and sat down. She seemed just like her normal dumb-headed self. So I left and went about my business.

After school I pretty much forgot about Kurt and his disgusting suicide, which we all know is the biggest sin ever. What a stupid idiot. Even his mother said so on the radio, which Carol Leigh was listening to when I got to her house. That's about the most pitiful thing I ever heard in my life, someone's own mother saying how they joined the *Stupid Club*. We worked on the diorama. Then I had dinner over there. Then I went home.

Carol Leigh lives in a real house by the way. Over on Fern.

I went in and went to our room. Lissa's things were on the bed. Then I went to the bathroom or I should say, tried to go to the bathroom, but the door was locked. Which is against the rules of our household. I mean you're just supposed to respect everyone's privacy.

I was knocking and knocking and then I started really banging on that door until I thought it might come clear off its hinges. I could hear the bath water splashing so I started knocking again. I don't mean to be disgusting or anything, but I really had to pee. I tried yelling for Lissa and called her an idiot and everything but she was ignoring me. Every once in awhile I go next door to pee, but its like totally embarrassing, so I decided to wait.

I did my math homework. I called Carol Leigh on the phone to see about going over there later. By this time I was getting really mad because the dork was in there for like half an hour which is strictly breaking the rules. Ten minutes for showers, fifteen for baths.

Patience is a virtue! I just waited patiently and by the time Mama got home from work I was fit to be tied. I usually don't tell on people, I'm not a tattler, even if I hate someone. But I was so mad. It was like all the madness of my whole life with my sister Julissa started coming out and once it started it was like an avalanche.

I started yelling and screaming—like a banshee, Mama said later. Mama got really upset too. Me and Mama both banged on the door, but nothing. Then I suddenly remembered about Kurt killing himself and that was when I got scared. I shouldn't have said it until we knew for sure, because it upset Mama so bad. But I told her all about Kurt Cobain and I even told about Julissa's disgusting ritual of the other night, just so Mama would know how serious things were.

Then I said, "Mama, maybe Lissa's dead."

*   *   *

Luckily Dad got home, because Mama was about to call 911.

Dad figured out what we were saying even though we were screaming like lunatics at that point and he went storming over to the bathroom and started yanking on that door and it finally did come right off its hinges.

Mama and me were behind him and we all sort of fell into the bathroom. Lissa was lying in the bath water, no bubbles or anything, just Lissa, with her stupid Walkman on. Her eyes were closed. She had on the big polka-dotted shower cap and this stream of blood was dripping out from under it and trickling down her neck and her arm, which was like dangling over the tub. So there was this little pool of Lissa's bright red blood on the floor.

"Dad," I yelled. "She's dead! And she's bleeding like a stickpig."

Dad corrected me, saying, "'Stuck pig,' Joanie, 'stuck pig.'" I guess he was just so freaked out. Then he did this dive into the tub and pulled Lissa out by her underarms, and right when he grabbed her, her eyes popped open and her one eye fixed straight on me, just like it did the other night when I busted her in the act of you-know-what. That eye was staring at me so cold it nearly scared the life out of me.

Dad was holding Lissa with one hand and he pulled the shower cap off with the other, because I guess even if she wasn't dead we had to see where all the blood was coming from. The Walkman headphones plopped into the tub. Never worked again either.

Well, if you're waiting for a big ending just forget it. Because the red stuff wasn't blood; it was stupid red hair dye, the same as her stupid dead boyfriend must have used. Like she wanted to be *twins* with him or something.

Lissa's hair was the biggest mess you ever saw. She just stood there with the red dye dripping all down her pitiful naked self and onto the floor, making a major mess which yours truly was *not* going to clean up. No way, even if it *was* my turn on chores. Dad said, "I can't even look at you." He was so mad he was shaking. Lissa started to cry.

Mama put a towel around Julissa; you could tell she felt sorry for her or something. Then Dad went stomping into our room and ripped all the photos of Kurt Cobain off the walls. He was so mad I thought he might start breaking stuff. But he only ripped the photos down and grabbed up the shrine and took it all into the kitchen and jammed it into the trash compactor.

Later, while everyone was finishing dinner, I scraped the little corners of the magazine pictures off the paneling in our room with a razor blade. The Scotch tape was sticking real bad; it was like Kurt was having his last fight to stay in my life. But of course it was good riddance and rest in peace, and that was that. The only thing I felt guilty for was how I kind of wished Lissa really was dead. But I only wished it for like one minute, maybe two.

Never Mind

madison smartt bell

KURT COBAIN WAS TEACHING ME how to play "Lithium." One of two songs off that record I ever liked well enough to care to learn it. How the changes were just so brutally stupid, like they went out of their way to pick the exact wrong chords. The funny thing was I was playing guitar. Kurt was explaining to me, you got to keep it rough. Which it seems like rough was built into the chord progression anyway but maybe it wasn't quite so simple as I thought. So he was reaching for the guitar to show me what he meant but somehow the guitar sort of went tilting away from both of us and that's how I woke up.

The girl was up. That's what it was. She was so pretty. Getting her clothes. Kind of a sack dress with some discreet little flower print on it, she was just now diving into. When her arms came out of the sleeves, I touched her on the elbow, to slow her down—I didn't necessarily want her to come back to me but she didn't need to feel so rushed. She shied away from my hand, eyes spinning white like the eyes of a spooked horse, and I wanted to call her name, like you might with a horse to quieten it, bring it back to itself, only I couldn't just then think what it was. She'd turned her face away from me, toward the other bed, and when she saw the smear of snarled hair and snoring across the pillows there she snapped her head back in the other direction, dropping it so her hair swung in her face. Straight black hair as glossy as a grackle's wing, just long enough to graze her col-

88

larbones where they showed out of the V of that thin cotton dress. Long enough it hid her face. She turned around toward the door, stuffing something in her purse, her bra. I saw our faces swimming together in the mirror for a second, in the dim green water light that came through the curtain from outside.

What time was it? Daylight slapped my head when she snatched the door open, a red hot hammer opening my headache up a little wider. I was still hearing the Lithium run in my head, that awkward shift over G-flat, D-flat to A. And at some point I must have jumped into my jeans because there I was blinking in the motel parking lot, bare foot and bare chest but at least with my pants on. What motel was it, anyway? This bright daylight was just messing me up even more.

"Hey," I said to her, "Hold up—" And she did stop to face me for a second, barefoot too, holding her Doc Martens in the other hand from the purse. The clunky shoes looked cute because they were so little.

"Let me take you to breakfast anyway," I said. Smile felt dry and cracking on my face. "Something—"

"I gotta go." She dropped her head again so the black hair swung, such a sweet movement, but I knew I shouldn't touch her. She would be thinking that people might be watching us from behind the curtains on all three sides of the motel courtyard. I was looking down on the part in her hair, which was kind of unusual cause I'm pretty small myself. Then following her as she stalked across the asphalt, which was soft and hot already—must be pretty late.

"Let me give you a ride somewhere?" The name, Karen, Sharon— Damn it. She glanced back.

"I got my car I gotta go." Without a pause. Now she was in it too, red VW Rabbit, shying away from her own face in the rearview mirror and then adjusting it to drive. I was moving up to tap on the window but she just flashed me a quick unhappy smile through the glass and almost ran my bare toes over, peeling out of there.

I waved at her tailpipe, kind of limp. Oh well.

Ocean City, that's where we were. Been there for a three-week run so it ought not to been such a trick to remember. Older motel of the type Perry favored. They got more character, he would say, then Chris would go, sarcastic, yeah and whole lot cheaper too, right, Perry?

In a way they both were right. Somebody'd planted roses around to pretty it up and there was a fresh painted metal spring rocker by the door of every room. But when you got inside the bathroom was mildewed and the beds all sagged in the middle—matter of fact we had kept rolling together in the swag of my bed, which I really thought was kind of nice, and we even woke up and did it once again before morning. So what was her hurry? Unless that had been a dream too.

Daylight changes your mind about it all, maybe. I don't know.

The motel was a couple of blocks off the beach, but you could smell the salt from there, and I even thought I could hear the ocean except maybe it was just traffic. I went shambling over toward the restaurant, concrete cracked and stubbled with weeds under my bare feet, til I remembered they wouldn't want to serve me without a shirt, maybe not without shoes either. There were quarters enough in my jeans pocket to buy a Coke out of the machine so I did that. Thought I might carry it over to the beach, but when I got to the roadside of the motel the traffic started slicing into my head like a saw blade and I knew on the boardwalk, Saturday morning, it would be like I was trapped in a pinball machine.

So I went back in the motel courtyard and sat on the back bumper of the van, drinking my Coke and partly wishing for a cigarette, partly knowing it would just make me feel worse if I had one. I did wish I had my sunglasses for sure. And "Lithium" still slamming in time to my hangover. Cobain was right, I thought then, I'd been trying to pretty it up, soften it and sweeten up a melody, when what it really needed to do was just pound.

I crumpled up the empty can and headed back toward the room, thinking I'd like to actually try playing the song. Trick was I didn't have a guitar along this whole trip, 'cause I joined Perry's band as a bass player, but I figured I could borrow one of Chris's. I didn't have my key when I felt my pocket but as it happened the door wasn't locked. I might have been in there as long as a minute before it registered that Chris and his girl had woke up and were going at it again. Maybe they didn't know I was in there or maybe they did and didn't care or maybe they did and liked the idea. I felt a kind of weight drop down from under the waist button of my jeans, and that sick anticipation in the back of my throat and in one way I wanted to sit down and watch or join in or whatever—do the absolute worst that was in me. Then I caught sight of myself in the mirror again so I just grabbed my sunglasses and a shirt and went back out.

Chris had snagged his usual big-blonde-hair babe, looked like she had just stepped out of a *Playboy* centerfold or at least would be willing to step into one. Last night I remembered her in this little white leather miniskirt and a fringy top that showed off her belly button and at the same time more or less jammed her tits in your face. The fringe had little beads that whipped around while she danced. My girl, meanwhile, her little friend, had been a good deal more subdued. The granny dress with the Docs clashing against it—and socks with a little pompom if I remembered right. Not so much make-up. She wore black lipstick and black nail polish—on her toes too. But that was all. And she danced the Deadhead way, like something swinging from a hook. Eyes mostly closed in that slow dreamy sway like she was high on something or more likely wanted you to think so. Definitely she was dancing by herself, not like Big Blondie whose dance routine was just as plainly meant to catch the eye of everybody in the room. They'd been coming in every couple nights for about ten days, with a gang of some other women and a few guys too, but nobody really paired off or anything.

Sunglasses helped, but I wished I'd took the time to hook some aspirins out of the bottle in the bathroom back there. I crossed the soft asphalt of the parking again, still barefoot, buttoning up my shirt and letting the tails swing loose. Ought to be enough to get me into the motel restaurant, where I could charge, 'cause I still hadn't picked up any money either.

I caught sight of my face again in the glass of the door as I pulled it toward me, heavy on its pressure hinge. That was the face she would have seen, without the sunglasses obviously. Black hair like hers with a little wave, slicked back with the natural oil to frame big longlashed eyes—Bambi eyes, like the girls would say. Small gold circle through the right ear and the eyes molten in my olive face. The dark skin would have made her take me for some kind of Latino like a lot of people did. It was the soft eyes and long lashes that made the face too pretty for a man. "Pretty boy," like my father used to say, leading up to another beatdown or coming off of one or maybe sometimes in the middle. I known it without him telling me, since my first teens. Same for me as for a good-looking woman I thought sometimes—it would get you attention all right only half the time it was attention you didn't want. And the Big Blondie types always wanted to mother me, press me into the space between their Playmate breasts, but I didn't want that. Fact of it was, I never met my mother.

Inside, I went toward where Perry was sitting at a table by himself, hearing the door puff shut on the pressure hinge behind me. I was at that point on the hangover curve where everything was just too loud, that door hinge and crockery banging and the waitress hollering to the cook and people clanging their knives and forks together—even though it really was quiet in there, midmorning lull and only a couple tables full besides the one where Perry was at.

He looked up at me as I pulled back a chair, his eyes pale green under the faded yellow brows. Perry had started out as a redhead they say but now all his hair was that washed-out yellow, yellow sprigs of hair covering the freckles on his arms. He had the local paper folded to the funnies beside his plate and he was eating sausage and eggs and grits. Breakfast was Perry's favorite meal he always said—he'd hunt the places where you can get it twenty-four hours a day. I sat down and pushed back the sunglasses to rub my eyes a minute.

"Having too much fun," Perry said.

"Shut up and give me some aspirin." I pulled the shades back down like a visor—can't say I really liked the light. All of a sudden the waitress was at my elbow.

"Just coffee," I said. "And a large orange juice." She wrote on her pad and went off.

"Didn't work up no appetite last night?" Perry said. Grumbling 'cause he went home by himself I guess. I waved him off like you would a fly, but Perry wasn't flyweight. He was a solid ten years older than the rest of us and he'd always been the leader of the band.

Coffee hot on my mouth and burning in my throat. I was looking over Perry's shoulder at the traffic going silent on the street beyond the plate glass window—whatever. And when I blinked I'd see flashes of Chris and Big Blondie working, half under the sheet and half coming out. Was that just now, this morning, or last night? I remembered the time with my girl in the middle of the night when it was quiet and dark but the rest of was foggy and I couldn't remember anything at all about when we first had got back to the room.

A click against my saucer and I saw Perry had flipped me his little plastic box of Bayer. He wasn't looking at me now, just folded his paper a new way and started studying Ann Landers. I took three and chased them with the orange juice. Then flicked the box back over to him, pinwheeling over the red flecks in the formica.

"Thanks," I said.

"Anything else?" Perry goes, mock-servile.

"I'd take a cigarette if you had one," I said. Perry shot me over his pack of Camel straights. But it was too early for a smoke, and I was too slung. Almost gagged on the thing when I lit it. Perry forked a link sausage into his mouth and then pushed it partway back out and gave the end a greasy wiggle of his lips.

"Now what does that remind you of?"

I closed my eyes behind the sunglasses, sucking on my cotton-mouth, and here came the eyelid movies again, Blondie with Chris and flashes of my girl too. Didn't quite know how to put it all together, if it had been anything weirder or nastier than just the four of us using the same room. I'd always draw the one that didn't usu-ally do that sort of thing, maybe because I didn't either—not usually, I mean.

Chris was working on Big Blondie every time we took a break, laying out the flash pick-up lines he of course had to go with the loud bright lead lines he laid out on guitar. But you'd be surprised how often Big Blondie turns out to have this little bit mousier friend. And some pause in the conversation where she'll turn to me and go, "oh, so you must be the quiet one"—that's where it usually starts. Karen, Sharon—Susan, that was it. There'd been a point, some time at the afterhours place we went with them after our last set, when I started calling her Brown-eyed Sue. Then she smiled and ducked and swung her hair and maybe even blushed a little. That ice-white skin, not dark like mine. But our eyes were the same color.

The cigarette Perry'd given me was smoking itself in the ashtray. I held my left hand against the coffee for the heat, and rubbed along the joint of my thumb where it would hurt from reaching for the bass notes, cause my hands are small. I had just started feeling that, wait-ing for the aspirin to kick in. Perry was stirring egg yolk with his fork, which I didn't want to look at but it seemed like too much work to look away.

"When you once get above Virginia they can't make grits no more," Perry was beefing. "Just look at it running around on my plate."

"Thanks anyway." I drained off the orange juice and somehow I stood up. Perry kind of glared at me. He was peeved for real, I saw, not at me but something about the set last night.

"Just sign the check, okay boss-man?" I said, and I went out.

Sunlight was still stabbing down into my face when I came out, and I was starting to feel that bitter crumble of the aspirins in my belly. Allston was up on the berm that divided the motel from the highway, doing one of his nunchuk patterns, just wearing his ninja pants and barechested to show off his drummer muscle, or just for the heat. He quit when he saw me and waved me to come up. I shook my head, only then I thought maybe it still wasn't a good time to go back to the room.

"Better move around a little," Allston said. "You know you'll feel better."

I climbed the last few feet of the berm on all fours, it was that steep, scrabbling in the stubble of the grass. Felt queasy light-headed when I straightened at the top, and my head was still thumping me too. I told Allston to keep on what he was doing while I sat down to stretch a little, fanning my knees on the warm grass and watching him whip the chuks around his head, fast or faster than he would his drumsticks. Working out or beating the drums, his time was rock-solid, muscles rolling smooth under his chocolate skin. Being a regular black dude he was darker than me, enough that the scar over his belly showed up white across the ridges. I didn't know what it came from though—you didn't ask Allston that kind of a personal question. It wasn't the first time I sort of wished I was bunking in with him instead of Chris. We depended on each other, bass and drums, so it would have made sense in that way. Allston was a clean-living character. He would drink maybe one beer for every set we played and at the end of the night he'd have himself a glass of soda water and go back to his room and eat carrots out of his cooler I think. Didn't run with no girls on the road—never happen. He always took a room by himself on the idea he'd fill it up with drums and all, except half the time the drums were just left set up wherever we were playing.

He finished and stuck the chuks in his waistband, came over and gave me a hand to lift me out of my split. We did some karate type kicks and punches together, then a monkey-style form he'd been teaching me while he learned it himself. After that we played push hands for a while, trying to unbalance each other off the top of the berm. I'd never be a real match for Allston, partly cause of natural talent I guess and partly cause he gave a lot more time to it, hunting out different hot-shot instructors and different styles and things. When Allston was going good, you just couldn't hit him—I'd rather stick my hand in a meatgrinder. But push hands is softer, gentle feeling, or at least it seems that way till Allston's got you and down you go streaking grass stains all over your shirt while you slide down the berm. It was just about a yard wide at the top, so that kind of added some interest. On the highway side there was a metal barrier at the bottom before the pavement so we didn't have worry about rolling right out in the roadbed to get mashed by the cars streaming by. It was a Saturday, end of the season, and people were pouring out the cities for a last day at the beach.

Allston took me down a few times, though it took him a while to do it, and I'd be laughing while I skidded through the grass and dandelions, every time I took a fall. It was true, I did start to feel better once I'd broken a sweat. Allston and me had a pretty good feel for each other from doing this together off and on since high school times when he first talked me into training with him. It didn't interest me like it did him, I wasn't cut out for a fighter, but he had guessed it out somehow that it would be worth my while to teach myself how to not get hit. Like the teachers would sometimes guess at it too, even though Daddy didn't mark up my face—he would cuss it but not hit it. I guess you can know if a dog's getting whipped even if a dog skin don't show bruises. But that was a kindness from Allston to me, even though we never talked about the reasons—I never told nobody none of it in those days or since. And Allston trained me well enough that now, up on the berm, when he thought he was pushing me he was leaning on air instead and I gave him a little help on the way, so down he went sliding through the grass himself, laughing and shouting "whoa" while he went.

"Done," I huffed, when Allston stood up. "Quit while I'm ahead, I think."

"Cool," says Allston. "Guess I take a shower."

He went on off to his room and I started for mine. I did feel better for the exercise—stomach was steadier and my head had quit hurting. The room looked empty when I opened the door, only there wasn't no evidence anybody had put on their clothes. Then the water started in the bathroom along with some giggling, then some grunts. Big fun was still going on, it looked like. I found my swimming suit and put my pants back on over it. It took a few minutes to figure out where I hid my wallet the night before, when it seemed like maybe a good idea, you know, with strangers.

So I walked on over to the beach and did a turn on the boardwalk, which was jumping by this time, all bells and whistles and buzzers, the barkers calling and the smell of beer and old fry oil and mallets thumping from people playing Whack-a-Mole. I was watching the girls from behind my sunglasses, half wondering would I run into Brown-eyed Sue, but not really thinking about it or thinking I would. I still felt a little woozy but it was pleasant now, more like a high, and it felt like I was invisible to the people I was watching, not just my eyes behind the shades but all of me. Maybe so. Half my head was somewhere else, back in the workout with Allston or further than that, but I didn't want to make that next connection. I went down the next stairs and walked across the burning sand, through the people laid out on towels or lounge chairs all shining with oil, kids digging or running and kicking up sand. Just above the high water line I laid down my shoes and my shirt and my pants rolled up around my wallet and the room key. People were jumping and shouting in the low surf and the gulls were calling while they dived for scraps and trash.

The water was warm where I waded in, foam sizzling around my ankles, then my knees. I walked out through the kids with their balls and floats in the shallows, letting the low breakers slap across my waist and ribs. Then came a good-size wave curling up and over me like a wall of rolling green glass, and I dived under. It was colder, deep under the wave, then I came through it, up among the easy rollers, sucking air. I swam for while parallel to the beach but far enough out that a life guard stood and shaded his eyes to study me a minute before he sat back down. For a few hundred yards I swam against the northways drag, then rolled onto my back and floated, letting the current carry me back, my eyes closed and glowing red with the sun shining on the lids.

Push-hands is something like waves, says Allston, finding the current in yourself and the other guy and how they mix together. I was feeling pleased to have caught him the way I had earlier, which was rare enough it counted for something and I liked replaying it in my head. The wave lifted me under the shoulders and let me down easy in the next trough and on the red screen of my eyelids appeared the figure of my father, that first time he couldn't connect his punch—he swung through the place he thought I was so hard he damn near threw his own self on the kitchen floor. I knew right then it was all over, he'd never get a hand on me again—I just wasn't gonna be there where his fist was, not no more. And of course I could have nailed him then and there, he was wide open to any one of Allston's hits or kicks. Payback time—I could have put it all back in his hide, everything he'd ever taken out of mine. That would have pleased him in a way, confirmed his notion of the way things were—it might've made him almost happy. Maybe it hurt him more I didn't do it than if I had, but that wasn't why I didn't. I known all along he beat on me for other reasons, didn't have a lot to do with me myself, and if I was to wail on him it wouldn't've solved my problems either. So after a minute I just walked out of the kitchen—then, a year or so later, on out of the house.

I had this other dream, a few months after I first got in my own place, where Daddy was himself but not, like he had a beard and one of those stupid hats you see in movies about England. Our house was ours but it wasn't either, and everything was like that. In the dream he was holding us prisoner and doing all kinds of bad stuff he never really did in real life, *us* because I dreamed there was another one, like my brother or my twin or something, anyway it looked enough like me, what Daddy told me in the beatdowns, *like a goddamn Melungeon, goddamn Melungeon is what you are.* Then I thought, well, I don't have to keep putting up with this. I dreamed Daddy was asleep on the couch so of course we could kill him that way and the only question was should we cut his throat like a hog with a knife or stove in his head with the fireplace poker (in real life there wasn't no poker, or fireplace either one). Me and this twin person were arguing about it when I woke up, spitting salt water cause I must have got crossways to a wave, and realizing then that the other one wasn't my twin this time at all, it was the brown-eyed girl. It was because of her I'd been thinking this old stuff I usually never thought about, because of love.

I swam in closer to the beach and started body-surfing, catching a wave to ride up on the sand and then running back to catch another one. That song was running in my head in time with the waves, and I could feel my hand holding down the power chords: E, G-flat, D-flat, A—it was almost my voice singing the words, and nothing else to think about because the guitar brang was washing it all away. But when I sat up in the sand from my last ride, I thought, *Daddy loved me too, cause he taught me how to swim. Did it so I wouldn't drown.*

I rinsed off from a shower head by the boardwalk steps, then walked on the beach carrying my clothes, splashing ankle-deep till the sun dried the rest of me. Not a thought in my head and that was just fine. The light was changing as the sun tilted to the west, and out over the deep part of the ocean the water changed from green to darker blue. Fresh wind was raising white caps out there, among the little pale triangles of the boat sails. A flight of pelicans came along and dumped in the water one two three, then sat there rocking on the waves, like I had. Getting fish, I thought, and then I knew I was hungry.

I sat on the steps to brush the sand off my feet before I put on my shoes, then strolled the boardwalk looking in the booths, beginning to figure what I wanted. Pretty soon here was Perry and Chris standing at a chest-high table in a stand by the Whack-a-Mole game, eating shrimp and drinking draft beer out of tall clear plastic cups. What they had looked good to me, so I swung in beside them before I realized they were having a fight.

Too late to book without being obvious, so I got myself a beer and some boiled shrimp, and turned off my ears so I wouldn't have to listen. I could sit there peeling shrimp and eating and sipping, thinking my way through that chord progression again so as to be doing something worthwhile. This argument of Perry and Chris was same-o same-o anyway—even Chris didn't have to listen too close cause he already knew the script. I could shut down to where I could watch Perry's mouth moving but not hardly hear anything coming out but the chords of "Lithium," with the Whack-a-Mole mallets next door keeping time and a bell at the end of each line like a cymbal. I knew all the same what Perry was telling him, *When you showboat like that you wreck the whole gig,* 'cause last night Chris had been soloing too loud and too long, and splicing in lines of his originals into the standard which was all we ever played, so Perry would have to be telling him now, *Don't nobody want to hear some shit you made up, they want to hear the stuff they already know they like.* Chris wasn't saying much. He looked like he'd been through the wars and swallowed the canary at the same time, if that was possible. Big Blondie was nowhere in sight, although the trouble was probably mostly over her if you boiled it down. I went and got some more shrimp and beer 'cause it was good and besides I hadn't had anything all day. Time I got back Perry was coming to the part about *if you want to use that guitar just to talk to the place between some chick's legs then save it till you get back in your room, you up there to play for everybody not just for your sluts—*

I thought I could face up to a cigarette by this time, and one more beer. When I got back from getting it, Chris was gone.

Perry was drumming his fingers on the table, the two picking nails on his right hand making clicks on the wood.

"Lord, Lord," he said. "Lord have mercy." On Chris, he meant, for making Perry be disgusted with him—that was what I supposed. People turned their heads at the counter when Perry dropped his voice deep. He used to preach the revival circuit when he was younger and his voice would get your attention that way. It was all bogus, Perry said, his preaching, just another hustle he'd done right well at for a few years—but now it had all gone on the TV, so Perry said.

I lit my smoke and watched Perry suck his lips in tight and chew at the insides of his mouth. "What do you do with a feller like that?" Like he was asking the whole boardwalk, but I didn't answer him— I knew he wasn't talking to me. I just put my mind to blowing one smoke ring inside of another—a skill I'd developed in front of the bathroom mirror back when Daddy would be out at work when I came home from school. Perry was talking to himself, had really been talking to himself the whole time he was jawing at Chris as well. His opinions about how the lead guitar ought to do was the same kind of thing as how he thought his grits ought to be cooked, you couldn't quite figure where he got them from but they were wrote in stone. It was Perry's notions that held the band together, but he could drive you crazy sometimes, and I didn't really blame Chris for walking. I finished my smoke and told Perry, "Dig you later," and I walked on back to the motel.

Chris wasn't in the room when I got there. The motel people had been to make up the beds and straighten up so there wasn't no evidence of last night except for about one finger of Southern Comfort in a pint bottle there on the glass-top dresser. Made my stomach do a small flip-flop to see it. Big Blondie had come up with that out of her purse when we left the afterhours place, and we had all been passing it around in the car. Lucky not to get arrested. I could sort of chain from that memory to the four of us tumbling back into the room, and after that there still were some blank patches but it didn't seem like there had been any swapping or group stuff or anything that would specially horrify somebody who didn't usually do that kind of thing when they woke up next day.

I took off my shoes and laid down on the neat tight coverlet of my bed and slept for almost four hours without dreaming. Rap on the door woke me up finally, and a voice calling, "Twenty minutes." I couldn't make out if it was Allston or Perry because it was through the door and I was asleep anyway. My hair was stiff and my skin crackling with salt in spite of the rinse I had under the boardwalk shower head, so I took another fast shower and then shaved and stood soaking my hand in the sink, to loosen the stiff tendon of my thumb, watching my face come clear in mirror as the shower steam melted off. The Melungeon face, whatever that meant. It had something to do with why my mother booked as soon as I was born, but I didn't really know if it was her or Daddy that was one or if maybe they were both renegade Melungeons. They must have been renegades because we sure didn't associate with any other ones and Daddy seemed to hate them anyhow. Or maybe my mother went back to them, that's where she went. I didn't know, I never even knew if it was something you just were like being black or something you had to do along with it, like being a Jew. The first time some kid in school started talking how I had nigger blood I didn't know whether to get mad and fight, because it was plain I didn't look like the black kids either, plain enough to them at least. Never really one thing or another—it didn't matter now.

Perry and Allston were in the van when I came into the dark parking lot, dim lights on the motel eaves and a crescent moon shining down. I slung my bass in the side door and climbed in after it. Perry gunned the motor.

"Where's Chris at?" he said.

"Dunno," I said. "He took his guitars wherever he went." Cause I had noticed they were gone from the room.

Allston looked around the parking lot from the shotgun seat he was buckled into—big believer in seatbelts, Allston. "His car's gone too."

Chris had decided to drive his own car this trip, a bright yellow Trans Am he claimed matched his hair. You wouldn't have missed it if it had been there.

"So I guess he'll meet us at the place," I said, not knowing if I believed it or not. I didn't know if Perry did either, but he didn't say nothing one way or the other, just dropped the van in gear and steered it onto the road.

The place was on a strip toward the edge of town, a few miles out the four-lane highway. The name of it was something like Rebel's Roost but Perry called it the Black Cat. We played roadhouses like that one all up and down the east coast, following the weather, and Perry called all of them the Black Cat; it was one of his notions. He said you didn't have to remember the name as long as you knew how to find the place. The original Black Cat was up in New Hampshire, a cinderblock biker joint without any windows, but this one in Ocean City was a big old wooden barn. A poster for the Road Warriors—that was us—was peeling off the door, with a way-back promo picture from when Meredith was still singing with the band.

Inside there were a few people at the pool tables in the front bar area and maybe twenty more in the big back room where the stage was. The place felt empty (it would hold a hundred or so), and you could smell the old smoke and stale beer. Later on when it filled up you wouldn't notice that smell anymore; it would be people, sweat, perfume, fresh cigarettes. I saw right off, walking to the stage, that Chris's guitars were set up there, the Strat and Les Paul too, which was a big relief because there'd been no sign of his car out front. There was more parking, though, around the back.

I climbed on the stage after Allston and plugged in my bass and switched on the amp, then slapped it around a little just to show I knew how. Perry was fussing around with the PA. I put the bass on a stand and slung on the Les Paul, but goddamn it was heavy, so I sat down on a stool to shed the weight. They were playing a Clapton album of old blues stuff, and I followed a little bit of his lead, leaving Chris's amp turned low. The fretboard felt nice and natural to me—it was no-frets like the one I had before I sold it when I switched to bass.

Allston was sitting at his drum set, he gave everything a sort of pat and tightened the spring on his snare. The Clapton tape had run out, so I turned up a little and hit the low E hard, letting it throb till the snare talked back to it from behind me. Then E, G-flat, D-flat, A, and louder, C, D, hold on B and back to the top, except Cobain, the dead guy, was shaking his head—*uh-uh, it turns around on D before it repeats* and that was it, you could hear it in the lyrics too even they were sort of mismatched with the chords, sort of slip-sliding around on top of the progression. I stood up, not noticing the guitar weight much any more. In the verse it was all power chords, you just had to hold down the major triads, vamp it just a little. I had the rhythm now, damping a little with the heel of my hand, but the tone needed a little sand in it or something. Chris had this effects thing on the floor that looked like he might have pried it off the dashboard of an inter-galactic spaceship, and I kicked the foot switches till I found something that sounded like the flanger. Now the chords were shimmering and crunching at once, and that was more like it. Cobain would be nodding his head except in reality he didn't have a head since he'd blown it off with that shotgun. Then in the chorus you want to open it up and play more of the full chord without damping, and all of a sudden Allston was backing me on the drums and we didn't sound half bad. I thought, "I *like* it I'm not gonna—"

Perry swung around from the mixing board and killed my amp.

"The hell you think you're doing?" he snarled. "People don't want to hear that crap."

So he was still in his same lovely mood, I could tell. But all right, we didn't play Nirvana, we didn't play punk and we didn't play grunge, we definitely didn't play any originals and we also (praise the Lord!) didn't play top 40. We did play Chicago blues standards, and white-boy blues like Clapton and Allmans and Stevie Ray Vaughan, plus rock warhorses from Hendrix and the Stones and Neil Young, or we might even take it a little bit country too if that's what people seemed to want. Which was in fact the way I liked it—I never was a Nirvana fancier, it was just this one odd thing.

I unslung the Les Paul, but Perry was going, "I didn't *say* put it down."

I looked at him.

"He ain't here, Jesse," Perry told me. "So guess what?"

"Don't tell me," I said, and I went on and set the guitar on the stand.

"Hey," Perry said. "Wasn't *my* idea to play fruitbasket-turnover."

My hand was twinging me already. I jumped off the stage and headed for the front bar, taking a long look at everybody. Some more people had been coming in, mostly guys so far but none of them was Chris. Mike poured me a double shot of bourbon and I sat there nursing it and looking at my hand—it didn't seem to be shaking at least, though I could feel butterflies in my stomach. The pain wasn't *there*

there, but I could just feel it waiting. When I did use to be on guitar it would get so bad sometimes I couldn't even pick up a coffee cup with my left hand, much less hold down a bar chord. Tendonitis, the doctor said, from repetitive motion. I could rest it and soak and eat aspirins on it. But what really helped was playing bass instead, which meant it had to be partly a head thing because I had to work my hand harder on bass. The good thing about bass was I could hang back with Allston and keep my head down and be "the quiet one," nobody paying me much mind—except tonight it wasn't gonna be that way.

"Jesse," Perry was calling me over the mike. Ten minutes or so had gone by somehow, and I saw I had drunk up my whiskey. I got a beer to have on the stand, and I went back to the other room.

"'One Way Out,'" Perry told me when I got up on the stage. He had my bass strapped on him already. Our usual line-up was Perry on an acoustic/electric Gibson, singing and strumming or Travis picking while Chris did the major guitar work. But Perry could play passable bass and sing over it if he had to, and it was do-what-you-have-to time.

I flipped the Les Paul to the front pick-up and stomped the floor controller for clean. The basic riff was simple enough—Perry would usually play it himself on the L-5. *Bap Bap Badda da DOT dot da dadda dadda*—I went through it a few times for an intro, long enough to start turning people toward the stage. Next should have been Chris coming in on the Strat with slide but this wasn't available so Allston just landed hard on the drums and then Perry stepped to the mike for the first verse. He had a passable voice, Perry, sounded something like Greg Allman, on a good day. Then the verse was done and I didn't quite know what to do next being that I was out there all by myself, so I just kept on with the riff over the I chord, vamped the IV, riff over I, vamp the V and back. Perry was giving me a look that said *That's pretty lame,* which it was, and me shooting one back that wanted to say *Yeah but this is supposed to be a two-guitar project* and quite a few other things as well.

I hit the turnaround so Perry had to start singing. At the end of the second verse I thought I'd better try the solo, since Perry looked like he was fixing to kick me or something if I didn't. I could've handled it if there'd been the other guitar to keep the riff going behind it or better yet, me doing that while Chris took the lead, but it was too thin with one guitar, plus I was trying to come back and quote the riff fairly often so people would remember what it was they were hearing. Two things at once was too many for me, and I got lost, couldn't hear the progression, dropped out the bottom on the wrong note and then I couldn't hit the riff again, just could not play it. I had a handful of broken matchsticks where my fingers had been, and there was sweat breaking out all over my body. I thought the weight of the Les Paul was going to bring me right down. I had stopped playing, just stopped cold, and Perry wouldn't even look at me. He was having to sing the third verse over just bass and cymbals while I stood there frozen, wondering if I was going to puke or pass out first. I was thinking I should have borrowed Cobain's shotgun instead of his song. Then my ears started working again and I realized it didn't sound bad that way, kind of cool actually. My hands came back and I started throwing in some fills. At the end of the verse Perry mouthed something at me and I knew he meant to try and pull it out by doing the first verse one more time, so we did that, and Allston smashed it out and we were done.

I looked over the room and what do you know? The people in front were stamping and hooting and the usual turkey was hollering, "'Whipping Post!'" (which we probably would get around to sooner or later). Everybody that was listening was already drunk and the people that weren't drunk weren't really listening. Same as every Black Cat from Key West to Alaska—no problem.

Meanwhile Perry was leaning across and kind of bellering in my ear. "Why? Why does he have to do this to me?" Meaning Chris dusting off like he apparently had.

This was a question that might have long answer—wasn't the first time Chris had pulled such a trick. Always after Perry had come down a little too hard on his case. If he really wanted to leave us screwed and tattooed, he would have taken his guitars along with him when he booked, but what he wanted to prove instead was that we needed him. Which was a fact. He'd come back once he made this point, sometimes by the second or third set but sometimes not till the next night. The catch this time was it was the last night of this entire strip. Sometimes we stopped out at the Black Cats of Virginia on the way down, but tomorrow we were just headed straight home.

"You maybe were ragging on him too hard," I told Perry. "Could be it makes him think you don't love him."

"Jesus Christ on a cracker," Perry said. "Ain't enough I carry the son of a bitch." His voice went down to the preaching register, gloomy and dour like he'd just had to shoulder the whole entire burden of God. "Ain't enough I carry him—he wants me to love him too."

Then Perry appeared to think this was funny 'cause he all of a sudden bust out laughing.

"What the hell," Perry said. "Let's try and make'm happy."

So we played "Sweet Home Alabama." This went over well enough, the usual turkey started hollering for "Free Bird." We did "Cajun Moon," and the turkey hollered for "Cocaine," which made him a smarter turkey than I'd have suspected. But Perry seemed like he really wanted to mess with the guy, take it out on him more or less, so we did "After Midnight"—not Clapton-style but the J. J. way, which is right and true but also a little narcotized for the first set at the Black Cat on a Saturday night. People were drifting when we got done with that one, and the turkey didn't holler for anything at all.

Then we did "Wicked Game," to throw a curve—the girls seemed to like that one. There were more of them there by this time, the place was filling up. Almost an even-steven mix of blue-collar and college types, with the turkey and his friends sort of on the fence in between, over-the-hill underemployed fratboys with their livers starting to go bad. Chris Isaak didn't seem to say anything to that sector, so we did "Sympathy for the Devil" and "Jumping Jack Flash." This started up some dancing. The turkey hollered for "Brown Sugar," but we did "Midnight Rambler," which seemed to put Perry in a straight blues mood, so we did "Gypsy Woman," "I'm a Man," "Red House," and "Statesboro Blues." The turkey hollered for "Whipping Post" again, naturally, after "Statesboro."

"'Blue Sky,'" Perry said to me off-mike, and threw a wink.

"Duane's dead, don't you know?" I said. "I ain't trying that one with just one guitar." I had been holding my own up to then, was even beginning to somewhat enjoy myself, so I felt like I had a right to refuse one.

Perry shrugged. "'Cinnamon Girl.'"

When we got done with that the turkey hollered for "Down By the River," of course, but Perry called "Tonight's the Night." Actually what he did first was yell for tequila, then stood there waiting 'til it came—a water glass about half-full of something that looked like old fry oil. Perry killed half of it and showed it to Allston, who of course shook his head. Perry passed the glass to me.

"Just do it," he said. I took a sniff. I didn't know what he had in mind but we'd been up there an hour or so, so what the—*Aaargh*. Never wished for a lemon so bad.

"Tonight's the niiiight," Perry sang, and hit the signature bass line. For a second I thought I was playing it myself—the tequila had smashed between my eyes like a bullet and I almost forgot I had the guitar. Then I recovered, partly, and hit the foot controller for max distortion. Perry was singing over the slow bass walkdown. "Tonight's the ni-i-i-i-ight—*waaarrgghhh-aauuwmpp*." That last part was me. By now I was feeling no pain whatsoever, but luckily this song only has about one and a half chords in it so I could get away with almost anything. By the end I was doing knee bends behind the amp and turning the Les Paul belly up to scoop huge bowlfulls of black feedback and dump them out over the crowd while Perry muttered and groaned the words and I wondered how much of this it would take to frenchfry the P.A. altogether—was thinking I better pull back a little when I came up halfway out of a crouch and "there she was." The stage was only about a foot high so we were almost nose to nose. She was dressed different, cigarette jeans and a loose white shirt, hair pulled back tight instead of swinging like the night before. It was her. Her look was clear and unintelligible (I don't know what mine would have said to her either) but still I could see well enough that whatever had happened between us hadn't harmed her, which was, I guess, what I'd been hoping to learn somehow all day.

I wanted to play something just for her, something to show I got that message, but Perry was going to take us on break, I knew, once this song ended. I straightened up, holding the feedback crescendo still, while Perry stared at me wondering when I'd ever let it drop. They had opened the second bar in the band room and I saw Chris was standing there with Big Blondie. I felt relieved, a little disappointed too. This would be my last one. "Brown-Eyed Girl"—Perry wouldn't sing it; "Beautiful Brown Eyes"—too country for tonight; "Brown Eyes Blue"—not without Meredith. Then I found it, or my hand did; I could just swing over on the same note into A-minor. I was already playing the hook and Perry was giving me the hairy eyeball, but he was stuck, he had to sing it now or else look stupid.

Didn't matter, it wasn't my voice singing, I was talking with guitar, my fingers humming on the strings and my eyes connected straight to hers. I took the middle solo as close to the sound barrier as it would fit, hand running deep in the cut-out. I saw the sound wave lifting her wings, billowing the white cloth of her shirt, like she was standing in a wind tunnel or a cyclone. *Like a hurricane*—Perry was belting it out. She twirled, a maple seed in a windstorm, and I lost her in the crowd. I held that last note hanging in the air like a sheet of hammered foil, till Allston shattered it with a cymbal smash and the shreds came glittering down on everything like snow.

"We'll be back," Perry was saying. The Les Paul was on the stand and I was down, pushing through the people toward the back bar. A couple of strangers said stuff to me—my ears were ringing and I couldn't hear, but they were smiling. A bartender threw on a Little Feat tape, which sounded thin and far away compared to us. I had a cigarette stuck in my mouth and was feeling for a match, but at the bar Chris snapped his lighter and waved me over for a drink, which I was more than ready for. The girl was gone, but it didn't matter.

Belgrade, New York

ava chin

IN VIENNA, IT'S CALLED THE DANUBE, the Duna in the twin cities of Buda & Pest, but in Belgrade we sit on the banks of the Dunav where the river meets the Sava and we do not hold hands. In the distance, medieval towers point to the ruin of the sky. Dragan throws a stone on the water. He says, "You can't stay here," green eyes turning brown. It ripples three times before sinking.

Stephen thinks the reason I sneeze is that I left Dragan in Yugoslavia. Since I returned, every morning waking means a thick chest, drippy nose, arms reaching past the sheets to gasp for air.

At first it seemed like hayfever—the kind that's kept my mother addicted to antihistamines for years. Other times it was the spy-like sneeze upon exiting the apartment, the sunlight streaming down Avenue A. But this was no ordinary pollen or smoke from the bar downstairs, seeping its way through the floor boards.

Stephen has had severe allergies since he was five and practically lived his twenties in a plastic bubble. Friends with allergic babies call him, desperate for advice. Wailing in arms, their soft noses drip. Mouths gape small fish. "They need love," he tells me from behind the register. Not shots or innoculations or plastic pillows and sheets. "I can tell," he says, packing CDs in a brown wrapper, his tattoos winking 15-plus years of faded colors. Like many old-time musicians who never made it to the big stage, Stephen has the hungry look of a dog but the softness of pumpkin pie. He raises an eyebrow before saying, "These children crave touch."

Yeah, yeah. The air outside is brisk on Broadway, nursing tea and honey to a suffering nose. The air is brisk in Belgrade, too—but that's yesterday's weather. On such a clear day you can see straight to the Empire State Building from my apartment, a giant needle shimmering in the sky. Along the avenue, students are walking, noonday hits the shop windows, their mannequins, their perfect nails. It's good to be back in the West, where the bathrooms gleam whiter than cocaine dust. It's good to be back in New York, I tell myself. Stephen is crazy, allergies are genetic. These kids need drugs so they can breathe. *Breathe*: Sinbads of New York, little lords of Brooklyn. Battle the unseen enemy. An immune system in overdrive.

Late to soundcheck, hand in traffic, I beat a businessman to a cab, his doughy nose wrinkling as I shut the door. Inside, tea sloshing and spilling, the driver asks the time, and I pause a second to do the math, my watch set ahead six hours. *See, it's proof*, I'm not really in New York, dial hands reaching into the future from the past. We weave through broken traffic like dust in a blue vein, the cold heart of Belgrade, but I'm six time-zones and 4,000 miles away.

Jaya, chronically on time, is annoyed and Sabine murmurs a low warning as she tunes her walrus bass. Walking into a cabaret during the day is Dorothy's entrance to Oz in reverse: you're swallowed into the whiskey of silence.

While my eyes adjust, Jaya snorts hard, hands full of cords. "S'about time."

"Sorry," I say, jumping over a strangle-hold of black cables. Consider showing her my watch. "I'm still jet-lagging."

"We've been home for weeks now." Jaya has been living a transatlantic lifestyle for ten years. Studio sessions in Berlin, Hamburg, and New York. She doesn't know the meaning of jet-lag. She's the kind of person who only needs four hours' sleep—which of course, she is able to get on the plane.

Sabine interrupts, bass leaning against her shoulder. "I think we need to go over the set-list."

Jaya pulls out the paper and Sabine cranes her long neck, peering over her shoulder. Sabine has also left a boyfriend in Europe, and it shows across her face in dark red blotches. Sabine can throw herself headlong into her work though, and not lose sleep over it. I walk around limp all day and have trouble getting out of bed.

While she and Jaya plan out the order, I walk the hull of the stage—hollow like a tooth, the belly of a ship. My footsteps make cold echoes in the room. Sometimes theater companies produce plays, their track-lighting running up and down in clusters of licorice and grape. Sometimes bands like us are booked, downtown art-rock, black-clad singers acting out Lotte Lenya before the red curtain. I used to think stages were holy places like the gap in your lover's mouth or the foothills where your grandparents are buried. Words were a charm against darkness, that space between us and them, my voice straightening the crooked frame of the world. But those days of medicinal rhymes are a long time ago, and it no longer seems possible to fill this room with my voice alone. I could open my lungs wide and only marbles would run out.

Back home, fumbling in the dark I answer the phone before the machine goes off. It is Nola, my grand-dame auntie, returned from her sister's in San Diego. Her voice draws the shutters back—she wants to know everything—how was Germany and England and when can she see me? It's been half a year and don't I remember I have a family?

"Yes, Nola," I reassure her, taking off my coat. It's cold and the heat my landlord gives is of little consequence. Frost collects on the windows. "The performances went well. Berlin is Berlin, and London is London."

"What about your friend? That guy you spent so much time with? Is he here?"

Dragan teched our shows in Eastern Europe, and unfortunately, in a sentimental moment, I wrote Nola and my mother about him. As if writing would make it more concrete.

"He can't come over Nola. He's home in Belgrade."

"He's from Serbia? Oh, I see," she pauses and then in a confidential whisper, "You know they're not like us."

I almost laugh. Nola is short, Chinese-Filippina and born seventy-five years ago on Mott Street. Last year she punched a mugger who tried to take her purse. Most would assume she's a frail, old lady.

"You're way too free for them. They're very, very macho, " she pauses. "I never told you this, but back in my day, before I met your uncle, I dated a Hungarian man…"

I have never heard this story of post-war interracial romance and punch a pillow for my head, but in that way elderly women have, she quickly changes the subject and wants to know what time the show is, whether or not there'll be lots of smoke and if she can bring a friend.

In the shadows, Nola's words fade wallpaper to the clock on the ledge. It reads midnight, and against my will the math is automatic: 6 A.M. in Serbia. A month ago, we would just be stumbling into the apartment from the studio and after a few cigarettes, going to sleep. Dragan would draw the curtains against dawn and crawl into my back.

In the dark, the light from the restaurant across the street blinks blue in the room. The phone goes dead with barely a click. Dragan and I have not spoken since I returned, and it's hard. I am reminded of him every time someone asks about the tour. Pictures and jewelry are in a box on the floor, pushed past the books and tissues and CDs, the laundry and unpaid phone bills. I have no will to pick up old reminders, to read last month's newspapers, or even throw away the stack of immigration papers under the bed inside the envelope that will never be used.

And as I blow my nose, I think of allergic babies and small fish, of parents concerned with life and death, of the blue-grey tones of Belgrade. There's the Danube coursing solemnly eastward to the Black Sea. Islands off Croatian coastlines and the salt contained in tears.

At the bar, under fading light, tall men coddle cocktails and buy drinks for journalists. Sabine finds me backstage, on the floor, behind the high hats and a jumble of dismantled drum kits like broken arms. Her shaved head peers behind the red curtain and murmurs comforting clucking sounds. I feign congestion and wave her away, looking up to see the soundproofed ceiling shake with the heavy bass mixed by the house DJ. I have never before noticed the fine layer of cork that coats the floor, a new layer of dust every ten days.

Outside, Nola is sitting alone, a Shirley Temple on the table. She politely waves away smoke with a folded AARP newletter from her bag. A few feet over, hair askew and forearms flexing, Stephen talks to some publicists awaiting their lawyer boyfriends.

"Okay, ten minutes," Jaya announces, headphones a perfect frame to her curly hair. Record cued and levels set, turntables and mixers steady. Pedals co-mingle with cords. Sabine's bass is wired. Leaning over, her head touches Jaya. They turn to me, a question.

Instead of responding, I fiddle with the mike. The mike is a spindly septum sensitive to the slightest touch. It is a miniature penis. No feedback, no distortion. The receiver responds to my quivering breath.

When I was a child, a popcorn kernel bore its way along the corridor of my ear. It took over a dozen visits to the pediatrician to remove it. This may well explain my resistance to visiting the doctor for my allergy. I dig into my pocket for nasal spray and inhale. I'm in junior high sniffing glue.

"Hey, smile," Jaya says. "There's a lot of money riding on this gig."

I am a happy girl and happy girls don't like to be told to smile. Instead, I frown.

Sabine leans, tuning her bass, round eyes sympathetic. Even in this light, her skin is red and uneven.

"I'm fine," I say, testily. "Just 'cause I'm not smiling on the outside doesn't mean I'm not smiling on the inside."

Jaya doesn't appreciate sarcasm and is about to embark on a lecture, but the engineer interrupts. Problems with the levels.

"Why is it that happy people are never allowed to be upset?" I doggedly tail Sabine, but she's too busy adjusting the amp and isn't listening. Her back to me.

"Everyone freaks out. What's the big deal?" I am shouting, but she shushes me.

Jumping on a chair, I yell, "I will not be silenced!" but the bar continues, business as usual. Even Jaya can't be bothered.

From the stage I can see Nola, waving to me from her high stool. Stephen sits with her, tired of trying to court the execs, leaning into it, waiting for me to begin. I attempt a smile and get off the chair.

Sometimes when we perform, the trio breathes together as if a single one-cell organism. Swaying, ten thousand beats of light. Jaya's needle hits the grooves, jumping Willy Wonka to Sabine's abusive use of toys. Her hollow cheeks breathe life into the melodica. Her weapons of choice: an egg slicer, a trash can, a plastic bird whistle. Tonight, my voice is the dissonant chord in our town, the foreigner in the crowd. Reaching out under this sea of floodlights and overhead projections, there's only the mike to hold on to. I used to think it cheesy when I heard performers yell for love from the audience, hoping to gather support like some autumn crop. I've a fit of emotions to harvest, to get back from these suits and arms and glued-on mouths and pasted hands. I want to pray for love with Nola and Stephen and my girls, no matter how angry and blemished they may be. Above the smoke and rush of beer on tap. The clink of tips collected at the bar.

*   *   *

He stands lonely like a knife in song, and I hum the bars like old memory. Melody can drown words like the rush of a river. Here, where two currents meet along the Danube's 1,775-mile stretch, through Hungary as through Belgrade, it is pointless to speak. Love, I have learned, cannot conquer time or distance or national borders or civil war. We lack the strength to make ourselves refugees, to slap history across our pages with bared teeth. I did not come to Europe for love, after all, but for business and art, music and capital. Love—I remind myself, while the sun hangs distant—is for novels and teenagers and amateur hearts. The fodder of bad songs and university poets, of lonely schoolgirls and misguided musicians.

"Hey, yo, that was great," Stephen says, mug in my face.

"Thanks," I say, focusing past his left shoulder. I never know how to respond after a show that doesn't seem disingenuous. Nor do I enjoy just smiling and soaking it in.

"No, no, I mean it," Stephen says unconvinced, Jack Daniels on the breath. A habit he picked up in the army. "Listen, I want you to come see my band play…"

He digs into his pockets. "These are for you."

A handful of tissues and a folded yellow flyer. The hard currency of downtown musicians. Usually, I just shove invites into my back pocket until a lump forms in the wash. This time I read it, taking it gently from him and do something I never do, which is look into Stephen's potato-brown eyes, and say, yes, that I'll be there.

It's one of those blue-black nights when we wait in the corridor, shivering with our breaths in front of us like another body on line. It is packed for Stephen's show, and the added layers of elbows and boots and other people's clothing help keep me warm. Stephen offered to put our names at the door, but I know every head counts when the venue is taking first cut, and refused to let him soak the ticket. At the register, though, the girl in the orange hat and gloves squints at me for a moment, smiles, and stamps my hand without taking money.

Inside, the room is filled with the smokey, sweaty, cigarette-ash smells that stain every club across the continents from the Lower East Side to East Berlin. The comfort of sanctioned anarchy—beer and graffitied toilets—familiar like a mall. In front is the stage, its metal instruments lit up like scapels. I wait in the dark on a rise in the floor in a part of the room that has the best sound and I see no known faces. Jaya and I used to come frequently, when the trio was barely a duo, but neither of us has set foot in the venue since long before Europe. Stephen is busy tooling with his amp on stage, ignoring the noise. The house lights hit the bald crown he's developing, a monk at the bass. He adjusts, listens, corrects. It's a care I used to take, too, even at the smallest venues. Even the ones like this, that pay the lowest, that pay in beer.

When the band enters, there is a tension I have felt before and a rise in the audience. It is in Stephen's face. On stage, where a minute is a century and at the same time less than a second, the extraneous is stripped away like bones in the floor of the Atlantic and you treat every moment like it's both forever and lost in a child's song. You do not think of last months rent or yesterday's weather, only of what you do. Someone once watched me from such a distance, as I watch Stephen, eyes turning from green to brown. One who kissed with a mouth burned by foreign words and promises and time stretching medieval towers. Who knew me by the edge of the river, as surely as the Danube knows the continent from southwestern Germany to eastern Baltic shores. And while Stephen does his solo, fingers flying over the thick chords, we clap, we smile. A woman yells. Stephen laughs. And I know now what I had forgotten all these weeks. That even a girl who drowns in some other country's river, who loses her voice in the current, can relearn old rhymes by starting slowly, going backwards, to make the words heard on a torn page as well as an empty stage. To open her voice and find the world in a marble and fling it back into the sea. As surely as the river counts its countries and recognizes all its names: Danube, Duna, Dunav.

And as I push my way to the bar, the bartender, says, "Hey! aren't you—?"

I just smile, spreading the coins like stones.

'Til There Was You

kim addonizio

PRACTICE

The band practices in the basement of the keyboard player's mother's house in San Jose. Every Wednesday, the mother's bowling night, the band members set up their amps and mikes and instruments in a tiny room whose walls are covered with carpet remnants from the warehouse where the lead guitarist works. The keyboard player's girlfriend watches TV in the mother's bedroom—*90210,* then *Party of Five,* then the news, or she restlessly surfs through the channels. She keeps the TV turned up loud to try and drown out the electric bass thumping up through the floor. The band members come upstairs to take a piss, to grab beers from the fridge and roll joints from the baggie of pot on the kitchen table. When the girlfriend goes into the kitchen they say, "Hey. How's it goin'." She can tell they've forgotten her name. They are large men, in their thirties and forties— older than her and her boyfriend. She is twenty, and her boyfriend just turned twenty-two. The bass player has a long gray ponytail, the drummer has hair plugs, the lead guitarist remembers when Eric Clapton played with some band named Cream. They are losers, playing loser music that the lead singer, Tony, writes for them. The keyboard player's girlfriend hates Wednesday nights but she always comes to practice, because she loves her boyfriend, and if he becomes a famous rock musician one day she will be able to say, I was with him from the beginning. Not that it's going to happen with this loser

121

band, but the girlfriend keeps this opinion to herself. Her boyfriend is actually not that good on keyboards. At least, not yet. She is sure he'll improve, though. Tony says he has soul. Soul, like it's the fucking sixties. What a loser Tony is.

Three Gigs

I.

Tony gets them a gig in a local club. They play in the back room, a cavernous space with a balcony and black walls, where the stage is. In the front room, where the bar is, the place is packed. People at the bar are talking and laughing and putting dollars in the jukebox. In the back room there's no one but Tony's girlfriend, the keyboard player's girlfriend, and a drunk Texan in a white ten-gallon hat looking for the men's room. The band plays for an hour and a half, and between songs Tony talks to an imaginary crowd, saying things like, "All right, people! Let's rock 'n' roll!" At one point he introduces each band member, and the two girlfriends clap. Tony says, "Here's a song I wrote called 'Downtown Streets.' Feel free to get up and get down and *dance* to this one." Tony's girlfriend gets up and dances, alone in the center of the room. The drunk Texan wobbles toward her like he's going to dance with her, but he runs into a chair on the way. His hat falls off. He bends down to pick it up, falls over and decides to stay there. He takes off his jacket, folds it into a pillow, and curls up on the floor. Tony's girlfriend raises her arms in the air, twirling around, her hair flying. She has a degree in music from Curtis Institute in Philadelphia, and plays weird experimental oboe in a different loser band. The keyboard player's girlfriend thinks, Well, there's someone for everyone. She goes off to the bar to get drunk.

2.

They play at a bar on Sixth Street in San Francisco—a neighborhood of junkies, crackheads, whores, alcoholics, and other people too poor or fucked up to be anywhere else. In the middle of the second set a fight breaks out between a man with a beer bottle and another man with a pool cue. Instead of going into the next song on the set list— a slow ballad called "Need to Need You"—Tony calls for "Starving," and starts singing at the top of his lungs: *You just chew me up / and spit me out / like I'm rotten meat / well there's just no doubt / that you'll be starving for my lo-o-ove, babe / 'cause when push comes to sho-o-ove, babe...* That's as far as he gets before the man with the cue chases the man with the bottle onstage and into the drumset, knocking over the toms and cymbal stand. Everyone stops playing and watches the man wildly swinging his pool cue, narrowly missing the drummer. The man with the bottle runs into the street. "Well, shit," the other man says, kicks over the snare and goes back to the pool table. By way of apology, the bar owner books them for another gig the following month. When they show up, the bar is gone and a Vietnamese restaurant is in its place. They lock their equipment in the bass player's van, sit down, and order dinner.

3.

They play at the Bay to Breakers, a race through the streets of San Francisco, at 6 A.M. on a Sunday. Thousands of runners stream past the outdoor stage. Tony shouts, sings, and stomps. He struts back and forth like an oversized Mick Jagger, a sleeveless black tank top riding up his beer belly, his bandanna headband soaked with sweat. "San Francisco, I love you!" he screams. "Rock and roll forever!" Runner after runner glances up at the stage and waves before pounding uphill and disappearing over the horizon. The keyboard player's girlfriend stands in front of the stage, one of the few stationary people, and even she is swept up in the excitement of the crowds and noise and color. "Yeah!" she cries after every song. She looks up at her boyfriend in his leather vest and torn jeans, standing at his KS-32 pounding out chord progressions, and thinks with pride: I have fucked him. I have tasted his cock in my mouth. A feeling of love and power surges through her. This is my future, she thinks; this is my fate.

Personnel Changes

The drummer quits after the bar fight. The band auditions a new guy, who happens to be blind. He hits his head going down the stairs to the basement. The friend who brought him refuses to leave the car; he sits in an old station wagon in the driveway, drinking beer and smoking cigarettes. The keyboard player's girlfriend walks into the kitchen and sees the friend through the window, his head thrown back, eyes closed, like he is listening to music on the radio. Good music, she thinks. Successful music. She can hear the new drummer trying to keep up while Tony sings, *Never gonna die / never gonna give up. / Gonna make the world / fill my loving cup.* She hears her boyfriend play a wrong chord, and then another one. In fact, he sounds like he's playing in a whole different key. By now she knows all Tony's songs by heart, and she can tell when somebody messes up. A sense of hopelessness overtakes her, but as she listens to Tony sing she feels a promise in the words. *I got my own vision / I got my own song. / Look out, world, / 'cause it won't be long.* Tony says they are going to cut a demo soon. He says a guy from a local cable-access TV show is going to come to the next gig. He says the band is going to play at the Great American Music Hall in San Francisco. Downstairs the music stops, and they start the song again. This time the drummer nails the beat, and her boyfriend gets most of the chords right. She closes her eyes, pretending she is blind, and stands in the kitchen listening until the song ends.

Romance

Tony's girlfriend gets pregnant and they decide to get married. At the wedding, which is held on a ship that has been permanently docked and turned into a restaurant, Tony asks the hired band if he can do a number with them. Tony's band members, looking uncomfortable in suits and ties, sit holding plastic glasses of champagne while Tony sings an old Beatles song, "Til There Was You," to his new bride. Usually, Tony's band is so loud that Tony is practically drowned out. But today, for the first time, the keyboard player's girlfriend can hear his voice clearly, and she realizes that Tony can't sing very well. In fact, he has a tendency to sing a little flat. It's hard to tell if he notices; he stands holding the mike in both hands, gazing into his bride's eyes, while she weeps under her veil. The keyboard player is nowhere in sight. When his girlfriend goes to look for him she finds him in the coat room with one of the bridesmaids, his tongue in her mouth, his soulful hands slipped up under her shirt. The girlfriend screams at him, and in the next room, Tony hits the last high phrase of "Til There Was You," and his voice cracks.

Where They Are Now
One by one, everyone quit the band. The blind drummer played two gigs with them and disappeared; the old drummer came back for a while but then moved to Florida. The bass player got a job as Banquet Captain at the Ramada Inn by the airport and was too busy to be in a band anymore. The lead guitarist, who could actually play—he was the only reason they got any gigs at all—moved to L.A. and started doing session work. The keyboard player decided to quit music entirely because it was too fucking hard, and he hated practicing. Now he does computer graphics for a firm in Silicon Valley. Tony's wife had a girl; she's five now, and Tony, after a long break to cope with fatherhood and unemployment, is working in a music store and putting together a new band.

The keyboard player's girlfriend—now his ex-girlfriend—bought herself an electric bass guitar. She joined an all-female band named V. Dentata. Their debut album, *Hose Me Down*, has just gone platinum. Two of the singles from it—the title song and another one she herself wrote, "All F**ked Up and No Place to Go"—are on the *Billboard* Top Twenty. When she looks back on her time with the keyboard player, she can barely remember him. He's a pair of torn jeans, a Wednesday night TV schedule, a weak left hand. All she remembers with any clarity is Tony, her inspiration, the person who taught her everything important about the music.

YOU'VE REALLY GOT A HOLD ON ME

Rock & Roll Heaven

t. coraghessan boyle

I DIED AND WENT TO ROCK & ROLL HEAVEN. It looked like Houston Street. This can't be rock & roll heaven, I thought.

A fat black man in a dirty white suit was sitting on a suitcase toodling on a saxophone. "No, this be-bop heaven," he said. "You want two blocks down."

I passed a knishery on the way. The sign said: Yonah Shimmel, 97 Years in Business. I hadn't eaten since I died. The smell of hot knishes was a siren song to a man who has no qualms about mixing metaphors. I stepped in. It was dark, but non-threatening. After all, this was heaven.

Two men in open-to-the-navel shirts were sitting on a table, making music. One of them had an acoustic guitar, the other had a mouth harp. What they were playing sounded a lot like rock & roll. "Hey," I said, "that rock & roll you're playing?"

The man with the mouth harp stopped sawing the instrument across his lips. His hair was ringlets, his eyes were blue. "Where's your ear, man? This is blue-eyed blues." He pulled a second mouth-harp from a glass of water and shot through a series of high stops, sucking and puffing. Music filled the room.

I took a table in the back and rested my axe against a chair. The waiter was bald. I ordered a kasha knish and homemade yogurt. The waiter held the steaming knish in his hands and sang, "Lassù in cielo" from *Rigoletto*.

129

"I had the impression this was blue-eyed-blues heaven," I said.

"This ain't my neighborhood," the waiter said. "I live over on the other side of town. In opera heaven."

The next block was choked with organ grinders and dancing monkeys. I was confused. I stopped to listen to a thick-eared man in Pinocchio hat. He ground out a rendition of *The Dance of the Sugar-Plum Fairy* while his monkey executed a tricky series of glissades and entrechats. When it was over the man handed me a quarter. I put it in the monkey's cup. "Thank-a-you," the man said.

I followed my ears. They took me through reggae heaven, disco heaven, punk heaven, and mariachi heaven. In punk heaven people were cutting themselves with razor blades and amplifying air-raid sounds. There was dancing in the streets in mariachi heaven.

I heard a sound like thunder in the distance. It could have been rock & roll. I hurried toward it. Three blocks down I turned a corner and found myself in St. Celia's Square. All the buildings round the square had organ pipes, bronze like the sun, instead of chimneys. In the middle of the square, just under the statue, a man in a periwig sat at an organ. His fingers made mountains quake, his feet toppled buildings in distant parts of the city. No one had to tell me. I was in toccata and fugue heaven.

In showtime heaven I met Frieda. She was wearing a peasant blouse, chamois jumper, and patent-leather shoes.

I'd just turned down a street of sand-blasted brownstones, dejected, axe under my arm, when a man in a ducktail haircut came bounding up to me. He vaulted a fire hydrant and a phalanx of parking meters. His mouth was open. "I'm the luckiest guy in the world!" he sang. Shutters opened up and down the block. Faces leaned from them. "He's the luckiest guy in the world!" they howl. He spread his arms and threw his head back. "In love with the love-liest girl!" The faces retreated coyly, but reappeared on the upbeat to shriek, "He's in love with the loveliest girl!"

"I don't mean to be a wet blanket," I said, "but I'm really not all that interested in your private ecstasies or the state of your soul. Not that I have anything against ecstasy per se, but the fact is I'm trying to get to rock & roll heaven."

"Rock & roll heaven?" he warbled interrogatively.

"Rock & roll heaven?" the faces returned.

He planted his feet and swelled himself with a titanic breath of air.

"Neverrrrrr," he began.

"Neverrrr," echoed the faces.

"Hearrrrrd—of it."

"He's never heard of it!" sang the voices on high.

I sat down on my sturdy masonite axe case and buried my face in my hands. When I looked up, the street was deserted and Frieda stood before me. Her cheeks were stuffed with cotton, her hair was in braids.

"Looks like you stumbled into the wrong heaven," she said.

"I'm looking for rock & roll heaven," I said.

She held out her hand.

Frieda was not in costume. Actually she lived in polka heaven, but worked musicals on the other side. Her outfit pretty much restricted her to *Fiddler on the Roof* and revivals of *Heidi*. She took me home with her.

Frieda's father weighed about three hundred pounds. He was wearing lederhosen and a cap with a tassel. He played accordion. Frieda's mother played tuba. Neighbors roasted chestnuts, kartoffels and bratwurst, raised steins of black beer and stamped over the floorboards of the tiny apartment. I danced with Frieda. She took me into a corner and held a wet sausage to my lips. Then she drew the cotton from her cheeks and kissed me. It was all very gemutlich. And yet it wasn't rock & roll.

Frieda's directions led me straight to rock & roll heaven by way of turkey-in-the-straw heaven and bossa nova heaven. Rock & roll heaven looked a lot like the Felt Forum. There were lines of people outside. The people were drinking white port from the bottle and smoking dope. Some of them were hawking tickets. I heard the strains of "Jumpin' Jack Flash" and knew I was home.

I pushed through the crowd with my axe held high. A man in a *Vita Brevis, Ars Longa* T-shirt stopped me at the gate. "Where you think you're going?" he said.

"Inside," I said.

His hair was like plant life. He was big enough to break the backs of normal people like breadsticks. "Oh, yeah?" he said. "Well let me tell you something: I don't recognize you."

I unhoused my axe, plugged it into one of hundreds of amps stacked up round the gate, and gave him a dose of "Treetorn Boogie" from our last album.

He folded his arms. "Still don't recognize you," he said.

"Lead guitar with the Toads."

"Never heard of them."

I was stunned. "Never heard of us? We cut eleven albums for Elektra. Cover of *Rolling Stone,* coast-to-coast TV. When I split up with Krista, I got 20,000 letters in one day."

"Sorry." He struck a match on his bicep and lit a cigarette.

I lashed into "Serengetti Serenade," our big single. The chords mounted like leapfrogging thunderstorms. I played the savanna, the spring of the springbok, the roar of the lion. I played the heat of midday, the solitude of the baobab, the deathscream of the hyena. I played my heart out.

He was laughing. "You couldn't even make session man around here, brother," he said. "I mean, this is rock & roll heaven. We got the King here. And everybody else you ever heard of. What do you think, we let just any hack off the street in here?"

I stretched my axe on the blacktop like a crucified Christ. Feedback hissed through the amp. Inside they were playing "Rock & Roll

Never Forgets." I turned my back on the gate and made my way through the crowd, wondering how long it would take to learn the tuba.

Sticks

lewis shiner

HE HAD A 12-INCH SONY BLACK-AND-WHITE, tuned to MTV, sitting
on a chair at the end of the bed. He could barely hear it over the fan
in the window. He sat in the middle of the bed because of the sag,
drumming along absently to Steve Winwood's "Higher Love."

The sticks were Regal Tip 5Bs. They were thinner than 2Bs—
marching band sticks—but almost as long. Over the years Stan had
moved farther out over the ends. Now the butts of the sticks fit into
the heels of his palms, about an inch up from the wrist. He flipped the
right stick away when the phone rang.

"Stan, dude! You want to work tomorrow?"

"Yeah, probably. What have you got, Darryl? You don't sound
right."

"Does the name Keven Stacey mean anything to you?"

"Wait a minute." Stan switched the phone to his other ear. "Did
you say Keven Stacey? As in Foolsgold, Keven Stacey? She's going to
record at CSR?"

"You heard me." Stan could see Darryl sitting in the control
room, feet up on the console, wearing double-knit slacks and a T-
shirt, sweat coming up on his balding forehead.

"This is some kind of bullshit, right? She's coming in for a jingle
or a PSA."

"No bullshit, Stanley. She's cutting a track for a solo album she's
going to pitch to Warner's. Not a demo, but a real, honest-to-Christ

134

track. Probably a single. Now if you're not interested, there's plenty of other drummers in L.A...."

"I'm interested. I just don't understand why she wants to fuck with a rinky-dink studio like yours. No offense."

"Don't harsh me, bud. She's hot. She's got a song and she wants to put it in the can. Everybody else is booked. You try to get into Record One or Sunset Sound. Not for six months you won't get in. Even if you're Keven Stacey. You listening, Stan?" He heard Darryl hitting the phone on the edge of the console. "That's the Big Time, dude. Knocking on your door."

Just the night before, Stan had watched Foolsgold in concert on HBO. Everybody knew the story: Keven used to fuck the guitar player and they broke up. It was ugly and they spread it all over the *Goldrush* album. It was soap opera on vinyl and the public ate it up.

Stan, too.

The set was blue-lit and smoky, so hot that the drummer looked like somebody was watering him down with a garden hose. Every time the lead player snapped his head back the sweat flew off like spray from a breaking wave.

Keven stood in the middle of the stage, holding a thin white jacket around her shoulders like there was a chill in the air. When she sang she held on to the mike stand with both hands, swaying a little as the music thundered over her. Her eyes didn't go with the rest of her face, the teased yellow hair, fine as fiberglass, the thin model's nose, the carefully painted mouth. The eyes were murky and brown and looked like they were connected to brains and a sense of humor. And something else, passion and something more. A kind of conviction. It made Stan believe everything she was singing.

Stan finished his Dr. Pepper and went into Studio B. The rest of Darryl's first-string house band was already there, working out their nerves in a quiet, strangely frenzied jam. Stan had turned over his drums to Dr. Jackson Sax, one of the more underrated reed players in the city and a decent amateur on a trap set. Jackson's trademark was a dark suit and a pork-pie hat that made him look like a cross between a preacher and a plain-clothes cop. Stan was one of the few people he ever talked to. Nobody knew if he was crazy or just cultivating an image.

Stan himself liked to keep it simple. He was wearing a new pair of Lee riders and a long-sleeved white shirt. The shirt set off the dark skin and straight black hair he'd inherited from his half-breed Comanche father. He had two new pairs of Regal Tip 5Bs in his back pocket and Converse All-Stars on his feet, the better to grip the pedals.

The drums were set up in a kind of elevated garden gazebo against one wall. There were boom mikes on all sides and a wooden rail across the front. If they had to they could move in wheeled walls of acoustical tile and isolate him completely from the mix. Stan leaned with his right foot up against the back wall.

There was some action in the booth and the music staggered and died. Gregg Rosen had showed up so everybody was looking for Keven. Rosen was her producer and also her boyfriend, if you paid attention to the gossip. Which Stan did. The glass in the control booth was tinted and there was a lot of glare, but Stan could make out a Motley Crue T-shirt, purple jams, and glasses on a gold chain. Rosen's hair was crewcut on top and long enough at the sides to hit his shoulders.

They each gave Rosen some preliminary levels and then cooked for a couple of minutes. Rosen came out on the floor and moved a couple of microphones. Darryl got on the intercom from the control room and told them to shut up for a minute. He played back what he'd just taped and Whitebread Walker, the albino keyboard player, started playing fills against the tape.

"Sounds okay," Rosen said.

"Uh, listen," Stan said. "I think the hi-hat's overmodulating."

Rosen stared at him for a good five seconds. The tape ran out and the studio got very quiet. Finally Rosen circled one finger in the air for a replay. The tape ran and then Darryl came on the speakers, "Uh, Gregg, I think the top end is, uh, breaking up a little on that hi-hat."

"Well, fix the fucking thing," Rosen said.

He walked out. As soon as the soundproof door closed there were a few low whistles and some applause. Stan leaned over until his cheek rested against the cool plastic skin of his riding tom. He could feel all the dents his sticks had left in it. Wonderful, he thought. We haven't even started and I've already pissed off the top producer in L.A.

When Rosen came back Keven was with him.

Jorge Martin, the fifteen-year-old boy wonder, fiddled with the tailpiece on his Kramer. Whitebread pretended to hear something wrong with the high E on his electric piano. Art, the bass player, cleaned his glasses. Stan just went ahead and stared at her, but tried to make it a nice kind of stare.

She was small. He'd known that, but the fluorescent lights made her seem terribly fragile. She wore high-heeled boots, jeans rolled up tight at the cuffs, a fringe jacket, and a white ribbed tank top. She looked around at the setup, nodding, working on her lower lip with her teeth. Finally her eyes met Stan's, just for a second. The rest of the room went out of focus. Stan tried to smile back at her and ended up looking down at his snare. He had a folded-up piece of newspaper duct-taped off to one side of the head to kill overtones. The tape was coming loose. He smoothed the tape with his thumbnail until he was sure she wasn't looking at him any more and he could breathe again.

"The song is called 'Sticks,'" she said. She was standing at White-bread's Fender Rhodes and her hands were jammed nervously into the pockets of her jacket. "I don't even have a demo or anything. Sorry. But it's pretty simple. Basically what I want is a real African sound, lots of drums, lots of backing vocals, chanting, all like that. Okay. Well, this is what it sounds like."

She started playing. Stan was disarmed by her shyness. On the other hand she was not kidding around with the piano. She had both hands on the keys and she pumped out a driving rhythm with a solid hook. She started singing. Suddenly she wasn't a skinny, shy little blonde any more. She was Keven Stacey. Everybody in the room knew it.

Stan's stomach hurt. It felt like ice was forming in there. The cold went out through his chest and down his arms and legs.

One by one they started falling in. Stan played a roll on the hi-hat and punched accents on the kick drum. It sounded too disco but he couldn't think of anything else to play. It helped just to be moving his hands. After one verse Keven backed off and let Whitebread take over the piano. She walked around and nodded and pointed, talking into people's ears.

She walked up to the drum riser and put her forearms on the railing. Stan could see the fine golden hair on her wrists. "Hi," she said. "You're Stan, right?"

"Right," he said. Somehow he kept his hands and feet moving.

"Hi, Stan. Do you think you could give me something a little more—I don't know. More primitive, or something?"

"More toms, maybe?"

"Yeah. More of a 'Not Fade Away' kind of feel."

Buddy Holly was only Stan's all-time favorite. He nodded. He couldn't seem to look away from her. His hands moved over to the toms, right crossing over left as he switched from the riding tom to the floor toms. It was a bit of flash left over from the solos he'd played back when he was a kid. He mixed it up with a half-beat of press roll here and there and kept the accents floating around.

"That's nice," Keven said. She was watching his eyes and not his hands. He was staring at her again but she didn't look away.

"Thanks," he said.

"I like that a lot," she said, flicking the side of the high tom with her fingernail. "A whole lot." She smiled again and walked away.

The basic track of drums, bass, and guitar went down in two takes. It was Stan's pride that they never had to put a click track on him to keep him steady. Keven and Rosen listened to the playback and nodded. Then they emptied the percussion closet. Stan put down a second drum track, just fills and punctuation, and the rest of the band loaded up another track with timbales, shakers, bongos and congas. Keven stood on top of a chair, clapping her hands over her head and moving with the music.

The tape ran out. Everybody kept playing and Rosen finally came down out of the booth to break it up, tapping on the diamond face of his Rolex. Keven got down off her chair and everything went quiet. Stan took the wing-nuts off his cymbal stands and started packing the brass away.

"Do you sing?"

Stan looked up. Keven was leaning on the railing again, watching him.

"Yeah, a little bit. Harmonies and stuff."

"Yeah? If you're not doing anything you could stick around for a while. I could maybe use you later on."

"Sure," Stan said. "Why not?"

Rosen wrapped the session at ten that night. Stan had spent five hours on hard plastic folding chairs, reading *Spin* and *Guitar for the Practicing Musician,* listening to Whitebread and Jorge lay down their solos, waiting for Rosen and Keven to fool with the mix. Keven found him there in the lounge.

"You're not doing the vocals tonight," he said.

She shook her head.

"You weren't even planning to."

"Probably not." She was smiling.

"So what am I doing here?"

"I just said I could maybe use you. I didn't say for what."

Her smile was on crooked and her shawl hung loose and open. Stan could see a small mole just below her collarbone. The skin around it was perfect, soft and golden. This isn't happening, he thought.

There was a second where he felt his life poised on a single balance point. Then he said, "You like Thai food?"

He took her to the Siam on Ventura Boulevard. They left her car at the studio and took Stan's white CRX. The night air was cool and sweet and ZZ Top was on KLOS. The pumping, pedal-point bass and Billy Gibbon's pinched harmonics were like musk and hot sauce. Stan looked over at Keven, her hair blown back, her eyes closed, into the music. There was a stillness in the very center of Stan's being. Time seemed to have stopped.

Over dinner he told her about the time he'd backed up the sensitive singer-songwriter who'd gotten his start in junk food commercials. The guy always used pick-up musicians and then complained because they didn't know his songs. The only thing he actually took along on tour with him was his oversized white Baldwin grand piano.

The gig was in a hotel ballroom. Stan and the lead trumpet player were set up right next to the piano and got to listen to his complaints through the entire first set. During the break they collected sixteen place settings of silver and laid them across the piano strings. The second set was supposed to open with "Claire de Lune" on solo piano. After the first chord the famous singer-songwriter walked offstage and just kept walking. Stan would have lost his union card over that one, only nobody would testify against him.

Keven had done the same sort of time. After high school she'd been so broke she'd played piano in one of those red-jacket, soft-pop bands at the Hyatt Edgewater in Long Beach. When she wouldn't put out for the lead player he kept upstaging her and sticking his guitar neck in her face. One night she reached over and detuned his strings, one at a time, in the middle of his solo on "Blue Moon." The stage was so small he couldn't get away from her without falling into the first row of tables. It was the last song of the night and the audience loved it. The manager of the Hyatt wanted them to keep it in the act. Instead Keven got fired and the guitarist found another blonde piano player from L.A.'s nearly infinite supply.

Halfway through dinner Stan felt the calf of her leg press gently against his. He returned the pressure, ever so slightly. She didn't move away.

The chopsticks fit in Stan's hands like Regal Tip 5Bs. He found himself nervously playing his empty plate and water glass. Keven put the dinner on her American Express and told him Warner's would end up paying for it eventually.

In the parking lot Stan walked her to the passenger side of his car and stopped with his hand on the door. His throat was suddenly dry and his heart had lost the beat. "Well," he said. "Where to?"

She shrugged, watched his face.

"I have a place just over on Sunshine Terrace. If you want to, you know, have a drink. Or something."

"Sure," she said. "Why not?"

Some of the houses around him were multi-million-dollar jobs, sprawling up and down the hillside, hidden behind trees and privacy fences. Stan had a one-bedroom apartment in a cluster of four, squeezed in between the mansions. Everything inside was wood—the paneling on the walls, the cabinets, the louvered doors and shutters. Through the open windows the cool summer wind rattled the leaves like tambourines.

Keven walked slowly around the living room, touching the shelves along the one wall that wasn't filled with windows, finally settling in an armchair and pulling her shawl around her shoulders. "I guess you're tired of people telling you how they expected to find your clothes all over the place and junk food boxes in the corners."

"People have said that, yeah."

"I'm a slob. My place looks like somebody played Tilt-A-Whirl with the rooms. And all those goddamn stuffed animals." Word had gotten out that Keven loved stuffed animals and her fans had started handing them up to her at Foolsgold concerts. "What's that?"

"It was my grandfather's," Stan said. It was the trunk of a sapling, six feet long, maybe an inch and a half in diameter at its thickest, the bark peeled away, feathers hanging off the end. Stan took it down from the wall and handed it to her. "It's a coup stick."

"Acoustic? Like a guitar?"

"Coup, with a 'p.' The Indians used it to help exterminate themselves. They thought there was more honor in touching an enemy with one of these than killing him. So they'd ride into a bunch of cavalry and poke them with their coup sticks and the cavalry would blow their heads off."

"Is that what happened to your grandfather?"

"No, he burned out his liver drinking Sterno. He was supposed to have whacked a cop with it once. All it got him was a beating and a night in jail."

"Why'd he do it?"

"Life in the big city, I guess. He had to put up with whatever people did to him and he couldn't fight back or they'd kill him. He didn't have any options under the white man's rules so he went back to the old rules. My old man said Grandpa was laughing when the cop dragged him away. You want a beer?"

She nodded and Stan brought two cans of Oly from the kitchen. Keven was rummaging through her purse. "You want a little coke with that?"

"No thanks," he said. "But you go ahead."

She cut two lines and snorted them through a short piece of plastic straw. "You're a funny kind of guy, you know that?"

"What do you mean?"

"You seem like you're just waiting for other people to catch up to you. Like you're just waiting for somebody to come up and ask you what you want. And you're ready to lay it all out for them."

"I guess maybe that's so."

"So what do you want, Stan? What you do want, right this second?"

"You really want to know? I'd like to take a shower. I really sweated it up in the studio."

"Go ahead," she said. "No, really. I'm not going anywhere. We took your car, remember?"

The heat from the water went right into his muscles and he started to relax for the first time since Darryl's call the day before. And he wasn't completely surprised when he heard a tapping on the glass.

She was leaning on the sink, posed for him, when he opened the sliding door. Her hair stuck out to one side where she'd pulled her tank top over her head. Her small, soft breasts seemed to sway just a little. One smooth hip was turned toward him in a kind of unconscious modesty, not quite hiding the dark tangle of her pubic hair.

"I guess you're tired of people telling you how beautiful you are."

"Try me," she said, and got in next to him.

Her mouth was soft and enveloping. He could feel the pressure of her breasts and the small, exquisite muscles of her back as he held her. Her small hands moved over him and he thought he might pass out.

Later, in bed, she showed him what she liked, how to touch her and where. It seemed to Stan as if she'd offered him a present. She had condoms in her purse. He used his fingers and his tongue and later came inside her. She was high from the cocaine and not ready to sleep. Stan was half crazy from the touch and scent of her and never wanted to sleep again. Sometime around dawn she told him she was cold and he brought her a blanket. She curled up inside his arm, building an elaborate nest out of the pillows and covers.

They made love again in the morning. She whispered his name in his ear. Later they showered again and he made her coffee and toast.

Stan offered her one of his T-shirts but she shook her head and dressed in yesterday's clothes. Time seemed to pick up speed as she dressed. She looked at the clock and said, "Christ, it's almost noon. Gregg is going to be waiting on us."

He stood in a circle with the other singers, blending his voice on an African chant that Keven had played them from a tape. He knew the gossip had started the minute he and Keven came in together. Rosen was curt and irritable and everybody seemed to be watching Stan out of the corners of their eyes.

Stan couldn't have cared less.

When the backing tracks were down, Keven disappeared into the vocal booth. Jackson packed up his horn and sat down next to Stan. "Got to make a thing over at Sunset. You working this evening?"

"I don't know yet."

"Yeah," he said. "Be cool."

Rosen put the playback over the speakers. The song was about break-ups and betrayals:

> *...broke down all my fences*
> *And left me here alone*
> *Picking up sticks...*

As she stretched out the last word the percussion came up in the mix, drowning her in jungle rhythm. The weight of the drums was a perfect balance for the shallow sentiment. Together they sounded to Stan like number one with a bullet.

She nailed the vocal on the third try. When she came out of the booth she walked up to him and said, "Hey."

"Hey, yourself. It's going to be a monster, you know. It's really great."

"You think so? Really?"

"Really," he said. She brushed his cheek with her hand.

"Listen," he said.

"No. I can't. I've got a dinner date with Warner's tonight. Gregg's dubbing down a cassette and we're going to play it for them. So I'm tied up until late."

"Okay," he said.

She started to walk away and then came back.

"Do you sleep with your door locked?"

He managed to fall asleep. It was an effort of will that surprised even him. When he heard the door open it was 3 A.M. The door closed again and he heard a slightly drunken laugh and a gentle bumping of furniture. He saw a darker shadow in the doorway of the bedroom. There was a rustle of clothing. It seemed to Stan to be the single most erotic moment of his life.

She pulled back the covers and slid on top of him. Her skin was soft and cool and rich with perfume. When she kissed him he tasted expensive alcohol on her breath.

"How were the Warner Brothers?" he whispered.

"They loved me. I'm going to be a star."

"You're already a star."

"Shhhhhh," she said.

He opened his eyes in the morning and saw her fully dressed.

"I've got to go," she said. It was only nine o'clock. "I'll call you."

It was only later that he realized that the session was over. He'd never been to her place, he didn't even have a phone number where he could call her.

It was like he'd never had empty time to fill before. He spent most of the afternoon on the concrete stoop in front of his apartment, listening to Buddy Holly on his boombox. A mist had blown in from the Pacific and not burned off. His hands were nervous and spun his drumsticks through his fingers, over and over.

She called late that night. He should have been asleep but wasn't. There was a lot of traffic noise in the background and he had trouble hearing her.

"I'll be by tomorrow night," she said. "We can go to a movie or something."

"Keven—"

"I have to go. See you tomorrow, okay?"

"Okay," Stan said.

She was sitting on the stoop when he came home from a session the next afternoon. She was wrapped in her shawl and the clouds overhead all seemed to be in a hurry to get somewhere.

She let him kiss her, but her lips were awkward. "I can't make tonight," she said.

"Okay."

"Something came up. We'll try it another night, okay?"

"Sure," Stan said. "Why don't you give me your number?"

She stood up, took his hands as if to keep him from touching her. "I'll call you." She stopped at the gate. "I'm crazy, you know." She wouldn't look at him.

"I don't care."

"I'll call you," she said again, and ran across the street to her bright red sports car. Stan held up one hand as she drove away but she didn't seem to see him.

After two days he started to look for her. Darryl reluctantly gave him Gregg Rosen's unlisted number. Stan asked Rosen for Keven's phone number and he just laughed. "Are you crazy, or what?"

"She won't care if you give it to me. I'm the guy from the CSR session—"

"I know who you are," Rosen said, and hung up.

He left a call for her at the Warner offices in Burbank and with Foolsgold's agent. He tried all the K. Staceys in all three L.A. area codes.

He called Rosen again. "Look," Rosen said. "Are you stupid, or what? Do you think you're the only kid in town that's had a piece of Keven Stacey's ass? End to end you guys would probably stretch to Tucson. Do you think she doesn't know you've been calling? Now are you going to quit hassling me or are you going to fuck over what little career you may have left?"

The check for Keven's session came in the mail. It was on CSR's account and Darryl had signed it, but there was no note in the envelope with it. On the phone Darryl said, "Face it, bud, you've been an asshole. Gregg Rosen is way pissed off. You're going to have to kick back for a while, pay some dues. Give it a couple months, maybe you can cruise back."

"Fuck you too, Darryl."

L.A. dried up. Stan hit the music stores and the musicians' classifieds. Most of the ads were drummers looking for work. The union offered him a six-month tour of the southern states with a revival of *Bye Bye Birdie*.

Jesus, Stan thought. Show tunes. Rednecks. Every night another Motel 6. I'm too old for this.

The phone rang.

Stan snatched it up.

"Stan. This is Dave Harris. Remember me?"

Harris was another session drummer, nothing special. He'd filled in for Stan a couple of times.

"Yeah, Dave. What's up?"

"I was, uh, I was just listening to a cassette of that Keven Stacey song? I was just wondering, like, what the hell were you doing there? I can't follow that part at all."

"What are you doing with a cassette of that song?"

"Uh oh."

"C'mon, Dave, spill it."

"They didn't tell you? Warner's going to use it as the first single from the album. So they're getting ready to shoot the video. They didn't even tell you? Oh man, that really sucks."

"Yeah, it sucks all right."

"Really, Stan, I didn't know, man. I swear. They told me you couldn't make the gig."

"Yeah, okay, Dave, hang on, all right? I'm trying to figure something out, here."

Stan showed up at the Universal lot at six in the morning. He cranked down his window and smelled the dampness in the air. Birds were chattering somewhere in the distance. Stan had the pass he'd gotten from Dave Harris. He showed it to the guard and the guard gave him directions to the Jungle Lot.

A Port-A-Sign on the edge of the road marked his turnoff. Stan parked behind the other cars and vans under the palm trees. A crew in matching blue T-shirts and caps was positioning the VTRs and laying down an Astro-turf carpet for the band.

He started setting up his drums. This was as far as his imagination had been able to take him. From here on he was winging it. His nerves had tunneled his vision down to the wood and plastic and chrome under his hands and he jumped when a voice behind him said, "They gonna fry your ass, boy."

Stan turned to face a six-foot-six apparition in a feathered hat, leopard scarf, chains, purple silk shirt, green leather pants, and lizard boots.

"Jackson?" Stan asked carefully.

"Something wrong?"

"Jesus Christ, man, where did you get those clothes?"

Jackson stared at him without expression. "I'm a star now. Not trash like you, boy, a *star*. Do you know who I was talking to yesterday? Bruce. That's Bruce *Springsteen*. He says Clarence may be splitting and he might need me for his next tour."

"That's great, Jackson. I hope it works out."

"You laugh, boy, but when Rosen see you, he gonna shit a picket fence."

Rosen, Keven, and some blond kid pulled up in a Jeep. Stan slipped deeper into the shade of a palm tree to watch. Keven and the blond kid were holding hands. The kid was dressed in a white bush jacket and Bermuda shorts. Keven was in a matching outfit that had been artfully torn and smudged by the costume crew. The blond kid said something to Keven and she laughed softly in his face. The director called places and the rest of the band settled in behind their instruments.

"Where the fuck is the drummer?" Rosen shouted.

Stan stepped out from behind the trees.

"Oh Christ," Rosen said. "Okay, take ten everybody. You, Stan. Off the set."

Stan was looking at Keven. Say the word, he thought. Tell him I can stay.

Keven glanced at him with mild irritation and walked away. She had hold of the blond kid's hand.

Stan looked back at Rosen. A couple of grips, ex-bikers by the size of them, were headed toward him. Stan held up his hands. "Okay," he said. He put his sticks in his back pocket and pointed at his drums. "Just let me—"

"No way," Rosen said. "Leave them here. We'll get them back to you. Right now you're trespassing and I want your ass *out* of here."

On the other side of the road was a tall, grassy hill. Stan could see Keven and the blond kid halfway up it. "Okay," he said. He walked past Rosen and got in his car, started it, and got back onto the road.

Past the first switchback he pulled over and started up the hill on foot. He was still a hundred yards away from Keven when she spotted him and sent the blond kid down to cut him off.

"Don't even think about it," Stan said. The blond kid looked at Stan's face and swerved downhill toward the jungle set at a run.

"Keven!" She stopped at the top of the hill and turned back to look at him. The blond kid would be back with the bikers any minute. Stan didn't know what to say. "You're killing me," he said. "Rosen won't let me work. Did you know that?"

"Go away, Stan," she said.

"Goddammit," he said. "How was I supposed to *not* to fall in love with you? What the hell did you expect? Do you ever listen to the words of all those songs you sing?"

A hand appeared on his shoulder, spinning him around. Stan tried to duck and ended up on his back as Rosen's fist cut the air above him. No bikers then, Stan thought giddily. Not yet. He rolled a few feet, off balance. One of his drumsticks fell out of his pocket and he grabbed for it.

Rosen looked more annoyed than anything else. "You stupid piece of shit," he said. Stan scuttled around the hillside on his palms and his ass and his feet, dodging two more wild punches. The slope made it tricky. Finally he was up again. He kept moving, letting Rosen come after him. He outweighed Rosen by at least forty pounds and had the reach on him besides. And if he actually hit Rosen he might as well throw his drums into the Pacific. On the other hand, if he waited around long enough, the bikers might just beat him to death.

It was what his grandfather would have called a classic no-win situation.

Kill me then, Stan thought, and to hell with you. He stepped inside Rosen's next swing and tapped him, very lightly, on the chest with his drumstick. Then he stepped back, smiling, into Rosen's roundhouse left.

"Hey, Sitting Bull," a voice said. It was Keven, kneeling next to him. "I think Custer just kicked your ass."

Stan propped himself up on his elbows. He could see Rosen walking down the hill, rubbing his knuckles. "Who'd have thought the little bastard could hit so hard? Did you call him off?"

"I wasn't going to let him kill you. Even if you did deserve it." She took his face in both her hands. "Stan. What am I going to do with you?"

Stan didn't have an answer for that one.

"This doesn't change anything," she said. "It's over. It's going to stay over."

"You never called me."

She sat back, arms wrapped around herself. "Okay. I should have called. But you're a scary guy, Stan. You're just so... intense, you know? You've got so much hunger in you that it's... it's hard to be around."

Stan looked at his hands.

"I wasn't like, just playing with you, okay? What there was, what happened, it was real. I just, I changed my mind. That's all. I'm just a person, you know. Just like anybody else."

She believed that, Stan thought, but it wasn't true. She wasn't like other people. She didn't have that fist in her stomach, pushing her, tearing up her insides. Not any more. That was what made her different, but there wasn't any point trying to tell her that.

She stood up and walked away from him, breaking into a run as she moved downhill. Rosen was there at the bottom. She took him by the arm and talked to him but Stan couldn't hear any of it. He watched the clouds for a while then headed down.

Rosen walked over, holding out his hand. "Sorry I lost my temper." Keven was back at the jungle set.

Stan took his hand. "No hard feelings."

"Keven says she wants you to do the video." Rosen clearly didn't like the idea. "She says nobody else can really do that drum part. She says there won't be any more trouble."

"No," Stan said. "No more trouble."

The worst part was hearing her voice on the radio, but in time Stan even got used to that.

Her album was out just before Thanksgiving and that week they premiered the video on MTV. It opened with Keven and her boyfriend in their jungle suits, then cut back and forth between a sort of stylized Tarzan plot and the synched-up footage of the band playing under the palm trees.

The phone rang. "Dude, you watching?"

"Yeah, Darryl. I'm watching."

"Totally crucial video, bud. I'm serious."

"Good drummer," Stan said.

"The best. This is going to make your career. You are on the map."

"I could live with that. Listen, Darryl, I'll see you tomorrow, okay? I want to catch the rest of this."

Stan squatted in front of the TV. Keven sang hard into the camera. Stan could read the words of the song on her face. She turned and looked over her shoulder and the camera followed, panning past her to the drummer, a good-looking, muscular guy in his middle thirties, with black hair that hung straight to his collar. The drummer smiled at Keven and then bent back to his work.

The clear, insistent power of his drumming echoed through the jungle afternoon.

Over the Line

linda gray sexton

TIRED OF WAITING FOR HER MOTHER at the hospital clinic, Reenie looked at her watch again and slid the smiling-face medallion she wore around her neck up and down its leather thong. Her mother was always late, always had one more patient to see. She scratched at the pale skin of her wrist. The molded plastic chair hurt her butt and she slumped, then crossed her arms over her chest, blowing her long straight bangs out of her eyes with a disgruntled puff of air. She was fourteen years old, already tall and full-breasted, but long sessions with the full-length mirror in her bedroom had shown her that there was still something unfinished about her body, and that she could look either graceful or awkward, depending on how she handled herself. She spent a lot of time in front of the mirror, alternating between pleasure and dissatisfaction as she tried to figure out which poses favored grace.

An incredibly tall black boy came into the waiting room and slouched down in the chair opposite her, stretching his long legs out so that his basketball sneakers were nearly touching her feet in the cramped waiting room.

Reenie peeked at him from the corner of her eye as he turned toward the window; he looked powerful in some way she couldn't describe, nothing like any of the boys she knew at school. Of course, she didn't hang around with many black kids—even if you were friends in class or in club activities, there were still invisible, un-

154

breakable barriers. In the cafeteria, for instance, separate tables according to color. Reenie had been on exactly three group dates, to the movies, white kids only.

This guy was the first boy she'd seen with a mustache, and because it was thin, as if it were drawn on with a pencil, it outlined the narrow shape of his upper lip. She wondered how it would feel to touch it. Two small braided pigtails hung down over his collar. None of the guys at school, not one of them, wore his hair tightly cropped plus the braids in back—it was awesome, she decided.

He looked at his watch and swore under his breath.

"You waiting, too?" she asked, taking a chance at conversation.

"No, I'm just sittin' here for my health."

Reenie's eyes grew wide. "Sor-ry."

He looked up at her then, seeing her for the first time. "Hey, no— I'm just kinda pissed, is all." She looked right back at him and for a second they didn't look away from each other. Reenie felt her face get warm. It was something she'd only recently discovered: you could tell how old a guy was by whether he looked straight at you, or chickened out and stared at the floor instead. When she locked eyes with someone a hollow feeling opened in the bottom of her stomach, and then she felt a strange charge, a strong beat that pumped up her body.

"My name's Reenie Walker," she said boldly.

"You here visiting?"

She shook her head, a frown crossing her face. "My mother's a doctor. We were supposed to leave for Macy's forty-five minutes ago, but she's still seeing patients."

"Your mom—she's Dr. Walker?"

Reenie nodded. "Why?"

He smiled, an odd smile that carried secrets in it. "My nephew, Miles, he a patient here. Dr. Walker *his* doctor."

Reenie shook her long hair back over her shoulder. "My mother's *always* late. She always promises she'll never do it again and I hate it."

"Sounds like you and her don't get along."

"She's on another planet most of the time," Reenie answered disdainfully. Only a year ago she and her mother had been close, like best friends. She could tell—or ask—her mother anything. This year, though, as Reenie had wanted to go out and do more things with kids her own age, her mother seemed to take it personally. A lot of the time she said no. They argued now about everything.

In the silence Reenie picked at her cuticles self-consciously, wishing she knew the right conversation, the kind of remarks a cool, experienced girl would have in her back pocket. She'd watched that kind of girl, a senior usually, talking with the boys in the cafeteria, reeling them in and out with her detached, teasing responses as if they were fish on a line.

But after a minute, he laughed. "Another planet. That's real good."

Encouraged, Reenie went on. "I don't like shopping with her, you know, but—" she shrugged, "—it keeps things cool."

"Mmm hmm."

"How come you're still here?"

He shrugged. "I'm waiting on my mother, she's visiting with my nephew, but I gotta get to work."

"Where do you work?" Reenie asked, not wanting him to leave, realizing suddenly that he might actually be so much older than she that he had already graduated.

"My real work, that's two nights a week, I play at the Valdez. In Palo Alto?"

Reenie nodded. "Sure, I've been there," she lied.

"Yeah, well, weekends I got a gig. Lead guitar."

Reenie tried not to look too impressed. "And tonight?"

"Night shift at McD's, on Willow. The manager there, he's one real bitch. And already I'm late." He looked at his watch. "It pay the bills, if he don't fire me first. Man," he tapped his foot, "I *told* her I got to go!"

Reenie smiled, absorbing each little fact gleaned as if it were the shards of a secret. She couldn't wait to get home and call her best friend Marlene, to tell her she'd actually met and talked with a guy who played at the Valdez! She wished she had on one of her short skirts instead of the baggy jeans she wore to school because everyone did.

He stood. "I'm outta here," he said. "You want I give you a ride?"

"A ride?" A million ideas crowded her mind: what would she say to him, how would she get home, had her deodorant worn off, what would it be like to be so close to him in the dark secret space of a car? "Oh, I couldn't. I mean, I have to wait…"

He looked at her slowly, a small grin playing at the edges of his lips. "How old you say you were?" He stood up and suddenly Reenie felt how tall he was, how lean, his broad shoulders straining at the seams of his shirt.

"Sixteen," she said quickly, nearly without thinking. "A junior."

"That right?" He looked her up and down, his eyes kindling, lighting her up, settling for an instant on her breasts, then moving back to linger on her mouth.

She couldn't possibly go with him, she thought, imagining her mother's horrified reaction. Her resolve melted a little at the edges. "That's right," Reenie said, sticking her hands in her back pockets.

"Sixteen a little young." He shook his head.

"Depends on who the sixteen is."

He grinned at her. "Didn't your mama teach you not to take rides from strangers?"

"We won't be strangers," she answered, flipping her hair back from her face. "Once you tell me your name."

Jesse's car was an old maroon Pontiac with a bench seat in front and a string of guitar picks swinging from the rearview mirror. As Reenie climbed in an unreal sense swamped her: she buckled her seatbelt at the same time she was thinking that maybe she should just get out of the car. Even though she had left a note for her mother with the nurse at the main desk, there would be questions and anger to face later; still, her mother already knew this boy's family, plus Reenie didn't plan to be gone very long. She would page her mother in a half hour and tell her to meet her at Macy's.

"Pick us some driving music," Jesse said, jerking his head toward the rear seat as he started the car. "It's all done up real alphabetical."

Reenie turned, and her eyes widened when she saw the shoeboxes full of CD's. She undid her seatbelt and leaned over the top of the seat to run her index finger up and down the rows, as if she were shopping with someone else's credit card in Tower Records. Allman Brothers. Bad Religion. Beastie Boys. Beatles. Dr. Dre. Hendrix. Ice Cube. Ice T. Metallica. Motley Crue. Nirvana. 2PAC. Pearl Jam. Pink Floyd. Prince. Rancid. REM. Rolling Stones. Skid Row. Snoop Doggy Dog. Sound Garden. Stone Temple Pilots. Too many choices, too much that made her mouth water. What if he didn't like what she chose?

"Think you've got enough?" she asked as he pulled out of the parking lot with a squeal of his tires.

"No such thing as enough." He grinned. "Go ahead."

Reenie chose *Miscellaneous Debris* by Primus, her current favorite. She opened it, pinched up the cool silver disc with her middle finger and thumb spread wide, and then slid it into the machine.

"You like *Tales from the Punch Bowl?*" he asked.

"Okay," she said, "but not as much as this." She took a deep breath, scared to say too much, scared to say not enough. "Even *Frizzle Fry*'s better, I think."

He nodded; she thought he seemed pleased that she had an opinion.

"Intruder" started up: on this track the drums were the first thing that hit you, like congas almost, maybe they were congas for all she knew, but in any case they whapped down into your bloodstream the way she imagined a drug would—suddenly, like a grab from behind.

The car had big speakers and the enclosed space boomed with the sound, the windows vibrated, the metal trim buzzed. Jesse started following the inexorable river of rhythm with his hands against the steering wheel. There was an edgy space-age sound to the song, with a lot of distortion; Reenie really liked that, the way it matched the current inside of her, the feeling that she was on the edge and about to fall off.

"I like to feel the suspense," she sang.

"I like the smell of the pretty dresses you wear," he sang back, his voice a low growl.

Their eyes met and Reenie looked away, trying for breath. She'd never been near a boy who looked at her so long and hard. She liked it, but at the same time it made her nervous.

By the time Primus had gotten to "Sinister Exaggerator," Jesse was swinging through the parking lot at the shopping center.

"My mother says this one sounds like a bunch of nuts howling in a loony bin," Reenie said, stalling.

Jesse laughed.

"You're so lucky to have a CD player in your car," she said wistfully, as he pulled up at the curb in front of Macy's and put the car into park, but left the engine running.

"You don't?"

She shook her head. "Only a radio—my Mom and I argue about which station all the time."

"Don't have your own car yet?"

Reenie thought fast: no way out except to go around the truth. "My mother's pretty strict. Hey, listen thanks for the ride." She lingered, her hand on the cool metal door handle. "Really, thanks for the ride."

Jesse ran his hand over the steering wheel and grinned. "Maybe

I come with you and call work, tell 'em how late I gonna be. Like, *too late*."

A small pulse of joy beat at the side of Reenie's neck. "There's a pay phone, right outside Macy's."

As they walked past the shops, excitement kept her smiling, tossing her hair; maybe they would run into someone she knew. She looked at him out the corner of her eye: he was humming "Intruder" as if he couldn't leave it behind. Maybe when he heard it again it would have transformed itself into memory; maybe he'd remember the bleached blue cotton of the late afternoon sky, the way her hair hung straight down her back, how she knew the words to all the songs.

She saw a denim vest in the window of the Limited and stopped to look at it.

Jesse stood beside her, hands stuck in his pockets. "That would be powerful on you," he said, staring at her breasts again. *I like the smell of the pretty dresses you wear,* he hummed.

"Think so?" she said, her heart racing, the tune gone straight out of her mind now. "Maybe I'll go in."

"I make my call and then I be back."

Reenie stood in front of the mirror, examining herself from every angle, *I like to feel the suspense,* she sang softly to herself. It was very snug, with a shiny brass zipper up the front that stopped just on her cleavage, a zipper that made you think about one thing: unzipping it. In warm weather she would wear it without anything underneath. She could hear Jesse ask a salesgirl about a leather jacket in the window, and she came out of the changing room to see what he thought. He lounged back against the counter with his elbows and laughed. "Girl, watch yourself!"

Looking in the big mirror at the center of the store, watching Jesse watch her—he was humming the song again—Reenie could hear her mother disapprove of the way the vest fit, so nice and tight, "revealing" she'd say, in that bossy tone of hers. She took it off, slung her purse over her shoulder and went to the cash register to pay.

As they walked through the mall, Reenie kept thinking she'd never met anyone who knew so much about music as he did. He talked about groups he liked that Reenie hadn't heard of yet and she just nodded, pretending, agreeing, hoping he wouldn't ask a question that would betray her ignorance. She planned to spend all of next week's allowance on Bad Religion, which had, he said, the greatest lyrics going about alienation. Even the word felt grown up in her mouth.

Surreptitiously she checked her watch. It might be better to see if she could get Jesse to take her home, rather than to page her mother. That way, if she beat her mother it would be easy to fudge how long she'd been out. And if not, she could just explain that Jesse had had a quick errand to do on his way home and seeing as he was being nice enough to give her a ride she could hardly say no. They got into the car and she fished for her seatbelt.

He watched her with amusement. "Think that'll keep you safe?"

"The way you drive? Wouldn't be caught without it."

He grinned. "Here." He slid *Stranger than Fiction* into the CD player. "This one's my favorite." The guitar hit like a fist, bruising the nerves of her ears, the lyric filled with desperation. *"Tonight the windows are watching, the streets all conspire, and the lamppost can't stop crying."* When the song finished, Jesse hit the stop button. "Doesn't sound too different from some of the hard rock they played back in the sixties, seventies. Stones, Allman Brothers maybe. Guitar just hammering that tune. You can *sing* this one and that ain't true of a lot of the shit out there today."

"Totally cool," Reenie said, shivering with nerves and wondering if she dared slide a little closer to him, maybe make it look accidental. He put his arm out along the back of the seat and she could feel his hand, resting just behind her head. She wanted him to touch her.

Those times at the movies with the boys from school, she'd fooled around a little, kissing, letting them touch her breasts through her shirt. It hadn't felt that great, but Marlene always said the best sex was with older guys. Marlene wasn't a virgin anymore. Marlene carried condoms in her purse.

"This your favorite song on the whole CD?" she asked

"Yeah," he looked over at her. "That one verse where Greg Graffin goes, *'The world is scratching at my door.'*" He grinned. "Reminds me of places I been."

"But not where you are now?"

"Where I could be again—just one thing goes bad on me," he answered, moving his arm off the seat. Reenie felt a wash of disappointment. He held a pack of Marlboros to his lips, and pulled one out, punched the car lighter and lit it. He held the pack out to her. Reenie knew she'd give herself away if she tried to smoke, probably choke or throw up or something, so she shook her head and looked out the window. He shrugged. "Feel like a burger? Oasis is close."

Reenie opened her mouth to explain she had to get home, but the pressure of not seeming young suddenly seemed greater than the pressure of facing her mother's anger when she didn't turn up for supper. She gulped, swallowing a sudden nauseating rush of saliva in her mouth. "Sure."

"You don't gotta get home?" He looked at her curiously.

She looked away. "My mother's hardly ever home for dinner anyway."

"Your father, he don't cook?"

"They're divorced." She looked away, out the window; thinking about her father, living separately in a small apartment, still made her sad. She saw him, of course, but nothing was the same.

They drove up El Camino. Jesse broke the speed limit, ran red lights, cursed at slower drivers, made Reenie giggle with nerves. She liked the adroit way he muscled his car lane to lane, but at the same

time it scared her. There were those accidents you passed on the highway: glass across all three lanes, bumpers and metal trim strewn over
concrete, people strapped down on stretchers and hauled off by
ambulance—or worse, in bags that zipped head to toe. Reenie
gripped her door handle tightly.

They swerved into the lot behind the O and walked in. The chain
of his wallet jangled as he held the door open for her and she barely
had to duck to pass under his arm. The smoke and noise hit her as
they ordered burgers at the counter, and took their food to a booth in
the back. The television at the bar and the pinball machines made a
racket.

He swigged his beer straight from the bottle, tipping his head
back, and Reenie watched his Adam's apple move in his throat under
the dark blue-black of his skin. She loved his color: it was beautiful
to her—though she would never have admitted that to anyone,
because she felt ashamed of even noticing it. She had been brought
up to ignore color, to be blind to it like a dog at a stoplight—no red,
yellow or green—only gray, everything and everyone the same. But
Reenie saw the richness and sheen of Jesse's ebony, she noticed the
way the creases on the inside of his elbows ripened into a purple the
color of summer plums, the way his eyes glinted pure black like no
white person's ever could. And all of it made her want to reach out
across the table that separated them and touch the pinkness of his
palms, discover the texture of his hair, trace his thin mustache with
her fingertips. She was more aware of his body that she ever had been
with any other boy.

He wiped the top of his beer bottle with his hand and offered it
to her.

She hesitated. Her mother would say one thing and her father
another but it would all add up to no.

A challenge played in his eyes, and that same little smile she'd
seen back in the waiting room curved up around the edges of his lips.

Reenie took a deep breath and grasped the cold bottle in her hand, quickly gulping three big mouthfuls. She smiled at him non-chalantly. "Thanks."

"Wasn't sure you drank."

"Doesn't everyone?"

He smiled, got up and went to the bar for another beer, which he slid into the middle of the table in her direction. "Want to go to the Edge after we finish—or do you have to be getting home?"

"The Edge?" Reenie drank some more beer, focusing on making it look natural.

"California Street, down near the train station—been there?"

The Edge was a nightclub frequented mostly by kids much older, college kids, though Marlene had been there on nights they had Under Eighteen, but Reenie's mother had refused to let her go. Reenie had called her father on the phone hoping he would contra-dict her mother and say yes, but when her parents caught on, she'd gotten in trouble. She'd been stuck at home that night in her bed-room with some dumb book while all the rest of her friends were off moshing.

"Could I get in?" she asked skeptically.

Jesse smiled. "Manager's a friend of mine."

"Have you ever played the Edge?"

"Not yet." He took the last bite of his burger and crumpled his napkin. "Edge is next step up." He finished his beer. "Still pretty early over there, but we could go see what's happening—if you want."

Reenie looked at her watch: it might be early for the Edge but it was late for her. She bit her lip, thinking ahead. If her mother ever found out—but how would she, unless Reenie told her?

Jesse waited, humming softly again. *I like to feel the suspense.*

She could tell her mother that he had had to stop by work and then she'd had to wait and then they'd had a burger. She could even tell her mother his car broke down. She would make something up, she decided suddenly, whatever. The beer had kicked in, and she felt strong and willing to take the risk of explanations that would come later.

The Edge was quiet, as Jesse had predicted. The group was yawning, plugging in their amps, tuning guitars, drinking coffee and beer, smoking. Real musicians. Reenie stood in the corner, leaning against the bar, electrified.

They started warming up, trying out a few songs, and the lights went down then, the black-painted walls got blacker and the band started up a set with "Alive," an old song by Pearl Jam. Reenie let the sound lap at her, then enter; the bass line lifted her up, the drums made her blood jump again. There was a place in the second verse where the guitar riffs were a duet, like voices singing back and forth across the space of the room to each other, with the drums lacing them up tight. The ache of it was a wail that shivered down the length of her veins. *"I'm still alive,"* she sang, closing her eyes because the music moved in her better that way. *"Is there anything wrong she said. Do I deserve to be?"*

"Like it?" Jesse's voice broke in on her, and she came back down, feeling silly. He handed her a beer and casually put his arm around her.

"'Like' doesn't exactly describe it." Leaning into him, she drank, awkwardness gone, feeling relaxed and a little hazy around the edges. Up close like this she could smell him—a dusky fresh sweat smell; she inhaled it deep to remember it better.

"You like to sing," he observed.

"Kinda," she said, unwilling to admit that the best she could do at school was sing in a stupid madrigal group. Or that she'd taught herself acoustic guitar so she'd have some accompaniment, so that when she sang her voice could rise up out of her as if she had vanished and there would be only her sound soaring out like a bird riding the currents over the ocean.

"You got a real nice sound," he observed, grinning at her again. "Hey, Saturday night I'm at the Valdez. It's nowhere like this—but if you want to come?"

"Really? Really!" Somehow she'd get there, even if she had to lie to do it.

After a while, they walked back to the car and Jesse unlocked the doors. "I like to warm it up if it's been sitting," he said, starting the engine but not putting the car into drive. He twisted to reach into the back seat and clicked on the overhead light to rummage for something. Then he turned back around, slid in a new CD and fiddled with the remote. Once again it was something that Reenie had never heard before.

"What's this?" she asked, taking a chance at ignorance this time.

"Dylan."

Don't let her see where you're going, don't put yourself over the line.

Reenie wrinkled her nose. "My Mom's got that one."

"Sometimes you got to listen to something different," Jesse observed, tilting his head back and sliding down in the seat. "Slow, sweet, easy." He looked at her as music filled the car once again—but this was a sound completely different from everything they'd been listening to before. "You love music?"

She nodded.

"Then you got to listen to everything and everyone. Old or new—don't make no difference."

"But it's so simple," she objected. "A tambourine? And it's *slow*, too."

"Hey, this wasn't ever released, Dylan didn't like it good enough. Recorded it live in New Orleans in '81, though—how it got onto this set, *Biograph*. Probably a shitload of stuff in my back seat you never heard before."

She listened for a minute and then snorted. "'If you can't do the time, don't do the crime'—isn't that some line from a TV ad?"

He laughed. "Yeah, well, they ripped Dylan off."

"No shit?"

"No shit."

Reenie shook her head, impressed. Jesse knew a lot about a lot. The song ended and another began.

"You really listen, you be surprised at what you hear. Sounds change—some. But what they say—" he laughed and shook his head, turned the volume down just a little. "Hardly at all."

She put her head back on the seat and listened to the plaintive notes, the rough voice that seemed to struggle. *I want you, I want you.*

Jesse softly struck the steering wheel with the infectious rhythm on the steering wheel with his fist. "Great guitar figure here—it's famous now. And it wasn't recorded in no studio, got no studio sound, just the man and his instrument. Watch you don't get used to listening to so much shit that's manufactured that you can't hear pure playing no more."

Rebuked, Reenie didn't answer. How was she supposed to know what to say to Jesse—he had obviously been listening to all kinds of music for a long time, not just the stuff everyone listened to, not just the stuff they played at the dances. Suddenly he seemed so far beyond her that she wondered what she was doing here in the front seat of his car, as gravity-free as an astronaut suspended weightless in space. Her heart beat faster and she turned her face to the window in disappointment. "Jesse, it's kind of late. I better get back before my Mom kills me."

He turned to her, his dark eyes amused, and said, "Hey, sweet girl, didn't mean to make you mad." He sighed. "I get talking about tunes—hell, you know."

She turned back to him, just a fraction, just so she could see him.

"Just listen to this last one," he said, playing with the hair at the back of her neck, teasing it real lightly with his fingers, "and then I take you home. Written a long time ago, it's steel guitar, but you know you feel it here—" he spread his fingers and rubbed his palms back and forth across his thighs. "It eats on me, like from the inside."

Lay, lady, lay. A dark voice, a promise, magic. Reenie sat very still as the song spun out dark and slow, sweet as caramel, and Jesse began to touch her, a little stroke, just a feather, ears and neck, lips. *Lay across my big brass bed.*

She thought about pushing him away because she'd only known him a few hours, but she didn't. She closed her eyes and thoughts of being late and her mother receded as he touched her body and the warmth started up in her like a tide slowly coming in. His breath whispered in her ear and goosebumps rose up and down her arms. The pulse of the bass pulled at her.

She ached for his lips against her neck, and she moved a little closer, wanting to be touched like that again, and he took gentle bites of her skin with his teeth, then made a long wet path up into her ear. She turned her face to him and he kissed her, his tongue sucking hers out into a dance, and she stopped thinking at all except for wishing she could just let him kiss her everywhere because his lips seemed to know what she wanted.

The music kept wrapping around them, melting her down. *Why wait any longer for the world to begin?* She reached out and put her hand on his cheek, running her finger over his mouth against the prickle of his mustache, so different from anything she'd ever felt before. Her hand was a thrill of white, paper white, against the dark color of his skin; under her fingers his hair was wiry and oiled, and he smelled like beer and cigarettes and something else she didn't know.

Jesse caught her hand and started sucking on her wrist, licking over her palm and then down each finger, sucking on the very tip. It was so different than being with the boys from school, at the dances, where they ground their hips into you and you wanted to shove them away, nothing like enduring their sloppy kisses, or their uncertain hands that poked and prodded at her body the way the doctor did when he gave her her annual exam.

She put both arms around him, hands wandering to feel his shoulders and arms and chest, the roundness of his muscles as they flexed when his hands moved over her shirt, brushing her breasts. He went back to her neck, just below her ear, and started licking and kissing and sucking, something no one had ever done before and a groan rolled out of her mouth. She rocked back into the deep cushion of the seat, and his hand went smooth and swift up under her T-shirt and she leaned into him as he squeezed her breast through the thin fabric of her bra, her nipple hardening against the calluses of his palm and then he pushed the bra down and started to roll her nipple between his fingers harder and harder and the music kept playing and he kept sucking and after a while there was nothing in her mind but the music of the wet ache between her legs.

He reached down and unzipped his pants with one hand, then took her hand and guided it over to his crotch. Reenie stiffened—it was the first time she had ever touched a boy's penis. It throbbed in her hand, humid and hard as a spike of iron, bigger and thicker than she could have ever imagined. She wanted to pull away from the shock of its size, but she forced herself to sit still and just grip it the way he seemed to want. She didn't know what she was meant to do. He took her hand and moved it up and down on him, showing her the rhythm, the stroke, as if this were a dance and he was teaching her the steps. Her hand pumped, sheet-white against the purple dark of him, and her arm no longer seemed attached to her body: it ached, deadweight. The spell of her own sensations was broken now, and her mind was suddenly clear, clicking along like a train on a track as she wondered what she was doing. She kept waiting for it to be over, a sudden gush into her hand the way Marlene had said always happened, but it wasn't like that, he was still hard and turned toward her now, starting to unzip her jeans. The warm sweet rock of the alcohol had evaporated, her body was cold, the car was full of ugly colors, the music leered in her face. She pushed his hand away from her pants.

"What're you doing?" she cried, struggling to pull her shirt back down over her breasts.

"C'mon, baby." He began kissing her ear again, put her hand back down on his penis. "Jus' give me some relief here."

"I want to go home," she said. "Please take me home."

He kissed her again, trying to draw her back to him but she pulled back, stiff.

He sighed, leaned back in his seat.

She averted her face, pressed her nose to the window, feeling supremely confused and somehow humiliated. She stifled an urge to cry.

After a minute, she heard him grunt, then the rasp of the zipper as he struggled with his fly.

"I'm sorry," she managed to choke out.

"Hey, I don't take nothing not freely given."

"I'm sorry," she repeated dully. "I guess I'm not good at this yet."

He put his hand on her shoulder. "It's okay," he said, patting her back. "I move too fast for you, I get carried away by your pretty face."

She looked up at him. "You're not mad at me?"

He laughed and held her chin in his hand. "How many guys you been with?"

She looked away, ashamed.

"Right," he said. "I think it time to get you home. But you got to show me how to get there."

And then, as if nothing at all had happened between them, he switched the CD back to Primus and drove her back to the house, talking about music all the way.

By the time Reenie got out of Jesse's car and walked down her own driveway, she had an excuse ready for her mother but she knew it would probably not help her escape some sort of punishment. She went up the back steps with a lingering feeling of humiliation. And maybe even regret. She'd had an opportunity and she'd blown it. Somehow touching his penis had panicked her. How could something so big actually be expected to fit inside her someday?

She took a deep breath and reached out for the door handle. Through the window, she could see her mother waiting for her at the kitchen table. The hardest thing right now was that she didn't really understand what had happened to her—not the way she had wanted the sex or the way she had not—and, for the first time in her life, she wasn't going to be able to ask her mother to explain it.

A Hunk of Burning Love

françois camoin

GENE IS ALREADY THERE when I come through the door of the New Deal Cafe and Bar. There's a sausage speared on the end of his fork and he's waving it in Rita's face. Gene's a fat man but a long way from jolly; he can in fact be mean as a snake if you give him half a chance. His hat is on the stool beside him, upside down with his work gloves folded in it. This morning we'll he digging post-holes for a new fence in old man Hazzard's pasture.

"This sausage looks more like a dog turd," he says. I like Rita. We have been to bed together now and then, after a hard Saturday night, in her little trailer out back of the cafe.

"Ease up, Gene," I tell him.

He turns around on the stool and gives me his Monday-morning stare, cold and nasty, as if I was some Dallas-Fort Worth traveling salesman cutting in on his time, instead of the man he has been working along side of, off and on, for the past three years since I came down from Chicago.

"Can I have the number three?" I ask Rita. "And lots of coffee?"

Gene is still giving me the stare. "I know what you've been doing," he says.

"What's that?"

"Never mind," he says. "I know, that's all."

"Eat your breakfast," I tell him. "It's going to he a hard day. Mellow out, buddy."

He looks after Rita, who is jiggling her way into the kitchen with my order.

"Yeah?" he says.

His eyes show white all around like a spooky horse. I'm watching him carefully, ready to slide off my stool and give him room but he blinks and heaves a big sigh. "One of these times they are by pure accident going to get somebody back there that knows how to cook and then I am going to have to start eating my breakfast in some other cafe because my stomach couldn't stand the surprise. Dog turds," he says, shoving the sausage in his mouth and chewing loud enough to make the salesmen at the table behind us turn around and look.

Gene looks back at them and smiles his best affable smile; they have the good sense to smile back.

Rita puts my breakfast down in front of me and swipes at the counter with a wet cloth. "Don't mind him," she says.

As soon as we get settled in the truck Gene slips the same old eight-track in the stereo; we ride the fifteen miles out to Hazzard's property listening to "Hound Dog" and "Blue Suede Shoes" and the rest of this tormented music that Gene likes so well.

He lights up a joint big as a dollar cigar and passes it across to me. In no time we are driving along in a cloud so thick it's a wonder he can find the road through the windshield.

"It was all them drugs give him by Jewish doctors," Gene says. "That killed him I mean."

"How do you know they were Jewish?"

"I read about it," he says. "You telling me they weren't?"

"I don't know."

"You don't know much," he says. His truck is an old four-wheel-drive Ford with balloon tires and a worn-out suspension; every little bump sends us swooping across the highway almost into the ditch on the far side.

"You think I'm some kind of bigot, don't you?" he says.

"No."

"Yeah you do."

"Watch the road," I tell him. "It's all right."

"No it ain't all right." He takes a deep drag, adds to the cloud. The truck bounces; Elvis sings. The heater is on and I feel dopey and too warm.

"The King," Gene says finally. "Being from Chicago you wouldn't know what that means."

"Why not? I watched Elvis the first time he was ever on TV, on *The Ed Sullivan Show*. I know the songs."

"Nope," Gene says. His voice is final. It reminds me of the bumper sticker on his tailgate. GOD SAID IT. I BELIEVE IT. THAT SETTLES IT. In blue and yellow. Not that I've ever heard of him going to church; he's religious in a patriotic, formal kind of way. It goes with the Confederate flag on the other side of the tailgate. I kidded him about fighting losing battles once, until he got mad, but it seems to me that's what the South is all about—how to get beaten and somehow come out on top morally.

"You been living down here with real folks three years now," Gene says. "You wear Dingo boots and a big buckle on your belt, and I taught you to drink Lone Star, but that don't mean you know." Somebody coming the other way in a station wagon honks his horn and flashes the lights to tell us to get back on our own side of the road. Gene gives them the finger without letting himself get worked up about it.

The King sings about the child born in the ghetto. Gene turns him down.

"Hey, Lawrence," he says.

"Larry," I tell him for the hundredth time.

"Law-rence," he says. "You ever think what it's all about? Life, I mean. You ever stop to think how we're all going to die?"

"Monday's always bad," I tell him. "We'll be there in a minute and we'll work up a good sweat. You'll feel better."

"No," he says. "I don't think I will."

The tape is hung up between tracks and I give it a kick to get it started again, and turn up the volume; I'd rather listen to Elvis than to Gene getting himself spooked by life.

"I ought to be running fence around my own place instead of old man Hazzard's," he says. "Have some kids. You ever have kids, Lawrence?"

"Two."

"Where they at?"

"Chicago."

"You just left them there?" He shakes his head as if he can't believe a man could do such a thing.

By lunchtime we are down to just pants and boots. It's January and not much above freezing but we have worked up a fine sweat putting up half a dozen lengths of new split-rail. Hazzard's pasture is mostly what they call *caliche,* hard as good Chicago cement. Here and there a little bit of bunch-grass rises out of it, barely alive. It's a pasture the same way the New Deal Cafe is a restaurant.

Gene stretches out on the ground and uncaps a Lone Star. He hasn't said anything for the past couple of hours, but I can tell it's still Blue Monday.

"You and Rita," he says.

"What about me and Rita?"

He rubs his thumb and forefinger together and grins. "I know what you've been doing."

"It's no secret."

"I guess not," he says. We both stare at the sky, which is, like most always, enormous and blue, Now and then down here there is some sort of weather, usually violent. The rest of the time the sky is like a TV screen when the station is off the air, a blank waiting to be filled in.

"Not that I give a damn," Gene says.

"About Rita and me?"

"That's right," he says. He sits up and drinks the rest of the bottle in one gulp and throws the empty carefully into the back of the pickup with the fenceposts, the tools, the other empties.

With his shirt off Gene looks pretty bad, though I can see how strong he still is. But everything is beginning to slump and settle and dry out and crack. His chest looks like the fields out there after a hard rain and a couple of days of sun.

"Gene?"

"You son of a bitch," he says.

About four o'clock I am taking a turn with the digging bar, a piece of wrought iron six feet long and as big around as an ax handle, which we use to break up the caliche before we can dig it out. Gene is leaning on the two-handled scoop waiting for me to get done.

"Indians," he says.

"What about Indians?"

"There used to be Indians all around here," he says.

I take another shot at the caliche. The bar feels like it weighs a hundred pounds. "What happened to them?"

Gene looks at me like I've asked a dumb question.

"They died out," he says. "Or they went someplace else. See any Indians in Chicago?"

"I guess so."

"That's what I should do," he says. "Go someplace else."

"And do what?" I ask him. If I could only talk to Gene I think something important might happen. But it's a dream: I can't talk to him. We dig for a while. He takes a turn; I take a turn. Over our heads the sky is like a page from a book that hasn't been written.

"Sometimes you can find old bones out here. I found a tooth once," Gene says. He fumbles in his pocket and brings out a little piece of yellow ivory; it looks like a tooth from a six-year-old. "Indian," he says, holding it out to me cupped in his hand.

It feels so light it has no consequence at all. "Probably a thousand years old" he says. "I was going to have it made into a ring but I never did."

I hand it back to him, but he shakes his head. "Keep it," he says. "Give it to Rita, she likes stuff like that."

"You're sore about me and Rita, aren't you."

"No," he says. He's standing in front of me with the bar raised, ready to take another lick at the hole. With his arms up like this, his chest looks like a young man's: not so devastated. We're out here about fifteen miles from nowhere, just Gene and me alone. The muscles are like blow-up balloons. Put a pipe in his mouth and he'd look like Popeye. He could kill me without thinking about it, and your average Texas jury would let him off with a year or two.

"I lost her fair and square," he says. "Before you ever come down here from Chicago. She don't believe in love." His face is both sad and puzzled; the whites of his eyes are showing. There might be a tear in his eye, or it might be only the wind, which is blowing cold and mean, coming from that part of the world Gene doesn't believe in.

"Well, Law-rence," he says. "It's about time to quit for the day. Let's go home."

In the truck we listen to Elvis some more but Gene doesn't talk. He drives it slow and easy, listening to the King, nodding his head now and then as if he's just said something to himself that he agrees with. The stereo is going bad and sometimes Elvis comes out from the left speaker, or the right, or quits altogether until I kick the dashboard and get him singing again, I get my feet as close to the heater as I can; now that I'm just sitting I'm cold and a little puzzled and sad myself. I wish we had this day over again, so we could do it different.

*   *   *

"You're a dumb-ass, Law-rence," Gene says.

It's like a judgment; he might be right. I'm not feeling any better about the day. We're sitting in the New Deal Cafe and Bar; it's two in the morning and all but a couple of really serious drinkers have gone home for the night.

"A real dumb-ass," he says.

One of the drunks puts a half-dollar in the jukebox and picks out a tune.

"Seems like that's all anybody plays anymore since he died," Rita says.

Gene looks up at her. "We could still get ourselves married," he says.

"Time for you to go on home when you start talking like that." She puts a hand over his. "Go get yourself some sleep," she says. We have been taking turns explaining this day to her and it's clear she doesn't like the sound of it any more than we do.

"Love," Gene says. He waves his free hand at the jukebox; the drunk is leaning on it, staring at the record going round and round, caught up in some kind of personal tragedy.

"Don't you care about love?" Gene says.

"No," Rita says.

"I can't believe that," he says.

"Go home, Gene," she tells him.

The King is singing "Jailhouse Rock" and Gene does a clumsy little dance step on his way out of the New Deal; he stops at the door and waves good-bye to us, then he stops grinning and gives me a narrow look.

"Chicago," he says. He rubs his thumb and forefinger together and nods at Rita without taking his eyes off me. It's his Monday-morning stare.

Rita's trailer is about fifteen feet long, and set up like one room with a bed smack up against the back wall and a little kitchen up front. There's a tiny toilet, but if she wants to take a shower she has to go into the cafe, where there's a tin stall behind the kitchen that the help can use. It isn't much of a place to live, but I've been in there with her one or two times when it was pouring rain and lightning and thundering, and it's the coziest place you can imagine, lying in the bed listening to the water and the wind beating on the sheet-metal six inches away from your head while you're warm and safe under the covers.

"It was just a lousy day," I tell her.

"Let me see the tooth," she says. "Is it really a thousand years old?"

I have to reach out and fumble around on the floor until I find my Levis, and there it is in the back pocket. She holds it up to the light.

"That's so goddamned sad," she says.

I put my arm around her; there's plenty of flesh there, too much, some people might say, but tonight I wish there was more, so much I couldn't get my arms around it all. She's a giving woman, but tonight I maybe want more than she can give.

"I like it when you hold me like that," she says.

"Yeah?" My nose is buried in her hair, which smells like cigarette smoke.

"Don't you go thinking about love," she says.

"That's Gene," I tell her. "Not me."

"Let it sell the songs," she says. "I don't want any of it in my personal life."

"You don't have to worry about me."

"That's what I hope," she says.

After a while she gets up and turns off the overhead light, leaving the little lamp on over the kitchen sink, and we make love, very slow and sweet, driving it easy, and go to sleep tangled up with each other. One of her legs is over mine, my arm is under her head, and with my free hand I'm holding her breast, which is a comfort.

What wakes me up is at first not clear. The trailer is rocking a little but I figure it's in my head, a hangover from the dream I was having in which every one of old man's Hazzard's fenceposts was rising slowly out of the ground. In the dream I didn't want to know what was pushing them up. Rita is already sitting up, looking around wild-eyed, still more than half in a dream herself.

"It's Gene," she says.

"We were just dreaming," I tell her. "Come on down here and go back to sleep."

I hear footsteps outside and a fist begins to beat slowly on the trailer door; the glasses in the kitchen rattle like dry bones, and something in the sink falls over.

"Rita," Gene's voice says, very drunk and very loud. "Rita, honey, it's me." He begins to pound on the door again, pulls on the handle, rocks our little trailer. It's a big one-man storm going on out there. "I love you," he shouts. "I know that son of a bitch Lawrence is in there with you, but it don't matter. We'll have kids; I'll build you a regular house. I'll be tender with you. Love me, goddamn it."

He runs around to the other side of the trailer and bangs on the metal wall; it sounds like thunder. Rita puts her hands over her ears. "Oh God," she says. "I can't stand it."

There's a little window just over the bed. I pull the curtain back and look out, but it's too dark—the only thing I can make out is my own face staring back at me with a peculiar lost expression.

"He's going to keep it up, l just know it," Rita says.

The footsteps are coming back around; they stop just under the window. Gene knows where the bed is. He says something but his voice is funny and I can't understand the words.

"What's he doing?" Rita says. She takes her hand away from her ears so she can hear better.

"I think he's singing."

It gets louder and I can start to make it out. I can see him out there, standing on his toes to get his mouth up to the window, one hand pressed on each side of it to keep his balance, hugging our trailer.

"I'm just a hunk, a hunk-a burning love," he sings.

I pull Rita down in the bed beside me and lay the covers over our heads. I put my arms around her. It's the coziest thing you can imagine.

WELCOME TO THE JUNGLE

The Unfinished Business of Childhood

lee k. abbott

I.

BEFORE THEY BECAME OUR NATIONAL SENSATION, Bobby Stoops billed his rock and rollers as the Feet of Yemen, a contrary and twice-mad group that sang of the Condition: "It is hell," he told an audience one night, "I can't wait to get back." During this period, he was Dr. Filth, what the skinny writer from *The Musician* called a "juiced-up fag-out of mock murder, the wrecked specter fathers fear most." Later he became Dwana Lynne Cootey, country girl, and made his hair shoot up like a wheat field. Other times, he was a state of mind—disquiet, want, Lutheranism—a thought upright, with ankle and mouth; and his group became the Dogs of New Jersey, More Facts About Beavers, and Wet Places at Noon.

"I put it to you this way," his manager, Putt Fenno, said finally. "In Arkansas, you have no fans, only confusion. They have mistaken you for a conifer." Fenno himself looked like a two-hundred-pound tool box. "Stop breaking my neck. Give me something I can peddle to Finns."

So during those months when their records remained on *Billboard*'s Top 40, and until Bobby menaced that teenage woman in the Cleveland Agora, they were the Eldest of Things, he the frontmost of a fivesome that played "I Want It All" and "Kill the Rich/Eat the Poor." These were tunes, he told the *Times-Herald*, that seized belligerence to make it toil for the dispossessed.

Eventually, in a way he would one day understand as inevitable, Bobby developed contempt for the whole process. "I have a dark place in me," he told Putt Fenno. "The light of love does not reach." At the Palamino in North Hollywood, he called the crowd cowards, simpletons. "The principal enemy of art is fame," he said. He could hear a woman in the back screeching, "Shove it in here, Dimitri! I want to swell up like a Turk." Once, hours late for a session at the Record Plant, he ate a thousand-dollar bill. "I would only spend it on myself," he told his bass player, Nate Creer. "I would still be sad." On Quaaludes, he carried a Vestin-M .38, a nastiness which he pointed at everybody; on speed, he taped a filet knife to his leg and made Putt Fenno weep.

"It is an odd life," he confessed to a reporter, "a march from one desire to the next."

In the end, the months ran together until, while performing miraculous figures on his Fender that night in Cleveland, he saw nothing left for himself but reckless despair. During "Lesser Stars We Shine Among," he spotted her at the edge of the stage, her face bright with rapture. "Come to me," he said, "I am empty inside." In the wings, Putt Fenno had the look of a man with many debts. "I am to make a statement," Bobby shouted over the PA. The girl stood beside him, thirsty as an adder. She represented them all, he told the crowd that night—the drossy, the fevered, the displaced, all of us who'd lost our way in the brillig, tulgey wood. "I am here to make a statement," he hollered. There was a howl of feedback. Eyes ablaze, he informed them that his was an immodest rearguard action in the service of, well, in the service of goodness—said action to be dispensed by this thing here, which was an ugly bone-handled skinning blade, said service to be performed by driving his point right smack into the thumping, sticky center of her, and our, plight.

"Forgive me," he said, "large times demand large gestures."

*　　*　　*

He hadn't cut her, it developed, but there was undesired publicity, expensive attorneys and a weekend in the Justice Center holding tank.

"Let us welcome you," one prisoner said, and four others, all heavily scarred black men in shower caps and Aunt Pecos hair curlers, bounded to their feet. They could have been a group themselves, one whose themes were morphinism and pox.

Said one: "I have sampled the treasures of Safeway and J. C. Penney, ain't nothing compares to the sweets of Miss Laticia."

Said a second: "Pray with us, white boy, that we might go forth and burgle."

That Monday, the judge lectured Bobby for half an hour. "Perhaps you have heard of me, as well," he said, his face that of a darksome animal. "Years ago, I wrestled under the name the Love of Britomart. I once tangled with the immortal Augustine Crespi of Argentina. In Public Hall, we went many rounds in a tropical heat. He had the growl, I the nimble feet. In the seventh, he pulled a trowel from his shorts. I was disheartened. Now, with similar enthusiasm, I battle perfidy."

Bobby felt a muscle let go in his chest. "I am a battler, too," he said. "I stand against dirty talk and self-neglect. Let's do this together, your judgeship. You can be the bow, I the lilting lyre."

The judge leveled a finger at him. He appeared to be having slanderous thoughts.

"Go away, defendant Stoops. I am feeling the call of the spinning toe-hold."

"You disappoint me," Putt Fenno told him at the Greyhound station. "We had possibilities. I saw us in a Swiss vault, bathing in coin. I was fond of you, too. Now, I'm off—what?—to make fruit famous."

For twenty-six hours, Bobby rode, slumped in his seat. He looked at his hand. It could have belonged to a sloth, his heart to a lizard. With every mile, he felt less like that celebrated outlaw he'd been for so long; and by the time the bus pulled into Deming, New Mexico, he knew that for a long time—six years, it would turn out—he would not be the Night Crawler, nor the Wicked Dwarf of the Western Shore, nor another demon from the nether quarters of his undermind.

"Shake this hand," he told the driver as he got off. "This belongs to Bobby Stoops and he has a lifetime to figure out how to tell the world what is wrong with it."

He rented an apartment on Olive Street, a dozen blocks from his mother and father, and worked at Buzz King's Chevron on US 70; in time, no one remembered he was the fellow who'd sung "Sick Figure in the Neighborhood" or "Old Fool Back on Earth," or that at the Park West in Chicago he'd spoken of the Tattooers of La Dominica and the Order of the Golden Dawn. Only once was he recognized, by Onan Motley, the kid who worked the pumps.

"I know 'Experiment in India.'" Onan looked like he had a fist in his throat. "I know 'Datalife.'" He hummed the bridge in which the shoo-bops sound like an army in retreat.

Bobby Stoops was not encouraged.

"I am an ex-ag major from Texas Tech," Bobby said. Covered in bearing grease from a California Ford LTD, he felt no more like his former self than he did gravel. "Perhaps you'd care to know details about the swamp potato. Or lichen."

"I was in II Corps then," Onan was saying. "You were heavy shit to a lot of us. We'd put on 'Orders for the Library' and rock out with Victor Charles. It was bullets and LZ Thelma. I liked best that thing you called forethought."

"I know you," Bobby said, "you are interested in moss and phytogenesis."

"I used to be a bad character." Motley was serious. "You turned me toward the good path."

In the spring, Bobby discovered he was a legend. He'd been seen, it was reported, in Cambodia with a Communist combo called

Modern Slavery. They sang "Let's Play Under the Bed" and "Important Moments in the History of Russia," and for state engagements they dressed up like KGB Samaritans named Roxy and Do Ling. One publication—was it *Circus?*—claimed that, in his first week as sheriff of Brownfield, Texas, he had vanquished a felon while speaking Jacobean. "Hark, ye motherfucker," he reportedly had ordered, "little availeth. Unhand that purloined raiment!" The article suggested he was feral, with a heart as insubordinate as lighting. An old picture (the one to promote "Stockings That Think") appeared on the *Newsweek* people page. The paragraph below it, Bobby was sure, was written by an iguana, for it spoke of a "constricted world of misgivings" in which "beings such as he tempted beings such as us into the worship of tumult and shudder."

He liked living in New Mexico, especially its desert. "Greatness could happen here," he told Buzz King. This was a place, he decided, like his past: scorched, flat, and unremarkable but for its twisted, gnarled, and needled plant life. (During this time—from Easter '74 to Xmas '78—he began developing himself. He bowled at the Thunderbird Lanes, found he could do it well, even liked it. He received permission from the Wildcat wrestling coach to use the weight room and there he exercised three times a week, doing ten reps for the major muscle groups—the flexors, the extensors, even Gimbernat's ligament.)

Yet, when he thought about the past, he felt dazed, as if his thinking meats had suddenly dried, had fractured and now were already crumbling along the fissure of Rolando; and once the coach caught him with 180 pounds braced over his head—he'd been that way for an hour, it appeared. The man said Bobby's eyes seemed, well, to drift in his face.

"You take it easy," the coach suggested. "Skip a week, then start again. But small this time. You ain't no Hercules."

"Right, sure," Bobby said. There was nothing in his brain but wind and light.

Somewhere in here he married, but even after the climactic WJKO speech and the complete return to the normal life, which were both many years away, he remembered little more than her name, Evelyn Greathouse, and that she was the ER nurse at the Mimbres Valley Hospital who bandaged the wrist he'd whanged with a tire iron. He did recall that she was pretty—as few seemed to be—and that one week they drove south to Las Palomas, were wedded by a Mexican JP and bebopped at Tillie's, on the juke box his record that had gone to number four, "Instantly Jealous of Grain." She lived in the Olive Street apartment for many months and wore a perfume called White Shoulders, and then she was gone: for all her skill in the healing arts, she'd been too interested in that difficult, absent creature he'd been, that one who had sung to us in the big world about disorder, swill, and common trespass.

2.

One day, while he nailed new roofing felt on his garage, he heard talk. It was that comic-strip scene of self-illumination: light bulb overhead, a way to save the world, the problem solved. With a start, he realized that, despite the frenzy of those early years, he hadn't yet said what needed saying. "I did not state it as Victor Fears," he allowed. "Nor in Black Music From Two Worlds. Nor as Men Without Rhyme."

At the horizon the sun appeared tilted at a peculiar angle. The desert shimmered, heat waves everywhere and rising, an empire of thunderclouds tumbling toward him. He had his shirt off, his hands black with roofing tar, stomach slick with sweat. Titles came to him: "Daughters of Rich Men," "We Destroy the Family"; in the middle distances, a picture of himself emerged, shining and uninvaded. He could smell something, too, like new earth—soil from the vacated marl of accomplishment.

"I mean to swell up and bristle," he whispered. "I mean to scold."

An hour later he had sent telegrams to Rolling Stone, to Tiger Beat, to the *Village Voice*—to all the press that had followed his career. "Mr. Stoops's exile is ended," the messages read. "He has recovered himself and seeks now to pass along his ideas. P.S. You may not recognize him as he is bald and affects the aspect of a haunted man."

The following Saturday, Bobby greeted a writer-photographer from the *Trouser Press*.

"I have missed the spotlights," Bobby said. "And the way trouble looks from the high road." He made muscles to demonstrate that a new spirit had entered his body as well as his mind.

The man had the penmanship of a Goth. The article, when it appeared, asserted that Bobby had uttered Iroquois. There were allusions to lodge poles and beaded wampum.

"Attend to your latter ends," Bobby said. "For example, the end of mirth is heaviness."

The fellow snapped a photo that showed Bobby with a torso firm as a tusk.

"Fierce wars and faithful loves shall moralize my songs." Bobby was looking into the man's eyes. There were flecks in the iris that could have been produced only by amphetamines. "I suspect I will be vast, as well as a mighty turmoil to the ignorant many."

Until he heard from Putt Fenno, Bobby practiced hard, delighted in his expert fingerwork, the way he caressed the fretboard. "Digits," he said, "you have lost nothing but time." His voice, too, had remained in splendid shape—still able, when he needed it, to wail and cause the blood to tremble. He told his mother and father that they were not to worry, that he would be leaving soon, but would one day return to them, a risen and everlasting thing. He informed the Wildcat coach that he no longer had need of iron and inert flange, but that the ache of exertion had made him appreciate the physical world of tendon, joint, and bone.

On his last day of work at Buzz King's, he told the kid who'd recognized him that several paths existed in this life, not one or two, and that down all, marsh or slough, jungle or avenue, lay miracle and tragedy both—the fudged and deprived, respectively.

"Yeah, I heard that before." Onan Motley's face—gaunt and held together, it seemed, by hope alone—grew dark, as if he'd spied a hairy item with a dozen legs dart from the dirt at his feet. "Our CO, Captain Fooley, used to say that just after we got dumped on. He'd stroll out on the char, where the smoke and screaming was coming from, and say, 'Men, ain't life lovely?' I didn't believe it then."

Bobby grabbed Onan by the shoulders, planted a saint's kiss on the boy's gritty forehead.

"Bless you," he said. "You are from rancor and clatter, and all shall be over soon."

His return, as expected, was swift. At LAX, in the breathdefeated embrace of Putt Fenno, Bobby spoke the three words that had seized his thoughts since he'd boarded the AA flight in El Paso: blight, spoilage, mendacity.

"I have no humor left in me," Putt Fenno said. "Listen, you must agree to the following. You may not batter, maim, or slap around. You may not shoot, stab, pummel, or coldcock. I have sent your luggage back. There was a bazooka in it."

Bobby glanced at the document Putt Fenno was holding. It forbade the use of anything manufactured by Uzi or Messrs. Smith & Wesson. It forbade reference to catamites or Tyuratum vertebrates. It disallowed anaphraxis and sleep standing up.

"I feel a hundred years old," Putt Fenno was saying. "Make us rich again, okay?"

Bobby grinned. More words had occurred and he wondered if there was a tune among them: filament, continence, ghastly.

"Hug me again," Fenno said. "It's been a long time since I drank for pleasure."

After a month's rehearsal in a warehouse off Los Feliz Boulevard, the band began a six-date tour, starting in Tampa, as the Unfinished Business of Childhood.

"It is good," Bobby told the crowd that first night. He had concluded "Lunch in Tunisia," the hall glowing with a million sparkles. "It will get better. The point of evolution is perfection. In time, you will twinkle and glitter above." In the back of the hall massed a legion of Spanish pirates and dispersed Apaches. They had skin the color of week-old pork. "Ease your pain," he told them, and, almost a hundred strong, eyes aglow with what Bobby knew were ardors and mordancies, they lurched forward. Bobby was touched, as if in them, in the smokes and swirling lights, he had glimpsed parts of himself—the hungry, condemned parts.

"Larger spirits are using me," he told Putt Fenno after the show. He was dressed in a velveteen jumpsuit, the ensemble that had made hair fashionable several seasons ago. "Tomorrow night, I shall shower them with fur."

"I have a confession." In Fenno's face was something like pain. "I have an ulcer. My ears ring all the time. Be nice to me."

Across the room, Nate Creer, the bass player, was wooing a woman. Bobby could read his lips: he was discussing, in the context of the discarnate, humbug, and pluck.

"I am writing a new tune," Bobby said. "It is called 'Yonder Wall in Japan' and suggests ruin."

The following night, after the performance in Birmingham, he found a surprise in his hotel. They were, he figured, heathen—on account of their breastplates and appealing smiles, not to mention exposed, muscular thighs. This, evidently, was to be that male-female principle he'd read much about.

"I have hitched many miles," the brunette was saying, "show me something vile." She was taller and had a reptile's lip curl Bobby found fascinating. The other was blonde, clearly from the Triassic age. Bobby envisioned a man, like himself, in climbing boots and leathers, adrool astride them, the welts on his pectorals those of combat and extirpation.

He showed them the bed, which seemed as large now as a great white sea, and they dashed to it in a style Bobby took to be species-specific. In a moment, all was flurry and a thunderclap of peeled outerware. A thought, obvious as a brick, struck him: If I can have this, why am I not happy?

"Now we will demonstrate the difference between curiosity and interest," a voice from the pile said. "You may ask questions later."

Reckless as a nightmare, they roiled, bed linen flying, at once a huddle and a tempest. He found them amazing, like poultry that could fox-trot and add by twos.

For a time, he sat on the coffee table, watchful as a sentry. A garment, heavy with buckles and bows, flopped over the table lamp. Another song occurred to him: "All About the Whites." He saw hank and thatch and a certain square of skin that could have belonged to either. "Ah, wretchedness," the blonde was groaning. "Ah, excess," sighed the brunette, eyeballs rolling. His heart virtually frozen, Bobby saw tongue and root and, after an hour, a flank of such delectation his lungs withered with a wheeze.

"We are lonely," the brunette declared. "Help us into the upper airs."

Bobby made his leg stop shaking. "What is your name?"

"Suzy," she said. "Though I am often known as Hellenora. Or Florimel."

"Yes, I have heard of you."

There was a profound instant, itself bittersweet as nightshade, during which Suzy studied the breathless sprawl of flesh beneath her. It moaned of ecstasy and a fetching work of nature called Chaco.

"This is Adele," Suzy said. "Many claim she invented shelter."

In Atlanta the next day, after the load-in and the sound check, Bobby told Putt Fenno he was going for a ride, visit the landmarks. "I have received a message." He'd spotted a sentence on the wall in his dressing room, its letters bunched and clumped, as if etched with an adze. "I am to venture among them. Ideas are surfacing. There are rumors of exuberance and enmity."

"I have an idea, too. It involves retirement comforts," Putt Fenno said. "What's that sound?"

"My liver," Bobby said.

Putt Fenno's eyes snapped out of focus, came back. "Convince me. I am skeptical."

"It is Greek," Bobby said. "I believe it endeavors to be free and live on a verdant isle."

All afternoon, warmed by a strangely Persian sun, he toured Atlanta, from Washington Park to Georgia Tech and Peachtree Center, his silver Cadillac limousine driven by a man whose face brought to Bobby's mind the terms *figwort* and *thermocline*.

"You have suffered a recent loss," Bobby said at last.

"Ain't that the goddamn truth."

The car pulled onto Chapel Street, near Terminal Station.

"It involves a woman," Bobby added, "and an ex-New Orleans banker named Fudge."

The man looked like a broke farmer in receipt of yet more bad news.

"Her name is Lou Ann, from the house of Akers," Bobby said. "Yours is—?"

"Al. Alfred," he said, "from the, uh, house of Boozer."

"Cheer up, Alfred Boozer." Bobby clapped him on the shoulder. It felt like stone. "They are an inconstant pair. This minute they squabble in a Cobb County bungalow. She holds a stick, he a tennis sock. They are discussing the pineal body and what to do with unnecessary fibrous matter." Bobby felt removed from this, as if he'd come from another, less complicated orb. "Yearning for a glamorous career, she has dyed her hair henna; he, alas, comes from a tribe which used to compute in yods."

"He's an investment broker with a five-thousand-dollar Rolex, is what he is." Alfred Boozer had the car stopped in the street. "Lou Ann says he's got a heinie like a teenager."

Bobby was pleased he'd worn this Arab costume—these robes, this warrior's burnoose.

"At this moment Lou Ann is seminaked but dismal in her mind. Where they are, it has rained for the seventh time in as many days; and last night she saw the rusted hulk of an Oldsmobile wagon tumble past on the nasty river behind their dwelling." Cars were honking, a knot of motorists waving. "She is holding herself at the bosom. Where I come from, we call these features glomerules; often they can be the source of our strength."

"My source is George Dickel and Four Roses," Alfred Boozer was saying. "The house of Boozer's a grim joint."

It was then, while he informed Mr. Boozer of his woman's affection for benthic fauna, that Bobby noticed they were parked in front of a pawn shop. Innards, he thought, be still.

"Wait here," he said, opening his door. A voice could be heard—his own perhaps after centuries of sleep: *Robert Virgil Stoops, this is why you've come.*

"Tell me about Fudge," Alfred was hollering. "Is he standing or does he have his fist up his wazoo?"

Inside, Bobby approached the woman behind the cash register. She had wet lips, the air around her as special as blood. "Madam, you have what I need. Please, take my monies." In a few seconds, he sat again in the Cadillac, now clutching a heavy paper sack. He felt calm, none of his organs in riot. He could have been at the North Pole, alone except for expansive plains of white and a rhapsody of Arctic night noise.

"That woman spit on you." Alfred Boozer, his face wrinkled as a prune, was pointing. "What'd you buy?"

Bobby held the bag aloft. It contained a .44 with six WCF cartridges and possessed the heft, Bobby thought, of a thousand things.

"In my homeland," he said, "this is an instrument of peace, a speedy exit from the hollow world."

3.

That night, Bobby Stoops, once known as Dr. Filth, a maker of statements, formerly of the American deserts, flew. During "Themes From Great Cities," in the chorus where the Pakistani finger cymbals are clinked to imitate icy, tinkling rains, Bobby felt himself harden in a dozen spots—calf, hips, small of back; then, stiffened by the thump and amplified thwang behind him, he rose. An inch. Finally two.

Nearby, mouth set hard as a doorknob, stood Nate Creer, pumping his bass feverishly. He'd been to Baylor, a physics major with several hours in Aquinas.

"Be watchful, Mr. Creer," Bobby said. "Three weeks from now you will pass from one medium to the next. I see the letters ICU, plus a flock of grave men in smocks."

Creer edged closer, adrift in the music. They were in the section that mentioned the Lip of Truth, the Froward Tongue.

"Observe," Bobby said, "I am risen. Verily."

"Right on," Nate agreed. "We are all risen in this venue. It's the pharmaceuticals."

Bobby felt sorrow clunk in him like a weight. "Give me your hand, Nathaniel, and let us shuffle together."

Afterward, backstage, amid a milling crowd of crew and well-wishers, Bobby stared into the littered bottom of his handbag. He cocked his head and all the objects in his vision—all the objects in his life, it seemed—were at the far end of this room. He felt remarkable, like a boxer dog wearing eyeshadow and Lady Astor's rubies.

"Rejoice in the habitable reaches of this earth," he said. "Hear my instructions and be wise."

Putt Fenno, his face like the floor of a horsebarn, approached.

"About that radio interview in Miami tomorrow——" he began.

"My friend, you look wretched," Bobby said. "I prescribe the high road of reason, plus yellow vegetables."

Nearby, Bobby's drummer, Wang-chi, was giving his real name. It was composed of c's and x's and possessed a primitive association with jaculation.

"Let me impress you," Putt Fenno was saying. "It is our understanding that the Pope will be listening. Also, tapes are being made for Fidel's boys. You have an international following."

"Trust me," Bobby said. "I already have an outfit in mind: It will say sleek and travel in the outer darkness."

Before he slept, hovering above the bed, Bobby entertained a vision. Images of fire rolled overhead, as well as scenes of salvation. Unbridled steeds, ears flattened, ran free amid the collapse of a crystal empire. In another, a fallen creature in gypsy headgear yelled of polymorphs and misogyny. In the last, almost familiar, a universe of eight dimensions, including the glandular, dissolved into itself and became, he knew, a grain of blackness as dense as a tear. Cold, his spine knocking, Bobby tugged the blanket to his chin.

"Ours is a mutable kind," he said. "We believe in naught but a future of joy."

In the morning, he dressed slowly. He desired a mytholyrical effect. In the mirror, he saw himself in a green Lycra bodysuit, the pistol in the red plastic box strapped to his chest.

"My astro-pack," he told everyone aboard the charter jet. "Today will be one of irreducible mysteries and some flitting about."

Airborne, he spoke of greenswards and leafy ensconcements, Phoebus and enswarmed furies. "We should be thinking of Keats and the fourth realm of space," he said over the intercom. "Not needments and habits that made us blue."

In the charter terminal, he addressed dozens of his fans. "Bobby

Stoops has been away too long," he said. "But he has learned much. For example, he has learned that machines have a dark and sly plan for us all. The question is this: What is to be done with the delirious among us, the floccose?" Putt Fenno made him quit when the talk turned to occultism, particularly a belief in woody tissues.

At the radio station, WJKO, he was introduced to a disc jockey who wore a T-shirt that said "Resist All Change."

"Yes, I have met you before," Bobby said. "You were riding with Cortez. You were called, I believe, Bernal of Almeria."

"Buenos dias," the man laughed, ushering Bobby into a studio. "I am Xavier Mendoza Gonzalez-Boit. You may call me Jake." He was Cuban, with a floppy hairpiece, and had the shine of a man making ninety thousand dollars a year. "We are gigante," he was saying. "We got waves going all around whole world. You mas big, too. All day long phones ring. It is Stoops, Stoops, Stoops. Everybody adores hombres who fly."

In the tiny room with them paced Putt Fenno, his tie undone and collar open. He had the stuffed expression of a bottom-feeding sea fish.

"You have been hopeless too long," Bobby said to him. "I shall give you something to glimmer for."

Jake was fiddling with a bank of dials. He adjusted the boom mike. "That light turns rojo, we are go for blastoff." Above a glass panel was the fixture. "Listo?"

Bobby felt the pistol against his ribs. His thoughts, gay and light, concerned recompense and the useful charms of the past. Within minutes, he knew, this episode in his life would be over.

"I am ready, my son."

The light flashed on and Jake rushed into extended remarks that cited sierra, viento y fuego—earth, wind and fire. He was mucho honored, he said, to have this numero uno rock-and-roll hombre on his show. It was a thrill, muchachos, like maybe having El Presidente himself or Old Señor Elvis. "Right now this gringo is touching my cabeza and I am feeling hot stuff go up my spine."

The room, Bobby imagined, except for the sluggish thud of his heart, was quiet. On the other side of the glass wall, people were busy, many smiling. Children, he was thinking, come unto me. I am neither sinister nor a member of low estates. Then he heard himself speaking, his voice music itself

"My true name is Jor-El and I come from the planet Alderon, which lies outside what you know as the Vega galaxy."

There was light, blinding as if from a flashbulb, and acrid smoke. It seemed he had fired the pistol into the ceiling tiles. Debris fell in a blizzard.

"Do not be alarmed, citizens of earth," he said. "This is perturbation only, not violence."

Jake had cast himself into a corner, his hair in a lump in his lap. "Carumba!" he was shouting. The good humor had vanished from his face in a flash. In the adjacent studio, folks shook in spasms, as if they had been touched, however briefly, by an electric wand.

Somewhere, Putt Fenno was blubbering.

"We are discreet people, tall and lean of build. Our fortunes, which we have no interest in hoarding, are made in the export of gummy exhudates. We talk of heths and locomote using an energy we measure in fardads. In our mountains, which resemble your Rockies in composition, we mine a mineral precious to us as the erg or dyne. Courtship in our world is without anxiety—in part because we subscribe to the wonderments of the temporary pleasures. Individuals have stepped forward to lead us in this enterprise and we consult them daily."

Jake, all Jolson eyes and kidney sweat, went many directions at once. The pistol had gone off again.

"Years ago, it was determined to make contact with you. I was selected as an infant and fitted into a uniquely designed vehicle. This was parsecs ago—three hundred years by your calendar. My transport landed in the New Mexico desert and I was taken in by the Stoops family, beautician Mildred and plumber Earl. Living among you as a scholar, I have learned your language and can use with confidence the words *gout* and *epicene*. I have eaten your foods and found them chewy. Your cities I enjoy very much, though they lack the splash and gleam of our capital, El-Dor. My mission is simple: I bring you greetings and counsel from our Circle of Elders."

In his corner, Jake was striking himself in an alarmingly private manner. "Holy mother," he was saying, "holy mother."

Putt Fenno, his eyes blank with panic, was collapsed on the floor.

"I have information about betterments," Bobby was saying. "The details will make you frolic and gambol."

The ceiling moved, and Bobby felt a comforting tingle: he was flying, as carefree as he had been on Alderon an epoch ago.

"Remain stouthearted," he advised. "Shirk not the resolve of your forebears, nor worry much of the dark arts. Fortify yourself with all faiths and claim perseverance as your chief virtue. Do not babble. Practice not the disciplines of demolishment and such. You are matter. It must be saved."

Now he could hear Putt Fenno. "Aarrgghh," the man was groaning. "Ooommpphh." He looked like he'd just lost his hands.

"Bear with me, my audience of earthlings," Bobby said, the weapon spilling from his hand. He had only a little more to say, specifically facts about souls and assurances of the next worlds, then this business would be finished; and soon—no more than a delfine, certainly—he would be home again, in that land of his infancy, that place of twelve red skies and crooked, hearty trees of gold.

Ma donna

harold jaffe

MADONNA wanted to live in the San Remo, a hincty high-rise in New York City, but her application was turned down by the tenant-owners, including other celebs, though Madonna appeared at the crucial interview with three crucifixes around her neck, or maybe it was four, she had (she is firm on this point) a "very" Catholic childhood, so that her *nom de video*, Madonna, serves the practical dual purpose of alloy and allegory, each encouraged and denied, likewise in her smash-hit single "Material Girl," material is of course lucre while being a timely reminder of our composition as vile matter, ditto Madonna's participation in a '79 soft-core flick in the Big Apple for which she was paid the princely sum of $100, and what was billed as the real scuz was not-so-deftly simulated, ditto her nudie photos disinterred, but my dialectical (so to speak) gloss on US iconizing-commodifying was evidently lost on Paul Simon, Dustin Hoffman, and the others on the application committee of the San Remo, the higher you climb the ladder of success the more your (pardon my Greek) arse is exposed applies in spades to Madonna, though she'd rather expose her navel, I've seen more female navels in rainy London this summer, Madonna-invoked, than you would imagine: Earl's Court, Shoreditch, Chelsea, King's Cross, saw a brace on Princess Street, Edinburgh, in the pouring rain, why *shouldn't* she issue a "restraining order" on the redistribution of her porn flick, on the publication of her nudies in both *Penthouse* and *Playboy*, the year was '79 (before

AIDS), Hamilton Jordan was deftly counseling Jimmy Carter on "Human Rights," Madonna was an eighteen-year-old tyro called Louise Ciccone, slim but breasty, brown hair and lush bush and sexy hair on her belly and lots under her arms, her "look" Lower-East-Side-sulky, even then she was religious as heck, in her way, only Diane Keaton among the bigs voted Yea on Madonna's application to live in the San Remo, perhaps on the grounds of sisterhood, I can only speculate, perhaps on the grounds of charity, we are in the grip of BAND AID, aid to the strife-torn in Africa, if only those Marxists would let our $$$ get through to the folks that need them: the good poor (in Mathew Arnold's father's phrase), Poverty Sucks, like the bumper sticker says, but isn't it just the incentive you need to get rich, a buffer (I mean poverty) against getting poor, as AIDS discourages congress with Haitians, homos, hemos, so wear your necktie munch on irradiated bean sprouts phone your broker *don't* bend over, "Like a Virgin," Madonna's first mega-smash, has got it all if you alter the words, while inserting Mother Teresa in her habit for Madonna in her confection of silks, no big deal, not with our technology, I think of the poor when I eat Tandoori, you wouldn't believe how many Indian/Pakistani restaurants there are throughout the U.K., Sikhs though scarce, evidently because of their continuing dispute with India, because of their stubborn insistence on possessing their skins, tough for a male Sikh to hide when you think of it, appearance isn't everything, well, it's darn close, take Madonna's navel, truthfully, I prefer reading about her navel from a distance, the U.K. isn't distant enough, and I'd prefer reading about her navel in another tongue, Basque, say, or Punjabi (as spoken by the Sikhs in northwest India), gosh, she's the very incarnation of Marilyn Monroe, a tramp with style, a composite of styles, a xeroxed composite of apparent styles accessed, video'd, transmitted via satellite, take the incessant rain in London, filthy weather and the thing is we have the technology to do something about it, the Brits though would like it both ways: the Queen Mother at Ascot and creeping Americanization on the telly, *Dallas* reruns are all the rage, "MERRY MPS DANGLED A TOPLESS GIRL OVER THE RIVER THAMES IN A STAGGERING EARLY-HOURS RAVE-UP" [this wasn't Madonna though it might have been], "ONE LABOUR MEMBER SWUNG THE GIGGLING GIRL OVER THE EDGE OF THE COMMONS TERRACE WITH HIS ARMS ROUND HER LEGS— AND SUDDENLY HER CHARMS POPPED OUT," according to *The Sun*, but why Madonna rather than video'd chanteuses like Blondie or Sade (pronounced "Sharday"), well, consider her hair, I think of Bernini's St. Theresa in her passion, or Barbara Stanwyck in a 40s betrayed-husband flick with moody camera angles, polymorphous perversity, AC-DC and whatever other C's you come up with (these *are* the pluralistic, pentecostal '80s), Madonna's hair—I want to put this plainly—is, like Ahab's doubloon, everything to everybody and nothing, like the foamy head of my draft Guinness, without the draft, now if we can only convince our Secretary of Defense, who, like Madonna, as of this writing, is on a bad roll, he's an honorable man, a proud man, and when he closes his eyes to respond to a question we know that the teleprompter on the inside of his eyelids will be American-made without Japanese anything, I imagine the unwinding of a bloody bandage and underneath, red and never not festering: *Communism* (reads the teleprompter) in *Our* hemisphere, when the talk turns to politics Madonna and her entourage commence to yawn, and who can blame them?, like that enduring silliness about what does the Scottie wear under his kilt, here in Inverness where I'm nursing my pint (it's late morning but raining bullets), I scan the OxBridge weeklies wherein the splenetic-exotic Scot is as ever good sport, as the Hindus under the Raj, as the "kaffirs" to the Afrikaners, but note: there is, as the intelligent writer demonstrated conclusively in a *New Yorker* article a while back, a distinct though subtle difference between fashion and style, the latter as you might expect being the more refined species, where then would you situate Madonna?, don't answer too quickly, don't answer surely on the basis of Madonna representing "low" as against "high" culture, I'm tempted to quote the playwright Tom Stoppard but compositionally I can't fit him in, here he is: "There's an essential distinction between countries where the abuse of human rights represents the system in triumph, and the countries in which it represents the failure of the system," Stoppard of course is clever and wealthy, and clever about being wealthy, beneath his neat formulation resides the oak-panneled soul of OxBridge, Sandhurst too, I remind you that it was not in benighted Moscow nor in Pretoria's whited sepulchre nor in Managua Nicaragua, but in the demotic Big Apple where they denied Madonna, oh well, it's Thursday and I'm off to the National Film Institute to see Joseph Losey's remake of Fritz Lang's *M*, and what can one say that hasn't been said about the ringworm of child molestation, is it really happening?, is it lurid imagining erected on lurid imagining in the service of classic-formula COKE and the New Old Vigilance?, Losey did his *M* in '51, twenty years after Lang, with (improbably) David Wayne in the Peter Lorre role, Losey, you recall, an American who did most of his strong work in England, best known for his collusion with Pinter in *The Servant*, Pinter incidentally just back from Turkey where he and Monroe's ex, Arthur Miller, were sent by PEN to pose certain queries about the systematic violation of certain Turkish artists' human rights, Pinter didn't hit it off with the American ambassador, in fact exchanged vivid Pintersque insults, slinging at each other from a stagey distance, the ambassador with the provisional last word: Pinter was incapable, he put it, of seeing Turkey's policy "in the round," which evidently is our Secretary of Defense's position, judging from his recent telepropmpted remarks re Turkey's "alleged" genocide of Armenians, the Secretary's guiding principle/missile here being Turkey's good will re U.S. bases in Turkey to bolster defense against Communism world-wide and intergalactically as well since the Soviets are, please remember, Asiatics, possessing that Asian mentality derived from Attila, limitless aggression, absolutely, Madonna about the eyes is Asian, dancing in circles like a benign ringworm, like a houri or odalisque, she doesn't touch us like Mary Pickford, touch is scarcely the point, nor is her coolness Garbo's with its insinuation of depths, Madonna glitters like neon viewed from the wrong side of the scope, she's there and not there, making contact with our nervous system like an electrified dentist's implement tap-tapping our tooth, no longer "the victim's information, but the *victim*, that torture needs to win—or reduce to powerlessness. By expanding the types and frequency of torture, by acquiring and exploiting a more exact knowledge of psychology and neurology, torture in the late 20th century has become able to inflict an immense variety of relatively graded degrees of pain upon anyone" (Edward Peters, *Torture*, Blackwell, '85), here in the U.K. there are only four television channels (though satellite dish antennas are making their bid) but any number of labels of beer, what happened to that honest mug of English bitter that is not ice-cold after the American fashion?, let's face it, short of cauterization (large-scale), homogenization American-style (Japanese-accented) is irresistible, and, yes, it is up to the artist (the who?) to extract, extrapolate, extort the esthetic principle no longer orbiting neck-deep in contaminant, such an immense variety of flavors, besides you can blend them yourselves, Madonna is (grant me this trope) a dervish, her mobile navel, slender, spike-heeled feet administering delicately graded degrees of pain, her Asian eyes, polymorphous hair (since shorn), her broader and broader wake of agents and investment advisers, which is probably the toughest job of the lot given the wild fluctuation of the dollar, mind you, I'm not implying that there aren't good, sound, economic heads in control: rock-solid Volcker at the Fed, the incorruptible Stockman, who was a peace activist in the Sixties and recently left the administration for Wall Street and a real salary (seven figures allegedly), Reagan's *doppel* Regan (exorcized in the wake of

"Irangate"), the estimable Meese (he's at Justice but ranges widely), who then are our torturers? Well, I'd like to cite Arendt's banality of evil (you thought I'd have something off-the-wall up my sleeve), in fact it's more appropriate than ever, dissociate while administering pain hi-ho, in front of the console, faxing your broker, stroking your hairless leg, "evil" itself can stand redefining, which perhaps I'll get to, though in a roundabout way, since it is harder than ever to be plain, that is, *you* are are plain but is it plain that's received?, heck no, the language all unstuck, thus Madonna and her whirling navel will describe a broad sphere of effluence, so to speak, inflicting all species of pleasure, so to speak, and if this seems elusive, take heart, there are these constants: dollars and power, though their acquisition and implementation signify a more various collusion, collusion in what?, in keeping the good poor good and poor, in keeping the electrified wire (now wireless) hooked to your genitals, yes yours.

U.K., 6.85
U.S., 9.86, 8.87

Kama Quyntifonic

lance olsen

THEY SEND IN THE UNDERFED GIRL, thirteen years old, maybe four-teen if you really stretch your imagination, bald except for that filthy yellow Plughead tassel dangling from her forehead, to pull off the final-dining.

Only the camera fails to record her as it spirals down through the darkness toward the white flash of stage below in the Royal Albert Hall on one of the hottest nights of the year, almost thirty degrees C and here it is November 30, atmosphere gray and close and damp. The camera fails to document her elbowing toward the nearest bodyguard like some little expressionless animal, canister cradled in her arms.

Instead it chronicles the radiant sense of promise spreading over these people, a sheet of flames over a pool of jet fuel. They stand in aisles. Perch on seats frothing foam rubber. Teeter on friends' shoul-ders, waving at the lens recording this event, making it part of global memory.

They're used to being filmed from above, these people, earth from the space shuttle or GSA station, riot scenes from police VTOLs, football throngs from low-gliding blimps. The guy lapping air, dia-mond stud flickering on his tongue. The couple, lawyers from nine to five, sporting lilac Aramis head-injury makeup, spinning in some magical private dance down front. The woman with two black eyes, a human raccoon, hoisted between two tall thin boys dressed as late-stage AIDS victims, laughing and rolling back her gray-knit T-shirt to reveal the startling alabaster scars of her cosmetic mastectomy.

Post-verbalists primped in golden nose rings and prosthetic neck burns toast the camera with Dixi-Cups of warm brown lager. Technogoths tricked out in crimson contacts and white sunscreen, SPF 65, swig whiskey from plastic bottles smuggled in strapped to their ankles. But those in the know realize pills are the future. Shiny pills in fluorescent colors and useless shapes. Lime triangles. Poppy-red hexagons. Lemon squares. Passed from palm to palm in a chain of secret handshakes. So you can see, actually see, every note float into being at this concert, feel each one clap your eardrums.

Everyone's talking at once, a rumble of language through the crammed auditorium as the electrical crew crisscrosses the stage, checking the relays, checking the computer terminals and projectors. As bodyguards gather in the wings, plump hairy arms folded across chests, black teardrops tattooed at eyecorners. As bobbies in plastic-visored helmets, flak jackets, and 50,000-volt stunguns on their belts line the back of the hall by the main doors, legs slightly apart, hands on hips, fifty ominous reminders of what can always happen.

The huge ventilation system convulses, shivers on, a monstrous fan stirring up soggy heat, tangy perspiration and urine, fruity perfume teenage girls wear, strawberry and cherry, diesel exhaust drifting in from Kensington Road, moist hair, alcohol vapors.

These people are the faithful. They've tubed from the Docklands. Hitchhiked from Birmingham. Trained from Newcastle. They've stayed awake the last seventy-two hours straight through a series of crashing headaches, bouts with low-grade hunger-nausea, chemo-fatigue, oil-scented rain clattering on the upper decks of ferries and car bonnets, making connections from Amsterdam, Berlin, Corfu, finagling credit from strangers, finessing rides from acquaintances who've owed them favors for years now and never thought they'd have to pay up this time around.

They're a nation for which it was never a question of *if* they would make it, only *how*. In a sense theirs is a journey that's been underway for months. They are the unwavering, working nowhere jobs to eke out a small line of credit, cleaning tables in a Camden Town pub, collecting fares on an Edinburgh bus. They've been part of this process for so long it hardly seems believable they've finally arrived, they've finally stood in the last queue, passed through the last gate, collected with others in this one prodigious body. They're finally where they've been imagining themselves all this while.

And they're ready. Hooting, whacking their hands together, stamping their feet.

The camera flies in, unable to capture the stark density of this congregation, the neophilic energy swarming at its center, the passion, the manic vortex, the bright suspense.

And then the stage goes black.

The first computer-enhanced chord reverberates, numbing as the blast from a tactical nuclear warhead.

A spotlight zaps Tango Deltoid, lead guitarist for Dr. Teeth, who launches into a speed riff. The holounit throws his image far above the mob, cuts to his right hand sheathed in the Fender electronic glove that metamorphoses his gestures into complex synthetic sounds. Cycla Propain, female percussionist, kicks in with a power roll. Right behind her come bassist Kupid Zitch and keyboardist Rheum Goldbug.

The decibel level soars like fourteen military jets taking off in unison in a one-room flat, shakes like the L.A. Shudder on Black Tuesday.

People don't *hear* Dr. Teeth. They *feel* them. They lean into the shockwaves, surrender to the tempest of static bursts slapping their spleens.

And they send up a great unified howl.

Begin to ululate into soundjolts.

*   *   *

And then she appears.

First as a sixteen-meter head levitating over the multitude, blond hair teased like Monroe's, features dipped in shadow like the Virgin's.

Then the face tilts up, huge and glaucous as a geisha's, to reveal the black-and-blue splotches around her browless methyl-yellow eyes, across her left cheek, the dried-blood look at the corners of her carmine lips, and that world-famous patented smile aglitter with teeth filed to wickedly sharp points.

The clamor increases.

The gigantic mouth opens and a thirty-meter-long gold-leafed cobra springs across the ceiling. Slithers down a wall. Disappears into the audience as on stage the real Kama Quyntifonic swoops in with the vocal, part primal-scream, part haunting melody, part tribal chant, camera riveted on her spectacular lingerie, raven corset rimmed in red, on those shiny Mylar thigh-boots, real nazi, that brass chastity belt with the medieval lock and that sexy nail-studded dog collar that just cries out *Wake up, you Quayles, I'm a marketing strategy!* while caving in the heart of every male and every third female in the place.

Dancers in tattered army pants and body suits, shoeless, skin blotched with ersatz scabs, flood around her, crawling on their knees, wriggling on their bellies, hobbling on wooden crutches, and Tango Deltoid, velvet hangman's noose around his neck whipping crazily back and forth, blue hair spattering sweat-beads, leads into the chorus with a compu-guitar solo electronically altered to sound more like frightened rapidfire human cries at 2 A.M. on some mews in the East End than any musical notes anyone on this planet's ever heard.

> *Burn this place*
> *Burn your face*
> *Burn this case*
> *Cuz I don't care*

I don't care
Cuz I been here
and I been there

Fans charge the stage, throw themselves at the bodyguards who now begin doing their work, unused to the sheer *numbers* of the devout, the sheer *concentration* of their zeal.

They catch torsos in midflight and catapult them back into the rabble that's become a living version of a stuntman's air mattress, but the fans keep coming, they keep massing in.

Some carry brass knuckles, some sand-socks, some offerings—jewelry, credit slabs, cans of mace—and they scrabble over each other, dive from each other's shoulders, cast themselves headlong at the strong-armed men who are breathless, nonplussed, increasingly agitated in the face of this assault.

At the rear of the auditorium bobbies shout into two-way radios, secure those flak jackets, lower those plastic visors, adjust those chin straps.

The holounit zeros in on the woman dancer whose eyes seem to have melted into myriad epicanthic folds, the scrawny Arab guy in seizures on the floor, then *(keep the camera on the credit, keep the camera on the credit)* Quyntifonic again who's begun shoving her way through these invalids, pushing them onto their sides, kicking their crutches out from under them while she begins the bridge to "Happy Daze" and behind her a ten-by-fifteen-meter screen drops and a black-and-white film, shaky, deliberately amateurish, loops images from Epidemics Hostels around Britain. Rows upon rows of beds. Skin stretched mummy-like over skulls of the dying. Arms the thickness of pencils. Legs the thickness of cricket bats. Specters in wheelchairs. IVs pumping in the morphine, keeping the flow heavy and steady. Quick cuts to the South American war, military jets defoliating what'd been left of the rainforest, tunnels of napalm seething.

Remains of L.A. the morning after the Shudder, megalithic shards of concrete and steel and cable heaved into smoky streets, flames from ruptured gas lines blooming around public housing projects, water spewing from fractured mains, shirtless people in ragged jeans staring into the camera as they stagger through the radioactive wreckage, muddled and embarrassed at what has gone on around them, at what part they took in all this, not even beginning to figure out yet things only get worse after this.

But the camera fails to record the underfed girl, thirteen years old, maybe fourteen if you really stretch your imagination, bald except for that filthy yellow Plughead tassel dangling from her forehead, eyes the color of Wedgwood, right ear vangoghed, hovering at the corner of the stage, just a meter away from the nearest bodyguard, an Iraqi who's struggling with another girl who's trying to shinny over him and deliver a cluster of artificial roses to Kama Quyntifonic's feet. He's holding her by a fistful of lavender hair as she writhes and snaps at his face like a Diacomm Doberman-tiger chimera. The underfed girl cradles the canister in her arms, some metallic doll, rocking it gently, scanning the situation around her, patiently taking stock as the lavender-haired fan bites down on the bodyguard's hand, fiercely, for the count of three, seven, and when he screams she bursts by him and almost attains her goal. Four more guards sweep her over their heads before she can reach Quyntifonic, and they toss her into the free-for-all in the orchestra pit. The camera catches her body spin awkwardly through the smoggy air and land at an unnatural angle on a suddenly bare patch of concrete.

Quyntifonic's holographic head releases a ten-meter-long rat.
A bat.
A scorpion.
These creatures dive at the spectators, who send up a communal

shout of delighted horror, and then engage in fierce battle on the vaulted ceiling, stinging, gnawing, sucking, while the film keeps looping images of destruction behind the authentic Quyntifonic standing among staged corpses and carving crosses and circles into her right arm with a dagger.

Dr. Teeth's in a frenzy.

Tango Deltoid's sunk deep into soundfields reminiscent of the mumbles and fumbled words you hear during the hypnagogic span just before sleep.

Cycla Propain and Kupid Zitch're pounding out an electronic seizure, wet hair slicked to temples.

And the temperature in the hall is rising, the air thickening, and Rheum Goldbug's zipping along the keyboard in rill after throbbing rill of sick sonics that're just pure clicking mega nazi.

The thirteen-year-old twists a valve at one end of the canister.

She eyes the spectacle before her, raises the bullet-shaped capsule above her head.

Throws.

Thin blood zags down Quyntifonic's right arm and Dr. Teeth has never played better than right now, this very second, and a Virus Baby's upper torso loops on the screen (it'd fit comfortably in a shoe-box, silently opening and closing its mouth like some goldfish) and the bobbies enter the rabble to retrieve the lavender-haired girl with the injured spine and the dancers lie motionless at Quyntifonic's feet and a line of gas jets opens at the rear of the stage freeing a hundred plumes of brilliant combustion.

Burn this place
Burn your face
Burn this case

Cuz I don't care
I don't care
Cuz I been here
and I been there

And then: the silver glint wobbling like a football in the fracas of laser lights, halting at the apex of its flight for the shortest period of time you can imagine, revolving, then plummeting among the dancers and musicians, mist from its nozzle spraying a wide white V and, just like that, a vast wave of people rolls back from the stage and Quyntifonic's down.

Kupid Zitch and Rheum Goldbug too.

Tango Deltoid's twitching, grand-mal-style, hugging his guitar, his glove generating a brain-splitting screech, coiled into himself like worms when you touch them with something hot.

Cycla Propain sprawls forward into her drumset.

The dancers try standing but are flat and still all at once. The bodyguards and roadies go to their knees. The holounit shuts off. Deafening feedback shoots through the speaker system.

For three heartbeats the audience falls silent.

Then a colossal animal sound of fear rises into the hot atmosphere, and the stampede begins.

The bobbies barely have time to lift their stunguns before the mass belts into them, the momentum kicking them back, someone on the PA system pleading for calm. Feedback rams through the hall. Shouts for help go up everywhere. The press of wild-eyed fans slams against the exit doors. A Datacidist wearing small nails through her ears trips and her ribcage implodes; her lover's elbows crack as he bends to wrestle her up. A guy in L.A. Gear desert camouflage propels into a wall and hears his own lower jaw disengage; a disoriented boy yanks on the complicated blue scarab-and-iron jewelry jangling around the downed guy's neck. An überthrasher who's just lost her tongue attempts clambering over a hill of people but slips back into the fray. Some suffocate in the immense army of bodies surging forward. Others lose fingers to the dying who struggle to the very end, only dimly aware of the explosion somewhere above and behind them as the gas jets on stage touch the screen, and the screen ignites and touches the holounit, and a cloud thick as burning tar churns along the ceiling, flames tonguing fuchsia and tangerine, the sprinkler system cutting in only to make the smoke thicker, like inhaling battery acid, like drinking lye.

And all across the globe dead-channel ash rains on television screens.

Ursus Major

roberta smoodin

"**W**ELL, AIN'T THIS CUTE," Bobo says, his dog eye looking like a large hole in his face because of the increasing gloom of sunset, the lack of any type of artificial light inside the bus. "While you guys been snoozin', we got us a club date." The bear awakens in a flash, sensing adversity, but the two women, languid and unimpressed by Bobo's hostility, stretch, rub their eyes with fists like little mitts, gather small pieces of clothing which look interchangeable to the bear, able to fit on any body part, and apply these to the nearest naked piece of their own flesh.

"That mean we work tonight?" Cassy whines, a child grumpy after a truncated nap.

"That's right, honey. You *are* a singer. Unless you want to hit the highway and thumb it back to S.F., where you might get a job waiting on tables," Bobo says. "How about it? You gonna get up and help, or do I have to stomp on you?"

"Okay, man."

"Jeez, what a Nazi."

"And how 'bout you, bear? You forgiven me for my indiscretions of this afternoon? Or you just gonna lie there like a sultan, smoke some opium, write some poetry, and wait for us workers to come home with the bread?"

"I'll help," the bear says, rising to his full height in an instinctual gesture of intimidation, then slumping back down into his

217

normal posture. "What can I do?"

"Well, big strong dude like you sure could carry in amps and equipment while me and Hank and Wayne do the close work, the wiring and plugging and stuff," Bobo says, ingratiating, his magnetic eye looking nearly human. "C'mon, then," he commands, and the four of them walk outside into the purple and pink and brown mountain sunset, the remarkable sunset you see when you are that much closer to the heavenly bodies involved in the celestial changing of the guard, where the very air gets you high, makes your head tingle at its top as if some bubbles were trying to escape like the gushing froth of a just uncorked champagne bottle, makes your lungs choke out giggles.

In among forties-style office buildings (no chrome, no brown reflecting glass), restaurants, and shops stands the anomaly, the obvious recent addition making passersby yearn for the good taste of the old days. A small, charcoal-colored building with the modern architect's disdain for the crassness of corners: everything curves, the places where the walls meet, the entryway (of course down two steps, making the whole affair seem subterranean and very hip), the atrocious roof which rises half-domed like some Kremlin reject, and, certainly, no windows. Above the sunken, concave doorway like a mouth, the sign seems to bloom like a series of mushrooms from the loamy surface of the building: HOLLYWOOD, each letter gigantic, each made up of not neon, not paint, but thousands of tiny, clearglass light bulbs with golden filament inside so that the letters seem to pulsate when viewed from more than twenty feet away, hurt your eyes when viewed from underneath, make the interior of the club seem gloomy by comparison, a sought effect, the slow adjustment of eyes taken into consideration by nouveau-decadent designers trying for a cross between Hollywood in the twenties and Berlin in the thirties; in smaller letters, half the size, right after the HOLLYWOOD and hardly noticeable in comparison, *Cafe* written in script and light-bulb-dotted just like its big brother, almost an afterthought. A rock and roll palace in Denver named the Hollywood Cafe would be a natural except for one thing: the absolute dearth of rock and roll talent passing through these parts. Young people come and sit at the small, modern California-style tables, buy piña coladas, and more often than not listen to recorded music because the Hollywood can't get anyone to come and play. So the unheralded arrival of the Ungrateful Wretches, certainly no big name, no record company backing, no album to plug, creates an instant stir, causes joints of Colombian marijuana to light up in the club manager's office, causes contracts to spring from file drawers, hands to shake, and an instant three-night gig to materialize better than any phony medium can summon into being the requisite ectoplasm hand over her wired crystal ball. As the bear and Hank and Wayne and Bobo cart equipment from the Datsun and the bus into the club, a small crowd of modishly tattered young people gathers, the box office opens mysteriously and a line begins to form, the air grows thick and sweet with the smell of marijuana as hands touch furtively in the ritual passing of the glowing ciggy. With darkness, the crowd grows larger, obviously stoned or the gleaming, living, hideously glowing Hollywood sign would deter them with promises of permanent eye damage similar to that gotten from watching the slow path of a solar eclipse.

Hank and Wayne wolf down hamburgers in front of the dressing room mirrors lit just like the ostentatious Hollywood sign: potential gigs always make them hungry, especially when they've been driving and smoking all day. Bobo, unaffected by this syndrome because of his dog eye, because of his more sensitive, more hostile, more excitable nature (closer to that of a trapped beast, of a leopard in a zoo), paces back and forth from the open door of the dressing room to the mirrored area taken by Hank, Wayne, and their hamburgers, hamburger wrappings, discarded bits of bun, condiment containers, salt and pepper packets, crumpled straw snakes. His cowboy boots, worn only at show times, clatter on the tile floor in the four-four rhythm so that the bear, even in bondage, shakes his hips. The bear's arms stretch to their utmost wingspan, each wrist tied with a long red ribbon, the ends of which the twins alternately hold in their teeth and in their hands as they try to lace the bear up to two tambourines. After many attempts, the bear has shown himself to be pitifully unable to hold tambourines, even one tambourine, and dance at the same time. By a gross contortion of his hands, he can hook his claws into a tambourine, but when he dances, they fly off like discuses, and the club wishes to avoid lawsuits and other related disturbances. Bobo suggested a single tambourine as the answer, but when the bear mustered his all in concentration to hold the small instrument between his flattened, pressing paws, his eyes crossing from strain as if the line if his vision, unimpaired and focused, keeps the thing in the air, he could not dance a step, dance flowing from a free-floating, unencumbered brain, certainly not from a bear brain intent upon levitation: he looked like a bear hero out of Ovid's *Metamorphoses,* about to turn into a tree, already half-rooted and growing a pelt of bark. So he ends up getting tied to the tambourines, the red ribbon going once around his wrist, then threaded through the holes of the tambourine, then down through a couple of digits and around the wrist again, uncomfortable and itchy, but Bobo says that a purely visual member of the band, a non-music maker, cannot be allowed; that everyone must contribute to the total auditory aesthetic; this sounds reasonable to everyone, and the bear accepts the handcuffing with docility and strain.

"Hey, Wayne won't mind sharing percussion with you, will ya?" Hank asks, making peace though no altercation exists. Wayne smiles and stuffs the last bit of his third hamburger into his widened mouth.

"The club manager really likes the idea of the bear," Bobo says. "He's sure we're the first rock and roll band with a nonhuman member, a real breakthrough. He says that if it goes okay tonight, and if one of you chicks screws him, that he'll do what he can about getting us a recording contract."

"Hey, really?" Hank says.

"I hope you told him to get lost," Cassy says, putting her fist up so that the bear's lace job becomes suspended in midair for the moment.

"You lousy pimp," Polly says. Before they begin speaking in their own language, spitting out consonants like sunflower seed shells, Bobo holds his hands up in the air placatingly.

"Just kidding," he says, though he keeps his dog eye turned to the floor. "That kinda stuff doesn't happen anymore. Unfortunately."

"He doesn't mean it," Wayne says, though this gets lost in a garbled mass of half-chewed hamburger.

"Doesn't matter," Hank says, "doesn't matter. Tonight's gonna be groovy, guaranteed. Who's gonna sing?"

"Not me," they say spontaneously together, then giggle and speak in code, words full of *z*'s sounding like male epithets; their complete lack of awareness of the real world during their secret conversation makes the bear invisible, the classic sensation of "pinch me, I must be dreaming," though in the bear's case he jiggles his toes in an unconscious affirmation of his existence: "I dance, therefore I am (*Salto ergo sum*)."

"What is this, a mutiny?" Bobo asks, throwing his hands up in the air, his hands which seem to the bear to wear white masks, which seem as incongruous as his dog eye. "Someone's gotta sing, the contract spells out two female singers to perform on alternating nights. The bear's not gonna sing, and I can't do all those pseudo-Joplin numbers, I'd break my throat. Shit, you know how long it's been since we had a decent gig?"

"No, how long?" Polly asks sweetly, as if seeking the answer to a troubling riddle. The bear perceives the rise in tension in the room as a human would be aware that the temperature has suddenly gone up twenty degrees: the fur on the back of his neck prickles, his muscles tense, his heartbeat accelerates in preparation for flight or fight, his head clears out fast as if someone had just turned on a wind machine, cobwebs shiver on their moorings, images flee, until a big blank space exists between his ears like a blank page inserted into a typewriter waiting for the first words to be written upon it, a tabula rasa, self-erasing, anticipating danger to imprint itself with rapidity, and with the grace of the kill. Bobo's arms flutter for an instant, wings or weapons, either way out of control. Wayne's chest becomes concave, his face pallid and hard as dry cement. Hank remains expressionless and interested as a sports commentator ready to describe one prize-fighter beating another's head to the consistency of mashed bananas. The bear's blood hammers through his heart as top speed, sent from there to assignment at one of the vital organs to wait for death, though the preparation proves to be unnecessary, kind of a hot dog gesture his body can't resist, like a diver's double-gainer with a half twist when a simple swan would do.

"Oh, for heaven's sake, I'll sing." Cassy sighs. "You guys take everything so seriously." The bear's body deflates, blood seeking out normal paths so that his legs and arms feel full of armies of ants rushing to the remains of a picnic; Bobo, too, resembles an inflated balloon let loose, allowed to whoosh and sputter and shrink and wrinkle into a feigned old age, his predator's body, after the rage and readiness to pounce, flaccid and directionless, his cowboy boots silent upon the tile floor.

"Hey, all right," Hank says, as if he has just engineered a world disarmament treaty. "I knew everything was gonna be far out. Maybe I'll even play the stand-up in a couple of numbers tonight."

"Man," Bobo says, wrath still evident upon his face, dog eye blooming darker than ever, "anybody plays that piece of wood, it's me. You just ain't no stand-up player yet, dude. Anyhow, I don't think Colorado's ready for a rock band with a stand-up bass. They just want to boogie."

The bear moves his arms with deliberation, listening to the tinkling of the tambourines (the image of a small gray hare caught in the steel shark jaws of a forest trap flies across his movie-screen consciousness) that attach to his wrists by pretty red ribbon. "When do we go on?" he asks, always professional. As if sleepwalking, moving through a dream without a sound, motion slightly slowed, Polly begins to fix Cassy's hair, to paint her eyes and cheeks, then speaks in a soft, singsong, mysterious voice which might be a Hindu prayer. Hank and Wayne nibble leftover fries.

"This bear's the only one of you who's right on," Bobo says, his voice high-pitched and dangerous. He throws his arms around the bear's arms and chest in a wild embrace from which the bear cannot free himself, his paws useless because of tambourine shackles. "You all think that all you gotta do is smoke dope and talk cool and you magically become rock and roll musicians. From now on this bear's my main man, and all the rest of you are amateurs."

"I've always taken my work seriously," the bear says, shimmying his captive shoulders within Bobo's grasp.

Wayne's eyes grow clouded with liquid and he says, "I never claimed to be Ginger Baker, or even Ringo Starr," but Hank's noisy animation drowns him out: Hank stomps up to Bobo, who must loose the bear in case he needs his fists to defend himself.

"I practice that stand-up every day, man, and I drive our equipment around in that hot little car while you get the bus, and I put up with those babbling chicks and I even found the bear who's now your main man, man," Hank yells to Bobo's magnetic eye which seems to be the seat of his consciousness, at least as far as conversation is concerned.

"We're not supposed to fight until we all become millionaire superstars with differing artistic visions," Wayne says.

The bear works and reworks this collection of syllables through the maze of his brain, much as a computer juggles an insoluble problem, sure that the answer lies in some unexplored region, before it overheats and throws up the tilt sign: Bobo and Hank look at Wayne as if they might have to beat him up, but then their shoulders relax from punch-out posture and Hank smiles into Bobo's dog eye, which fades from a deep chocolate brown-black to its normal medium brown.

"Right," Bobo says. "We split up after we make our first million a piece, and then all cut solo albums using the Grateful Dead as sidemen."

"Well, I'm ready," Cassy says, emerging from the dream like a butterfly from a cocoon, her hair curling on many levels like a diagram of strata, eyes kohled so that they look huge, cheeks reddened, her mole painted black and with tiny lines radiating out from it as if it were a black star in a pale firmament. "When do we go on?"

"Any minute, sweetheart," Bobo says, his voice all syrup, all 1940's Hollywood agent: incongruous for a black man with a dog eye. "Everything's set up on stage. All we need is for you to wail your little head off. Bear, can you handle those tambourines all right?"

"Yes, but I'd feel better if I knew your songs," the bear says, his hands feeling like they belong to some other bear, a classic horror-film ploy in which a concert pianist turns into a psychopathic killer because of an unfounded (who knows—?) belief that grafted onto his own musical wrists are criminal paws full of hatred for mankind.

"No time," Bobo says. "Just wing it for tonight, and tomorrow we'll rehearse. It's not like we're doin' Mozart's concertos or anything. It's real old fashioned rock and roll, I thought you had that in your blood."

"Hey, no prob for the bear man, man, you saw how this guy can dance, he's hot stuff," Hank says.

"I'll do my best," the bear says, waiting for his legs to readjust to the demands of reality.

The sound of the applause ricochets around the small wooden room until it comes to resemble a full-fledged echo, ringing and buzzing with resonance in the bear's ears. Then a knock on the door, a real percussion solo which straightens all their spines and sends Hank's hands in a simulated bass riff on an invisible instrument, a kind of warm-up exercise. The bears needs no warm-up (artists at the pinnacle of their profession don't need to practice, to warm up, to rehearse: whatever they do is art, transcending time and place and circumstance. The bear, unaware of this, knows that Dance pulses through his veins, sees no separation between himself and the Dance, feels the Dance to be an inherent portion of himself, his soul, whatever the most basic unit of bear-ness might be); he follows Bobo out onto the stage of the Hollywood Cafe, and senses the prescience of many beings sitting out behind the blinding lights as the musicians and the singer take their places by the already set-up microphones. Confused, startled by the assortment of equipment, the lights, the invisible audience, the bear stands at the edge of the stage until Bobo whistles in a high clear, nearly audible dog whistle which the other members of the band don't seem to hear; when the bear looks at him, he inclines his head to the right of Cassy, where the bear then stations himself in a readiness to boogie, to dance.

"How you're all doin' out there?" Hank yells, one arm upraised, at the audience.

"All right!"

"Fucked up!"

"Rock and roll!" come voices from various parts of a room the size of which the bear cannot gauge, topless and bottomless and of infinite depth: like the light of the sun unfiltered by prismatic layers of atmosphere, the lights sting his eyes with blackness, make the world a world of shadows, of stark blacks and whites like the reversed world of photographic negatives. Cassy, the nearest one to him and the only one he can clearly make out, wears a startling halo, a thin shimmering nimbus surrounding her being like an aura, so pale yellow that it nears white, moving with her like another, ethereal layer of skin which must disappear in daylight, seeable only in the heightened atmosphere of performance and of music. The others move slowly, darkly, like black holes in the space of the stage; when a couple of trial chords and notes sound out to test the hookups and the amps the bear leaps into the air, his tambourines clattering, because the music surrounds him, hammers in upon his sensitive ears, feels like the pressure of water, twenty feet beneath the surface, to his body. The two shadows that are Hank and Bobo nod to one another, and move in western shoot-out parody.

"Ya ready?" Hank yells again, and rhythmic clapping comes from the infinite room, not from all of it, part reticent, involved in something else, not yet giving themselves to the mere promise of music, but enough. "Far out!" he yells, and the opening riffs cut the bear's ears.

The first chords, familiar, full of cultural resonance, send the bear's knees moving in and out sensually before he can even perceive the barrage of noise coming at him: from behind, out of the huge stack of amps, from in front, from the small screened boxes that send the sound of the music as heard by the audience back at the musicians, from everywhere, bouncing off ceilings, floors, faces, tables. The music frees him of the idea of tambourines, his hands flying off into the air like eagles; his ears straighten, his neck grows limp, fluid, his hips cut the air as a mermaid's propel her through her thick liquid environment. When his heels Mash Potato, his arms windmill so that the tambourines ring out, he's lost in the music, an unconscious dancing machine; the lyrics begin and he's in heaven. The audience whistles, stamps, then as if sudden, spontaneous inspiration claps along, the perfect, catchy beginning to a rock show: a woman singing "Johnny B. Goode," an unwritten rule broken immediately, nothing rock and roll audiences like better than iconoclasm. Cassy's voice, high, strident, on a rocky edge of something not human, something akin to the howlings and bayings of coyotes, something barely controlled: how it sends shivers up and down the bear's spine, how it twists his back into dancing postures never before invented, how it rolls his eyes back into his head as if trance is imminent, as if the whole world were this voice, as if all senses combined into one to tickle his ears past pleasure into a new, unknown realm where he can only dance off the druglike effects of this laser beam of sound, dance unceasingly until it might end.

The bear Boogalooes his whole body down Funky Broadway, his arms blocking arrows of sound that tingle and sting his skin way down past the fur, but this seems much too tame, too loose, too laid back a dance to go with this voice, and his bear butt snaps in and out, suggestive and quick, while his arms Monkey, the tambourines punctuating Cassy's singing with their four-four clatter. His knees grow weak, so he Jerks down into a slouching posture, his hands shivering at the tops of his arms, high as they can go, like captive butterflies; he rises with a leap, his legs scissoring, then falls into a split that defies gravity as it drags him back up to standing with its own momentum which sends him Twisting, outrageous calves and thighs and hips moving in contrasting directions.

Cassy sings, about the country boy, railroad tracks, rhythms of the train, guitar in a gunny sack, which catapults the bear up unto the sound-waving air again until he falls with his shoulders and upper back arching, then touching the ground while his hips and legs remain elevated and his arms backstroke wildly, punishing the tambourines, gyrating his hips like a supine Elvis. And she sings the *go-go-goes* in this song-dream of splendid virtuosity, and the bear stands again, this time with languor, all grace, and starts a Freddy, arms tracing circles in the air, legs shaking loose, thigh not attached to hip, calf free from the bondage of knee, foot tied to ankle by a rubber band. Each new dance feeling like it could last forever, like it could consume him with its perfection, its fullness, but the song moves on from verse to chorus and back to verse, and the bear's body tells him in muscle twitches and unknown spasms that he too must move on, that a dance of all one step is not the Dance.

With his head rolled back as far as it can go, his elbows swinging and strutting, he slides into a high-kneed Stomp, one foot kicking out in front of the other in parody of forward movement, a bear mime practicing his walking against the wind. Cassy's voice lifts higher with each chorus, the effect that of a rocket straining to escape the shackles of earth's offensive, limiting gravity, to escape to the void cruise of space, to infinite possibilities, and she points her child's chin at the ceiling to hit the notes, her neck showing strained and thin. Each word a scream, a howl, a curse, a moan lifting the bear off the stage like sudden wings, turning his mime into a crushing back bend, then carrying him up on his toes, on ballet pointe for instant, before the flow of the dance resumes as if nothing but a dream has interrupted it. For the last verse he falls to his knees, shimmying his hips and shoulders while his arms Swim every stroke of the civilized world, the butterfly, the crawl, the backstroke, the breaststroke, the tambourines going crazy with the delirium of underwater, his knees numb to the hardwood, his feet twitching in air and rotating on his ankles, the movement fast and unrelated to reality like the flicking of a sleeping cat's tail.

Cassy sings, her hips swinging, her back arched and sensitive to the crackling of her own voice. She looks over at the bear, at his holy-rolling, grabs the mike from its stand and struts over to him, doing her own brand of the Dance, California-style, all limbs loose and sensual, each move of the hips a rehearsal for sexual encounter. The bear senses her nearness before he sees her, the electricity of his performance creating a radar aura around him as potent as the electric fences that protect the mansions of wealthy paranoiacs. With a motion as lithe as the snap of a whip, he leaps up and dances next to her, their steps unique but in tandem until as if by accident, by the slightest miscalculations, their hips brush, right to left, and the image of lightening striking both bodies simultaneously crosses the bear's black-as-outer-space consciousness, his eyes nearly blinded by the metaphor, and he whirls around, a full three sixty, and does it again, this time left to right, and Cassy swings into him with the ease of a pendulum, then swings away, dancing a few light, febrile steps of her own, unnamed steps without conscious inspiration, separate from art unlike the bear's but with magnetic, sexual appeal no bear could duplicate (sexual suggestion for bears being a whiff of something on a breeze; but the bear feels lightheaded as he sees her hips slowly circle above her legs, as lissome as the rings of Saturn about their unchanging, luminous center, feels a tingling starting in his legs rather than his spine, a chill calling for the right tender touch, the cure for the fever). They bump hips again, side to side, then away with an intricate walking Funky Chicken with the knees, Mashed Potato with the heels, then back, butt to butt, then Swimming away, side to side while Bobo strums, plucks, pounds on the electrified strings of his gleaming instrument as high-pitched band ear-cutting as Cassy's screaming voice but with the metallic edge, the machine hum that might cause dogs to run wailing into the night after a phantom fire engine. The emblematic riffs that began the instrumental bridge sound again, and Cassy plants her feet as if her voice comes from her whole body, or as if she were no more than an antenna, a lightning rod, a receiver and transmitter for this voice which is her essence, her audible souls sprung out through her mouth:

> *Go, go Johnny, go, go, go Johnny go*
> *Go, oh Johnny B. Goode,*

and the bear whirls on a single toe, his arms outstretched and vibrating the tambourines, a gorgeous pirouette liberated from the music, from the corporeal limitations of the body, before he falls straight as a two-by-four to the ground, his arms catching him in the ultimate pushup, then catapulting him up again where his legs scissor, then fall into a perfect split when his body lands without a sound just as the last chord, the last tremulous echoing of Cassy's voice, bounces off the back wall, the ceiling, the teeth of smiling and yelling faces and flutters to the stage at his feet like an exhausted carrier pigeon.

"All right!" Hank yells through a barrier of screams, thrown napkins, whistles, through aircraft and antiaircraft, the aftermaths of the music as noisy and reminiscent of movie apocalypse as the music itself. "Rock and Roll!" Hank yells.

Cassy stands at the mike waiting, untransformed, a regular small woman without her secret identity as double agent; the bear remains split, legs like clock hands pointing to an early evening hour, his body limp, tambourines silent. What *danseur noble* would be required to solo immediately after a pas de deux? But when the first chords of the next song sound, the bear knows without knowing that his legs will propel him up, up again, that he will soar with the joy of Dance and forget the limitations of muscles and bones, that his eyes will close and his tongue will loll and the music will run through his veins in place of blood, faster than blood, jet propelled and outside the bounds of all natural laws, of the inevitability of gravity and death.

ROCK AND ROLL IS HERE TO STAY

Bigger Than Jesus

lucinda ebersole

ONE MORNING SAMUEL WINKLER WOKE UP in bed and looked down and discovered he was a Beatle.

Wipe that smarmy I've-read-Kafka look off your face. I didn't say he looked down and discovered he was a beetle—I said a Beatle! With a capital "B."

A Fab Four capital "B."

A capital John, Paul, George, and Sammy "B."

That's right. John, Paul, George and Sammy! Who did you *think* he would replace—John? Oh sure, have you ever heard one song that Sammy has ever written? Of course not. And furthermore, Sammy is not sleeping with that Yoko chick, no matter how weird the story gets.

Paul is out. Paul is dead. Ok, he's not dead yet. Maybe he never was. But Paul is the cute one. Sammy is definitely not the cute one. Beside, Sammy can't write music. I told you this already, so try to keep up. If you think doing it with Yoko would freak Sammy out, just imagine what it would be like if he started hanging around with some maharishi dude. Sammy and an old gray-haired Indian guy preaching religion in an airport of your choice. No way. Not my Sammy. So all that's left is Ringo. Besides, last one in, first one out. So Sammy is now the fourth Beatle.

If Sammy was really a sixties kinda guy, he would be thinking, "Wow, man, am I tripping." But Sammy is not a sixties kinda guy,

234 · lucinda ebersole

which makes waking up as a Beatle pretty fucking strange. Sure, Sammy said it over and over again, "I wish I'd been around in the sixties," but he didn't really mean it. He never once said, "Gee, maybe one day I'll wake up and be a Beatle." It was a primitive nostalgia thing. Sammy longed for sex without condoms, LSD, watered-down heroin, the kind that didn't blow your head off the first go round. Sammy longed for bell bottoms, Twiggy, and marches where the blacks and whites and Jews were all in it together. Sammy wanted to fight injustice, fight the war, and fight the establishment. It all sounded so cool.

Sammy wanted to be in the romanticized sixties. The television sixties. The Janis, Jimi, Jim Morrison, died-before-our-time sixties. The only real person from the sixties Sammy knew was the father of a cheerleader he dated. He was balding and sold insurance and he told Sammy about being at Altamont and Woodstock. He would rub his balding head every time he told the story of listening to Hendrix play the national anthem. He would say, "There'll never be another president like JFK." He would say he could remember exactly where he was when he heard JFK was shot.

"The Cubans killed him," he would say.

"It was the Mob who killed him," his wife would say.

Sammy thought it was Lee Harvey Oswald.

Sammy remembered hearing his great-grandfather talk the same way about FDR.

"There'll never be another FDR," his grandfather would say.

Sammy would agree. They found a cure for polio. There'll never be another president who will be able to hide a major illness. With today's press, a president can't hide a hemorrhoid or an ingrown toenail. There'll never be another president who married his cousin and if Eleanor had been young in the sixties, she would have never married Franklin, she'd have become a Lesbian Avenger. But the old man remembered where he was the day FDR died.

Sammy remembered where he was the day Kurt Cobain died. He was at the McDonald's and it came on the radio. Kurt put a gun in his mouth at about the same time Sammy was putting the Big Mac in his. But Sammy couldn't imagine a day when he would sit back at the dinner table and tell a bunch of kids that he knew where he was the day Kurt Cobain died. He was hoping to have more of a life.

The past was not what Sammy had expected for the future, but it sure gave him a leg up on everybody else. Think of the possibilities. He could stop Janis and Jimi and Jim at least one time. He could call the Secret Service and tell them that the Cubans or the Mob or maybe LBJ but definitely Lee Harvey Oswald was going to kill the President. Or he could just revolutionize rock and roll. Sammy jumped out of bed and headed for the Cave Club.

"You're late," John says to Sammy. Then Paul shows up late. John is really pissed off and he screams at Paul.

"You're late," John says.

"Yea, yea, yea," Paul says.

"That's it," Sammy says. "Yea, yea, yea."

Paul and John look at each other, shaking their heads.

"We should've kept Pete Best," John says. John won't give it up and he turns to Paul. "What have I got to do, hold your hand?"

Sammy says, "I want to hold your hand!"

"Jesus, John, another Stu Sutcliff," Paul says. That really pisses John off.

"We are never going to get anywhere with this fucking band," John says.

"John," Sammy says, "one day you'll say we're bigger than Jesus."

John tells Sammy to shut up. He's got an idea, a "look." He wants the band to slick their hair back in greasy DA's and wear motorcycle jackets.

"No way, " Sammy says. "The fifties are over." He says they should wear shaggy hair. Hair that looks like someone put a bowl over their heads and cut. Paul agrees because he's in one of those moods to disagree with anything John says. George's girlfriend says she can cut hair with a bowl and soon they all have these similar bobs. John says they'll never sell any records. He wants to play it safe and cover old Little Richard hits.

"No way," Sammy says. "New stuff. We need new stuff that you and Paul write."

John says Paul can't write and Paul says he can and sings, "I want to hold your hand." John says its in the wrong key. George says its catchy. Sammy insists they play it in Hamburg.

Sammy had never been more than a hundred miles from home and now he was in Hamburg.

"Play the song," Sammy says.

John looks at Paul and they begin. Paul can't get used to the hair-cut and he keeps shaking his head. The more he shakes his head, the louder the girls scream. The girls scream. It's an amazing thing. They never screamed at the Little Richard songs. They never screamed at the slicked-back hair. Now they're screaming. The record company's screaming, too. They can't press enough vinyl.

"This song is going to be Number One," Paul says.

"We're going to be rich," George says.

"We're going to be on *The Ed Sullivan Show*," Sammy says.

"Don't get your hopes up," John says.

Their manager bought the boys matching suits to match their matching hair. Their debut album went gold. They were booked on a tour of the United States. When the plane landed you could hear the roar of the crowd over the roar of the engines. John looked out the window and saw thousands of screaming fans.

"We are bigger than Jesus," he said.

Girls screamed and fainted. Cameras recorded the chaos. The Fab Four laid on the floorboards of the cars as they were smuggled into the theater where *The Ed Sullivan Show* was filmed. Ed didn't know what to do with Fab Four. He had survived Elvis, but this was much bigger. Girls screamed at him when he arrived at the theater. They wept when he introduced them.

"Ladies and Gentleman. From Liverpool, England. The *Beatles.*"

Sammy looked out at the crowd. All the faces ran together until he saw her. A familiar face. She looked like the cheerleader he had dated in a past life. Sammy wondered if she could be her mother.

"It was the high point of my young life," she had said about the time she had seen the Beatles.

Sammy saw her again as they left the theater. He reached out and touched her hand, holding it for a brief moment. She was more beautiful than her daughter would be, but he couldn't tell her that. He couldn't tell any of them. He couldn't save JFK or John. He couldn't save Janis or Jimi or Jim. He couldn't save Kurt. Sammy worried for a minute, then he thought, "What the hell." Sammy Winkler wasn't put on this earth to save the world or to save himself. There was a time Sammy didn't have a clue what he was on this earth for, but that was then. Now Sammy knows. He is going to change the way people listen to music. He is going to change music itself. He is going to be bigger than Jesus.

Brazzaville Teenager

bruce jay friedman

HE HAD ALWAYS FELT THAT PERHAPS a deathbed scene would unite them; he and his father would clutch at each other in a sicklied fusion of sweetness and truth, the older man dropping his lifelong cool, finally spilling the beans, telling Gunther what it was all about, philosophy, stories of extramarital rascality, the straight dope on how much dough he had to the penny, was Mom any good in the hay. Did it hurt to be old? Was death a breeze?

This may or not have been a deathbed scene. You could not tell and perhaps that was the trouble. His father hung before him in harnesses and nettings, elaborate pullied contraptions. Two weeks before, the old man had suddenly collapsed into himself, accordion-style, pinching off nerves. Undreamed of pain. A classic new high. He had to be kept stretched out indefinitely. Later, they would see. Gunther pulled up a chair, not too close.

"How's it feel, Dad?"

His father faced the ceiling, chin high, as though he wore the world's tightest collar, a steel ascot.

"It's no picnic."

"What do they say?" asked Gunther.

"What do they know? This one gives you one kind of pill. Then you get another. They're nice guys. You should see how young they are these days. Clean-cut, you know. Not wise guys. And you'd be surprised. They think nothing of treating a man much older than

238

they are. Way older. I'd say I'm a good thirty, thirty-five years older than one fellow they had working on me. I told him and he laughed, but it didn't bother him."

Did you ever make it with an actress, Gunther wanted to ask. Ever catch a dose? What's the worst thing you ever pulled? Let him dare ask one of these: his father would somehow get out of the contraptions and smack him in the mouth.

"You'll be out of there in no time." Said Gunther.

"I'll tell you one thing about this," said the old man. "It's bad, very bad. It's one of those things where they don't know. Don't ever get this, kid. You're a hundred per cent better off without it. To tell you the truth, I think I'm finished."

"Don't say that, Dad. You'll get better."

Later that night Gunther thought of his father's enlarged knuckles. The contraptions had not bothered him quite that much. Somehow you could get free of them. The old man's body had been whittled all the way down, but there were force-feedings. You could get back the weight. The knuckles were the tip-off, though. Once knuckles got out of hand, you were washed up. Still later that night, the idea came to him that only if he Gunther, were to debase himself, to do something painful beyond belief, the most embarrassing act he could imagine, only then would his dad recover. Grimly, he shopped along the noisy streets of his mind. The instant his plan formed, he wanted to tear it from his head.

The following day, Gunther, a voucher clerk, was summoned to the office of his boss, Hartman, a tall gray-haired man with steady bomber-pilot eyes. Although Hartman had never scolded him, Gunther feared the man, came to work an hour early each morning so there would be no chance of a time-clock slip-up. The boss's quiet gaze had sent others in the office writhing into colitis attacks.

Before Hartman could speak, Gunther himself raced into words. "Sir, if you don't mind, I've got this thing going on. My father's very sick, I've never really asked you for anything, but I've got this thing to ask."

"I'm sorry," said Hartman. "All right, go ahead."

Gunther took a deep breath, as though about to swim a pool underwater. Perhaps if he just asked, just said it, that alone would keep his father's fever down.

"The only thing that can possibly save him is if you make a recording with Little Sigmund and the Flipouts, three kids, doing the background doo-wah, doo-wahs and the second-chorus yeh, yeh, yehs."

"I'm not following any of this," said Hartman, his calm reaction throwing Gunther into panic.

"The recording is called 'Brazzaville Teenager.' It's about a young boy whose father is a mercenary and gets sent to the Congo. The boy goes along and writes this letter back to his girl in the States, talking about how great it was surfing and holding hands and now here he is in Brazzaville. Little Sigmund and the Flipouts are a new group, with only one other recording to their credit, 'Berlin Wall Teenager.' If this goes, the idea is coming up with an album of teenagers at the world's trouble spots. In any case, you're involved in only one record, Mr. Hartman."

"You're still not coming through," said Hartman, throwing his legs up on his desk, a movement that terrified Gunther, as did most of Hartman's movements. "What's the connection between all this and your father's sickness?"

"I can't explain it," said Gunther, amazed he was still talking. "There is just one. I've learned that if I can get you to do this thing, which of course is way out of your line, the bottling business and everything, Dad will recover."

"What do you mean, you've learned?" said Hartman.

"I know it," said Gunther. "I don't know much, but I do know this. Can we forget the logic part for just a second? I'm asking you to do this thing. It's no fun asking, believe me. I wish I could tell you what I feel like. But will you please do it? I figure I've got one no-questions-asked favor coming."

"Do me a favor," said Hartman, taking his legs down.

"Anything," said Gunther.

"Go back inside and forget you ever made this little speech. You forget it and I promise I'll try to forget it."

At least I came out with it, Gunther thought, as he drove his car aimlessly through Manhattan. For no special reason, he owned a car in the city and had to pay a huge monthly garage bill for it. To get his money's worth, he took it out for pointless drives at night.

If I got myself to say something like that to a boss, there's no limit to what can I do.

His contentment lasted momentarily and before long, he was stifled, out of breath. Hands other than his seemed to sweep the car into a U-turn and out he drove to Westchester. As he entered the Hartman estate, platoons of dogs, signifying great wealth, yipped at his tires. Gunther had heard that worthless brothers-in-law, other no-goods and hangers-on lived in cottages on the grounds; he strained to see them in the darkness. At the main house, Gunther was ushered into the dining room where Hartman and his guests were completing their dinner. "Well, what is it?" said Hartman, pushing back from the table. "He works for me."

"One would think the poor fellow had driven all the way from Nairobi," said a bushy-haired man in a witty Viennese accent, to which the other guests tumbled back with laughter.

"You'll have to forgive Mr. Ortberg," said Mrs. Hartman, a charming woman with many jeweled coils at her neck. "He has trouble keeping his untrammeled sense of humor in tow."

Leaving the table, Hartman took Gunther off to a side room. "They're going to press the platter at 5 P.M. tomorrow," said Gunther. "Look I don't know how it would be if my father died. Maybe I'd be casual. Maybe I'd really fly off my cork. All I know is that I saw him, I don't think he weighs a hundred pounds, and I really want to have him around. Not that we ever exchanged two words that meant a goddamned thing in all our lives. Hell, I've talked more intimately with you, Mr. Hartman, and you know how I've kept my distance in the last eight years. Anyway, I really don't want to lose him. You should see the way they've got him rigged up. There's nothing left of him."

"Gunther, look, I've been in the bottling business for thirty-three years. Anyone will tell you I've never fired a man on the spot—"

"Why don't you go along with him, darling," said Mrs. Hartman, who had slipped into the room. "The poor fellow's obviously quite upset. It will cost you very little and it might be fun. My husband told me about it this morning, Mr. Gunther."

Hartman's jaw bunched up, then softened as he put his arm around his wife's waist, embarrassing Gunther. "Now what is it you want me to do again?" he asked.

"The doo-wah, doo-wah and yeh, yeh, yeh backgrounds, Mr. Hartman," said Gunther. "The A & R man at the studio will clue you in. Oh, Christ, thanks a lot, the both of you. Thank you, Mrs. Hartman. Sometimes you just meet someone out of the clear blue sky and they'll go along with you, no matter how crazy you sound."

In the handsomely paneled penthouse office of Conrad Jaggers, lunch hour the following day, Gunther momentarily lost his nerve. Meeting the young president of Dirty Bird Recordings at a bar the previous week, Gunther had no idea Jaggers headed such an elaborate operation. The pimpled young fellow sat on a fanback chair in a blizzard of phone calls, memos, stenographers; there seemed no way for Gunther to get back on the footing they had so quickly established at the bar, three in the morning, two fellows drifting quickly into a kind of cabaret intimacy, sliding capsule wisdoms back and forth around the table.

"Fantastic to see you, Gunther," said the young man when he had finally cleared his office.

"Nice to see you, Mr. Jaggers. I mean Conrad. Look, I'll go right into it. It would be easier to say this if it we were back at the bar. My dad's dying and I need a favor. It's got to be on trust alone, one of those that guys at a bar do for each other. You know that recording you told me about, 'Brazzaville Teenager.' You hummed it in my ear."

"We go on that this afternoon."

"Well, I want you to let a friend of mine work in with the Flipouts, you know the doo-wahs and yeh, yehs."

"You mean a singer buddy of yours just needs a fast credit, doesn't monkey around, that it?"

"Something like that," said Gunther. "What do you say."

"Let me meditate," said Jaggers, putting his head on the table. "Yogi." Thirty seconds later, he lifted his head. "Done," he said. "Like you say, two guys at a bar, one asks the other a favor. Operate that way and you never go wrong."

Later in the day, Gunther arrived at the recording studio with Hartman, who was introduced to Little Sigmund and the Flipouts, sullen, empty-eyed boys with patched, beginning beards.

"You stand in here, Hartman baby," said Jaggers, "between Raymond and Alfredo. You know about the doo-wahs. Now listen, can you girl it at all?"

"He hasn't done that much work," said Gunther.

"What do you mean?" asked Hartman.

"You know, the falsetto thing. If we can get that working in the record, we can cut through all the strings I plan to use. Anyway, try it on the first press, you know, do a high-pitched little-boy thing and if it works, we'll keep it. Ready, Sigmund? Ready, kids?"

I'm writing you, my darling,
From war-torn Brazzaville...

"I do hope it wasn't too much of an inconvenience," said Gunther, driving his boss to the railroad station.

"I'd rather not go into it," said Hartman. "The music does get to you, though, in a way I can't quite explain." Gunther drove carefully, his back stiff. How would it be to crack up with a boss inside your car. Cruising along Broadway, he passed a small restaurant with a crowds gathered out front, their eyes on a man in the window tossing flapjacks. Gunther suddenly began to perspire as though vaulted into the middle of a tropical sickness. Pulling on the brakes, he double-parked and then ran round to open his boss's door. "Sir, look," he said. "I know this is unforgivable after what I've put you through, but you've got to go into that store with me."

"Not on your life," said Hartman. "I think I've been jackass enough for one day. Not only that, but if you don't get right back into this car…"

"Where do you want me, on my knees?" said Gunther. "It just came to me that maybe the record wasn't enough. And just one more thing would put over the deal, get my dad out of there clean. I swear to Christ I'll work for a month, no salary. You've just got to go into that window and flip a batch."

"Your job's not worth a plugged nickel," said Hartman, but some people had turned toward the car and Hartman began to ease out of his seat. "I think I'm doing this for my wife," he said as Gunther took his arm and led him through the crowd into the restaurant.

"Christ, this is difficult for me to do," said Gunther, leading Hartman into the window-cooking area. "All right, all right," he said to the performing chef, taking out some new bills he had somehow anticipated he would need, "here's fifty if you let my man toss the next round."

"What have you got, a publicity thing?"

"Never mind," said Gunther, helping Hartman off with his jacket. "What's the matter with this town, doesn't money talk any more?"

A week later, Gunther arrived at the hospital to help his father pack. The old man walked cautiously, with a slight limp, but color had appeared in his cheeks and he had put on a few pounds.

"You know what I like about this place," the old man said. "They do all these things for you and don't charge you a cent. Isn't that a laugh. Not much they don't. Well, what the hell, they got to get paid. Otherwise, how would they run the place. Somebody's got to pay them, am I right?"

"Right, Dad. The important thing is that you are back on your feet."

In the car, the old man said, "I'll take it easy at first. No sense rushing into things. Otherwise you're just back where you started and what was the good."

Gunther spun the car into Central Park, a few miles from where his dad had his apartment. More than ever, Gunther wanted something from the old man, anything. Had he ever stolen anything? Could he still get it up at his age? What about broads? Was Mom the first he'd ever slept with? Had he ever gone to a cathouse?

"Dad," said Gunther.

"What's that?" the old man, whirling suddenly as though he had guessed Gunther's dirty thoughts and might throw a decrepit punch.

"Nothing," said Gunther.

"I thought you wanted something. For a second it sounded like it, but what the hell, everyone's wrong sometimes. The top men in the country."

Gunther double-parked, then helped his father to the apartment. Half an hour later, his father settled, Gunther entered the elevator and pressed the lobby button. But midway, he pulled the emergency switch and screamed up the shaft, " You son of a bitch, do you know what I had to go through to get you on your goddamned feet?"

In Winter the Snow Never Stops

michael covino

It was approaching four p.m. She sat in the living room in her easy chair, her small grey poodle snoozing in her lap, stroking it vaguely and looking out the first story window at the rain—the first real rain of the spring. She was thirty-two, single, unemployed, though she got enough freelance entertainment assignments from the newspaper to keep her going. She was also bright and agreeable—slight, with long, shiny dark hair and pupils so deep and black one could look into them for five or more minutes then come away not knowing if the eyes were blue or brown. Her shoulders hunched gently, as if she were always fearing a blow, and with more self-confidence, or perhaps a job, she'd have been pretty. It was a choppy period and, God knows, she needed the assignments. She needed, too, to keep one foot in the door, as she had for the past two years, hoping that a staff opening would eventually come up. Both the entertainment and the book editors liked her, steering many choice assignments her way. There was testimony to this too—the crates of records and ragged stacks of books, of reviewer's copies, columned high and more than a trifle shakily against all four living room walls: art books, music books, cookbooks, novels, books that she had been meaning to sell for the past two weeks, then two months, then two years.

But this interview had been her idea and now she was chain-smoking. She picked up one of his old album jackets from the floor and wondered what he looked like now. On the jackets he was handsome and stylish, with blue eyes so preposterously earnest you felt on guard for a joke. He dressed neatly, sometimes in a navy blazer and tie, more often in a maroon V-neck sweater with white trim. He wore his hair in a neat black pompadour, not too heavily lacquered or piled too momentarily skyward, and his ears stuck out just enough of an impulsive angle so that he didn't look letter-perfect. In the late 1950s and early 1960s, practicing the still nascent art of rock, he had been one of the best-selling instrumentalists. He'd toured constantly, appeared often on TV—and then, just like that, he'd retired to a cabin in the mountains. And hadn't been heard from in the twenty years since.

At least not until last month when a small but influential nightclub owner persuaded him to give a show. The club had been packed. And consequently his first major tour in twenty years had been hastily organized.

The paper had arranged, through the nightclub, for her to call him at four. Now she waited anxiously. Even more than tossing off an article that would maintain her in good standing with the entertainment editor—the sort of article that always appears and is always the same and whose author hardly matters—she wanted to write something worthy of this legendary figure.

At five to four a fat green iridescent horsefly began buzzsawing the living room—loud, sonorous, richly satisfied hums. Her poodle went wild. She spent the next five minutes with a rolled-up newspaper chasing the fly from bookshelf to phone stand to bookshelf to record player before finally swatting it out the open window, her little poodle yapping madly and leaping up to plant both furry front paws on the windowsill. She noticed that the poodle's hair was matted. A bit rattled, she lit another cigarette, then reached into the crack between the two green corduroy sofa cushions, felt around a bit, and fished out a hard brush clotted with balls of gray dog hair.

Almost immediately, though, she laid the brush down on the arm-rest, went into the kitchen, and returned with a glass of water. She continued to drag nervously on her cigarette, then dug around the layers of clutter on her writing desk for a pen. Then, finally, unavoidably, she crossed the living room to the small telephone table, placed the glass of water and her notebook with its list of questions beside the phone, sat down, picked up the receiver, and began—very meticulously—to dial.

He felt nervous. Standing by the picture window, he watched, with no real pleasure, a small sailboat, its white sail billowing, cutting across the icy waters of the enormous waters of the icy lake. Mountains hemmed the lake on all sides, rugged mountains which ranged in every direction, their snowy upper slopes falling away to great pine-forested ravines through which mountain streams, swelled by the melting snowpacks, splashed and tumbled. The youthful-looking man slowly sipped his vodka-and-tonic. He rarely drank before dinner, in fact, he rarely drank at all, and for someone in his mid-forties he was superbly fit. Right then, though, he didn't feel particularly fit or chipper. He turned to glance at the perfectly still black telephone in the hallway… and at that instant—no, it did-n't ring—at that instant the western sunlight slanting in through the picture window caught his profile in a rather pleasing light, as if the whole arrangement were a studio setup for the press photo of some notable country-and-western singer, now moving handsomely (if with a trace of winsome boyish nervousness) into middle age. Which is to say, he was handsome even if his ears, not quite camouflaged by his longish hair, stuck out a bit.

For the past fifteen years life had been relatively kind—kind, that is, once he'd adjusted to the role of rock royalty of the heroic early years too soon deposed. At the end of that first sweet boisterous passage of life, he had found no horrors waiting in ambush around the bend. He'd known other rock musicians who hadn't been as smart, who'd mishandled their money, who'd been exploited by agents and managers. For him, though, retirement hadn't been all that difficult. His house, reached by beautiful winding mountain roads, was large and spacious, full of windows, and stood at the edge of a high cliff amid a stand of towering tutelary redwoods overlooking the lake. And his hadn't exactly been a recluse's life. There'd been family. Old friends anxious to get out of the city for a weekend or a week—or a month, or two years—often visited. In the winter the area was a popular ski resort, in the summer an equally popular swimming and boating resort.

But then a phone call two months ago had changed everything. A small but influential nightclub owner had asked him to give a show. He hadn't immediately expressed interest, but when the club owner went on to promise that he could put together a backup band of the finest studio musicians in the industry, all longtime admirers of his, he had become interested. His ears perked up. And he had agreed. Then later, he had been amazed when, after the show, several famous rock musicians, all reputed to be unqualified megalomaniacs, had come backstage, completely humble, to pay tribute. It had all been a shock. And he'd realized too, how much he actually missed performing before a live audience as he had until the mid-sixties when the musical invasion from abroad had transformed him, at twenty-four, into a first generation rock relic.

A rich relic. But a relic. He had continued living in the city for a few more years, but he found he'd been forgotten overnight. Album sales, once in the millions, plummeted. He had an increasingly difficult time getting studio recording time, and when he did get it he found that all the delays and frustrations had killed whatever creative impulsive he'd had. So he had made what amounted to a military decision. To retreat. With a minimum of bitterness, he accepted what had happened—indeed, counted his blessings that so much good had been his lot in the first place—and had retired to this comfortable cabin in the mountains.

He glanced at his watch. It was just about four. The nightclub owner had called yesterday to say that a music reporter would be calling him today at four. Now he was even more nervous than he'd imagined. A reporter from the big metropolitan daily was going to call up and interview him—no one had interviewed him in twenty years. He imagined some young stylish woman in her early twenties, someone who liked the new music, a go-getter at the bustling center of a great metropolis's media life; that is, someone who'd been playing in the crib at the height of his popularity (probably cracking her daddy's records over her knobby knee) and so never really knew just how famous he'd been once—and he felt nervous. He wanted so much to have a second chance. He turned from the window with its panoramic lake view and made another vodka-and-tonic.

She was startled when, on the very first ring, she heard a soft and hesitant "Yes?"—none too resonant, none too firm—and suddenly, gratefully she felt relieved. Brushing her hair back from her forehead, she spoke boldly into the receiver, "Hi…"

"So I was pretty amazed," the man's voice came through, "to see the line winding around the block."

"What accounts for the renewed interest in you?"

"Who knows?" A suddenly grumpy silence ensued. "Novelty. Nostalgia. *Bore*dom."

She was taken aback. Testiness tinged his voice. It unnerved her.

She continued asking questions—how did you develop that famous guitar sound? do you think you'll record again? etc., etc.— and he answered carefully. She took a long drag on her cigarette and asked, "What made you move up there?" The question surprised her. She hadn't written it down, nor was it the logical follow-up to any of his answers.

"After going out of style, I continued to live in the city for a while. And I grew more and more depressed. So I moved up here. Up here people didn't make me feel like an old-timer at thirty."

She flinched—perceptibly enough so that her poodle, who lay curled in her lap, glanced up. At thirty-two she was sick of freelancing and wanted a full-time newspaper job in the worst way.

"I've noticed," his voice continued, "that when people get hot in this business they run for about five years. My first string of hits ran from '58 to late in '63—almost five years to the minute. Maybe I'm ready for another five years."

She leaned back into the armchair, depressed, and thought, "Astrological five-year plans. Don't use it. It'll make him sound dumb."

A sound over by the window made her abruptly turn. The neighbor's cat had stuck its furry black-and-white left front paw through her open window and was, quite deliberately, taunting her poodle. Almost simultaneously the poodle bounded out of her lap, yelping madly, and charged across the room.

"Ssssh. Go away "

"Huh?"

"Sorry. Not you. Neighbor's cat."

"Oh."

"Please go on."

He cleared his throat. "Where was I?"

"Uh—?"

"Oh yes. So I'm sick of hearing that rock and roll won't last. In the old days…"

His voice droned on. Her cigarette burned to its filter, so she fitted the receiver snugly against her left shoulder and tapped a cigarette out from the pack. She fumbled a bit lighting it, but then, after two quick restorative drags, immediately balanced it on the ashtray—and begin thinking how pretty it was up there, the snowy mountains, surrounding the enormous blue lake, the vast redwood forests, people probably still skiing. She wondered what he was doing at that moment, whether he was pacing some dark recessive hallway or sitting before a window with a spectacular view of the mountain lake...

In fact, at that moment, he sat by the window watching a motorboat draw a water-skier in trunks across the still freezing cold waters—not just watching but hoping, just a little, that the skier would spill and come up blue.

"So you like it up there?" he heard her ask.

"Of course," he snapped. He abruptly stood up, took a balsamic gulp of his vodka-and-tonic, and tried for a more congenial note. "When things slacked off, I accepted it. I realized I was happy just to be able to sit back and relax a bit. " He sat back down and tried very hard to relax a bit, but kept wondering if he was saying the right things. That five-year stuff had sounded awfully silly to his ears. It had been so long since he'd given an interview and he no longer knew what made good copy. He almost wished he could come right out and ask her to feed him lines. He stared at the mountains across the lake and wondered how bad the runoff would be this year.

"We were all spit and polish in those days," he said. "You couldn't even have a mustache. And of course there were no drugs— or groupies." He added as an afterthought, "In a way it was probably easier." But he thought he detected uncertainty in his own voice.

"Look, I really wish I had things to tell you but I've been living quietly and that's it. I mean I haven't been hitting the bottle, I haven't been shooting up drugs, I haven't even opened up a tourist restaurant or lent my name to a line of concert speakers. I haven't really been doing much of—" He fell silent. He hadn't been interviewed in years...

In her cluttered living room she scanned her notes, silently agreeing that he hadn't really told her anything. Most rock musicians had a stock repertoire of anecdotes that they knew made good copy, but he apparently had been out of circulation for so long, or the rules of the game had changed so radically in the intervening years, that he was completely at sea. She recalled a press conference she'd recently attended where a journalist asked the young musician, who had a reputation for surliness, why he'd even bothered to call a press conference. He'd replied, "So I don't have to talk to you individually. Besides, you all ask the same questions." She—and a few other reporters present—had been delighted. Now she felt sick.

"Listen. Is there a family I could say something about? The paper usually goes for family stuff."

"Well," he said carefully, "There've been several." And she laughed—and he did too—but then she coughed on some cigarette smoke, choked out, "One second," and reached for the glass of water, taking a long therapeutic gulp.

"Better?"

"Better," she said. Then suddenly, "Do you have any press photos?" She was thinking how photos immediately made a story seem more appealing to editors, how they'd be less likely to kill it.

There was a pause. Then he said, "I have to have some made up."

He was so courteous and sweet beneath the gruffness that she really wished she had better material. It had become apparent to her that he hadn't quite figured out what all the revival stuff was about. Suddenly she heard scraping and turned—her poodle emerged from under the green corduroy sofa, cheerfully dragging a week old T-bone.

"It really is beautiful up there," she said thinking aloud.

"For so long I was at the center of things," he said wistfully. She switched the receiver to her other hand—her left hand itched so she scratched it on the table edge. She switched back. He added, "In the winter it doesn't stop snowing."

"Huh?"

"The snow. It doesn't stop. Sometimes I stand in front of my window for hours, completely hypnotized, just watching it snow. The mountains across the lake recede until they're just dim bluish outlines. At times the snow gets so thick that even the nearby red-woods—as sturdy a tree as God ever made—become mere phantoms looming through the veils of snow. It's like a dream world."

"Ummmm."

"I live up here because it's beautiful," he said emphatically.

"I live down here because—" she searched, then had one of her brighter moments "—because it's the only place I can find work." And was rewarded by his laughter.

"Look. Send me the clipping when it comes out. Maybe..." His voice trailed off.

She said yes, of course, they exchanged farewell pleasantries, good-bye—and then she was replacing the receiver in its cradle. She had no idea what her story would be, or if she even had one, yet she didn't feel at a loss. In fact she was feeling a great deal refreshed and knew exactly what to do next. She went into the kitchen and put water on the stove for coffee. She returned to the living room and flipped over the record on the turntable. She squatted alongside her poodle—who immediately relinquished its T-bone then rolled onto its back—and began vigorously scratching its belly. And then, still in her squatting position, she watched the rain as it gently beat down in the new green leaves that brushed her window, and she listened to the music, and kept scratching the poodle's belly—and recalled the last time she'd driven up into the mountains, now more than two years ago, and how it had been snowing when she arrived—from the looks of things had been snowing for years and years—big, soft, fairyland-slow flakes. Her poodle, just a puppy then, had jumped from the car but was startled when it sank right up to its furry gray chin in the unfamiliar stuff. But then the puppy quickly got its bear-ings and began romping happily, if a trifle clumsily, from pine to pine, as though in its secret heart it had known of snow all along. Laughing, she had turned to get her camera from the car but then remembered she'd left it at home. And not far from the car, near where three wooden picnic tables stood buried up to their benches, a raging stream flashed through the steeply banked snow.

Like a Lead Balloon

kevin downs

HAVE YOU EVER BEEN HAUNTED BY A SONG? I don't mean haunted like Bogart in *Casablanca*. I mean haunted like the innocent victim in a horror film who hears an ominous theme right before the axe murderer shows up. This basically describes the feeling I have whenever Led Zeppelin's "Stairway to Heaven" begins. Why this pompous anthem above all others in the annals of classic rock? Sure, I could go on about its confusing lyrics and manipulative arrangement, but in reality my hatred has little to do with the song itself.

It all began in July 1977, a time I remember as the summer of punk and the year that I broke up with my high-school girlfriend, Cindy. I should have known it would never work out. She was a cheerleader and the squeaky-clean daughter of a prominent local businessman. I was the rhythm guitar player in a tone-deaf garage band called the Halfwits. We'd been going out together for almost six months, and as far as I knew we were getting along just fine. She had given in to all my requests to wear fishnet stockings, a black leather jacket, and a studded dog collar when we made love, but when it came to piercing herself in the cheek with a large safety pin, she had no other choice but to stand her ground.

The truth is, she had always been more the knee-socks and wraparound skirt type anyway. You know, like Chuck Berry's Sweet Little Rock and Roller or Buddy Holly's Peggy Sue. That's what it was like in the suburbs where we grew up. Every once in a while the Stones or some other band would do something to make you think the seventies were really progressive, but life in our generic little WASP community had been basically the same since the late 1950s. People still dreamed of following in the footsteps of their parents, marrying their high-school sweetheart, buying a ranch-style home—all the usual crap.

To me, punk was the battle-cry for a revolution that would change all that. The world would never be the same in its wake. What the world would become, I hadn't a clue, but that's not the point. The point is, I wanted Cindy to feel as passionately about punk as I did, so that when she did the pogo at a Halfwits gig it would mean more than just a quick release for her teenage hormones. But I could have been playing in a Top 40 cover band for all she cared. And it was on the night she decided to dump me for good that the trouble with "Stairway to Heaven" began.

Things seemed pretty usual on that hot Sunday afternoon: I went to band practice around 3:00, dropped a couple of homemade Quaaludes, drank a few beers, and stumbled through an hour of songs with the rest of the Halfwits. But when we stopped for a break, and somebody put on the new Sex Pistols forty-five, and the drummer pulled a handful of oversized safety pins from his pocket, the temptation to make the ultimate punk fashion statement grew too great to resist.

Cindy, meanwhile, was waiting for me to pick her up at the local Younglife meeting—Younglife being this holier-than-thou group of teenagers who got together every Sunday to act like Jesus was cool. So there she was sitting on the floor with the rest of these geeks, singing along with some preordained schmuck strumming an acoustic guitar to, you guessed it, "Stairway to Heaven," when in I walked, with blood splattered all over my Ramones T-shirt, and a safety pin proudly jutting out from just over my jaw.

The place fell so quiet you could have heard a pin drop (but not mine). After the shock wore off, the schmuck on the guitar started acting like he had dealt with misfits like me all the time, and he kicked Cindy and me out on the street. So much for Christian compassion.

Now, I had no problem with "Stairway to Heaven" before then. And although no self-respecting punk would ever admit it at the time, I secretly liked bloated arena bands like Led Zeppelin when I was in high school. But if you think that song sucks today, you should have heard the unplugged version in that church basement. Personally, I still think everyone in that room owes me a debt of thanks for bringing their god-awful wailing to an end.

But Cindy didn't see it quite that way. Since I was still high from the Quaaludes and the rush from piercing myself, she took the keys to my Volkswagen and drove us back to her house. Never had I seen anyone so mad in my entire life, and I tried hard to think of a way to make things up to her. Then, as I followed her past the white picket fence up to her parents' front porch, I fished out a second safety pin I had stashed in my jeans, dropped to one knee and asked her if she wanted to get engaged. For the first time that night she looked me directly in the eye, and as she took the safety pin from my hand, it seemed as if she was actually giving my proposal some serious thought.

There in the gleaming point of that pin were all the differences that ever stood between us. This was a time when anyone, no matter how little talent you had, could pick up a guitar or a camera or a typewriter and become famous. All you had to do was move to the East Village and wait for your muse to come. Was Cindy ready to stop playing punk for pretend and start playing for real? My cheek was hurting like hell as I waited for her to make up her mind.

"Jesus is a fisherman," she declared at last. "I can only pray that he puts his hook in your mouth instead of that safety pin someday."

I nearly barfed all over her, but she slammed the door in my face before I got the chance. I could barely contain my rage. I decided the mind-numbing effect of that "Stairway to Heaven" singalong must have turned her brain to mush, and I started screaming how everyone inside that nice little brick colonial home of hers, including her baby brother and eighty-year-old grandmother, should go fuck themselves. I was going places that Cindy, Jesus, and the rest of these self-righteous creeps could never imagine. My ranting continued, but no one bothered to respond or even cared enough to call the cops on me. All I heard in reply was someone inside turning up the family television. My jaw was hurting too badly to go on much longer. Heartbroken, I staggered back to my beat-up Volkswagen, fell face down in the back seat, and quickly passed out.

I never saw Cindy again after that night. And as the years went by, punk, the revolution I thought would change the world, turned out to be little more than a blip on the rock music radar screen. It was about 1987 by then, and I was firmly entrenched in the East Village with a railroad apartment several stories above an abandoned Polish banquet hall. The Halfwits had disbanded eons ago, my safety pin had been discarded for even longer, and in the meantime I had been in at least a dozen bands that had all gone nowhere. Still, I consoled myself by thinking that the speed metal and hardcore movements were just punk by another name, and that my luck would soon change. But then came my second disastrous encounter with "Stairway to Heaven."

This time it happened on a cold February night. I'd gone to see an early riot grrrl band called the Sisters of Fury play at CBGB's, and I fell madly in love with their drummer, Ilsa. She had a shock of pink dyed in the middle of a jet black mohawk and a fourteen-gauge nose ring hanging from her septum—in those days, pierced noses were rare. But what really attracted me to Ilsa was the way she played the drums. Never had I seen anyone, male or female, attack their instrument like she did that night. I could have cared less that the Sisters were rumored to be a bunch of man-hating dykes. It was all hype anyway, right? Besides, I had at last met a woman who could rock as hard as I did and nothing was going to stop me from getting her.

Being a groupie had never been my strong point, so you can imagine my embarrassment as I hung out at the bar with a dozen other wasted losers until the Sisters started their load-out at the end of the night. Then, with all the style of some smitten stray mutt, I made my way over to Ilsa and told her how much I enjoyed the show. Why she didn't just kick me in the balls and be done with it right then, I have no idea, but the next thing I knew I found myself crowded in the front of a rented U-Haul with the rest of the band, off to spend the night at their rehearsal space in Hoboken.

The trip through Lower Manhattan was a boisterous one, and with Ilsa, or someone in that truck, caressing my crotch as we sped through the Holland Tunnel I had never been more excited to drive into Jersey in my life. Finally, we came to a stop in front of the enormous warehouse the Sisters shared with two other bands, and I grew even more convinced that I had at last found my perfect soul-mate. The place looked like it hadn't seen a building inspector since World War II, and it was in an area so bad that even the crack dealers probably felt frightened at night. It was perfect for rock and roll. You could play as loud as you wanted and no one but the rats and junkies would ever complain.

The Sisters had the entire third floor to themselves, and after lugging close to a ton of their equipment up the stairs, Ilsa and I drifted off to a corner of the room she had partitioned off as her own. The mood couldn't have been any more romantic. She had a king-size mattress thrown on the floor. The pot I had copped from the reggae band on the first floor was excellent. And then, as if that wasn't enough, when Ilsa pulled out a small bag of cocaine, and I scratched out our initials in the powder instead of just making lines, anyone could see how much she dug my style. Our passion began to build. We reached for each other in a frenzy, but just as our lips were about to meet an earsplitting version of, yes, "Stairway to Heaven" filled the night and the moment was lost forever.

As bad luck would have it a fledgling heavy metal band rehearsed on the floor directly below us and their lead guitar player was also up late and feeling rather spiritual it seems. Visions of Cindy and her Moonie-like sing-along flashed through my brain, and I tried hard not to act too concerned. Ilsa, on the other hand, was livid. She started stamping on the floor, yelling for quiet, and then threatened to stuff a drumstick up the guitar player's ass if he didn't shut up. Finally, the big Marshall amp below us fell silent, and it was then that I knew I had more in common with Ilsa than just a mutual respect for the first Patti Smith LP. But unlike my own hostility, Ilsa's was directed less toward a particular song than toward Led Zeppelin in general, and specifically toward an event she referred to as the Fish Thing.

For those of you who don't know, the Fish Thing is a notorious incident that some say took place at a post-concert orgy when Led Zeppelin, or someone associated with the band, shoved a live salmon, tuna, or mackerel up the vagina of one of their groupies. Did it really happen? No one knows for sure, and, like most folklore, it has been passed around so many times that no one ever will. For my part, I've always believed it about as much as I believe Robert Plant singing about Heaven—total bullshit.

Ilsa, however, had no patience for such excuses. As soon as she knew I was hip, she launched into a tirade about misogyny and male-dominated art forms. She claimed to have proof that Jesus was a woman named Jessica and that virgin birth was an allegory for the role men should play in the world. She even revealed the secret behind her savage, power-packed drumming style. All she had to do was envision the jaded, leering faces of Jimmy Page and Robert Plant on her drumheads and the rest was easy: she just beat the shit out of them.

Now, if not for that late-night rendition of "Stairway to Heaven," chances are Ilsa and I would have had a night of great sex, realized we had nothing in common in the morning, and parted company with no harm done. But instead I tried to inject some levity back into the evening.

"Maybe the fish lady got into it," I suggested as I finished off the last of the coke.

"Then maybe your sweet ass should get a taste of what it's like to be my cheap piece of meat for awhile!" she shot back.

Pride keeps me from going into the graphic details of what happened next, but it was like being stuck in a mix between a sick letter to *Penthouse* and an X-rated outtake from a Quentin Tarantino movie. Ilsa had me in every way a man can imagine or fear. It never got to the point where the Sisters were passing me around like an inflatable sex toy, but it was close. The days turned into weeks, the weeks turned into months, and, much to my disgrace, I quickly became the laughing stock of the East Village and Hoboken combined.

Finally, at the end of what seemed a near eternity, the Sisters recorded their first CD and left for an extended tour of Europe and Japan. By then I had been reduced to nothing more than Ilsa's willing lackey, so I begged and pleaded for her to take me with them, but all I got in response was a slap on the ass and a half-hearted promise about flying me in to see their show in Berlin. But like thousands of groupies that came before me, I never saw or heard from my rock star again.

Ilsa had taken everything from me. My dignity, my self-respect, and (figuratively speaking) even the dangling reason that had inspired me to pick up a guitar in the first place. There was no sense kidding myself anymore, punk was finished, and so was I, and the only thing left for me to do was crawl back to the suburbs and try to start over again.

In the years that followed Led Zeppelin was inducted into the

Rock and Roll Hall of Fame, immortalized in several slickly packaged box sets, and with "Stairway To Heaven" leading the way, seduced an entire new generation of listeners. I, on the other hand, underwent countless hours of intense personal therapy and carefully avoided classic rock radio or any other situation that offered even the slightest chance of my hearing that song. Then, after several years of living with my parents, I borrowed some money from my father and invested in a small recording studio, where I recently produced an award-winning jingle for a local shoe store. As for any contact with the opposite sex during this time, I was as celibate and reclusive as a Benedictine monk. Sure, there were a couple of dates with the occasional horny high-school English teacher or oversexed dental technician, but whenever things moved into the bedroom there was nothing there for me. And thanks to Ilsa, I do mean nothing.

This would have been a fairly bleak end to my lifestory had it not been for a college intern I hired to help out around the studio last fall. Her name is Microdot, and she claims to have been born to a pair of notorious acidheads at a Grateful Dead concert in the mid-1970s. She has bright purple hair, a small bat tattooed on her back and more holes in her ears, nose, navel and other places than you can find in a five-pound slice of Swiss cheese. I knew she was perfect for me from the moment she walked into the studio and asked if I had a spare Jolt cola in the 'fridge, but due to my past experiences I decided to proceed with caution.

Was she grunge? Grunge had been dead since long before the suicide of Kurt Cobain, she assured me. What about alternative? That was far too commercial for her, I soon found out. How about Generation X, then? Microdot hated that term most of all, and finally admitted that she was really a vampire and into the industrial, techno, and gothic scenes.

Having no idea whether to laugh or run for my life, I simply nodded like I knew dozens of industrial-techno-gothic vampires and went back to mixing another shoe store commercial. It was obvious to me that I was officially washed-up and over-the-hill forever until I noticed Microdot giving me a curious look. She pointed to two small scars on my left cheek and commented on how much they looked like fang marks. When I explained they were all that remained from the time I pierced myself with a safety pin there, she gave me a brief approving nod and mumbled the word *cool*. And to my surprise, she started using that word more and more when referring to me.

It was *cool* when I said Green Day and Rancid were lightweight rip-offs of the Sex Pistols and the Clash. It was *cool* that I had lived in the East Village before it had a Gap. It was *cool* how I knew who Iggy Pop was before the soundtrack to *Trainspotting* came out. And although I refused to discuss the specific reasons involved, it was *cool* how I hated anything having to do with classic rock.

I, in turn, began to have a greater respect for Microdot. It began simply enough when she forced me to listen to her entire collection of Nine Inch Nails CDs at work one day, and continued to the point where I even began to enjoy the ambient sounds of Moby and Orbital. She even came close to talking me into having my scrotum pierced, but I backed out at the last minute for fear of not being able to sit at the mixing board for a week. Finally, when she turned on my car radio and showed me how many stations were moving away from their '60s, '70s, and '80s rock formats to more modern music and groups, it was like waking up from an intense bad dream. I had been freed from "Stairway to Heaven" forever, or so it seemed until just last night.

To fully understand the impact of what happened you have to realize that, despite my sordid past and Microdot's daily wardrobe of latex bondage outfits, our relationship had been strictly platonic over the past several months. Sure I entertained countless lurid fantasies about her during that time. But I had no reason to think she considered me as anything other than her employer, and I had been celibate for so long that I doubted I could even act on my passion.

So I didn't expect anything unusual to happen yesterday, either. I spent most of the day running off dubs and sending out demo tapes to shoe stores in neighboring suburbs. Microdot came in around 2:00 wearing a pair of custom-made fangs she ordered off the Internet and gave me a hand with a few odd chores. We called it quits around 6:00, went to a nearby health store for a couple of smart drinks, and made plans to meet later that night at a club she frequented called the Crypt.

In the past the Crypt had always left me unimpressed. Apart from a few ravers dressed like they'd just stepped out of a Dr. Suess book, there was nothing I hadn't seen or done better at the old Mudd Club twenty years ago; but last night was different. Maybe it was the extra drop of gingko-biloba Microdot ordered in my smart drink, or maybe it was all the X'ed-out gay guys pressing up against me as I made my way through the club's crowded front hallway. But whatever the reason, when I spotted Microdot dancing by herself under the wash of blacklights, I forgot all about the Mudd Club or any other landmarks of my youth. Suddenly it was great being in that strange new place, with all those strange new creatures, listening to all that strange new music. And, this feeling stayed with me until I drove Microdot home at the end of the night, and she invited me inside her small studio apartment for the first time.

Since I had never been in that box-like room she called home before, two things immediately struck me as odd. There was an enormous plastic crucifix hanging from the wall and several large halogen lamps were filling the room with a blinding white light. Seeing the near life-size likeness of Jesus created the usual rush of panicky thoughts about Cindy, but I dismissed them: Microdot probably just thought it looked trendy and cool hanging there. As for the halogen lamps, Microdot explained by clicking them off to reveal a field of a thousand glow-in-the-dark stars pasted on her ceiling and, much to her delight, a glowing Jesus as well.

She gave me a seductive look and took off her fangs. We kissed passionately for a few moments, then she led me to bed. It looked like my days as a Benedictine monk were over at last, and even though I still doubted my ability to consummate our relationship, I was hopeful it would all come back to me in time. But as Microdot stood to remove her earrings and some of her other, more cumbersome piercings, she absentmindedly began to hum a melody aloud. At first it sounded almost soothing, but as it grew increasingly familiar, a cold, clammy feeling set in. It can't be, I thought. No way. Not her. But when she softly started singing the lyric about "a lady who's sure all that glitters is gold," there was no mistaking it.

Countless morbid thoughts raced through my mind. What if this vampire thing wasn't a joke? What if Cindy and Ilsa were part of the Undead too? What if I ended up drained of blood and hanging on that cross with Jesus?

I managed to control myself long enough to ask Microdot why she had chosen that particular song, especially since she'd always claimed to hate such classic rock standards. But "Stairway to Heaven" was the only standard her hatred excused. In fact, she didn't think of it as a rock song at all. For her, it was only an innocent lullaby her acidhead mother used to sing, and Microdot often hummed it to herself before going to bed at night. Giving it no further thought, she then started to disrobe and shared a little-known fact from her Anthropology 211 class.

"Did you know that a woman's hymen is the only proof we have left that man once lived in the water just like the fish?" she asked, more for my own enlightenment than hers.

Out of all my perverted fantasies, the fact that Microdot had never been with another man, woman, or combination of the two had never occurred to me. I looked into her eyes, and although I can't really describe what it was, I saw the same thing in her that once led me to believe the Damned, the Dead Boys, the Slits, the Voidoids, and countless other punk bands would one day rule the world.

"You're a virgin?" I gave as my somewhat obvious, stunned response. And to this she simply nodded, kicked off her Doc Martens, and climbed into bed.

From somewhere deep inside me a nervous rumbling began. And for lack of a better analogy, it started to build in much the same fashion that the arrangement of "Stairway to Heaven" builds. Then, for some repressed reason, I can only assume, I felt a long forgotten part of myself harden in the front of my relaxed-fit Levi's, and I made love to another person for the first time in years.

Later that night, with Microdot sleeping by my side, I looked up at the dim light of the stars on her ceiling and the still glowing crucifix on the wall, and it was like everything in the world was perfectly interconnected. It was like Cindy, Ilsa, and Microdot had been put in my life with some divine purpose in mind. And it was like even the fish in the sea were part of the same master plan as the heavens above. And it was like punk did change the world. And it was like Jesus really did love me. And it was like "Stairway to Heaven" wasn't such a bad song in the end. But these thoughts soon passed, and as the light of the crucifix and the stars continued to fade, I looked up above me again and saw nothing at all.

Blues town

geoffrey becker

WHEN I WAS FIFTEEN, MY FATHER showed up at our high school and stood outside the door of Mr. Margin's history class wearing his leather jacket, waving a pink piece of paper. It was a September afternoon, sunny but not too hot, the sky bright blue. I had been alternately staring out the window and making eyes at Lucy Westbrook who sat opposite me, and had probably the nicest body in the whole school. Mr. Margin stopped lecturing (the subject was, I think, slavery) and went to the door, then gestured for me to step out into the hall with him.

"You're excused, Spencer," he said. "It seems you've forgotten something."

I didn't know what he was talking about, but the prospect of getting out of that stuffy classroom was an unexpected gift.

"Your doctor's appointment, Spence," said my dad, pointing to his watch. "We're late already." He had this concerned, fatherly expression on his face, and looked at Mr. Margin in commiseration. "I knew he'd forget. He's known about this for weeks."

"It's my experience," said Mr. Margin, "that given half a chance, these kids will forget anything. Get a move on, Spencer—read the next chapter for tomorrow's class." He gave me an affectionate smack on the shoulder.

"Kids," said my dad to him, then led me down the hall. When we got to the front entrance, he looked both ways, then began to run. He took off across the front lawn, past a group of kids sharing a joint, nearly tripping over a girl who was stretched out in the sun. I ran after him, thinking that this time he had finally, truly lost it. When I caught up with him at his car, a '67 Buick station wagon with a wired-on front bumper, I could see the back was loaded with equipment—all his guitars, an amplifier, and a suitcase. I got in the passenger side as he started up the engine.

"What's going on?" I asked when I'd caught my breath.

He slipped on a pair of aviator sunglasses. "It's way too nice a day to hang out in school," he said.

He loved to break rules—it was one of the things I liked best about him. It was also part of the reason he'd been banished, several years before, from the small ranch house where my mother and I still lived along with Hal, her new husband. My dad, a few gray traces just beginning to appear among the hair that fell over his ears, now inhab-ited a small apartment downtown, over Angelo's Pizza and Calzone. I still saw a lot of him, more than my mother would have liked. He was only supposed to get me one day a week, but I'd go over to his place after school and hang around listening to albums, or playing cards. Since his work, when he had any, was at night, he was home after-noons. He liked to talk about the old days, when rock and roll was still counter-culture and not just something else to show on TV. We'd sit on his second-hand sofabed, albums and cassette tapes strewn over the floor, the smell of pizza wafting up through the floorboards, and he'd tell me how he was never really cut out to be a family man. Possessions and responsibilities made him nervous, even things like his stereo and television. Even so, whenever he did get some money, he'd spend it on a new toy—a phase-shifter or a compressor, or maybe a graphic EQ, and together we'd spend hours fooling with the knobs and buttons.

He played me albums, everything from Robert Johnson and Lightnin' Hopkins to Jimi Hendrix and Duane Allman. Guitar, he said, was the only instrument on which you could really play the blues, and at fifteen I was a blues expert. I was familiar with all sorts of obscure, Chicago-based players, most of them named Milton or Melvin. I fully believed I knew what it meant to have the blues. In school I covered my notebooks with drawings of guitars and amps. My prize possession was a Muddy Waters T-shirt he once brought me back from New York, which I wore so often my mother had to swipe it from my room just to get it washed. With my friends I smoked cigarettes and kept my hands plunged deep into my pockets, nodding in time to an imaginary beat. What I liked above all things was the tortured sound of a guitar string, bent almost to the point of breaking.

I asked about all the equipment, and he explained that he had an audition in Montreal for a gig with a new band that had backing, a recording contract—everything but the right guitarist. This seemed major—there was an intensity on his face that I couldn't remember seeing. When I asked him how they happened to come up with *his* name, he just smiled and said "a friend of a friend." My dad had a lot of friends.

He made a living as a guitarist, more or less. It always seemed he was on the verge of success when something would happen. My mother said he brought it on himself, but as far as I could see, he just ran into a lot of bad luck. For a while he'd pinned his hopes on a local woman named Maddie Kelso—an emaciated redhead with an enormous, whiskey-steeped voice. He worked with her for about a year, but she got born again and moved to Wisconsin. Another time he left his car unlocked and all his instruments were stolen, so for months he had to borrow equipment. But he stayed optimistic, full of plans, and even my mom, on the uncomfortable occasion when she would run into him at the supermarket or the drugstore, found it hard to be angry with him. She didn't like us spending time together and said he was a bad role model, but he could always do something dumb, like wiggle his eyebrows at her, or juggle a couple of avocados, and at least get a laugh.

We went to the Dairy Queen and had black-and-white milk shakes. It was where the greasers hung out, and the parking lot was full of them: slicked-back hair, big combs sticking out of the back pockets of their polyester pants. They leaned against jacked-up cars, smoked cigarettes, ignored the girlfriends who lounged next to them, all hair spray and lip gloss, car radios blaring. With his leather jacket, worn-out jeans, and shades, my dad was easily the coolest-looking person there. I liked the way we could just hang out together on the hood of the Buick, feeling the hot metal under our legs, sipping a cold shake.

"Jimi," he said. It was something we'd done since I was little—calling each other by the names of dead guitarists. I got to be Jimi, and he was Duane, after Duane Allman, who was the closest thing to a hero in his life. Nobody'd ever played slide like Duane, or ever would. "They sent me expense money," he said.

"Great," I said. "That means they're serious."

He shrugged. "I guess. The way I see it, if I drive up, it costs me next to nothing and I pocket the difference. What do you say? Feel like a road trip?"

I could think of nothing I felt like more. An image of the two of us cruising north through New England flashed through my mind like the trailer for a sixties road movie. But, I pointed out, my mother was going to be a problem.

He lowered his voice. "We won't tell her—we'll just leave a note saying you're with me, and when we get back I'll take all the heat."

A note from him wasn't going to get me out of anything, but I wanted to go, so I convinced myself it was a workable plan. After all, it would just be a couple of days.

"It feels a little like running away from home," I said, enjoying the idea. A friend of mine, Nicky Dormer, had run away from home for four days the year before, and afterward he'd seemed to me years older.

"Jimi, my man," he answered, massaging my shoulders. "It is impossible to run away from home with your own father."

My mom was still at work. We drove by the house and I ran upstairs to get a toothbrush while he stood in the kitchen penciling a quick note in his own, peculiarly recognizable handwriting—an angular sort of chicken scratch. When I came back down he was still laboring over it. It was odd seeing him there, back in the house for the first time in years. He looked uncomfortable, out of place. I looked at what he wrote, but it wasn't until we were in the car and heading out of town that I asked him about it.

"Hey, Duane," I said, "How come you put down that we were going to Virginia?"

"Just a precaution," he said. "In case she decides to call the cops, it'll buy us some time."

As soon as we were on the road, he slipped in a cassette of the Allman Brothers doing "Statesboro Blues," and I kicked my feet up on the dashboard. The music almost seemed to be powering the car. I'd seen pictures from back when I was only about three or four, when my dad practically *was* Duane Allman. He wore his hair all the way down his back and had the same mutton-chop sideburns. The day after Duane died on his motorcycle, my dad managed to get into an accident on his. He broke a leg and an arm, but he also got an out-of-court settlement that was enough to buy our house, as well as a good PA system and a couple of guitars. He was twenty-five years old, a high-school graduate with a wife, a kid, and his own place. Things started to happen. Weird people would come over in the middle of the night to hang out, and in the morning there'd be spilled beer and cigarette burns in the carpet. My mom and he would fight, then he'd disappear for a couple of days at a time. Afterwards he'd always try to make up for it by doing something real normal, like mowing the lawn, or taking the three of us out to the movies.

Finally, she just told him to move. I was nine. "Buddy," he said to me, "I'm not going anywhere." He wrote his new phone number on the inside of a book of matches and put it in my hand.

We stopped for gas at a turnpike service station and he pulled out his wallet. It was stuffed with bills, more money than I'd ever seen him with at one time. He removed a ten and gave it to me. "Candy bars," he said, solemnly.

I got change and pushed quarters into the machine until I had extracted four Snickers, our favorite. Then, on impulse, I also bought a pair of cheap amber-tinted sunglasses that were aviators like his. They were small on me and rode high on the bridge of my nose. They cost six dollars and were probably worth about forty-nine cents, but I bought them anyway. When I got back to the car he lifted them off and bent the flimsy frame across the middle, just slightly, then put them back on me.

"That's it," he said. "Now you're cooking."

As we drove, we talked about Canada. Neither of us had ever been, so we made a list of things it was famous for.

"Canadian bacon," I offered.

"Salmon," he said.

"The Expos."

"Draft dodgers."

"Niagara Falls."

"That's in America."

"Only part of it. The other part is Canadian."

He looked over at me. "Who figured that out?"

"It makes sense. It's a natural divider. That's how they always divide up countries, states too." When he didn't say anything, I fell silent for a little while, thinking about how things divided. How did they know exactly where Canada stopped and America began? It was all just water—there couldn't be any clear line like on a map. I thought about me and my dad—I was halfway to thirty, and he was halfway to seventy. I always had an idea that when I turned eighteen I would experience some obvious transformation into adulthood, but now that I was getting closer, I wondered. The twenty years that separated me from my dad suddenly seemed like nothing at all, not in the larger scheme of things.

We crossed the Vermont border around sunset and stopped for burgers at a place with two enormous trucks parked outside. It was a classic roadside diner, but somehow not quite real—everything in it was brand-new, though styled to look mid-fifties. It was someone's idea of what a diner should have looked like—lots of chrome and mirrors and a big, colorful jukebox. I put a quarter in and selected two songs.

"If they like you, does that mean you'll have to move to Canada?" I asked, coming back to the table.

"Could be," he said. "I don't know. It all depends."

I pictured his apartment over the pizzeria and tried to imagine someone else living there, but it just didn't seem a real possibility. "I'd miss you," I said. "Where would I hang out?"

He tapped the table top with his fork. "Well, let's not count our chickens. They may not want me at all. I'm getting kind of old for this line of work."

"How can you say that? Look at the Stones. Look at—" I tried to think of someone else. "B. B. King. He's still going, and he must be about sixty."

He yawned. His eyes were red from all the driving, and he looked tired. "I don't know," he said. "The way I see it, this may be my last shot. If it isn't happening, I may just try to get into something respectable."

"Like Hal?" Hal was in insurance, and we had a fair amount of fun at his expense. Both of us thought insurance was about the most boring thing you could possibly do, and that by marrying Hal my mother had not so much found a mate as taken out a policy. Actually, though, I kind of liked him. He never tried to be my father, he was just Hal. He left me alone when I didn't want to be bothered, and he was an incredible cook.

"Exactly. How do you think I'd look in a suit and tie?" He picked up his glasses and pointed them at me, businesslike. "Let's talk coverage," he said in his best salesman's voice. "You tell me you play in a band? Fine. Say one day you get up there on stage, put a hand on your guitar, the other on the microphone. And let's just say that system isn't properly grounded. In one blue flash you get zapped right into the next state. What about your wife? Your kids? Who takes care of them? The musicians' union? You say you're not in the union? Well, I have a little policy designed just for you. We call it the Guitar Player's Friend—it provides all-purpose coverage for you and your loved ones, and it's issued by the Chuck Berry Mutual Accident and Life Insurance Company, a name you've known and trusted for years. Believe me, you won't want to plug in without it."

The waitress interrupted him with our food. I waved a french fry. "Brilliant," I said. "You could be rich."

"Yeah, maybe," he said modestly. "I'd like to think I'll be able to leave you something someday." He sipped his coffee. "If you had all the money you could ever want, what would you do?"

I chewed and thought. "I don't know, I guess I'd buy about ten guitars, a small recording studio, and some video equipment."

He nodded. "And live where?"

"Hawaii maybe. The Swiss Alps."

"Good choices," he said. "A little romantic, but you're supposed to be romantic at fifteen."

"So? What would you do?" I asked.

"I believe," he said, "I'd do exactly what I'm doing right now."

He was tired and didn't feel like driving much more, so we started looking around for a place to stay. Since we were in Vermont, he said, we ought to find one of those quaint country inns where you slept under thick goose down comforters and they served you up a big New England style breakfast in the morning. We must have spent an hour driving around trying to find one. Eventually we settled on a motor-court called Traveller's Rest, with a blinking neon sign of a sheep jumping over the name. The parking lot was empty, and my dad kept shaking his head over the fact that the one time he actually wanted to spend some money he couldn't find a way to do it, but I was happy. This was much more the kind of place I imagined crashing for the night, and as for the rest of that stuff, it wasn't really cold enough for a down comforter, and I supposed I could live without breakfast.

Our room was hooked up with cable television, and I immediately found an old movie that looked good, a British vampire flick with lots of gore and women nearly tumbling out of their bodices. My dad spent ten minutes going back and forth to the car bringing in all his guitars. It seemed a little odd to me that he'd bothered to take every single one of them along, but I didn't say anything. This was a very big audition for him, and I figured he needed the extra confidence. He took a pint bottle of Chivas Regal out of his bag, went into the bathroom and returned with two tissue-wrapped glasses. I'd never had Chivas, but I remembered reading on an album cover that it was John Lee Hooker's favorite drink. I squinched over to make room for him on the bed, then took the glass he handed me. He turned the sound on the television down.

"Your mother called me last week," he said, after a moment. "Says you're messing up in school."

"That's not true," I told him. "Just one class. I'm getting B's in everything else. Anyhow, why should she call you?"

"She wants us to stop hanging around together so much, at least till your grades pick up."

We almost never talked about school, except in the most general way, and having him speak to me like this—father to son, when we were now hundreds of miles from home—seemed a kind of betrayal.

"That's stupid," I said.

He nodded.

"I hope that's what you told her."

"I didn't tell her anything," he said. "I wanted to talk to you first."

I was suddenly angry at my mother for trying to interfere so blatantly with my life, and behind my back, too. I wasn't a kid anymore. I had been thinking about calling her, just to let her know I was all right, but now I felt like letting her stew a little.

"You know," he said, lying back on the bed and crossing his legs, "she's probably right. I'm thirty-five, still kicking around the same town I grew up in, still trying to land a steady gig. Being with me isn't going to help you become CEO of General Motors."

"Come on," I said. "You're my dad." I sipped at my drink, which made my eyes water.

"O.K.," he said, studying me. "I just wanted to make sure."

A question occurred that I was almost afraid to ask. "Could she do something? Something legal I mean?"

"I don't know," he said. "It's a possibility." He got up and went into the bathroom to pee.

I made a promise to myself that regardless of what happened, things would continue on between us the way they always had. It was hard to imagine my mother actually doing something so drastic, but taking off without her permission had already given me a sense of power. Things could be any way I wanted them to be, I thought. What were they going to do, put me under armed guard?

"How long do you think we'll stay in Montreal?" I asked when he came back.

He looked through the blinds out at the parking lot. "Not long. A couple of days, tops." Then he slapped a hand down on my leg. "What do you say we head out and see if there's any nightlife around here?"

I jumped up and turned off the set.

We drove around until we found a little roadside place called Mother's that had pick-up trucks parked outside and a flashing red Miller sign in the window. There were maybe twenty-five people inside, not counting the band—five bored-looking guys in checked shirts playing sleepy country tunes. The guitar player didn't look much older than me, in spite of an attempted mustache. When we walked in I immediately sensed hostility, but I just followed my dad. He walked to the bar, took a seat, ordered us drinks and helped himself to a handful of peanuts from a bowl they had out. I reached in and grabbed a couple too. The bartender pursed his lips and considered me for a moment, then shrugged and uncapped us two long-neck bottles of Bud.

"Never order anything fancy in a strange bar," said my dad, tipping back his bottle. "The first thing people notice about you in a place like this is what you're drinking."

I nodded. We sat for a while, just swigging beer. Then I got up to go to the bathroom, and when I got back he was in a conversation with a fat guy he introduced as Al. Al worked as a mechanic, he said. He had huge, grease-blackened hands.

"This your kid?" asked Al.

My dad smiled proudly and I stood there feeling like a prize hog. I wished I were still back in the motel room watching television.

"I got a kid," said Al. I waited for him to say something else, but for Al, the statement was a complete thought, and he just turned and faced the bar.

The band shuddered to a halt and went on break, and my dad ordered a round of shots for them, digging into his stuffed wallet and tossing a twenty onto the bar. Then he left me and Al sitting together, went over and got talking to the guitarist and bass player. I thought about all the bars in our town where he'd played. He was always in trouble with the club owners for showing up late, or mixing up dates, but he could smooth-talk them and manage to get hired again regardless. His ability in this respect was legendary. One time he got himself booked into two different places with different bands on the same night, and rather than cancel, he did half of one gig, then drove to the other and finished up the night there, using me as an excuse. "You came down with a convenient case of the mumps," he explained the next day. "I could never have made it without you." For two days after that, I walked around faking a cough and trying to look weak, just in case someone should want to check out his story.

Al wasn't much of a talker, so I drank at my beer and tried to pretend that hanging around in a bar was the most natural thing in the world for me. I counted the bottles of liquor lined up next to the cash register.

"Jimi," said my dad, coming over and poking me in the side. "We're going to sit in next set. What do you say?"

I looked into his eyes to see if he was kidding. I played a little guitar, but not very well, and never in front of people. The prospect terrified me, and I could see he was serious. "You go ahead," I said. "I'll watch."

"Come on, we'll do some blues." He smiled encouragingly.

"I can't," I said. "Really."

"Sure you can," he told me.

I felt something close to panic, but at the same time it didn't seem that I had any choice. They had an extra guitar on stage for me, and the band's guitarist handed his over to my dad. When he did that he gave me a little smile that made the few dark hairs spread out on his upper lip. I took it as a sign of encouragement and plugged in. My dad called out "Red House," a Hendrix tune he knew I knew, and started playing. I tried to follow along, but after a few seconds I realized something was off.

My guitar was tuned a peculiar way. The chords I formed were one disaster after another. My dad kept giving me furious looks, as if I was deliberately screwing around. Everything I played came out wrong. He leaned over and shouted something to me that I could not hear above the music. I could see the band's guitarist leaning against the bar, laughing. I did the only thing I could think of—I stopped playing. Or rather, I pretended to play, damping the strings with my left hand so that no sound came out. My dad shook his head, turned away and began to sing.

He played particularly well. Toward the end he picked up an empty Budweiser bottle and ran it along the strings for a slide, while I mimed along, numb, waiting for it to be over. We got hoots of approval and applause, but I barely heard them in my rush to get off.

The band's guitarist said something to me as he took the instrument out of my hands. I jumped down, ignoring the amusement in his eyes, and went and stood next to a shuffleboard table while my dad talked to some of the locals—bearded men in checked wool jackets who clapped him on the back and offered to buy him drinks. Finally he came over to me.

"Let's go," I said.

It was cold in the parking lot, the air smelling of pine, the muted sounds of the bar mixing with the swell and hush of the wind in the trees. My dad walked me to the car and unlocked it.

"It was in open tuning," he said, finally. "Set up for slide."

"Yeah?" I said. "How was I supposed to know that?"

"You know about open tuning. All you had to do was think."

"I *couldn't* think!" I practically shouted. "Nothing sounded right and I didn't know what to do!"

"So what?" he said. "You just quit? You can't let yourself get beat like that."

"I didn't."

"Well, what do you call it?" He was glaring at me, and I could see that he was really upset about this, more so even than I was.

"I didn't quit," I said quietly. "I stayed up there with you."

We drove in a silence that I was afraid to break; the longer it went on the more permanent it felt. He wouldn't look at me. He was speeding too, I noticed, but I wasn't going to say anything. Then, about a mile from our motel we got pulled over by the cops.

As the officer shined his flashlight into our faces, I thought about the note we'd left. If my mother really had reported us to the police, this was probably it. I wondered what, if anything, they could do to him. I suspected he could get in a lot of trouble. Mostly though, I was worried he might not get to the audition, and that it would somehow be my fault. I sat frozen in anticipation, the cold night air flowing against my face from the open window, hoping as hard as I could for nothing bad to happen.

"Been doing a little drinking tonight?" asked the policeman as he examined my dad's license.

"Yes sir," he said. "Two beers. But I'm sober."

The cop pointed his flashlight in my face. "Who's that?"

"My son."

"Is that right?" He turned the light away from me and back at my dad. "Taking a little vacation, are you?"

"You might say that."

"Please get out of the car."

I had to sit for ten minutes while they ran him through a series of tasks to determine whether he was drunk. It was hard to watch. He walked a straight line four times, and counted backwards from fifty twice. They made him balance on one leg, then the other. All the while, another cop sat behind us, just a silhouette under the flashing blue light, speaking into his radio. They were checking on us. They didn't believe he was my father.

Finally, they wrote out a ticket and let us go. Just like that. This seemed incredible luck to me, and as soon as we were back underway, I let out a little whoop.

"Man," I said. "That was close."

But he still wasn't talking. In fact, he wouldn't even look at me. I wanted to tell him it didn't matter, to just forget it, but I couldn't. He didn't say anything at all until we got back to the motel. He put out a hand and tugged at the top of my head, then ran it down the back of my neck.

"You could use a haircut," he said.

When I woke the next morning, he was in the bathroom, shaving. I went and leaned against the door, watching him slide the razor carefully along the contours of his throat. He put a finger on his nose and pushed it comically to one side to get at his upper lip, turned and made a face at me. I liked seeing him shave. Getting my toothbrush, I fought him for sink space. When he pushed back, I pushed harder, then scooped water out of the sink and splashed him. He dropped the razor, picked up the can of shaving cream and advanced toward me, his face spotted with islands of foam. I ran, but he cornered me by the television and emptied half the can onto my head before I managed to wrestle it out of his hands. We stood there for a while, the two of us covered in shaving cream, laughing. Then he took the can from my hands, flipped it once in the air and went back into the bathroom.

We reloaded the car and checked out. He paid cash for the room and asked the guy at the desk where we could get a good breakfast. He recommended a place about three miles away that turned out to be one of those country-style inns we'd been hoping to find the night before, and had in fact driven right past. We were both starved, and my dad told me to order a dream breakfast—anything I thought I could possibly eat. I had four eggs, home fries, sausages, waffles, toast, orange juice, and coffee. He had steak and eggs with fried onions. The waitress looked a little hassled bringing out all that food—there was barely room for the plates—but we got a kick out of being so extravagant, and we tipped her heavily when we were through. After all, it wasn't our money.

We hit the road about eleven, windows open, tape deck turned up full. We sang along with some old Traffic and Santana, and I beat out rhythms by banging one hand on the glove compartment and the other against the roof of the car. It was a perfect day to be driving, and North seemed the only direction possible. The Buick's big engine hummed powerfully in front of us, and even the air tasted like Canada—cool and fresh and full of promise.

"Hey," I said to him. "What do you say after Montreal we just keep on going? We could set a record. First station wagon to reach the North Pole."

"Bad idea," he said, adjusting his glasses with his forefinger.

"Why?"

"Because. Too much competition. The North Pole is swarming with guitarists already."

I kept quiet.

He closed his eyes for a moment. "They've got this little town up there. It's jointly owned by all the major record companies."

"Not a very pleasant place to live," I said.

"That's the whole point, it's a miserable place to live." He reached over and turned the stereo down. "'Bluestown,'" he said. "Most of the greats are up there, on salary, just biding their time. Muddy Waters, Jimi Hendrix, Duane Allman, Elmore James. All of them hanging out, drinking, jamming, and trying to keep warm."

I forced a laugh, but I wondered. Sometimes he seemed to have no notion of how old I was. Or even that I was there at all. "So what you're saying is that they're actually still alive?"

"That's exactly what I'm saying. Where do you think they keep getting those 'newly discovered' tapes from? The blues wasn't selling, so they figured this would be a good way to stir up interest. And let me tell you something, a couple of years from now the world is going to be in for one hell of a surprise. Because they're coming back, all of them."

"Return of the Killer Guitarists," I said in my best coming-attractions voice. "When is this going to happen?"

He shrugged his shoulders. "Who knows? When we're ready for them, I guess. When everyone has had enough of the crap they play on the radio."

"Bluestown," I said, flipping through the road atlas. "You know, it's not here on the map."

"It's there," he said. "Trust me. You just go to Chicago, then head due north."

"But," I pointed out, "the North Pole is due north of everywhere, not just Chicago."

"Hey," he said. "Don't argue with your father."

I nodded off for a while, imagining a town built entirely of ice, with fur-bundled shapes walking up and down the streets carrying guitar cases. I kept thinking, how do I know these people are who they say they are if I can't see their faces? Then we got off the highway and I woke up. We were a little south of St. Johnsbury. My dad said he wanted to take a few minutes and look at a typical New England town. The place was called Denton, and it was truly quaint: tree-lined streets, big old houses with well-kept yards, two neat white-steepled churches, only a couple of blocks apart. It was one of those picture-postcards of a town, and I thought it probably didn't look any different now than it had fifty years ago. I couldn't imagine what people there did for a living, but everyone we saw looked reasonably well-off. We drove up and down its few streets, looking at the houses, and just enjoying the simplicity of the place. It seemed that everything here was exactly the way it ought to be. In the center of town, he pulled over by the bus station and put the car in neutral.

"How about a couple of candy bars before we get going?" he said.

I was still stuffed from breakfast, and I couldn't imagine that he was actually hungry again, but I said sure and hopped out of the car. He stuck his hand out the window with a five-dollar bill in it. I took the money and went inside.

It was a tiny bus station, just a window, a bench and two vending machines. The guy at the window was out of singles, and I waited while he counted the whole five out in quarters, nickels and dimes. Then I bought two Snickers bars. With them in my hand, I stepped back out into the bright sunlight.

He was already gone. I could see the tailgate of the station wagon bouncing away from me down the street in the distance. I stood there watching him go, thinking that any moment now he would turn around and come back. It had to be a joke. But he kept going until the car disappeared over a crest.

I stared after him down the street. I was standing alone in the middle of a tiny Vermont town with two chocolate bars in my hand and no idea what to do next. Then I stuck my hand in my pocket and felt the wad of money. He had slipped it there somehow without my noticing, and when I took it out I counted nearly seven hundred dollars, most of it in fifties and twenties. I suddenly felt so strange I sat down right where I was on the curb.

It took a little while to collect myself. I walked up and down the main street of Denton, Vermont, looking into shop windows, kicking at loose stones on the street. I opened one of the candy bars and took a bite, but dropped the rest of it in a trash can. I took out the roll of money again, fanned through it bitterly, and a small slip of yellow paper fell out from between two of the fifties. Picking it up, I saw that it was a withdrawal slip for just over nine hundred dollars from my father's bank, and on it in a teller's handwriting were the words "Account Closed."

I stood for a while feeling the sun on my face, looking up at a solid blue sky that extended, unbroken, right up to the Canadian border and beyond. There was no audition. There had only been, for a brief while, an idea about the two of us starting over again someplace else, and maybe this time getting it right. I thought I understood what it felt like to look at your own future and see nothing but disappointment and failure stretching out like an endless series of clouds. The thing was, if he'd asked, I would have kept going. Taking all the change I had in my pockets, I began feeding the parking meters of downtown Denton, Vermont, pumping each one hard until it would take no more, then moving on to the next. After a while, when I ran out of coins, I stepped back into the dark little bus station and paid for a one-way ticket home.

287

LEE K. ABBOTT is the author of six collections of stories, most recently *Wet Places at Noon*. He directs the MFA Program in Creative Writing at Ohio State University in Columbus.

KIM ADDONIZIO is the author of a poetry collection, *The Philosopher's Club*, and a novel in verse, *Jimmy & Rita*. Her fiction has appeared in *Chelsea, Dick for a Day,* and *Penthouse*. The bands she has founded include Sixteen Scandals, Kim Doggy Dogg, and Dentata.

GEOFFREY BECKER is the author of a novel, *Bluestown,* and a collection of stories, *Dangerous Men,* which won the 1995 Drue Heinz Prize for Literature. He has received James Michener and NEA Fellowships, and currently teaches at Colorado College in Colorado Springs.

MADISON SMARTT BELL is the author of eight novels and two story collections. His most recent novel, *All Souls' Rising,* was a finalist for the National Book Award and was nominated for the PEN/Faulkner Award. He currently lives and teaches in Baltimore.

JODI BLOOM lives and writes in Washington, DC. Her fiction, essays, and poetry have appeared in *Happy, Caprice, WordWrights!, Potomac Review, UNo Mas, The Washington Review,* and *Gargoyle*.

T. CORAGHESSAN BOYLE is the PEN/Faulkner Award–winning author of *The Road to Wellville, World's End, East Is East, Water Music, Riven Rock,* and five other works of fiction. He lives near Santa Barbara, California.

FRANÇOIS CAMOIN was born in Nice, France, and came to the United States in 1951. He has published two novels and three collections of stories. He currently teaches fiction writing at the University of Utah.

AVA CHIN has performed poetry at Woodstock '94 and New York's Knitting Factory. Her work appears in *Dick for a Day* and *Not a War*. Currently, she is a Van Lier fellow in fiction at the Asian American Writers' Workshop.

MICHAEL COVINO's books include a novel, *The Negative,* and a collection of stories, *The Off-Season.* He has received a National Endowment for the Arts Fellowship and the *Paris Review* Aga Khan Prize for Fiction, among others. He lives in Northern California.

KEVIN DOWNS is a professor of screenwriting and film/video directing at Georgetown University in Washington, DC. He is also the award-winning author of numerous screenplays and the producer-director of several films and music videos.

LUCINDA EBERSOLE is the author of a novel, *Death in Equality.* She has edited six books, including *Mondo Barbie* and *Women, Creativity, and the Arts.* She is an editor at *Gargoyle* magazine and owns Atticus Books in Washington, DC.

JANICE EIDUS, the co-editor of this collection, has twice won the prestigious O. Henry Prize for her short stories, as well as the Pushcart Prize. She is the author of two books of stories, *The Celibacy Club* and *Vito Loves Geraldine,* and two novels, *Urban Bliss* and *Faithful Rebecca.*

BRUCE JAY FRIEDMAN is the author of the modern classics *A Mother's Kisses* and *Stern,* and more recently of *The Collected Short Fiction of Bruce Jay Friedman, The Slightly Older Guy,* and *The Lonely Guy's Book of Life.* He lives in Water Mill, New York.

KIM HERZINGER teaches at the University of Southern Mississippi, where he is at work on a biography of Donald Barthelme. "The Day I Met Buddy Holly" was his first piece of fiction.

HAROLD JAFFE is the author of three novels and six collections of short fiction, including *Straight Razor, Eros Anti-Eros, Beasts,* and *Madonna and Other Spectacles.* He is editor of *Fiction International.*

290

JOHN KASTAN, who co-edited this book with Janice Eidus, is a former rock drummer, and is currently affiliated with Mount Sinai Medical Center and the Columbia University School of Public Health. A sociologist, he has published articles on literature, ethnomusicology, and other topics.

JILL MCCORKLE is the author of four novels and a book of stories. Her short fiction has appeared in *Cosmopolitan, The Atlantic Monthly, The Southern Review,* and elsewhere. She lives near Boston.

LANCE OLSEN, Writer-in-Residence at the University of Idaho, is the author of two rock and roll science-fiction novels, *Tonguing the Zeitgeist* (from which "Kama Quyntifonic" is excerpted) and *Time Famine,* as well as a study of the writer William Gibson.

ROCHELLE RATNER's books include two novels, *Bobby's Girl* and *The Lion's Share,* and thirteen books of poetry, including *Practicing to Be a Woman: New and Selected Poems, Someday Songs,* and *Zodiac Arrest.*

LINDA GRAY SEXTON is the author of the memoir *Searching for Mercy Street: My Journey Back to My Mother, Anne Sexton,* as well as four novels. "Over the Line" is an excerpt from her current novel-in-progress. She lives on the West Coast.

LEWIS SHINER's rock and roll novel, *Glimpses,* won the World Fantasy Award. He is currently working on another novel, *Say Goodbye.*

ROBERTA SMOODIN raises thoroughbred horses on her ranch in North Texas. She is the author of four novels, most recently *White Horse Cafe.*

KATHLEEN WARNOCK is the author of the award-winning play, *To the Top,* and was a sportswriter for the Columbia (South Carolina) *Record.* Widely published, she is a contributing editor to *Rockrgrl* and assistant director of the Writer's Voice of the West Side Y in New York City.